VOLUME 2

Obsessions
of
an Otome Gamer
Middle School Years

NATSU

ILLUSTRATION BY SHOYU

Cross Infinite World

Obsessions of an Otome Gamer, Volume 2
Natsu

Translation by Charis Messier

Illustration by Shoyu
Editing by Alexis Ang
Proofreading by Yvonne Yeung and A.M. Perrone
Book Design by A.M. Perrone

Cross Infinite World
contact@crossinfworld.com
www.crossinfworld.com

Published in the United States of America

Visit us at www.crossinfworld.com
Facebook.com/crossinfworld
Twitter.com/crossinfworld
crossinfiniteworld.tumblr.com

First Digital Edition: April 2019
First Print Edition: March 2020

ISBN-13: 978-1-945341-34-2

TABLE OF CONTENTS

CG 21: Entrance Ceremony (Kou)

MY middle school uniform was a navy-blue sailor skirt with a matching blouse. I tied the dark-red tie over my blouse and quickly braided my hair. Stepping back, I posed in front of the mirror with my brand-new school bag hooked over my right wrist.

Yup, pretty cute if I do say so myself!

I glossed my lips, applied sunscreen, and rubbed on hand lotion.

I didn't realize I was hogging the bathroom sink until I looked up and saw Dad reflected in the corner of the mirror.

"Ack! S-Sorry, Dad! Wanna brush your teeth?"

"No. I was just standing here, coping with the realization that you're a real middle schooler now."

"How so?" I tilted my head at Dad in the mirror.

"Hana used to inspect her appearance every morning, too," he told me. "Puberty hits yet again." His eyebrows furrowed as his mouth drooped into a frown.

"It's not puberty, Dad!" I rushed to correct him. "I'm not dressing up for boys. I'm supposed to give a speech during the ceremony as the representative for the new students," I explained, which only resulted in getting him heated for an entirely different reason.

"You're the representative?! And giving a speech?! Tell me that sooner, Mashiro! I would've taken the day off work!"

Telling him I'd kept quiet about it because I didn't want him to come wasn't something I could say aloud. Having both of my parents there making a loud scene in front of all my friends would bring death by embarrassment!

Being embarrassed by my parents…am I sure this isn't puberty?

"Sorry, Dad."

The words "rebellious teenager" and "puberty" flashed through my mind, scaring me. Please, not now. Been there, done that. Once was enough.

"I'll go later," Mom said as I was on the way out the door.

"See you later," I replied just as Eri arrived out front with perfect timing.

I had walked to elementary school but was given the okay to bike to middle school. Both schools were about the same distance from home, but commuting to middle school became a million times easier. I don't get why we weren't allowed to bike to school younger!

"Good morning, Mashiro."

"Good morning."

Eri had informed me a while back that she'd graduated from calling me Mashiron. Reason being she felt too embarrassed by how childish she sounded.

Everyone is growing up! I thought emotionally, like a grandmother.

The public middle school I had enrolled in was composed of students from both Tada Elementary and Tada North Elementary. Altogether, there were 250 new students this year.

Eri and I made a beeline right for the display board with our class breakdown. First year students were broken into eight homeroom classes, creating quite a crowd in front of the board.

"Mornin', Mashiro! You're in Class 7!" Rin slipped out of the throng of pushing students and told me straightaway.

"Good morning. You checked for me? Thanks."

"Hi, Kinose. What about me?"

"You're in Class 3, with Majima."

"Woohoo! Thanks a million, Kinose!" Overjoyed to hear she was in the same class as her boyfriend, Eri grabbed Rin's hands and swung them up and down.

Dressed in his stand-up collar uniform, Rin had matured into even more of a hottie since elementary school. Something fierce gleamed in every girl's eyes when he was in their proximity.

Ah, this isn't gonna end well.

I poked Eri in the back and whispered a warning in her ear. Snapping back to her senses, she let go of his hands as if they were on fire.

"S-Sorry. I'm so happy, I couldn't help it."

"Doesn't bother me, but I don't want Majima picking a fight over it."

"Boo! D-Don't tease me!"

Eri was so cute, with her cheeks redder than a strawberry. I couldn't help but grin at her too.

"Mashiro, you seem happy today. Good luck with your speech!"

"Oh yeah! I wanted to complain to you about that, Rin!" I griped.

"I'm in Class 6. It's right next to yours, so come to me anytime you've got a problem."

"I've got a problem I want to lay into you about right now."

"Look, there's Hirato! See ya later!"

Curse him! He ran away!

Mr. Kumaja had originally asked Rin to give the new student speech. With his involvement in our elementary school's student council and sports teams, it totally made sense why Rin was picked. But he had the nerve to bring me up as a better candidate instead!

"'Shimao's the most talented girl in our school,' he said! I couldn't agree more. So, with that said and done, we're countin' on you, Shimao! Gahahaha!" Mr. Kumaja laughed like a bear as he entrusted the speech to me. I couldn't just say no. Doesn't help that he had asked me right after I saw him shedding tears during graduation.

The new student speech was given in turns by representatives from both elementary schools. And so, that's how I ended up representing our school this year.

The ceremony proceeded solemnly with the entire student body and the new students' guardians in attendance. Catching sight of the third-year boys out of the corner of my eye took me by surprise when I entered the auditorium.

Everybody was huge! Some kids stood over six feet tall! Female students in their third year also had a different aura about them. They had lost their childish features and looked closer to adult women than girls. They were younger than I was before I died, but I still found myself feeling overwhelmed in their presence.

Internally baffled by that feeling, I read the script I had memorized aloud.

"Did you hear that? She's Mashiro Shimao from Class 7."

"Do you think she's smart?"

"Beats me. But she's pretty cute."

Kids from Tada Elementary knew about my weirdness and said nothing during my speech. I knew right away that it was the kids from North Tada whispering about me. They seemed rather accepting in a good way, which was a relief.

Only new students remained in the auditorium after the ceremony. The homeroom teachers and different subject teachers were introduced in order next.

"Hello. I'm Tomoi Matsuda, the math teacher. Let's have a good year together!"

Yay! Tomoi really is a teacher here!

Tomoi must've noticed me gawking at him because he briefly glanced my way. His long black bangs had been cut short.

Was the distant and hard look about him an image he was putting up because this was school? Maybe the gentler impression I had of him was because I knew him as a friend of Hana and Shinji.

My mind was full of thoughts about Tomoi the whole time I was in class and on my way back home.

Something about him really got under my skin. Not knowing the reason why frustrated me to no end.

♩♩♩

THE social studies teacher, Ms. Sawajima, was Class 7's homeroom teacher. I took to her animated and energetic personality right away. Despite my class being made up of an equal number of students from both elementary schools, none of my friends were in it. But at least there were a few kids here and there that I felt comfortable greeting, so it wasn't the end of the world.

"You're amazing, Shimao! You gave the new student speech!" One of the girls in my class called out to me as I stumbled out of the classroom with my bag filled with heavy new textbooks. *Oh, she's the girl who sits behind me.*

She left one heck of an impression on me because she said, "reading historical novels is my hobby," during her self-introduction.

"You're Sugishita, right?"

"Yup. Call me Rei. Can I call you Mashiro?" She seemed like the outgoing type, speaking to me with a bright smile the way she did. She was a mature girl who kept her pretty, shoulder-length purple hair swept to one side.

"Of course you can! I was feeling a little nervous because all of my friends are in different classes. Thanks for talking to me!" I exclaimed.

Rei playfully winked and shrugged. "Same here. I was scanning the classroom to see if anyone else was alone and found you."

I immediately took a liking to Rei. Her straightforwardness was comforting.

Mom had gone home after the ceremony. Eri said she was going home with Majima, so I walked with Rei to the bicycle racks and parted ways with her there.

"Let's have a fun time in class tomorrow, Mashiro! See you then!"

"Yeah! Looking forward to it. Bye, Rei!"

Rei smiled when she saw me blush with embarrassment for calling her by her first name for the first time. My middle school days are getting off to a pretty good start, if I do say so myself.

Humming a little ditty, I began pedaling my bicycle towards home. I didn't notice the black Benz until my house was just around the corner.

The expensive-looking car parked beside the sidewalk in front of my house could belong to only one person—

"You're finally home?" Kou, dressed in a blazer with his middle school's design, stepped out of the back seat.

"Kou…."

I told Kon to give Kou the message I wouldn't see him again back in the middle of January. So this would mark the first time I'd seen him in three months. I didn't know if it was because of his different uniform or because he'd grown taller in the time I hadn't seen him, but my darling Kou was starting to look just like the fanbook Kou Narita I had fallen in love with at first sight.

That fact made my heart drop.

For whatever reason, I just couldn't forget my past self; the one who'd wholeheartedly devoted herself to studying music for Kou because she loved him more than was healthy. Every other memory may be a blur, but that one was engraved in the deepest reaches of my heart.

"Didn't Kon tell you I won't be seeing you ever again?" I shot and made a dash for the front door.

Kou swiftly caught hold of my arm. "I can't accept that. Give me one good reason."

"The reason…"

There were two reasons: I couldn't face Sou's best friend after how cruelly I'd treated him, and I thought that Sou would hate it if I did see Kou.

And the greatest reason of all was that being with Kou reminded me of Sou. Of the days the three of us made beautiful music together. Of the days we ate out together. The day we went to the beach. Sou was everywhere Kou was.

"…Fine. I'll explain. Then will you accept it?"

"Depends on what you say," Kou said arrogantly. I couldn't keep the smile off my face.

Don't act cocky when you're just as lonely without Sou, I thought, and then it dawned on me. *I get it. Even the great and mighty Kou feels lonely. Maybe he's hurt after losing Sou and being avoided by me on top of that.*

"Wanna come inside then?"

"Nah. I'd feel bad coming in unannounced. How about we go for a short drive and talk in the car instead?"

"Okay. I'll drop my stuff off inside and tell my mom. Be right back," I said, turning to go inside my house, but Kou wasn't letting go of my arm. "Kou?"

"…! Sorry." He released my hand when I looked up at him puzzled.

The great Kou stared at his own hand with a conflicted expression revealing his inner turmoil.

Heroine's Results
Target Character: Kou Narita
Encounter Event: Ambush
CLEAR

I stripped off my uniform and changed into a long-sleeved shirt and a pair of jeans.

Kou looked me over and sighed. "*That's* what you pick out to wear on a date with me?"

"I only changed so I wouldn't wrinkle my uniform. I won't go if it's that big of a deal to you."

"I'm just kidding. Don't pout. Come on, get in."

You're the one who's pouting! This guy's a real pain.

"It's nice to see you again," I greeted Mr. Mizusawa in the driver's seat as I slid into the car.

"I am also very pleased to be in your presence again," he replied with a charming smile.

Ah, his adult composure is dazzling! He puts me at ease when I'm with him, unlike a certain someone.

Kou snorted when he saw my dorky grin. I was starting to get scared that he could see through everything I was thinking.

Mr. Mizusawa drove at a leisurely pace towards no particular destination per Kou's orders. Kou didn't say much despite being the one who invited me out.

"You're mad that I hurt Sou, aren't you? I'm sorry," I apologized, feeling like I should breach the subject as the adult here.

"Nah." Kou shook his head. "I heard the gist of things from Sou. From Kon too. I'm not mad about what you did. I do think there could've been a better way to go about it though."

"Yeah… I wish I had persuaded him in a nicer way instead of hurting him. But when he said he'd give up his family and stop playing the cello, I lost it."

Talking about Sou killed me inside; the memory alone hurt. But Kou, having been Sou's friend longer than me, had a right to hear my side of the story. He patiently listened to what I had to say without interrupting me.

"I heard from Kon that Sou went to Germany. I think that was for the best, but it's made you lonely, huh, Kou?" I teased to keep the gloominess from my voice.

Kou roughly pulled my head towards him. It was so sudden; I fell on his shoulder without resistance. My breath caught in my throat from the masculine musk clinging to him.

"The one who's really lonely is you. Don't act tough."

Shocked as I was, I was forced to face the feelings I had fought not to acknowledge. The tender tone so unlike Kou brought tears to my eyes.

I'm lonely. I want to see you. I want you to always be smiling. The things I couldn't say to Sou flooded into my mind one after the other. *Stop it. Don't cry. You can't cry in front of this guy.*

"Cry if you want to cry. I won't tell anyone."

I heard his sweet voice beside my ear.

"You're an easy woman who'll cling to anybody as long as they comfort you."

The Kou from my memories sneered at me with a wicked smirk.

Which is real? I don't know anymore.

The kind Kou right before my eyes and the Kou who used to tease and torment me smashed together and became a swirling mess in my head. I dug my fingernails into my knees and squeezed the rough fabric of my jeans.

"Please, stop toying with me." Enduring the tears, I turned aside and swatted away Kou's arm.

Wincing, he pulled away. "…Do you hate me that much?"

"It's a real pain trying to figure out what's an act and what's real. You love those kinds of games, Kou, so why don't you find yourself a girl who'll play them with you?"

"Mashiro."

"Sou's gone now. What's the point in hanging around me?" I lashed out.

The second I looked straight at Kou, the dam holding back my tears broke. I swiped at the teardrops tumbling down my cheeks with my sleeve and fixed a hard stare on Kou through eyes blurred with tears.

"…Am I not even allowed to worry about you?" Kou whispered. His pained voice threw me for a loop.

Why are you making such a tormented expression? I really will come to hate you if this is a part of your game.

"If you really think of me as your friend, leave me alone right now." This clichéd response was all I could come up with after brooding.

Kou bit his lower lip and silently held my gaze until he relented and said, "Fine." He turned towards the front seat and addressed Mr. Mizusawa next. "Mizusawa, head for her house."

"Right away."

Mr. Mizusawa overheard our entire conversation, yet he calmly responded as if nothing had happened, making me want to cry all over again.

Why am I getting so emotional over everything? Why can't I handle things more like an adult? Today isn't the first time Kou's toyed with me.

"Kou…I'm sorry. I'm so sorry."

"Forget it. I wasn't trying to push you to your limits… It's my fault."

Being apologized to by the thirteen-year-old Kou made me want to dig a hole and bury myself in it. For whatever inexplicable reason, those words actually sounded like the truth to me, making it even more painful.

♪♪♪

I went straight upstairs as soon as I got home.

Wanting to clear my head, I stood in front of my desk to organize my new textbooks. My gaze locked on a single letter sitting there. I reached out with trembling hands and flipped over the envelope.

The sender was Sou Shiroyama. Mom must've gotten the mail while I was at school. I stared at Sou's handwriting for a good while.

Something to do with Sou right after Kou, huh? That's Hear My Heart's gimmicky world for you all right. The perfect timing of these events never ceases to amaze me.

Hands still shaking, I ripped open the seal to discover a three-dimensional origami frog inside.

My jaw dropped.

I thought that a scathing letter blaming me for what I'd said or officially telling me good riddance was going to be inside. The raw memory of Sou's ice-cold expression the last time I saw him left me staring at the envelope's contents feeling dissatisfied.

…This is it. Nothing else is inside aside from the origami. This is the origami he was attempting to make the last time he came over. He finally learned how to fold it right. It's a hard one, too. He worked really hard at it. Moved to tears, I took the paper frog in hand. The straight and clean fold lines were just like Sou.

But why go out of his way to send origami? And why a frog of all things? I tilted my head and stared at the green frog sitting neatly on my palm. *Maybe it's his way of saying he's coming back home, just like how frogs tend to return to the same pond they spawned from years later.*

Natsu

Were you practicing this origami because you were preparing to go to Germany someday, Sou?

"I'll definitely come back to you, Mashiro."

I simply shook my head at the pretty origami. I felt like I could hear Sou's soft voice echo from it.

Why do you forgive me? Why, after I hurt you with those horrible words? I slammed my hand against the desk. *That's it! I can't take it anymore. Are they all trying to make me cry? I don't even care if this is some stupid event flag!*

"Dang it! Both Kou and Sou are playing against the rules! Jerks! Dorks!" I fumed.

My first day of middle school ended in messy tears.

♩♩♩

IT doesn't matter how sad or heartbroken you are; time mercilessly passes by regardless. Every so often the passage of time can be a saving grace, while at other junctions in life it leads to despair. For me, it was the former.

Now's not the time to be a crybaby! I scolded myself. *The Junior Music Competition takes place in October of my second year. I have to polish up my piano skills by then.*

"Mashiro, have you picked what club to join yet?" Rei asked me at the beginning of Golden Week.

Joining an afterschool club was a requirement at our middle school. Rei was all excited about joining the Soft Tennis Club with her friends from North Tada. Eri and the gang had also decided on their clubs already.

"Why don't you join with me, Mashiro?" Rei suggested. "I went to observe the club, and tennis looks like a blast! They use soft rubber balls instead of the hard balls. I'll admit I'm scared to death of getting a sunburn though!" she laughed.

"I've been excused from club activities," I said, explaining my special circumstances to her. "I play the piano outside of school and have a hard schedule to keep up with."

Miss Ayumi had contacted the school on my behalf and got them to grant me an exemption from their policy on club membership. Apparently, participating in music competitions was the clincher that sealed the deal, doubling the amount of pressure on me to succeed.

"Neat! You play the piano, Mashiro?"

"Yeah. Honestly, I'm pretty serious about it."

I'd become very good friends with Rei, so I opened up to her about my dreams and aspirations as a pianist. She took me seriously, never once teasing me with the typical, "becoming a pianist is a pipe dream!" line.

"Cool. So that's why you always go straight home after school. You take forever to text me back, too. I was starting to worry that you didn't like me." Loneliness crept into her voice.

"No way! I definitely like you, Rei!" I rushed to assure her.

"Yeah, I understand that now." Rei nodded and took ahold of my hands. "I'll be cheering you on from the sidelines! Make your dreams come true, Mashiro!"

"Thanks! I'll work my hardest at it!" I exclaimed, then added, "Have fun with tennis, Rei!"

She beamed at me and gave me two thumbs-up. I pressed my thumbs against hers.

♪♪♪

CLUB activities weren't the only big change between elementary and middle school. Standardized and regular tests became the new norm. I pulled on knowledge from my past life to study for midterms before the subject matter was announced. The intense study sessions I'd undertaken to capture my darling Kou's heart had become a regular part of my life at this point. I was already mastering high school level workbooks. Middle school tests had nothing on me.

"Why are you so smart, Mashiro? You've got, like, superhuman intelligence acing a test with 500 questions! You're killing me here…the difference between us is so crazy!"

I gently rubbed Rei's back as she slouched in her chair. It's not like I could tell her, "it's because this is my second chance at life." Instead, I went with, "It's because I study like a maniac every single day."

"Really? I seriously love how you don't brag and say stuff like, 'acing tests is a piece of cake for me!'" Rei giggled and rubbed my back as well.

DURING lunch break some weeks after our first major test had ended, I scarfed down my lunch and hurried to the teacher's lounge to fulfill my duties as the class representative, responsible for checking what the students needed to bring to class the next day. All I had to do was check the board in front of the teacher's lounge, copy the schedule left out by the teachers, and write it on the blackboard in our homeroom class.

What should've been an easy job was made difficult by certain annoying teachers who forgot to put out their schedule by lunch! They really made it take longer than it should have. Science class' slot was empty again!

Grr! He forgot again!

The science teacher was an old coot with zero motivation who'd forgotten to write down his schedule over forty times and took every spare moment he had to smoke behind the teacher's lounge.

I don't care if you need to smoke, but do your job first! I balled my hands into fists in front of the board.

"Is something the matter, Shimao?" Tomoi asked, appearing in the teacher's lounge doorway with impeccable timing.

Tomoi never stopped treating me like just another new student. At first, his behavior made me want to ask him, "Excuse me? I'm Hanaka's younger sister. Don't you remember me?" But I quickly realized people would look at us funny if he was friendlier to me than the other students just because he's best friends with my sister's boyfriend. Tomoi's ability to make a clear distinction between his professional and private life amazed me. My affection for him soared.

I had developed feelings for him ever since Hanaka showed me his picture on her phone. His average looks had a way of putting me at ease. Maybe it's because I thought that he was cut from the same cloth as me.

Well, there was no guarantee he hadn't actually forgotten about me either.

"The science schedule is blank," I answered. "Is the responsible teacher inside the teacher's lounge?"

"No, I didn't see him."

Seeing him cock his head caused my heart to race. *Why do I have such a thing for cute older men?*

"You didn't? I guess I'll come back again during fifth period's break."

My agitation over having to come back must've shown on my face because Tomoi smiled wryly. "I'll make sure to tell him to do it when I see him."

"Thank you. Please do." I bowed once and started for the stairs when I saw him beckoning me closer with his index finger.

Hm? He wants me to come over? I jogged over to him.

"You studied hard for your test. It showed. Good job," Tomoi quietly praised me, his eyes softening around the corners.

Heat rushed to my cheeks.

"Ah, um, thanks."

"You take class seriously, turn in all your homework on time, and are an overall great student. You've really impressed me with how hard you have been working all this time. Your piano recital was really amazing, too. Keep up the good work!" He flashed an impish grin and disappeared inside the math prep room.

Oh my gosh! What is this feeling?! I'm too happy! He remembered my piano recital!

I returned to class excited and Rei noticed right away.

"Hmm? Hey, Mashiro, your face is redder than a tomato."

"Whaaat?! I-It is not!"

"Did you look in the mirror? And you look like you're on cloud nine right now." She leaned forward and stared a hole through my face.

"Mr. Matsuda complimented me on my test score," I whispered, quietly confiding the joy I'd just experienced. "It made me happy someone acknowledged my hard work!"

"Mr. Matsuda? ...Oh, you mean that gloomy math teacher?"

Rei's cruel evaluation of Tomoi made me snap back at her. "Gloomy?! He's cool!"

"Ick. Go see an eye doctor, Mashiro." Rei shook her head and waved her hand in dismissal. "He's outta the question. Not even worth a look," she flatly declared.

Tch! But, it's her loss. More of him for me, then! I thought.

"Well, it's their loss. I can be the only one who knows his good points, then," said another me, at another time.

STAB! THROB! A dull, throbbing headache hit me out of nowhere. The intense pain caused the notepad to slip from my hand and clatter onto the floor. Rei chalked my reaction up to shock over her not agreeing with my assessment of Tomoi and picked up the notepad with a big smile.

"Oh my gosh, what's with that exaggerated reaction! You're so funny sometimes, Mashiro!"

"A-Ahaha. Thanks."

The debilitating headache passed in a matter of seconds. What in the world was that?

It made me think of the time I went with Mom to the hospital. The medical test results came back negative. I got the unshakeable feeling that no matter how hard we looked into it, the cause would never be found.

♪♪♪

THE following Saturday I dropped by Kon's house after solfège as had become our custom. She handed me an envelope once we wrapped up practice.

"What's this?" I asked.

"Tickets to the operetta next month. My dad on the Genda side said to give it to you, Mashiro."

"F-For real?! Are you sure it's okay?!"

"Yeah. These are extra tickets anyway. I really wanted to go with you, but it falls on the same day as Seio's field trip. It's such a shame!" Kon knitted her brow with regret.

I comforted her, thanked her for the tickets, and left the Genda estate.

I hadn't seen an opera since *Madama Butterfly*. Operettas, literally "little opera", were comic or lighthearted operas, and this one was being performed by one of my favorite orchestras. I knew that they were coming to Japan, but the operetta tickets sold out the same day they went on sale, and the ticket prices were obscene anyways.

I tore open the envelope once I had settled down on my bed at home.

The tickets were for Franz Lehár's *The Merry Widow*, a famous operetta that's considered a masterpiece from the Silver Age of Viennese Operetta.

The three most famous composers in the Silver Age of operetta, which overtook the Golden Age of Johann Strauss Jr., were Franz Lehár, Emmerich Kálmán, and Oscar Straus. The Great Depression and the rise of movies spelled the end for Viennese operettas after the Silver Age, but *The Merry Widow* is said to be the work that captures the final sparks of genius from the age right before they were snuffed out.

Interestingly enough, the original German title is *Die Lustige Witwe*, but Japan goes by the English title instead. Similarly, *La Traviata*, an Italian opera in three acts by Giuseppe Verdi, literally means *The Fallen Woman*, but it also isn't known to most people in Japan by that name and is instead known as *The Lady of the Camellias*.

Singing the well-known "Vilja Song" from the operetta, I pulled the tickets out of the envelope and discovered there were four total!

Papa Genda, you're so generous! No wonder you're the sponsor!

I didn't delay in telling my family the news as soon as we sat around the dinner table.

"How nice. I'll call the Genda family and thank them later," Mom said with a smile, but then she snapped her fingers with sudden realization. "Oh, but I think the district athletic meet is that day."

"Yes, it is. Sorry, Mashiro. We're both working as volunteer staff for this year's meet. It's really too bad because it would've been a great chance for us to go out and spend some time as a family," Dad sighed, disappointed.

"I've got a great idea!" Hanaka suddenly exclaimed, clapping her hands together after watching our exchange with a smile. "I'll invite Shin and Tomoi, and the four of us can go together!"

"What?"

"We were just texting about how long it's been since we all got together. Would you rather not?"

"No, I'm okay with it, but what about Mr. Matsuda?"

"Mr. Matsuda, huh? Oh my goodness! That's got such a cool ring to it!"

It's no use! She's not listening to me!

It was decided that the four of us would go to the operetta together next month without much input from me.

I get to see Tomoi outside of school! The mere thought of it made the heat rise to my cheeks. *No, no, no! That's not it! It's not like I like him or anything!*

I think older men are cool, but that's it.

…What should I wear?

The operetta was more than a month away, but I ran to my closet, pulled out a bunch of clothes, and tried them on in front of the mirror until I found the perfect outfit.

Something's wrong with me. I was puzzled by my own actions, but I couldn't put my finger on why.

I was just so excited.

That night I had a hard time falling asleep after crawling into bed.

Interlude: A Letter from Mashiro (Sou's POV)

ELEMENTARY school in Germany ends in the fourth grade.

Truth be told, Dad told me to come to Germany then, but I convinced him to let me stay in Japan until graduation. I planned to push for middle school in Japan, too, but he'd hear nothing of it.

Dad's policy was that whether I followed the path of a musician or inherited the company someday, I needed to broaden my horizons and see the wider world while still young.

Either way works. Whatever they say goes. It's easier if I just do what they tell me to.

That's the way I always used to think—until I met her. Then, all my priorities shifted.

I don't want to be apart from Mashiro. I want to stay by her side and become an adult with her.

I knew she didn't see me as boyfriend material.

Mashiro always looked at me with kindness in her eyes. I had no doubt she'd give me a big smile and say "That's great!" if I told her I fell in love with another girl.

And I was okay with that. Because she never pushed me away, I took advantage of her kindness.

And the events of that horrible day were the result.

Her jaw had tightened, her lips had been set in a hard line, and her eyes had blazed with a cold fire. Mashiro looked me square in the eye and hit me hard with her blunt farewell.

I'd just been dumped, but I couldn't pry my eyes from her dignified expression and powerful gaze.

Sorry, Mashiro. I'm sorry I like you even now.

"*Tagchen.*" The older man who often went for strolls in the area greeted me while I was at the park near my house.

"*Tagchen. Das Wetter ist schön heute,*" I casually replied and sat on a bench to open the letter that had come by airmail from Japan.

Ever since I'd sent the letter to Mashiro, I'd been checking the mailbox every day and asking the housekeeper if anything had come for me. Even I thought I was being foolish. I couldn't fathom the possibility of her not sending me a response. Mashiro wasn't the type to do that. That's why she ended up with someone like me falling for her.

This was the letter that'd arrived at long last.

I took several deep breaths and opened it.

"Dear Shiroyama."

The salutation gouged out my heart. I'd forever erased the Mashiro who called me "Sou" with a big, bright smile.

The letter detailed Mashiro's current life. She wrote about the new friends she'd made in middle school, the piano songs she was currently practicing, and the horrible way Kou had treated her.

"I didn't want to deal with his crap anymore."

With that one line, I exhaled the breath caught in my throat. As soon as I sighed, I felt disgusted with myself. I'd rejoiced that Mashiro had rejected him, regardless of knowing how he felt about her. I had hoped that, just as she'd rejected me, she wouldn't let anybody else get close.

"How are you doing, Shiroyama?"

Mashiro was curious about my life too. Her calm and kind penmanship made me feel both relieved and hungry for more.

"Please stay healthy. Make sure to eat well. Don't push yourself too hard. If something bad happens, make sure to talk about it with an adult you can trust."

I unthinkingly laughed out loud at the lines that sounded just like what was in the letter I'd received from Mrs. Mie earlier.

It's a fact: Mashiro sees me as nothing more than a child. That cruel reality was thrust upon me once again.

But I was okay with that for now.

Finishing up *Realschule* would grant me the same qualifications as a middle school graduate. It was recommended that I advance on to a *Gymnasium*, a college-preparatory school, but I didn't want to be stuck in Germany through the twelfth grade. Dad finally broke down and gave in to my plea after I insisted I'd stay for only three years. I was fairly certain he'd send me back to Seio for high school.

Three years to go.

Three more years until I can see Mashiro.

She might've fallen in love with another man by then. Seeing me again might just be a nuisance for her.

And I'm okay with that.

As long as I can see her, I'm okay.

Interlude: Kou's Circumstances (Kon's POV)

"SO? Did she say she'll go?"

"Yup. She was ecstatic. Are you really sure it was smart to leave out that the tickets were from you, Kou?"

"She probably wouldn't accept if she knew."

I pitied my older brother who was incapable of giving Mashiro the sold-out operetta tickets he'd jumped through hoops to get ahold of.

But, in a sense, this was the inevitable result of his actions.

"I'm surprised you even got them. I thought all of the tickets sold out a while ago."

"I begged Dad for them."

"Wow! You went that far!"

Kou fidgeted in place, a miserable expression on his face. "It took me too long to realize it's her favorite orchestra. What other choice did I have?"

"That's not all you should've realized sooner."

Kou took a sip of tea, gave a short, "Ha!" and put on a show of bravado. "I only did it because Mashiro's so depressed I thought it'd rub off on me. There's no special meaning behind it."

"Hmm."

"What?"

"Nothing."

Kou clicked his tongue with annoyance but didn't stand to leave.

He always dropped by the Genda estate on Sundays. I knew all too well that he was eager to hear about how Mashiro, who always visited the day before, was doing.

He really is hopeless.

"Oh yeah. Yesterday, Mashiro…" I began. I told him about the piano songs Mashiro learned and how she was doing. He listened attentively with a face that said, "not interested." His behavior was always so funny and cute; I had a hard time keeping a straight face.

"I hope you can see her again."

"Doesn't matter to me. But I'll go see her if she asks me to."

Then you'll never see her again no matter how much time passes, Kou.

I hope you hurry up and realize just how ridiculously awkward you are when it comes to Mashiro.

CG 22: Heroine (Operetta)

A month passed in the blink of an eye.

I stood in front of the calendar hanging on my bedroom wall and tapped the date I had drawn a red heart around. *The Merry Widow* looked like it was shining brightly off the paper.

> *"Tisn't you and I, though*
> *Wish we didn't sigh so*
> *Lovers fall in love that way"*

I skipped down the stairs singing the German lyrics from the operetta's duet "Jogging in a One-horse Gig" sung by Hanna Glawari, a young widow who had inherited a massive fortune from her deceased husband, and her former sweetheart Count Danilo during Act 2.

A broad smile stretched across Hanaka's face when I appeared in the living room belting the lyrics. "Morning, Mashiro. You look stoked for today's operetta!"

"Good morning! How could I not be stoked when Hanna will be played by *THE* Thérèse Lichtenberg, and Valencienne by Malta Istelle? It's impossible not to be excited!"

"…Err, sorry, who are they?"

"You don't know the most famous soprano and mezzo-soprano singers in the world?!" I fell dramatically to my knees and banged my hands on the floor.

Hanaka cocked her head at me. "So they're opera singers? I wonder what they're like."

"You're in for a real surprise! They're both so talented and drop-dead gorgeous!"

Not that I've seen them in person before, but that's what they look like in their pictures. Where in the world do they pull that otherworldly voice range from with such tall and slender bodies? I just know Hanaka will be stunned when she sees them!

"Hey, can you do my hair after breakfast?" I asked.

"For sure! What're you going to wear?"

"I was thinking about going with that white and black dress."

"Oh, that one is cute. Then why don't we put your hair in a cute bun and curl your bangs?"

"Sounds good!"

I was positive Hanaka could make me look cute.

Humming, I fried up some omelets for Hanaka and me, and tossed together a lettuce and tomato salad. Dad and Mom left at six in the morning to set up the tents for the district meet, so they weren't home.

"Time to eat!"

"Thanks for the food, Mashiro. The omelet and salad are delicious!"

"Glad to hear it!"

My time with Hanaka had decreased since she started university. It'd been a while since we last had breakfast together like this.

♪♪♪

DOORS opened at 2 p.m.

Shinji was coming to pick us up just past one, so I decided to play the piano until he arrived. I was completely devoted to perfecting Bach now.

Miss Ayumi didn't know that Bach's "Sinfonia" was the qualifying song for the music competition I wanted to enter. Even without that knowledge, she still created a special lesson plan to prepare me for music competitions, which inevitably led back to Bach. I'd already discussed my desire to play Ravel's "Pavane for a Dead Princess" with her. Miss Ayumi contemplated my plan before agreeing.

"Well, if that is what you want to do, I won't stop you. The results of a music competition tend to change with the judging committee's tastes. We can revisit your selection choice once the guidelines are published."

Miss Ayumi had many connections with different circles, so I wouldn't put already knowing a large student music competition was going to be held next fall past her. Kon clued me in that Seio Academy's current board chairman and director were present during the competition when the heroine won in *Hear My Heart*, resulting in her being selected as a special scholarship student.

The scholarship covered tuition, uniforms, textbooks, and learning materials. It was a chance to receive a real music education without putting a burden on my parents. I wanted to win no matter what.

Three hours after sitting in front of my piano, a knock on the door brought me back from the music world.

"We should get ready to go soon. I was thinking about making pasta for lunch," Hanaka said from the doorway.

"Oh, I'll make it."

Hanaka still sucked at cooking. Mom would pass out if she found the kitchen looking like a war zone when she came home. Cleaning up the stovetop after Hanaka torched it last time was no easy feat.

Hanaka had set the pasta water to a roiling boil in the biggest pot we owned. We didn't need THAT much water, but it was an improvement to Hanaka burning the stovetop again. The worst cooking offense was the two peeled onions Hanaka left on the cutting board. Did she really think each person would eat a whole onion?

I smashed some tomatoes and added basil, salt, and olive oil to make a tomato sauce, which I quickly mixed with the drained al dente pasta. The onions had no place in this meal. I didn't want Tomoi to think that I smelled bad, so I put the pre-peeled onions in the freezer for later.

"You always make quick work of it, Mashiro. And it tastes heavenly, too. You can marry anytime you want!"

"Only if there's someone who wants to marry me," I replied casually, then pointed out, "Hey! I'm too young for marriage!"

Tomoi came to mind as I corrected her.

Why does Tomoi come to mind here?! I'm only twelve right now. He's twenty-four—that's a full twelve-year difference between us! Oh, but maybe that wouldn't be so bad when I'm twenty and he's thirty-two... Gah! What am I thinking?! That'd never happen!

Hanaka blinked at me several times, baffled by the weird faces I was making as I stabbed my pasta with a fork.

Natsu

♪♪♪

THE time to go finally arrived.

Shinji, looking like the hunk he was, pulled up to our house in a brand-new Japanese SUV.

"Hi, Mashiro. You're looking cute today!" He gently placed his hand on my head, careful not to mess up my hairdo.

Three years had gone by since he started dating Hanaka. I was starting to understand that despite his player looks, he was actually a faithful and serious guy, so I passively allowed him to pat me on the head.

"Okay, leave it at that, Shin. You're putting Shimao on the spot." Tomoi stepped out of the car a few seconds after Shinji. He looked younger than he did at school with his black jacket over his light-blue shirt and chino pants.

Hanaka looked up from her phone when Tomoi mentioned our last name. "Hm? Which one of us are you referring to?"

"Which? Ah, I guess it's hard to tell this way," Tomoi groaned, and without looking at Hanaka, he answered, "I meant Hanaka's little sister."

He said her name curtly, but Hanaka still innocently rejoiced, exclaiming, "Wow! You finally said my first name!"

Even Shinji looked happy. "Good for you, Hana. You finally graduated to having your name said. Tomoi is shy when it comes to stuff like this." He smiled.

Meanwhile, my heart throbbed painfully.

I had a hunch that the reason why Tomoi avoided calling Hanaka by her first name all these years had very little to do with being shy.

He stopped himself from saying her name to keep his hidden feelings for her in check.

Hanaka hopped into the passenger's seat without a second thought. I slid into the back seat with Tomoi and watched the happy couple chat away up front. There was little chance they would ever notice, now or in the future, how Tomoi felt watching them together from the back seat all these years.

"Lonely?"

Lost in my thoughts, I hadn't realized Tomoi was staring at my face. "Pardon?"

"I was wondering if you're lonely now that Shinji has taken your precious older sister away," Tomoi teased. He breached the silence between us out of consideration for me.

"I am not," I demurred with a laugh. "They've always been super close."

"That's for sure. I was surprised to receive their invitation to hang out today. I told them I would be a third wheel, but they said the ticket would be wasted without me."

"It really would be a waste! We received four of them, after all."

I'm glad I get to go with you, Mr. Matsuda. I so badly wanted to say that to him but couldn't bring myself to. Tomoi being a teacher at my school was one reason but not the main reason.

Seeing the way he looked at my sister made it very clear that Tomoi had been in love with Hanaka all this time.

♪♪♪

THE opera house was teeming with people by the time we got there. After much finagling, Shinji parked the car, and we entered the building.

Tomoi took ahold of my hand and said, "Just so we don't get separated."

"I-I'm fine on my own. I can keep up with you guys just fine."

My heart hammered painfully in my chest from the feel of his warm hand.

Won't Tomoi get in trouble if someone saw us like this? I thought bashfully, but those girlish feelings were brilliantly dashed by Tomoi's good-humored reply.

"Don't be silly. Children shouldn't be walking in a crowd without an adult."

"…Okay. Thank you," I muttered, my voice flat.

Child. That's what I am. He's not wrong, but it still hurts to hear.

The tickets from Kon were for some amazing seats. Celebrities and the rich and famous sat in the seats around us.

"How did you get these tickets?" Shinji whispered as soon as he, Hanaka, me, and Tomoi sat down in that order.

"I received them from my friend, Kon Genda."

"Genda? Wait, you can't possibly mean the daughter of *the* Genda

Group?!" Shinji's eyes bulged, and he pointed to the sponsor name listed in the libretto. I nodded in silence. He shook his head and loudly sighed. "Mashiro, your circle of friends is scary."

"Ahahaha. I get that a lot."

Kon, Kou, and Sou were all the heirs to major corporations. By all appearances, they shouldn't have any connection to a normal middle school student from an average household. Unable to explain it as the game world at work, I just laughed it off.

As for Hanaka, she was surprised by the sound of tuning coming from the orchestra pit and exclaimed, "There's people down there!" Shinji watched her reactions with a loving smile.

Tomoi seemed to have an interest in the operetta's storyline as he was attentively reading the commentary included in the libretto. Noticing my gaze, the corners of his eyes crinkled sheepishly.

"I know it's probably obvious to most people, but the lines and songs are all in German, huh? I'm worried I won't be able to follow the story."

"Do you want a simple rundown of it?"

"Oh, would you?"

"Of course!" I said and began explaining *The Merry Widow* to him.

Act I takes place at the Pontevedrian embassy in Paris, where a gala party is in progress. The highlight of this act is when Hanna Glawari, who has inherited twenty million francs from her late husband, reunites with her former sweetheart Count Danilo.

Count Danilo's family had forced the couple apart because Hanna used to be a poor commoner, but he never forgot her, though he refuses to tell her how he feels because he doesn't want to court her just for money, now that she's rich.

It's a classic tale of two people constantly being at cross-purposes and slowly growing agitated by it.

Things get complicated once the Pontevedrian Ambassador in Paris, Baron Mirko Zeta, his wife Valencienne, and his wife's French lover Camille get involved.

Tomoi frowned after hearing my brief explanation of the first act. "Aren't the baroness and her lover committing adultery?"

"They are. But during their duet, Valencienne tells Camille that, 'my

marriage is sacred to me' while he sings about his burning love for her."
I shrugged.

Tomoi raised a dubious eyebrow. "Weird," he sighed. "I don't really
get it, but does the story end happy?"

"Yup. The baron and baroness return to their former relationship
and Danilo proposes to Hanna at the end."

"Huh. Well, this is just one of those times I'm better off not thinking
too deeply about it."

I burst out laughing at Tomoi's all too serious tone.

"Hey," he warned, poking me in the shoulder as I giggled. "How is
that funny?"

"Because of the way you put it!" I said through my laughter.

The red curtain rose, and the lights dimmed as we squabbled.

"Oh, it's starting." I quickly sat up straight in my chair, dedicating my
full attention to the stage. Tomoi smiled warmly at me.

Heroine's Results
Target Character: None
Event Linked to Past Life: Unwitting Love
Clear

The curtain rose on an extravagant scene.

Clad in dazzling dresses and fancy tuxedos, the cast of characters
gallantly danced on stage to the playful overture performed by the
orchestra. Opera had a certain charm that pulled its audience into
another world.

In the first act, the poverty-stricken Balkan Principality of
Pontevedro's embassy in Paris is holding a ball to celebrate the birthday
of the Grand Duke.

The Pontevedrian Ambassador, Baron Mirko Zeta, boasts to
everyone at the gala that his wife Valencienne, a former dancer, "is the
shining example of wifely virtue—she's charming to everyone for my
sake." Meanwhile, the wife in question is flirting away with the handsome
Frenchman, Camille de Rosillon.

The handsome Frenchman takes hold of Valencienne's fan and writes, "I love you" on it in this scene. He flirtatiously tells her, "Since you forbid me to say it, I shall write it down instead."

She rejects his advances in turn, saying, "My marriage is sacred to me. I am a highly respectable wife."

I listened with rapt attention to their duet, "A Highly Respectable Wife".

Malta Istelle, Valencienne's actress, was a delicate and pretty soprano singer. *She's so slender! And beautiful! God is so unfair with the looks he grants some people! Or should I say the game developer is unfair?* I thought, staring into the distance.

The baron is old enough to be a grandfather, and his wife Valencienne is young enough to be his daughter.

Siegfried, who performed Camille's part, was a handsome man with sharp facial features. His tenor voice was literal music to my ears. I visually and audibly preferred this couple to the baron and baroness.

"Forget these feelings and get married," Valencienne asks of him.

Camille fervently appeals to her, "I'd rather die. But my love for you won't die. I know the dangers. You needn't have told me. But true love is fearless. And nothing shall hold me."

I felt a sharp throb in my chest as I listened to Camille singing his appeal to the beat of the cheerful melody.

I wonder if that's how Tomoi feels—that his feelings for Hanaka will never die. I took a furtive glance beside me. Tomoi looked surprised by his first opera. He watched the stage with the attention of a child glued to his favorite cartoon on TV.

Their duet ended, and Hanna came on stage next.

Thérèse Lichtenberg had breathtaking beauty befitting her role as Hanna. Women in the audience sighed in admiration of her refined features, feminine curves, and porcelain white skin.

Since she was supposed to be in mourning for her deceased husband, she wore a black dress with delicate lace, held a black feather fan, and had black pearls weaved through her intricately arranged bright-red coiffure. Her stunning outfit was apt for an affluent widow.

Henning Reger was performing the role of her former sweetheart, Danilo. He was a singer reputed for being a cut above the rest of the younger singers in the opera world, and he had manly features with a wild flare.

They were both still in love with each other, but Hanna was fixated on the reason they had broken up, and Danilo stubbornly held to the notion, "You think we can marry now? I don't want them to think I court you for your fortune."

Count Danilo's uncle had vehemently opposed his marriage to Hanna because she used to be poor. Hanna married a much older, wealthy man after she was forced to break up with Danilo, and Danilo remained single all this time because of his broken heart.

As the Pontevedrian Ambassador, Baron Zeta is on pins and needles about who Hanna will marry. She has the power to bankrupt the nation. If she marries a foreigner, Pontevedro will lose her fortune. Danilo uses various means to drive away the fortune-hunters flocking to Hanna.

Valencienne endorses Camille as a suitor for Hanna, but she secretly hopes he won't fall for her. The tactics at play here are another highlight of the first act.

Act I ends with Hanna and Danilo dancing the waltz once everyone has left the room.

Truly in love with each other, but afraid to admit it, the waltz they danced in silence was the most romantic scene.

♪♪♪

WE entered a twenty-minute intermission before the start of Act II.

I excused myself from the others and made a trip to the bathroom.

Wow, that was even better than I'd hoped! I can't wait to hear Thérèse's aria in the second act and to watch the "Merry Widow Waltz" during Act III! Brimming with excitement for the rest of the operetta, I stepped out of the bathroom and, of all the great misfortunes, I happened to spot a tuft of red hair in the VIP seating area.

Is that Kou? Kon said she couldn't come, but she said nothing about Kou. It'd be rude for me not to acknowledge him now that I've seen him here. The tickets did come from his uncle after all.

After some contemplation, I stepped forward to greet Kou, only to realize he wasn't alone. A girl with blue hair, so bright it was blinding, was sitting beside him. What I could see of her face through her pixie cut was very cute. Kou smoothly scooped up a lock of the petite girl's hair and tucked it behind her ear as she lovingly gazed up at him. He must've whispered sweet words in her ear for her face to be flushed that red.

Hmph.

Pretending not to see him, I attempted to return to my seat, which required me to walk right past him. This was the one time breaking into a brisk walk inside the opera house was called for. I shoved open the heavy door and tried to go inside.

"Mashiro!"

Someone caught hold of my elbow before I could vanish inside. I didn't have to turn around to know who that someone was.

"Hello. Sorry, I'm in a hurry," I rushed out in a bid to flee as fast as possible, but Kou pulled me to his side. He was probably being considerate by keeping me out of the foot traffic going through the door while we talked, but that consideration would be unnecessary if he had just let me go!

Kou said nothing to me. It made me wonder where in the world his usual sarcastic remarks were hiding.

I reluctantly peered up at him and was surprised by how troubled his expression looked.

Decked out in a fancy suit, Kou looked nothing like a middle schooler. His sleek red hair had grown to the nape of his neck where he had tied it in a casual ponytail. He left one lock unbound to frame his cheeks with the same calculated strategy he used when he left one shirt button undone and his tie loose. If only he wasn't so attractive, I could've come up with insults to hurl at him! How mortifying!

"Kou, let go of me," I ordered, my voice baleful.

"Huh? Oh, sorry."

I felt a death glare burrow into me from a distance. I glanced to where I felt the heat of that gaze and found Kou's date glaring at me. I couldn't blame her either. It's no laughing matter to be abandoned in the middle of a date so that the person you're out with can go chasing after another girl.

"Aren't you on a date? Hurry back to her." I jerked my chin toward the girl behind us, trying to draw his attention back to her.

Kou, however, disregarded my advice, and brought up an utterly unrelated question. "Are you enjoying the operetta?"

Huh? Seriously, what is this guy's deal?

"Didn't you say this was your favorite orchestra before?"

Now that he mentions it, I may or may not have said something like that before. His memory is amazing, as to be expected of the Great Kou.

"Yeah. Tell Kon's dad thank you for me as well, Kou. Let him know I really appreciated the tickets and that I'm so happy I came. That it's been the experience of a lifetime hearing them live."

"...Sure. I'll pass it on." Finally satisfied, Kou released my arm.

"Please do. Bye."

"Oh, and before I forget, you look stunning in that dress, Mashiro."

"...Are you trying to imitate Sou with that comment? Give it a rest, seriously!"

How far does he have to take his teasing and tormenting to be happy? I glowered at him with exasperation in my eyes. Kou pressed his lips together.

"But thanks anyways. You look as cool and dashing as always, Kou. All right, have fun on your date!" I said loudly, making sure his date overheard that last part, and turned on my heel. I didn't want to earn unjustified resentment from that girl.

Hanaka looked up at me with worry on her face when I returned to my seat. "That took a while. Was there a line for the bathroom?"

"No. I was detained by Kou."

"What?! Aww, I wish I could've seen him again. It's been a while!" Hanaka exclaimed, free of care from what that meeting entailed.

"What? Did Mashiro run into her boyfriend?" Shinji teased.

Tomoi looked over at me with a fatherly smile. His tranquil expression disappointed me in the way it seemed to imply, "how cute, you have a boyfriend." I knew he wouldn't care, but it still hurt.

"He is *so* not my boyfriend. He's a terrible friend I'm stuck with whether I want to be or not," I huffed, not hiding the disgust from my voice.

Hanaka pursed her lips and scolded, "You don't find hunks like him every day. You should try harder to be friends."

Yes, big sister, you can say that because you only know that little crimson devil's handsome exterior!

♪♪♪

ACT II began with Hanna's aria.

Clothed in an elegant white gown, Thérèse looked just like The White Queen. The long veil trailing behind the sparkling diamond crown on her head was equally as stunning.

"Vilja, o Vilja, Du Waldmägdelein."

"The Vilja Song" is a famous aria, so it wasn't far-fetched to say the audience was familiar with what it should sound like. In the face of that pressure, Thérèse's powerful and expressive voice swept the audience off their feet. If the human voice can be considered an instrument, then Thérèse's voice was irrefutably an exquisite instrument of the highest quality.

Unlike normal operas, operettas have some songs where encores, called refrains, are allowed. Thunderous applause exploded from the audience for Thérèse's sonorous soprano. Some people even cried out, "Brava!" The actors on stage applauded for her as well.

Thérèse smiled bashfully in response to the wildly enthusiastic reaction her singing received and gracefully raised her right hand. Taking that as the signal, the orchestra replayed the aria from the start.

Wow! She's singing the refrain!

I squeezed my hands together, shut my eyes, and immersed myself in her aria.

The dancing during the "You'll Find Me at Maxim's" scene held at Hanna's manor was riveting, and I was blown away by the "Merry Widow Waltz" during Act III. The audience clapped to the beat of Jacques Offenbach's "Orpheus in the Underworld". The beautifully colored water fountain behind them jetted water into the air.

After all of that, Hanna and Danilo finally confessed their mutual feelings for each other.

I sighed in awe during the part where Danilo lovingly accepts Hanna who had cast aside her black mourning gown for a passionate red dress. They sang and danced together to the sweet melody of the "Merry Widow Waltz". Both their duet and waltz were sensational. Naturally, the orchestra work was superb.

The energy coming from the audience made it clear that everyone was fully enjoying this luxurious moment. By the time the curtain fell for the final time, I was moved to tears.

"That was amazing! I always thought that operas were supposed to be boring!" Hanaka exclaimed during the car ride home. She was the most excited one after the opera.

"Operettas are considered the origin of musicals, so that's probably why. It helps that *The Merry Widow* is an easy to understand comedy. It makes it fun!"

"Yeah, yeah! I totally agree. My compliments and thanks to the almighty Mashiro who secured these awesome tickets for us!"

"Almighty, huh? I could get used to the sound of that."

Shinji and Tomoi burst out laughing at our banter. Since it was just past evening, the four of us went out to eat before going home. Being considerate of our driver Shinji, Tomoi didn't order any alcohol either.

"Don't hold back on my account, Tomoi. Get a drink," Shinji said.

"Nah, I'm good. Besides, it's not like I can drink in front of Shimao," Tomoi said with a wry smile.

"Do you actually like alcohol?" I whispered in his ear.

"Yeah. Keep it a secret at school," he requested in a hushed voice. "I don't want them to think I'm a heavy drinker."

My heart thudded loudly in response.

♪♪♪

A lot had changed since becoming a middle schooler.

I was now allowed to commute to Miss Ayumi's house by bicycle and was granted full reign of the kitchen to make lunches for myself. Being able to help out Mom, in any capacity, made me happy. The lunches consisted of anything I could toss together from what we had in the freezer, but since it made little difference to cook for one or three, I took it upon myself to make lunch for Dad and Mom too. Their extremely thrilled reactions tickled me pink.

Getting my own cell phone was another big change. While Dad and Mom debated whether to buy me a smartphone, I went straight for the old-school flip phones. Considering how much it would cost with the data plan each month, going the cheaper route of a phone without data charges was the best option. Having my own phone helped me keep in contact with my school friends more than before.

Thanks to texting, I didn't feel disconnected from Eri and the gang despite being in different classes. Kon and I texted at least once a day, too. Mostly about the piano.

"How far did you get today?"

"I made it to x and x part."

That was what a general conversation between us sounded like.

One day in July, I received a text from Kou. He must've asked Kon for my number. *Let me see just how egotistic his text is!* I thought wickedly, ready for a challenge, only to be surprised by how incredibly normal his text was. Did it make sense for someone to be more polite over text than in person?

"I'm here if you ever need anything."

I stared at that last text for several minutes before quickly typing up my response. I hadn't owned a cell phone for more than three months yet, but I could text with mad speed. Hanaka once commented, "Your fingers are scary!" as she watched my thumbs dash over the keypad.

"Thank you very much for the text. Your kindness is moving. I doubt I will ever need your help, but should the occasion ever arise, I will take you up on that offer," I texted in a formal tone.

Well, that should do it, I thought, satisfied with my work. I hit send and my phone started ringing a few seconds later.

"Mashiro?"

I grimaced hard when I saw the name of the caller. "…Hello."

"What's with your text?"

"What about it?"

"Do you normally text your friends that way?"

"It was a proper text."

"What part of it was?! I thought you were sarcastically trying to tell me to never text you again."

"Yup, you got the right idea."

"I was right?"

We noisily tossed complaints back and forth about how unreasonable the other one was being and hung up in a huff. I laughed after hanging up on him. It'd been so long since I last argued with Kou like this. Not since Sou left. The conversation I had earlier with Kon helped me open up with him more than before.

"I've put Kou into a horribly unreasonable situation since enrolling in Seio. We've let everyone know that I'm his twin sister, but the girls who fawn over him tend to hate my guts anyway."

"How's that affected Kou any differently than before?" I asked her.

"Well, you see," Kon started, sounding like she was having a hard time finding the right words, "he's been going on dates with each girl he used to casually brush off before. He drives home with them and goes shopping with them. I think he's trying to treat the girls with the most influence at school equally."

Geh! Sounds like such a pain! I immediately sympathized with Kou after hearing about his situation.

Kou Narita was written as a Femi who's nice to every girl in *Hear My Heart.* Maybe his current situation was the hidden backstory behind that setting. Perhaps he went out of his way to be nice to everyone so that the girls who crushed on him wouldn't fight.

The girl he took to the operetta might've just been another of his groupies.

There was no way for me to know the true reason for his personality when I had failed to play his route to the end. I only ever knew the prince-like Kou Narita who spoke sweetly to the heroine every time he saw her.

I had forced my unilateral game image on Kou, thinking that I was in love with him, and then started to hate him when the real Kou differed from my ideal view of him. Even I felt disgusted by how self-serving I had been.

That said, it was impossible for me to fall blindly in love with Kou like that again.

I got the unassailable sense that Kou hated girls who loved him.

He was very cautious around girls who interpreted his superficial sugary words in ways that benefited them. I still didn't understand why he bothered with me after Sou left, but I was positive the moment I fell for him, he'd change his mind about me faster than he changes suits.

"Don't tell me you took what I said seriously?" He'd scoff at me, driving me to the wall with cruelness gleaming in his eyes, and once he did that, I'd no doubt *stab* him. I was not some fragile doormat who'd let someone step all over my heart. Surely Kou wouldn't want me to stab him, and I certainly didn't want my future to end behind bars as a knife-wielding maniac.

So the distance between us right now was just right.

Sou had started sending me picture postcards. Postcards with nothing written on them aside from my name and address. Some had adorable illustrations of boys and girls on them. Others were pictures of gorgeous churches with stained-glass windows. There was one with a painting of an angel. I imagined Sou picking one picture postcard from the racks every time he went out.

I pinned the postcards from him to the cork bulletin board hanging on my bedroom wall. Sometimes, when I thought of him, I'd look at his postcards and wonder about his life in Germany.

Is he doing okay? Is he eating well? ...Are German sausages just as good in

Natsu

Germany?

♪♪♪

SUMMER vacation was just around the corner, and the student body was starting to get excited for their break when the schedule for finals was announced. I was worried about the health, computer, and art class tests, so I went to study in the library with Tomo. She'd called me saying she'd received the past test sheets from her older sister who was in her third year at our middle school.

I pedaled my bicycle to the library the following Sunday afternoon to find not only Tomo waiting for me out front, but Rin as well.

"Rin, you're here too?" I asked, hopping off my bike.

"Yup. I've formed an alliance with Miyano."

"An alliance? With Tomo?"

Tomo bashfully swept her shoulder-length straight hair behind her ears. She used to be the easy to overlook type, but she had exchanged her glasses for contacts and started growing out her hair. Lately, she was becoming super cute. Her hair gesture just now was enough to make even my heart skip a beat.

"An alliance to topple you from your rank as the best student at school."

"There you have it."

They looked at each other and grinned.

I wonder when they started getting close.

Excited, I carefully studied Rin's face.

"Wh-What?" he stammered, averting his eyes.

"Just thinking. I should stop calling you by your first name now," I teased.

"Don't be stupid!"

Ooh, he's turning red.

Tomo smiled as she watched Rin and I. But I didn't miss the dark shadow falling over that smile. Did she think she could pull one over me?

We haven't been friends since elementary school just for show, Tomo.

"Hey, Tomo, would you mind if I made a copy of the past test questions?"

"I don't mind, but aren't you going to study with us?"

"You don't need a third wheel." I lightly punched them both in the shoulder.

"Y-You aren't the third wheel! If anything, I'm the third wheel!"

I snatched the test sheet from a bright-red Tomo and headed for the copy machine on the library's first floor. "Rin, should you really let Tomo think that way?"

"...No."

"Wait there just a minute. I'll copy it faster than you can say third wheel."

I pulled coins out of the change purse I brought with me and quickly made a copy of the tests using the copy machine. It was impossible to hold back the stupid grin creeping onto my face as I made the copies. I wondered how long it'd been since Tomo developed feelings for Rin. It must've made her really sad seeing the relationship dynamics between us if she'd been pining for him since elementary school.

Tomo was a smart, kind, gentle, and incredible girl. I thought that Rin was the greatest for discovering her good qualities.

I'll have to teach him a lesson in the off-chance he cheats on Tomo and makes her cry! Muahaha! Laughing maniacally on the inside, I returned to my friends, who drew several steps back from me for some weird reason.

"Mashiro, what's with that evil look on your face?"

"I thought the same thing. What? Are you gloating that this test is going to be a cinch too?"

"I am not!" I objected. I returned the test sheets to Tomo and whispered in her ear, "Text me later about how it went. You can do this, Tomo!"

Tomo gave me a solid nod, her eyes misting.

Oh my gosh! She is too cute! Rin was watching her with adoration too. *I hope everything goes smoothly for them!* I thought as I waved goodbye to my friends.

"Help me out if I get a crush in middle school. We'll be even then." Rin had made that request of me last fall.

I kept my promise.

The summer breeze whooshing past me while I pedaled my bicycle felt magnificent.

That night I was able to confirm with Tomo that she had indeed been crushing on Rin since the fourth grade.

"Oh, but I really was hoping that things would go well between you two," she texted me.

I fell onto my bed reading her all-too-lovable texts. I rolled back and forth hugging Becchin.

Lucky! It's so bittersweet and romantic!

Rin sent me the short text, "I've got a girlfriend now. Thanks, Mashiro."

Putting all of my joy for them into a single text, I replied, "Well done, soldier!"

"What are you, a general in the army?!"

I laughed at his joking reply.

♪♪♪

I'D scored a hundred percent on the five core subjects and music finals, and over ninety percent on the remaining three subjects. The alliance to overthrow my reign as the best student at school still had a long way to go.

"Dang it! Watch your back! I'll get you next time!"

"Same here! I'm joining the alliance! I'm definitely beating you next quarter!"

Majima joined arms with Rin in trying to take me down. Rei's eyes went round when two of the most popular boys in our year barged into our classroom during lunch to declare war on me.

"M-Mashiro, what was that just now?"

"An alliance to overthrow my position as top student."

"Seriously?!" The rest of our classmates clamored over the news.

I waved my finger at Rei and our classmates while clicking my tongue. "No one can defeat me! You just have to score all 100s in every subject if you want to overthrow my reign!" I declared, imitating the way an army general speaks.

"Oh! Mashiro, you're so cool!" Rei's perfectly timed comment got the classroom roaring with laughter.

"Was Shimao always this weird?" Kids from the other elementary school watched on with their jaws dropped.

CG 23: Mashiro & Kon (Comparing Piano Skills)

I was taken by complete surprise when August rolled in, and Miss Ayumi informed me that she'd be leaving Japan. Apparently she was going on tour in Europe with her former university mentor. Interestingly enough, Miss Ayumi was a graduate of the University of Music and Performing Arts Vienna. She was a drop-dead gorgeous piano virtuoso from a distinguished family and fluent in English and German to boot—I felt grateful for how blessed I was having such a talented woman as my teacher. Someone of her esteem would've never taken a kid from an average household as a student under normal circumstances.

Thank the game gods for heroine power!

As grateful as I felt, it was still a bummer I wouldn't be able to attend Miss Ayumi's lessons for close to two whole months.

Miss Ayumi saw how dejected I was feeling during our lesson and clapped her hands together, as if striking upon a genius idea. "I know! How about you take lessons from another piano teacher while I'm away, Mashiro?" Her eyes glittered with the idea.

"With another teacher?"

"One of my friends from university is a Japanese pianist who will be returning to Japan right around the time I leave. What do you think? I'm fairly certain he will take you on as a student if I ask him to."

"Is it really okay to ask him at the last minute like this?" My head spun with reluctance and anticipation.

Miss Ayumi smiled softly at me. "You know, Mashiro, you won't become a professional pianist if you let once-in-a-lifetime chances within reach slip by. You have to be greedier. My friend is talented enough; he was a finalist in the International Chopin Piano Competition two years ago. I am of the opinion that it will be a good experience for you to be under his tutelage for a period of time."

Am I dreaming?! Isn't that Noboru Misaka she's talking about?!

Noboru Misaka was the only Japanese pianist to make it to the International Chopin Piano Competition finals two years ago.

I gasped. He was a young virtuoso and the only Asian to make it all the way to the finals in a competition dominated by Russian and Polish pianists. The judging committee that year was so torn on the decision that they decided not to pick a winner at all. I watched the video of his performance when it came on during a TV special. His Chopin had a heartrending quality that squeezes the chest.

"P-Please do ask him for me!" I loudly exclaimed, dropping into an extremely formal bow.

Miss Ayumi smiled encouragingly. "Okay, I will."

Miss Ayumi cracked down on us hard when it came to the piano, but whenever she smiled, her beauty was so great I couldn't look straight at it without being blinded. I could practically see roses blooming behind her like a scene from a game or manga!

♪♪♪

ON the last day of first quarter, Mom took the day off work for the parent teacher meeting at my school. She rained praises on me when she saw straight A's on my report card.

"I'm so impressed with you, sweetie! You've been working so hard! Your teachers were going on about how many friends you have and how much fun you're having at school!" Mom effused, happier about my results than even me.

Knowing her, she was likely rejoicing more about me having a fulfilling school life than my grades. During the second grade I had put my parents through a lot of worrying after regaining my memories. How shocked they must've been to see such a sudden and drastic change in their young daughter. And yet they didn't meddle in my life more than absolutely necessary. No doubt they had various opinions and thoughts on what was going on too.

"Mom."

"Hm?"

"…Thank you. I'm so blessed to have been born as your daughter, Mommy."

The older me insisted that I convey my feelings to my loved ones while I had the chance.

Why was that?

Because I knew how much you could come to regret not saying the words you shoved aside thinking you could say them anytime.

Moved to tears, Mom pulled a tissue out of her purse and pressed it to her eyes. Seeing her cry drew out my tears too. I left school holding my mother's hand. The baseball club kids running laps before practice ran by us, looking over their shoulder to see what all the fuss was.

The pounding of shoes on pavement faded into the distance while the cries of the cicada grew all the louder in my ears.

♪♪♪

A ridiculously hectic summer vacation came next.

Until last year, my triangle route from home to the library to the Genda estate was good enough, but now I wanted to add school as a fourth destination on the days it was open. School was only open for students taking summer school lessons, but other students were allowed to come and go as they pleased too.

Eri and the gang had zero interest in going to school during summer vacation, but a chance to see Tomoi more often was too irresistible for me. By checking the summer school program book I could confirm what classes Tomoi was teaching.

I can see Tomoi for three days! Using a pink highlighter, I drew hearts around his days.

Then there were the lessons with Maestro Noboru!

Kon and I were taking his lessons together, so Miss Ayumi picked us up in her Jaguar on the first Sunday of summer break and drove us to Maestro Noboru's house. I trembled with anticipation over what kind of grand manor he lived in, only to be surprised by it being an average and cozy single-family home. I felt ashamed for assuming that just because someone was Miss Ayumi's friend that meant they had to be some sort of rich celebrity.

Maestro Noboru's house was located in the rustic city outskirts about an hour's drive from Miss Ayumi's house. His house didn't have an address or nameplate anywhere.

As soon as she pressed the intercom button we heard the pitter-patter of running feet before the door was suddenly thrown wide open.

"Ayumi!" Maestro Noboru stepped outside and hugged Miss Ayumi without even glancing at Kon and me. "Aaah, it really is you, Ayumi! Do you know how happy you made me when you called?"

"I know. Come now, let go of me. You're scaring my students." Used to his eccentric behavior, Miss Ayumi simply rapped him lightly on the back with a sympathetic smile.

Maestro Noboru's first visual impression could be summed up with a single word: lanky.

He definitely stood over six feet tall. His weight was anybody's guess—I was too scared to know. He was so skinny I thought he might blow away with the faintest breeze!

It was impossible to make out his face under the mop of fuzzy green hair hanging over his eyes. His chin was covered in a bush of stubble. Big, black-rimmed glasses peeked out through gaps in his unkempt hair.

Y-Yeah, I can't even call him good-looking to be polite.

When I watched the TV special on his performance during the competition, he still had on those horrible glasses, but his hair was shorter. Honestly, I didn't remember what his face looked like. What I did remember was the intensity of his music and following his fingers dancing across the keyboard the entire time.

Kon stood beside me with an equally perplexed expression.

It probably didn't help that we'd been whispering fangirl comments in the back of the car on the way over, saying things like, "I hope he's cool!" and "He already has high marks in my book for being a piano virtuoso!" Now I felt bad for getting my hopes up and being disappointed.

"It's such a shame though! I would've stayed in Vienna if I'd known you were going to be on tour there!"

"Don't push yourself. You and I both know you flee to Japan this time of year because you don't want to see *those* people."

Left out by their intimate conversation, Kon and I exchanged bemused looks.

"E-Excuse me?" I timidly spoke up.

I didn't want to interrupt their heartwarming reunion, but we'd brought ice cream with us as a thank you gift!

Miss Ayumi glanced over at me and promptly pushed Maestro Noboru away. "Won't you let us inside already? The girls bought you ice cream. Isn't ice cream your favorite?"

"Yeah. I love it! Thanks a bunch!"

From what I could tell, his gratitude was directed toward us, but I couldn't see where his eyes were looking under all that hair.

He led us inside through an empty foyer into the even emptier living room where we ended up downing the melting ice cream in a rush— while standing. We actually brought five containers of ice cream for Maestro Noboru to eat later on, but things didn't go as planned.

"I can't believe it. At least buy a couch and a refrigerator! It's not like you're pinched for cash!" Miss Ayumi looked around the barren room with exasperation written all over her face.

Kon, Maestro Noboru, and I scarfed down the melting ice-cream cartons while trying to avoid brain freezes. Maestro Noboru silently shoveled ice cream from a second carton into his mouth as he shook his head in response to Miss Ayumi's accusation.

"It's too much of a hassle. I'm only here until the fall. I'm good as long as I can play the piano."

"There you go saying stuff like that again! Don't make me worry about you so much, Noboru." Miss Ayumi probably said it without much thought, but I caught a glimpse of the bright-red cheeks underneath Maestro Noboru's rat's nest of frizzy hair.

Ah, so that's how it is. Maestro Noboru has feelings for Miss Ayumi. That's why he took on our lessons without much notice.

We somehow managed to polish off the ice cream and followed Maestro Noboru to the second story where the piano was located.

He told us he had all the rooms on the second story knocked down and rebuilt the space to be completely soundproof. Unlike the first story, the second was air-conditioned and even had a couch. Two Steinway concert grand pianos glistened in the center of the room.

"You should've brought us to this room right off the bat!"

"I couldn't. No eating or drinking is allowed in here!"

Kon and I had broken out in a sweat from the heat downstairs, so we thoroughly agreed with Miss Ayumi's complaints. But Maestro Noboru firmly stuck to his guns, retorting, "This is where I play the piano. It's sacred."

Miss Ayumi didn't argue the point with him and instead went right over to the pianos to check out how they sounded. "Want to hear how well the girls can play first?" she asked him, stroking the piano keys.

"Yeah, I guess I should. They're your students, Ayumi, so let me know if there is anything I should be careful of or should look out for in advance."

"Let them play faithful to the sheet music."

"Ick…I'm not fond of that."

"I know you aren't. But don't make them stray from it yet."

The air surrounding Miss Ayumi and Maestro Noboru changed in the blink of an eye. Miss Ayumi directed her attention to us with the commanding air of our mentor.

"Kon, play the third movement from Beethoven's 'Moonlight Sonata'. Mashiro, play Ravel's 'Jeux d'eau'. You can decide who goes first."

Kon looked at me nervously. "What do you want to do, Mashiro?"

"You'll set the bar too high if you go first, Kon. Do you mind if I play first?"

"Go ahead."

"Which piano should I use?" I asked Maestro Noboru. My heart hammered in my chest, my hands dampened with sweat.

His hard expression gave way to a broad smile, and he patted me lightly on the head. "Play whichever one suits you. Don't feel nervous. Pretend like nobody is here."

"Pardon?"

"You're playing Ravel, right? Concentrate only on you, the piano, and the music in your head, Mashiro. Erase me, Ayumi, and Kon from the room. Understand?"

No, I didn't understand what he meant. I shifted my gaze to Miss Ayumi in search of help. For some reason she pressed her index finger to her chin and rubbed it thoughtfully. She said nothing though, leaving the instructing to the maestro for now.

Beyond confusion, I sat in front of the right piano. Testing the sound, I tapped one of the white keys.

Th-That's weird. Thrown off by the sound, I played several random chords. *Hmm. It sounds pretty and resounds well, but something about it just doesn't sit right with me.*

Bothered, I got up and tried out the left piano. Kon watched me in anticipation. They were both Steinway concert grand pianos, but I had a clear preference for the left one. I adjusted the bench height and laid my fingers on the keyboard.

Ravel – Jeux d'eau

Jeux d'eau, often translated as "Fountains" or as "Play of Water", is a piece infamous for using nonstandard keys included on larger models and for its nearly bitonal juxtaposition of two harmonies. Its infamy continues to this day as a difficult song that makes pianists cry. The ebb and flow of harmonic color is as near to a liquid state as music could ever achieve with its complex appregrios. You could say it's a distinctive trait of Ravel's to express beauty only through the sound of the piano by excluding the emotional melodies of the romantic school.

The true test of talent was just how smoothly the pianist could play the diverse arpeggios that incorporated not only natural overtones, but dissonance chords. The continuous *arpeggiations* and chromatic flourishes had an electric effect. Playing according to the *très doux* musical notation, I concentrated only on the music flowing beneath my fingertips.

The last note faded and I stood from the bench. No one said a word. I thought I'd played well, but maybe I had unknowingly screwed up somewhere along the way.

Feeling the blood drain from my face, I looked to Maestro Noboru. He gave me an impassive nod and simply said, "Kon, it's your turn."

Oh, I get it now. He won't appraise my performance till he hears Kon's.

Kon sat in front of the same piano I had and masterfully played the third movement from Beethoven's "Moonlight Sonata" with her usual masterful technique and expressive power.

Once both of our performances had ended, Maestro Noboru complimented us. "You both played marvelously."

Miss Ayumi stared at Maestro Noboru without saying anything.

Pushed by her nudging gaze, he took a short breath and looked at me. "Why did you choose the left piano?"

"The sound… I can't really explain it well, but it sounded like it was sulking," I answered truthfully.

He burst out laughing. "Buahaha! S-Sorry… You're an interesting girl, Mashiro. The right piano is the one I've been using ever since I was a small boy. And the piano you played is the one I have guests use when they come to this house. But I see. The piano is sulking, huh?"

Maestro Noboru stood in front of the right Steinway and played Chopin's "Black Key Étude" with a smile. The moment he started playing, the room filled with glistening and sparkling music, accented with real gaiety and tenderness.

"How does it sound to you now?"

"Like it is bubbling with joy," I answered with the first thing that came to mind since I had no idea how to explain it. Even Miss Ayumi laughed aloud at that one.

"I'll take them on as students, Ayumi. Things might just get interesting around here for the first time in a long time." Maestro Noboru shook hands with both me and Kon. His hands were surprisingly soft and supple.

"How was my performance?" Kon asked on our way out. She searched his face as if tormented.

"It was good. Your tragic resolve suits Beethoven well."

Kon's eyes went saucer-wide at Maestro Noboru's response.

Tragic resolve? Lost as to what that meant, I looked from Kon to the maestro.

"However," Noboru added, shrugging as he met Kon's drilling gaze head on, "if you keep this up your music will crumble to pieces sooner or later. Proceed carefully."

Kon merely nodded with her head hung low, her teeth cutting into her bottom lip.

Heroine and Original Heroine's Results
Target Character: None
Event Linked to Past Life: Warning
CLEAR

♪♪♪

THE weather was sickeningly hot. I threw open my curtain and the window when I woke up in the morning, letting in a gust of hot stuffy wind. Gazing up at the endless blue sky without a single cloud in sight, a smile stretched across my face.

The first summer school lesson is today! It's the day I get to see Tomoi!

Lessons with Maestro Noboru fell on that same evening, so I made plans with Kon to meet up in front of my middle school.

"Summer school? Mashiro, don't tell me you're…" Kon's voice instantly darkened with worry when I called her in the morning and told her I would be attending summer school lessons until 3 p.m.

Uh? Does she think I'm failing school?

"D-Don't finish that question!" I cut in. "I'm not required to attend summer school. I just thought I should take advantage of the school being open. It'll help my parents save money on A/C if I'm not home, too!" I rushed out to clear Kon's suspicions.

"You keep the A/C off to save money? …Mashiro, are you enduring this horrible heat whenever you're at home?" Kon sounded even more worried about me. That's what she latched onto this time?! "You're welcome to stay at my house every day until your parents come home."

"I can't do that to you."

Kon made a disappointed sigh through the receiver.

I was grateful for the offer, but I couldn't impose so much on someone who wasn't even related. It didn't matter how close we were; there were some points where you needed to draw a line.

"As it is, you're doing me a big favor by picking me up and dropping me off twice a week for Maestro Noboru's lessons. I couldn't be grateful enough, even if it kills—"

"DON'T SAY THAT!" Kon sharply cut me off. She must've sensed my shock through the silence on the line, because she took a small, shuddery breath. "Sorry. I'm tired… But really, don't think anything of it. I do these things for you because I want to." She sounded as if she were trying to force as much cheerfulness into her voice as possible.

"Kon? I've wondered this for a while, but are you doing okay? It seems like something is weighing you down."

"I-In what way do you mean?"

"Hmm, like there's something about the remake version of *Hear My Heart* that's hard for you to share with me? Or maybe not that exactly. Either way, it seems to me like you're extremely worried about something… Oh, but I hope it's not a nuisance for me to worry about you like this."

It'd been bothering me for forever. Her arguments with Prince Tobi, her cornered expression during the recital, her deathly pale side profile during the fireworks—signs of something being horribly wrong with her had been interlaced through our encounters for quite a long time.

But what if the problem she was facing was something incredibly personal, that she didn't want anyone to know about?

I didn't want to hurt her by overstepping my bounds.

Silence filled the line for what felt like hours. Just when I thought she might've hung up on me, I heard Kon's strained, wisp of a voice. "Mashiro."

"Yeah?"

"I'm always praying for your happiness, Mashiro."

"…Thanks."

"I don't have to be forgiven. I just—KOFF! KOFF!" Kon suddenly started hacking. The intense coughing fit made it sound like she was choking on blood. I heard her wheezing in a desperate gasp for air before everything went dead silent.

In a panic, I pressed my cell phone right against my ear. "Kon?! KON?! Are you okay?! KON!"

BEEP! BEEP! BEEP!

The disconnect tone suddenly kicked into the silence.

What should I do?! What was that just now?! Terrified, I dialed Kon's house phone number. I called several times, but no one picked up. Did that make any sense when her estate was supposedly filled with butlers and maids and housekeepers?!

Tears in my eyes, I dialed Kou's number. Now wasn't the time to argue with myself about not wanting to depend on him!

Kou picked up on the second ring. "Mashiro? What's wrong? It's unusual for you to call."

My heart lurched at the sound of his voice, and the tears spilled down my cheeks. I always ended up crying in front of this guy.

"K-Kon is…" My voice cracked through the sobs. I heard him gasp.

"Are you crying? What's wrong, Mashiro?!"

"No! It's not me! It's Kon! Sorry, I know you're busy, but please, please go straight to the Genda estate and check on Kon for me!" Through my tears I managed to explain how Kon suddenly had a coughing fit in the middle of our conversation, the line abruptly disconnecting, and how nobody picked up the phone when I called her house.

"Okay. I'll go right now. Don't get too worried," Kou replied and hung up.

Summer school lessons with Tomoi didn't mean squat to me anymore. I was worried sick about Kon. I clutched Becchin to my chest and paced circles in my bedroom. That coughing fit wasn't normal.

Is Kon sick? Is that what she's been hiding from me? Could she be—

"Kon…don't leave me," I cried out.

Saying it aloud only served to dredge up even worse anxiety that turned to sobs. Brooding for several laps around my room, I finally struck on the bright idea to ride my bike to the Genda estate. It'd take me an hour of hard pedaling to get there, but at least I'd be doing something instead of sitting still and moping in my bedroom.

I wish I had money to call a cab!

I shoved my cell phone and wallet into my pouch bag and noticed the black Benz rounding the corner as I was about to fly out the front door. The driver honked the horn once, and I squinted at the car against the bright sunlight.

"Lady Mashiro, I have come on orders from Master Kou to escort you to the house." Mr. Mizusawa stepped out of the Benz he parked in front of my house.

"Mr. Mizusawa! Kon is…Kon has…" Flustered, I flapped my lips unsure of how to explain the situation.

Mr. Mizusawa placed his hand on my trembling shoulder and gently directed me into the car. "Please get in. Lady Kon is all right. I will take you to the Genda estate right now."

"P-Please do!" I bit my bottom lip to fight back the tears. Mr. Mizusawa opened the backseat door for me, and I slid inside the air-conditioned space, pressing my handkerchief against my mouth to hold in the sobs.

At any rate, I needed to calm down. Mr. Mizusawa told me that Kon was all right. Panicking wasn't going to help anyone.

After an agonizingly long drive, we finally arrived at the Genda estate.

I entered the foyer with Mr. Mizusawa and was immediately escorted to Kon's room by one of the maids.

"I shall excuse myself here. Master Kou is already waiting inside," Mr. Mizusawa informed me.

"Okay. Thank you very much." I bowed deeply to him and knocked on the door.

"Come in," Kou's voice said calmly from inside the room. That's all I needed to hear to know the worst hadn't come to pass. Slightly relieved, I turned the doorknob. Kou appeared from the hallway connecting Kon's bedroom to the piano room.

"She just fell asleep. Thanks for contacting me. No one had noticed Kon had collapsed. The phones weren't working for some strange reason just like you'd said."

He beckoned me to sit on the couch, and I sat down without a word. Going crazy with concern for Kon, I just couldn't sit still.

Seeing me fidget, Kou gave a half smile. "You didn't clean up after your tears," he said softly as he sat beside me and wiped under my eyes with his thumb. His fingertips were callused from the violin strings. I surely would've pushed him away if there was even a hint of flirtation in that gesture. But deep down I could tell Kou was genuinely worried about me.

"Tell me the truth, please. Is Kon seriously ill?"

"Not as far as we can tell. She's suffered from sudden feverish attacks and coughing fits for a long time now, but there's nothing blatantly wrong with her body. She's been through complete physicals and thorough medical testing more times than I can count. She receives a clean bill of health every time. The attending physician said it might be linked to something mental," Kou explained, his voice grim.

That's the same as me. Hammering headaches. Bizarre bouts of sickness. Every test coming up clean. Does our shared identity as reincarnated souls have something to do with it?

I shook uncontrollably in the face of that frightening hunch. What was happening to us? Did Kon know what caused this abnormality in us?

"…I'm sorry. I'm so, so sorry.

No. That's not it. Don't cry.

You don't understand. It's all my fault. I was wrong.

Because…I actually knew everything all along."

STAB! THROB!

Skull-breaking pain shot through my head every time I nearly remembered something I knew was very important to me. Intense regret flooded through me from the blank space where my memories once existed. My head felt like it was being split open. It hurt so bad I wanted to throw up.

"Mashiro, calm down. Kon's okay." Kou put his arm around my shuddering shoulders.

"I probably…smell like…sweat right now," I squeezed out through the pain.

"Don't be silly. Even if you did smell, it'd only be because you were panicking to help Kon."

You always smell good Mashiro. That was the kind of sugar-coated line I expected to fly out of his mouth. But it didn't.

I leaned into Kou's arm without putting up a fight. He couldn't hide his surprise over me nestling up to him with zero resistance. I tightly shut my eyes to escape the relentless pain and nuzzled my cheek against his broad chest. Tears welled up when I heard the sound of his quickening heartbeat.

I might lose Kon forever. I don't even know if I'm going to get through this in one piece. A future might be out of the picture for us. Maybe my life will end again at eighteen.

The hopelessness suddenly rearing its ugly head amid my agonizing pain shook me to my core.

Daddy. Mommy. Hanaka.

I needed someone to hold me in their arms and tell me it was okay just this once. I longed for someone to capture the pieces of my crumbling body and anchor me to this place. Somewhere in the back of my mind I strongly thought how glad I was that it wasn't Sou with me right now.

I didn't want to give that sweet, precious boy the wrong idea. I didn't want to disappoint him when he viewed me like a surrogate mother.

"…Kou…I'm sorry…forgive me this once."

I heard Kou's sharp inhale. I had a feeling that Kou, with his lack of affection for me, would allow me this display of weakness and neediness. I always blamed him for being calculating, when I was the most calculating one. I forced back my feelings of guilt toward the middle school aged Kou and put a lid on them.

This world, my fate, myself; everything scared me beyond measure.

"Both you and Kon are hiding something from me," Kou whispered, the hurt audible in that tiny voice, and still he adjusted his hold on me to make our position more comfortable for us both.

I felt like he was really losing out at a time like this.

He should've just pushed me away and refused me with a snide remark like "don't lean on me when it's convenient for you."

Instead, he embraced me in silence with the gentlest touch until the pain and fear abated.

Interlude: Kon's Bad Day

Lacrimosa dies illa
Qua resurget ex favilla
Judicandus homo reus:

Huic ergo parce, Deus.
Pie Jesu Domine,
Dona eis requiem.

Amen.

IS that Mozart's Requiem? Yes, that's "Lacrimosa" playing.

I partially opened my eyes through the haze enshrouding my consciousness. *That man* was sitting on a chair next to my pillow singing those Latin lyrics like a lullaby, his blond tresses swaying with the rhythm. His perfectly clear voice sounded like an angel.

The irony twitched my lips into an unintentional sneer.

"You've come to?"

I nodded. He rested his hand on me.

"That was most marvelous, Kon. Mashiro was a real treat, too."

What did you do to her?! I tried to jump out of bed, but my body wouldn't move. My voice lodged in my throat.

"Haha. Despair, *Kon*. Relentless torment and despair for the future filled me most satisfyingly. I must thank you." He theatrically sighed at my killer glare. "It's your fault, *Kon*. All because you try and try again to break our deal. This world won't hold together if you refuse to stick one-hundred percent to the terms of our contract." He dolefully shook his head. "I'm the source of the contract and equally bound to it, after all."

He gently stroked my hair. "Five years to go. It's a real shame we can't play for more than five years." He blinked those stunning blue eyes identical to Tobi's. "The crimson prince has your divine protection and assistance. Sou's little knight offers up her own form of protection. Now then, how will the game play out?" He chuckled, his shoulders shaking with mirth.

He looked lovingly down at me. "Oh, on another note, I've set the stage by summoning your precious lover here as well."

Icy chills crawled up the length of my spine.

How dare you! I yelled at him in my thoughts. *You promised me you wouldn't involve him in this! He has nothing to do with our game!*

The man smirked with Tobi's flawless face. "It's a temporary form, of course. Multiple contracts with people from the same world aren't allowed, after all."

I swore I'd never see him again. It doesn't matter if he's in this world. I'm not getting involved, I retorted in my thoughts.

"Do you really mean that? Could you truly say the same thing after seeing him in person?" He pushed his blond bangs off his face and disappeared as suddenly as he had appeared.

"You're up?" Kou appeared from the hallway connecting my bedroom suite. Mashiro timidly popped her head out from behind him.

She looked whiter than a ghost. Her puffy red eyes and tear-streaked cheeks were painful to look at.

That wretched man… I'll never forgive him.

Kou and Mashiro became horribly flustered when they saw me in pain, biting down on my bottom lip until the tooth drew blood.

"Lay down if you're still in pain."

"Listen to Mashiro. Don't overdo it."

"I'm not. I'm fine now." The pain scorching my body from the inside out vanished as if it had never existed. "Sorry for worrying you."

But it's okay. It doesn't matter how much pain we're in. Both she and I are protected from "death" until the day we turn eighteen.

Mozart – Lacrimosa (English Lyrics)

Full of tears will be that day
When from the ashes shall arise
The guilty man to be judged;
Therefore spare him, O God,
Merciful Lord Jesus,
Grant them eternal rest.
Amen.

♪♪♪

IT was almost noon by the time Kon woke up. Our lesson with Maestro Noboru didn't start until 4 p.m. so I wanted to return home for a bit first, but Kon and Kou insisted I stay.

"But I don't have my lesson bag or any of my stuff with me," I protested.

"We can just leave earlier than usual and drop by your house on the way over, Mashiro. Okay?" Kon reasoned.

"Just do that, Mashiro."

"O-Okay."

The summer school lessons I had been so looking forward to came back to the forefront of my thoughts once I saw Kon looking like her usual self. *The lesson doesn't start until 1:30 p.m. If I make a mad dash for it now, I'll be able to slip into the lesson only a little late.*

"I really wanted to attend the summer school lessons at my school though," I muttered.

Kou's eyes went round. "Don't tell me you—"

"I'm not failing anything," I got out before he could finish the same sentence Kon tried to ask me earlier. "I'm not trying to brag, but failing a middle school test would be the same as forgetting how to breathe for me," I retorted.

He's the last person I want looking down on my intelligence!

Kou gave me a once-over, his eyebrow arched with suspicion. "Then why go to school during break?"

"B-Because…"

My motives were so impure, I hesitated to say them out loud. *Not getting to see Tomoi even once during summer break is too much for me to bear! I want to see his face, just for a little bit. If only I didn't have piano, I could've entered the badminton club he advises and seen him every day!*

I was shocked by the direction my thoughts took. Something was seriously wrong with me, wanting to spend time with someone more than the piano.

I must've been blushing, because a beautiful smile blossomed on Kon's face. Boy did she look amused and delighted as she shifted her gaze from me to Kou.

"Are you possibly meeting up with the guy you like at school? I sure feel bad for keeping you here if that's the case."

"N-No! I-I don't like him like that—Anyways, it's not what you think!"

I stood no chance against Kon. Could she see everything written on my face like an open book? Shaking my head back and forth as hard as I could, I averted my gaze from her. I shouldn't have let myself be distracted by her though, because Kou closed the gap between us on the couch and caught my cheeks between his hands. He forced my face toward him and searched my eyes.

"Mashiro, is Kon right?" he questioned, his voice husky.

"I-I just said it's not like that."

"Aren't you the one who said you won't date till high school? What's the big idea?"

I'm the one who wants to ask what the big idea here is!

"What's the big deal, anyway? It's not like you like me or anything. Or do you, Kou?" I came right out and asked him.

Don't be stupid—was what I had expected him to say in return for my directness. Instead, Kou grimaced, dropped his gaze, then suddenly returned his eyes to mine and held it. A dark shadow fell over his violet eyes and his face twisted into a heart-wrenching expression. Despite knowing it was all an act, I couldn't stop from being captivated by him.

"What if I said I do?"

There! It's come! Our trademark mind games have begun. How many times must I tell him I won't fall for his tricks for him to get it through his thick skull?!

"I can't trust the words of someone who answers a question with a question!" I pried his hands from my face and jumped to my feet. Kon, who was watching over our word war with bated breath, loudly sighed and slumped back against the sofa.

I should go home after all. This isn't the time to play with Kou. Missing out on today's lesson means I won't get to see Tomoi again for a while!

"Sorry, Kon. I'm going home."

"Okay. I'll have Nonaga drive you."

Kon saw me to the door and handed me a cute, decorated lunch box. "Eat this for lunch."

Kou looked irked as he stood beside Kon. His mouth was turned down in a nasty frown.

"See you later today. I'll be waiting for you in front of the school gates," I said to Kon, ignoring Kou.

"Sure. Good luck with your lessons. Thank you so much for today."

Once I finished speaking with Kon, I faced Kou. Wordlessly, he waited for me to address him.

I should at least thank him for letting me lean on him and for helping me calm down. My panic attack went away because he held me without saying anything. This is the one time I'm legit thankful for him being good with women.

"Kou."

"What?"

"Thanks. I'm glad you were here for me."

"…No problem." Kou's eyes rounded as if surprised by what I said. The slight pink hue of his earlobes betrayed his indifferent response.

Oh my gosh! Is this some sorta trick to make me fall for the gap between the bashful him and the player egomaniac him?!

Scary! It's insane how much effort he puts in! Girls haven't been falling all over themselves for him since childhood for no reason!

Impressed by the detail he put into his womanizing skills, I waved goodbye and exited the lavish foyer.

I heard Kon giggling behind me.

ONCE I got home, I scarfed down the lunch Kon gave me, brushed my teeth, and checked my appearance in the mirror. The summer uniform was a white, short-sleeved sailor style blouse and skirt. I was pretty fond of the cute pleated skirt, even though the extra lining to prevent it from becoming see-through made it hot. Lastly, I tied the aqua tie and skipped to the foyer. Honestly, I wanted to take a shower and blow my hair out first, but time wasn't on my side.

Tomoi wasn't in class when I arrived, meaning I barely made it in time. Around ten kids were taking the supplemental lessons. Some other students who were here for different reasons could be spotted here and there throughout the campus.

"Yo, Mashiro. What're you doin' here?" one of the boys from my class, Tazaki, asked when I entered the classroom. He looked like the delinquent type, down to his long, silver hair and pierced ears, but he actually seemed like a good guy with the way he always struck up a friendly conversation with me.

"To learn, of course."

"HUH?! Are you freakin' kiddin' me?!"

Yes, I lied—I bet if I told him the real reason it'd shock the socks off him.

"Nope, it's the truth!" I answered with a smile as I secured the seat next to the window and pressed my forehead against the glass to get a better look below.

The teachers' parking lot was visible from this classroom. A blue domestic car pulled into the lot with perfect timing. The cute, round standard car was Tomoi's favorite. One thing he had in common with Dad was the way he took care of his stuff—his car was always polished.

My heart pounded loudly in my chest when he stepped out of the driver's seat.

This has to be that feeling. Love is the only thing that explains it.

He looked a little tired even though it was past noon. Maybe he stayed up late last night since it was the weekend. *Oh, tufts of hair are sticking out a little from behind his ears. The way he rubs his eyes with his fists is such a cute gesture at his age! It shouldn't be legal!*

If Rei saw him now, she definitely would've struck him down with an instant, "So unattractive!" But I found his natural, unaffected looks just as lovable.

If this isn't love, then what is it? It's heartbreaking that he's still in love with my amazing older sister, but that might be the exact reason why I find him appealing.

I didn't have any overreaching ambitions like wanting a romantic relationship where we had mutual feelings for each other. My feelings were closer to that of a fan. I fell for him from a distance, always wishing that he would have an amazing day every day.

"To your seats! Class is starting now." Tomoi appeared inside the classroom not long after I watched him enter the school building. The kids who were talking in groups around the classroom each picked whichever seat they wanted.

"You're Mashiro, right? Can I sit here?"

"Of course you can. Minori, was it?"

"That's me! Thanks for remembering!"

A girl with orange hair in a wedge cut sat in the seat beside me. She was a member of the same soft tennis club as Rei and from Class 6 with Rin. I'd spoken to her on multiple occasions when she hung out with Rei.

"I didn't think you'd be here, Mashiro."

"Yeah, I was having a hard time studying at home."

"Me too! Would you mind teaching me the parts I don't know?"

"I'm not sure how good of a teacher I'll be, but I'd be happy to help."

Minori's face lit up in a bright smile.

Tomoi quickly went through roll call, then began handing out the math worksheets he'd made for the summer school students. The worksheet covered very basic math problems, but it was like gold to me because it was in his handwriting. I had to get a hold of one no matter what.

"Oh? Do you need one too, Mashiro?"

"Yes, I want one," I replied instantly.

"I don't think this will pose much of a challenge for you though," he whispered, inclining his head to the side in contemplation. "Well, it's not like it'll hurt." He turned and addressed the whole class, "Once you solve this worksheet, bring it up to me."

Tomoi returned to the teacher's desk at the front of the classroom. I immediately set about solving the worksheet problems. It was way too easy.

I finished in less than three minutes…

I glanced at Minori out of the corner of my eye and saw she had more than half left.

"I don't get it!" Tazaki groaned, giving up on trying already.

It wouldn't be easy going up to Tomoi's desk with my completed worksheet before everyone else got halfway through it. While I was at a loss about what to do next, I sensed someone looking at me from the front of the classroom.

Tomoi looked amused by me. I felt the heat rush to my cheeks. He beckoned me up front with his finger, so I obediently shoved to my feet and brought the worksheet to him.

"Are you freakin' kidding me?!"

"Tell me the answers!"

The boys in class threw complaints and pleas at my back as I made my way to Tomoi's desk.

"Should I assume you're all finished since you have enough time to grumble?" Tomoi threatened, exasperation coloring his voice. I silently showed him my worksheet. He quickly ran his eyes over my answers and circled them with practiced ease.

He wrote "very good" at the top of my 100% correct worksheet with a red pen, then flipped the paper over. After a moment of thought, he wrote down a new set of math problems.

※ **a, b, c, d, and e are nonnegative integer numbers from 1 to 9 and satisfy the following two conditions of (I) and (II):**

(I) $a > b > c > d > e$

(II) $(a + e)(b + c + d) = 273$

Calculate the value of ①$a + e$. Also find the value of ②d.

Tomoi finished writing down the problem and smiled up at me. His mischievous and boyish grin drew a smile out of me too.

You're trying to test my skills with a difficult problem, aren't you? But I won't be frazzled by a question of this level.

Answer:

①273 = 3 x 7 x 13

When a + e = 13, the sum of the remaining three is 21.

So the answer is 13.

②Since the difference between a and e is 4 or more according to (I), a = 9 and e = 4.

Since b + c + d = 21, b = 8, c = 7 and d = 6.

So the answer is 6.

Not even hesitating for a moment, I scribbled out the answer on the back of the paper. Tomoi raised an eyebrow and clapped his hands together in approval, careful not to make a sound. That alone was enough to send me over the moon with delight.

"Use the rest of the time to do your homework or whatever else you want to study. If you happen to have any math questions, which I doubt you do, bring them to me."

"Yes, Mr. Matsuda." I gave a cheerful reply and returned to my seat like I was walking on air.

Minori was waiting for me to come back and leaned over to whisper, "What were you talking to Mr. Matsuda about?"

She seemed interested in our secret conversation.

Is Minori a fan of Tomoi's, too? Join my fanclub! Grinning away like an idiot, I showed her the back of my worksheet.

She glanced over the question and answer and flopped onto her desk, grumbling, "I wish I'd never asked."

Why not?! How could you not be crushing on our teacher when he does such cute stuff like this?!

CG 24: Arrival of the Support Character (Mashiro & Kon)

TIME flew by until it was already the end of August. Today marked my ninth lesson and *solfège* with Maestro Noboru. From Bach to Chopin to Beethoven and Brahms, Maestro Noboru assigned me a rich variety of music styles. He didn't share Miss Ayumi's method of slowly taking apart my progress with each song. Instead, he allowed me free rein to play how I wanted and made perfunctory remarks about it in French such as "*J'aime* (I like it)" or "*Je n'aime pas* (I don't like it)." I was welcome to replay a song he'd given a disapproving shake of the head to, but if he shouted "*Non!*" a second time, he would never listen to me play that same song again. All of it made for thrilling lessons.

Living in Paris for a long time had given Maestro Noboru the habit of speaking in French whenever he got worked up.

"*Je ne comprends pas* (I don't understand)!" I exclaimed.

"S-Sorry. Um, I was trying to tell you to think harder about why this passage's tempo indicates allegro."

"You were? Okay, then should I replay this part?"

"Yes, from the beginning."

It's thanks to Maestro Noboru that I added French to my self-study lessons. Every day was crazy busy. A whole month passed by in the blink of an eye.

"Maestro Noboru is the devil incarnate!"

"You still have it easy, Mashiro! He's stuck me with composers who incorporate tons of Jazz elements like Piazzolla and Gershwin, you know? Worst of all, he never gives me the go-ahead to move on from it."

Kon made a good point. For whatever reason, Maestro Noboru employed completely different teaching methods for us. We had taken him up on his offer to sit through each other's lessons so that we didn't have to suffer in the heat downstairs. His different instructions seemed so weird to us.

On this particular day, he had Kon play Piazzolla's "Libertango". Amazingly, Maestro Noboru joined in on the other piano halfway through her performance and it became a jam session.

"Kon, empty out your thoughts. Pursue only the rhythm and sound. Feel the beat." Maestro Noboru freely mixed up the tempo, frustrating Kon to near tears. "Unfetter your heart, Kon. Come on, follow me."

Aggravated by his overly abstract instructions, Kon suddenly started applying improvisatory elements to the music.

After a period of great productivity as a composer, Astor Piazzolla suffered a heart attack in 1973 and that same year he moved to Italy, where he composed Libertango, a portmanteau merging "Libertad" (Spanish for liberty) and "Tango", symbolizing his break from Classical Tango to Tango Nuevo. The famous song has come to be symbolic with Piazzolla now.

I owned a CD of a famous cellist's rendition of the song, but this was my first time hearing "Libertango" played as a piano duet on two pianos. Compact, dynamic, and unforgiving didn't even begin to scratch the surface of describing this classical tango. The melody weaved between dark and intimate sentiments. Sorrow hung over the intense and gritty rhythm. The high notes beautifully descended. Kon struck to life every sorrow and burden she carried, turning them into a magnificent tango.

Tears welled in my eyes. I dropped my gaze to where gooseflesh rippled along my bare arm.

"*Tres bien!*" Maestro Noboru walked over to Kon, who was in a daze like she had her soul sucked out, and shook her right hand. "Kon, you can be more up-front about your passion for music. Acknowledge your own piano."

"…I'll try."

"Then let's tackle Liszt next week. I'm going to see how you play 'La Campanella.'"

Sounds like she finally gets to go back to the classics.

Kon answered him with a relieved nod.

Lucky! I love "La Campanella"!

I stared at Maestro Noboru with excitement, prompting a, "Do you want to play too, Mashiro?"

"I want to play! But I have zero confidence I can play it right by next week."

"Hmm. Next time then." He smiled and declared, "That's the end of today's lesson!"

Our lessons had no set end time, so Kon called Mr. Nonaga to pick us up once we were finished. Maestro Noboru always played a variety of songs for us until our ride arrived. The amazing thing about him was his ability to reproduce any song he'd ever heard, including ones he'd never seen the sheet music for.

Kon and I were getting carried away tossing all sorts of song requests at him when the lesson room door flew open.

"NOBORU!"

"…Hah," he sighed. "You found me then." His fingers stopped on the keys as he grimaced at the beautiful girl with indigo hair who'd suddenly appeared. She stormed right past us as we gawked and dove for Maestro Noboru who was still sitting in front of his piano.

"I've longed to see you! Say, don't you know just how much I've been dying to see you, Noboru?!"

I feel like I've heard this same line somewhere before…

The girl looked around the same age as us, while Maestro Noboru was in his thirties. Even if I tried not to think it, the words "Lolita complex" and "pedo" jumped to mind. The thought must've crossed Kon's mind too, because she took a big step back with me.

"It's not what you think, girls! This is my little sister." Maestro Noboru accurately read our looks of disgust and was trying to pry off the girl clinging to his neck. She wrapped her arms even tighter around him like an anaconda, cutting off his airway and causing him to gasp for air.

"U-Um, if you don't cut it out soon your older brother won't survive the afternoon," I timidly pointed out. I couldn't stand to watch my piano teacher get strangled to death.

The girl glanced over her shoulder at me and released Maestro

Noboru at long last. "Who are you people? Ah, right, I should introduce myself first. I'm Noboru's younger sister, Midori Misaka."

So her name's Midori Misaka, huh? Wait, what?!

"WHAT?!" Kon and I shouted in unison. Midori's eyes bulged with fright. Even Maestro Noboru stared at us in surprise, tears in his eyes as he sucked in air.

"Ah! S-Sorry. We overreacted because we've heard of you from a friend." Kon recovered faster than I did and hid her shock by introducing us. "I'm Kon Genda. This is Mashiro Shimao."

It was Midori's turn to be surprised by our names. "What? Are you two really *that* Kon and Mashiro?" We nodded. For reasons beyond my comprehension, Midori squeezed her hands together and broke out into a broad, ecstatic smile. "Then you're that Kou guy's little sister and the other girl is Sou's femme fatale! Who woulda thought we'd meet in a place like this!"

I gagged hard at being called Sou's femme fatale.

How did I become an attractive and dangerous woman fated for him?! Scary!

But that's beside the point! This girl really is Sou's fiancée, Midori Misaka. Hold up. What in the otome game craziness is going on here? I want to pull Kon aside and hash out what's going on right now!

Mr. Nonaga, get here soon!

One of the gaming gods must've heard my entreaty, because the second-story intercom connected to the front door went off seconds later. Maestro Noboru staggered to his feet and ambled over to check who was on the screen.

"Looks like your ride is here, girls."

"Let's go, Kon."

"Okay. Thank you, Maestro. We will be back next Saturday."

We hastily scooped up our lesson bags, dropped into a casual bow, and tried to escape from that room. Lo and behold, Midori trailed right behind us. Never exchanging so much as a single word, I slid on my sandals in the foyer and turned around to say goodbye to her. My eyes met smack-dab with Midori's Cheshire cat grin.

"Say, can I call you both by name?" she purred.

"Huh? Um, sure, be my guest," I fumbled.

"Sure, you're more than welcome to."

Why was she in such high spirits? I prepared myself to be shredded a new one with a clichéd, "Don't lay your dirty fingers on my Sou!" The next words out of Midori's mouth, however, caused my mouth to drop.

"Great! Hear me out. I want nothing more than for you to end up with Sou, Mashiro. I'll help you out in any way possible to make that happen! I'll crush any opposition Auntie Reimi poses!" she declared, putting her hands on her hips.

Auntie Reimi? Isn't that Sou's stepmom?

…Crush her? Scary! This girl is the extreme type!

"I heard that you are Shiroyama's fiancée though, Midori," Kon pointed out, her voice tight, earning the greatest grimace seen on Earth from Midori.

Her impeccable good looks were unfazed by the scrunched up expression. What kind of mechanism was in place that made even grimacing attractive?! If only the situation allowed, I would've fallen on my knees before the girl whose beauty was on par with Kon's.

"I so don't WANNA! I don't even like joking about marrying that crabby, unsociable, coldhearted jerk."

Who is she referring to? Sou's the adorable, puppy-dog type.

Unable to believe we were speaking about the same person, I asked, "Are you talking about Sou Shiroyama? You sure you don't mean a nice, lonely boy who gets easily attached?"

"*Sie machen wohl Scherze!*" she exclaimed in German. "As if! Sou Shiroyama just pretends to be that way with you. Every time he sees my face, he looks at me as if he just stepped in dog poop! It's not like I want to be with him either!"

I had no idea what she was recalling, but Midori started stamping her feet on the ground. That's Maestro Noboru's sister all right. She definitely matched him in eccentricity.

Kon held her head in her hand beside me as I escaped reality by being oddly impressed by Midori's personality.

Heroine and Original Heroine's Results

Target Character: None

Event: Sou's Ally?

CLEAR

KON stared out the window lost in thought during the car ride home from Maestro Noboru's house. The sudden appearance of an unexpected game character shocked me speechless as well. In the few moments before we left his house, Midori insisted the three of us get together again.

"Let's have lunch together after your *solfège* next Saturday. Okay? I won't be in Japan for long, so I'd love to get to know you better while I can. Unless you don't want to?"

I couldn't say no when she put it like that. I wasn't sure whether it was due to her living overseas for a long time or if it was just her personality, but Midori had a unique way of closing the space between her and others. Though, she managed not to be pushy about it either. Keeping that balance was a remarkable skill.

When I initially heard about Sou having a fiancée, I honestly thought, "Cool. The rich and powerful sure live different lives from us commoners." But now that I'd met Midori in person, I wrangled with mixed emotions. How could I not when it seemed like she seriously hated Sou's guts? I wanted Sou to have a happy life.

I didn't want him to have a loveless, miserable marriage. Was it impudent of me to worry about him in this way?

"Mashiro, are you okay?" Kon whispered, careful not to let Mr. Nonaga hear from the driver's seat.

"Why wouldn't I be? I'm fine. I'll admit it surprised me though. I just always assumed that I wouldn't meet the support character Midori until I enrolled in Seio," I answered in hush tones. When I looked from the window to her, Kon was carefully studying my face.

Her nebulous expression didn't reveal any emotion and she continued with the same vein of thought, saying, "If this world is progressing exactly like the remake version, then like you said, it shouldn't have been possible for you to encounter Midori at this point... I think we need to start thinking that this world is following a separate course from *Hear My Heart*." She paused there, fell silent, and tightly held my hands.

Surprised by the trembling of her cold hands, I returned her gaze.

"I had this false notion that I could predict the future somewhat because I was reincarnated with my past memories. But nothing is going according to plan… Life in any world just won't go the way I want it to."

I didn't know how to respond to the anguish lacing her voice.

Maybe it was beyond my comprehension to know how Kon really felt about this world when I'd never played the remake game. Be that as it may, I had one thing I needed to convey to her.

"I'm glad I was reincarnated," I confided.

"…You are?" Tears lightly misted Kon's eyes.

Wanting to encourage and comfort her, I squeezed her slender hands. "I barely have any memories of my past life left, but I know I was only eighteen at the time of my death. I'm sure I had lots of regrets. But ever since I was reincarnated into *Hear My Heart*'s world, I've been able to live every day to its fullest. I think it's all thanks to starting up the piano, and most of all, because I met you, Kon."

"Mashiro…" The tears welling up in her eyes finally rolled down her cheeks in big drops.

"I love you, Kon. I'm truly happy you're here with me."

Kon gasped and suddenly threw her arms around me. Her tight hug honestly took me by surprise. Kon was like a big sister to me since the day we met. She gave me advice and showed me the way.

I wonder if she was holding back all this time. Was she struggling alone, trying not to let me see her anxiety and sadness?

"I'm on your side, Kon, even if you are keeping secrets from me. Always remember that."

"I'm sorry…I'm so sorry," Kon repeated her apology through her tears. Was she apologizing for keeping secrets or for something entirely different? I didn't know.

♪♪♪

THE following Saturday arrived in no time. We pressed the intercom button next to Maestro Noboru's front door.

"Yes, come in," Maestro Noboru answered, so we went right ahead and opened the front door.

Kon and I gazed in wonder at the completely changed first-floor.

The living room was furnished with a big, comfy couch. A stainless-steel refrigerator glistened in the kitchen next to a matching oven and coffee maker. Susie Cooper china and dinnerware decorated cupboard shelves. A vase arranged with roses sat on top of a maple dining table.

His house looks like it was pulled straight from a catalogue!

"Do you think this is…" I started.

"Midori's handiwork," Kon finished in a whisper as we ascended the stairs to the second floor. There, we tasted our second jaw-dropping shock of the day.

"Today we'll be working on your aural skills and sight-reading…. What's wrong? Come all the way inside the room," a stranger beckoned us into the piano room.

The voice sounded just like Maestro Noboru's. Maybe he had another sibling aside from Midori. With how young the stranger looked, he could have been a younger brother. After all, his refreshingly short hair was the same shade of green as Maestro Noboru's. No prickly beard or glasses dashed the looks of this tall, dark, and handsome man. A perfectly straight nose and chiseled jaw complimented his big, olive-brown eyes. He had all the makings of a good-looking guy with nothing left to want.

"Excuse me…"

"Who might you be?"

Kon and I asked the strange man at the same time. He blinked his long lashes at us.

"Is that some kinda joke? Are you teasing me?"

His dumbfounded face was dreadfully familiar. I exchanged looks with Kon and then we both let out a loud cry. "WHAAAAT?!"

Cutting straight to the point, the incredibly dashing man in the room with us was Maestro Noboru himself. It had completely slipped my mind that this was a world governed by otome game mechanics. Handsome and beautiful sub-characters were a must. Apparently, Midori had invited herself over and gave both house and owner a massive makeover. Maestro Noboru looked like he found the efforts of his younger sister to be a big, fat nuisance.

"But you look great like this," Kon said in defense of Midori.

"Yeah! This is definitely a better look for you. I'm positive Miss Ayumi would agree," I threw in for good measure.

Maestro Noboru's face twitched. "You think so? Even though I'm still me?"

"Don't underestimate visuals. Miss Ayumi isn't the type to judge people by their looks, but a well-groomed hunk will leave a more favorable impression than a drab old fart," I spoke with fervor without mincing words. I only realized I ran my mouth once it was too late.

"A drab old fart…" Maestro Noboru's head drooped, his shoulders slumped forward.

Kon quickly rushed to amend what I said. "Some women are into men who don't care that they look like they're letting themselves go."

Granted, it only dealt a worse blow to the maestro.

Letting himself go. Doesn't care how he looks. Was her remark any better than my own?

"Okay, drop it, girls. Let's start the lesson before I take any more mental damage today."

I'm pretty sure we were at fault for the day's *solfège* being one of the strictest we'd ever had.

Boo. It's not my fault he shocked the truth out of me!

♪♪♪

TWO hours later: Midori strolled into the room right when our lessons ended. "Done for the day?"

"Yup, we just finished." Exhausted, I put my music paper and pen case inside my lesson bag.

Midori sauntered over to the table, her fluffy curls bouncing behind her. "Your hair is such a cute pink, Mashiro! Maybe I should dye my hair that color next time," she remarked as she fixed an envious gaze on my hair.

"Is that not your real hair color?" I asked.

"Nope. I used to have the same green hair as Noboru. It's ridiculous to have green hair and a name that literally means green, so I dyed it."

Midori was yet another victim to the bad naming scheme belonging to *Hear My Heart*'s developers.

Out of the corner of my eye I spied Kon nodding vehemently. "I totally understand your pain." Kon had been through a lot because of her name too.

"Noboru, we're going out for a bit! Catch you later!"

"You are? I wanna go too. I'm famished."

"*Absolut nicht!*" Midori shot him down in German. "Today is a girls-only lunch party." She stretched up on her tippy-toes and pecked him on the cheek, then slipped between Kon and me and linked arms with us. She flashed us the most charming of smiles. "I reserved the café in advance. I hope you like Italian. Can your chauffeur take us there, Kon?"

"Of course."

"Great! Then let's go!"

We piled into Kon's car with Midori. She didn't even bat an eye at the Rolls-Royce Mr. Nonaga drove exclusively for Kon.

The Misaka family had a historic financial conglomerate to its name that was even listed in contemporary history books. Midori gave us the short version of why Maestro Noboru, the son and heir to the prestigious Misaka family, lived such a paltry lifestyle.

"Noboru wants to live independently," she explained. "He got into an argument with our grandfather over it. Grandfather promised he'd allow him to leave the house if he made a lasting impact in the International Chopin Piano Competition. So Noboru entered the competition, even though he *hates* competing with a passion. Well, he didn't win, but came close enough that Father and Grandfather are letting him run free for now."

"I see. The rich have problems only rich people have," I commented. *Boy, am I glad I was born to a middle-class family*, I earnestly believed.

Midori started giggling. "You sound so disconnected from it! Most people would normally have stars in their eyes and try to get favors from friends like me and Kon."

"Meh, I'm satisfied with my current life."

I wasn't so naïve as to say I didn't want money. But growing up and earning money with my own skills was more my style. Some part of me was cowardly when it came to money, because my stomach killed me every time I received expensive gifts from Miss Sakurako and Miss Chisako.

I had only expressed my honest opinion, but it deepened Midori's grin. "I like you, Mashiro. This is the first time I've agreed with Sou's opinion on something."

"Uh...thanks?" I answered hesitantly, unsure of how else to reply. Midori happily wrapped her arms around me in a big hug. The way she became attached to people was on par with Sou. They were very similar.

Hating somebody who's just like you...yup, that fits for them.

WE eventually arrived at a chic restaurant that felt a lot like a place you might find in *The Secret Garden*.

Starting with the bruschetta, the waiters brought out mouthwatering dish after mouthwatering dish, including a mozzarella cheese and tomato salad, trofie with pesto alla Genovese, and oven-baked freshwater prawns.

I spent the whole time, until they brought out the espresso and homemade gelato, adding up the total price. Mom had given me a 5,000 yen allowance, but that didn't seem like it'd even dent the bill.

Kon must've noticed my sheer horror over the abysmal prices because she softly whispered in my ear. "I'll help you pay for it. Don't let it ruin your day, okay?"

"O-Okay. Would you mind advancing me the money then? I'll be sure to pay you back later."

Midori seemed to have overheard our conversation because she arched an eyebrow at us. "They won't charge us. I assume Father will pay for it later. I've never carried cash on me before."

What the heck kind of confession is that?! Feeling the energy drain from me, I narrowly avoided banging my forehead against the pure white lacey tablecloth. Was it okay to have a girl I'd only met twice pay for my meal?

"Anyways, can we start talking about Sou now? I'm dying to rant about him to someone else." Midori kicked my internal conflict to the curb and began her endless rant about just how horrible Sou was to her. "No matter what I say to him, he just gives me this frigid look with his arms crossed and barely acknowledges me. The few times he does open his mouth it's always 'Mashiro this' or 'Mashiro that.' I'm always like, sure, sure, you've made your point loud and clear. I mean, it's not like I want to see him either. Who does he think he is?!"

If he was just like his game version then he was supposed to be a pompous, overconfident, and narcissistic oresama.

"So I got the bright idea to become besties with you, Mashiro, and irritate him with our friendship! Take a selfie with me later, okay? I'm gonna brag his ear off once I go home." She must've had some serious resentment pent up because she snickered and gloated as she spoke.

Kon couldn't resist bursting into laughter over Midori's simple yet evil plan. "Are you really okay with things going well between Mashiro and Shiroyama? Wouldn't that only make him happy?"

"Well, Sou's had a pretty miserable life. I'd never wish for him to be eternally unhappy. I don't care what happens as long as we can get rid of this ridiculous engagement."

It was funny seeing Midori's face twist with annoyance over the whole ordeal. I was also relieved knowing she was aware of Sou's circumstances.

"But Sou and me dating is out of the question. I mean, I can't even begin to imagine us together. The potential problems only just begin with the fact that he's living all the way in Germany now," I explained.

Midori shrugged. "You don't really know Sou if you think he's going to be an obedient little boy and stay in Germany forever. Mashiro, you'd better mentally prepare yourself! Once Sou returns to Japan, he's going to be on your case more than ever before!"

"P-Please don't make scary predictions."

Midori giggled at my grimace.

♪♪♪

SEPTEMBER rolled around again, starting the new quarter at school.

Miss Ayumi wasn't returning to Japan until the end of September. October marked Seio's fall break when Kon and Kou had plans to vacation in Europe. Maestro Noboru was scheduled to leave in September too. Things were going to get lonely over the next few months.

The sun was still hot during the day, but the cool winds blowing in the evening informed all around that fall was coming, stimulating my sentimentality along with the fleeting dusk sky.

It was during this time of emotional weakness that seeing Tomoi during class or when he showed up to school in the morning became the center of my enjoyment.

I wanted to share in this giddiness with someone, but I just couldn't find anyone who was a fan. Rei obviously didn't see his charms, and the one time I'd brought it up with Eri and the girls, they flat-out declared, "Mr. Matsuda isn't even worth a look!"

Boo, he absolutely is worth it!

Now that I had made myself busy mastering piano, German, Italian, and French, I began thinking it was high time to start cutting back on my school studies. The whole reason I even started my hardcore study plan was for the impure motive of matching Kou's preference for smart girls. I made full use of TV and radio lectures, but learning three languages at once overloaded my brain.

But see, the problem I faced now was that I wanted Tomoi to compliment my intelligence and grades. How could I give up studying? My behavior was laughable; I hadn't learned my lesson from the first time around.

When all was said and done, every day of my life was packed with a crazy busy schedule that made my elementary school days look like a walk in the park.

As for Hanaka, she was finally going to be a university senior next year.

She was going to receive her kindergarten teacher license the same time she earned her diploma, but she groaned about the lack of practical training and hands-on experience. A teacher's employability greatly changed based on how much or how little experience they actually had working with children. She was working hard to fill in the gaps left by her college education through volunteer work and side jobs at preschools and private kindergartens. Being able to play the piano to some degree was a part of her job requirements, so I offered to teach her, but she formally turned me down.

"Why not? I could probably teach you Bayer."

"No way. Impossible. Not happening. Please spare me!" Hanaka begged, becoming teary-eyed toward the end of the conversation. I had to wonder what kind of torture she imagined me putting her through.

Oh, come on. Not even I would expect someone else to follow the same training regimen as me…I think.

The days flowed by faster than a coursing river and Midori left for her school in England. She was going to drop by Germany on the way to taunt Sou about her time with me. She took an insane number of pictures with me before she left.

"Hmm, guess that'll do. All that's left is…oh right, I want you to record your voice on my tablet. I want to use your voice for an alarm, Mashiro."

"Wh-What?! It's too embarrassing. I don't want to do that."

"Come on! Please!"

It was impossible to say "NO" to a beautiful girl with puppy-dog eyes, begging me to do something for her. It was a feat beyond me. I mean, she was just too cute! In the end, I whispered the lines Midori prepared for me with my face flushed bright red.

"Good morning."

"It's morning now."

"Hurry and wake up."

"Have a great day today!"

Midori demanded countless retakes like a sound director. "Say it cuter!"

"Say it like you're blowing kisses!"

Her absurd demands utterly stumped and embarrassed me.

"Okay, this should do it. Thanks, Mashiro. I'll make him completely in my debt for this. Mwahaha!"

Bothered by her disturbing remark, I confirmed, "You're going to be the one who uses those, right, Midori?"

"Of course I'm going to *use* them! You're such a meanie, doubting me like that!" She looked at me with misty eyes any good actress knew how to employ.

Dang it! Beautiful girls who know how to use their charm as a weapon are the worst type of all!

♪♪♪

MISS Ayumi finally returned to Japan on the last Sunday of September. She said she'd be present for our last lesson with Maestro Noboru, which made both Kon and I nervous.

Kanako had accomplished her dream of being accepted into the Paris Conservatory and had already left to study there. Aoi was a second year at Seio Music University. They'd both graduated from Miss Ayumi's lessons, leaving Kon, Rinko, and me as her only students now. She didn't plan on accepting any more students for the time being.

"I want to focus my full attention on both of you girls right now.

You are at the time and age a pianist grows the most."

I don't want to disappoint Miss Ayumi after she put so much faith in us, I thought, convinced once more to do my best.

"So, how was it? Are you glad you took Noboru's lessons?" Miss Ayumi asked from the driver's seat as she drove us to Maestro Noboru's house.

"I'm extremely glad I took it!"

"It was a great experience."

Kon and I gave similar answers at the exact same time.

Thanks to Maestro Noboru, I became more capable of considering how the listener might perceive my performance from an objective point of view, while Kon's piano music had taken on a clearly different sound. Explaining the change in words wasn't easy, but her music had a great deal more color and brightness to it than ever before.

As we were chatting about our experiences with Maestro Noboru, we eventually arrived in front of his house.

Miss Ayumi was so surprised by how well-stocked his house had become that she thought we might have the wrong house, yet she didn't seem too impressed by the drastic change in his appearance.

"Good to see you again, Noboru. Thank you very much for what you did these past few months."

"It was my pleasure... By the way, um...do you notice anything different about me?" Maestro Noboru fidgeted in anticipation of Miss Ayumi's compliments.

"What? Hmm... Oh, now that you mention it, you cut your hair."

"I did! I also set aside my glasses for contacts and started shaving my beard. What do you think?"

"I bet you feel cleaner and more refreshed this way. I'm glad you'll be able to see the sheet music better now."

...It's no use. He's not getting through to her at all.

Maestro Noboru's excitement withered like spinach under boiling hot water.

"He looks like Kou," Kon murmured.

What part of him is like Kou?! Isn't it being super rude to compare the sincere and innocent Maestro Noboru to the oresama, narcissist host Kou?!

"Okay," Miss Ayumi put an end to that conversation and turned toward us. "What will you play for me today?"

The gentleness about her vanished into thin air. I swallowed hard when I noticed Miss Ayumi's piano switch had clicked on.

"Can I play first today?" Kon requested.

I agreed without hesitation. She had let me start first last time.

"I'm going to play Liszt's 'La Campanella.'"

"I see. Go ahead then." Miss Ayumi sat in a nearby chair.

Maestro Noboru slowly walked to the back wall and leaned against it, seemingly declaring he wasn't going to say anything today.

Liszt – Grandes études de Paganini, S. 141 No. 3 "La Campanella"

Liszt was said to be a pianist with extremely large hands. The size of a pianist's hands is vitally important to their career. Size affects the pianist's breadth of expression, such as whether or not they can play through the octaves with ease. Ever since Kon and I began learning the piano, we'd never once forgotten to practice stretching and spreading our fingers. I secretly took pride in the fact that my fingers were a whole knuckle joint longer than the boys in my junior high class.

Kon chose to play at a faster tempo.

This song, played in continuous octaves, made it very hard to stress notes. The switch from fortissimo (very loud) to a crescendo (gradually getting louder) made me want to scream, "well, which is it?!"

Kon expressed the music dynamically by playing with her entire body. Her hands danced across the keyboard like she was pounding the keys, but some sort of magic had to be at play as she achieved a continuous ringing of tinkling high notes, producing the bell sound effects Liszt intended. It didn't even sound like music produced by a mere instrument anymore. Perhaps this was what sprinkling stardust would sound like.

She returned to the secondary theme and gave it the most spectacular treatment with a roaring crescendo of contrary-motion chromatic octaves. The music burst forward with an impassioned end-of-the-dance fanfare over an insistent bass figure and ever-widening crashes in both hands that made me sigh.

Maestro Noboru and Miss Ayumi broke into a loud round of applause for Kon when she removed her hands from the keyboard.

Naturally, I'd started applauding without even thinking.

Ah, how long and how far must I chase after you before I finally catch up?

I wordlessly passed by Kon, her cheeks flushed from exertion.

Even if there are no winners or losers in music, I want to perform side by side with you without being ashamed of my performance.

"I am going to play 'Rondeau' and 'Capriccio' from Bach's Partita No. 2," I informed my teachers, took a deep breath, and placed my hands on the keys.

Bach – Partita No. 2 in C minor, BWV 826

With great care, I played the songs which required superior technique and precision from note to note.

The song's demand on the pianist to use both the right and left hand in the same way makes it difficult to tell which is playing the primary melody. The tempo remains constant.

As I played the song, I repeated the instructions in my head. *Avoid stepping on the pedals as much as possible. The trailing notes must be maintained to a certain level. Gently stroke the piano part. Play the second half in a way that brings the music to a rollicking and dramatic ending.*

I lifted my hands from the final chord and was greeted by dead silence after the last note.

…U-Uh? They won't even applaud to be nice?

I glanced at Miss Ayumi and found her staring at me in disbelief. Kon had her eyes firmly pressed together, her hands tightly clasped over her lap.

"Brava! That was quite marvelous, Mashiro." Only Maestro Noboru clapped his hands for me after a slight delay.

"Mashiro…" Kon said in a feeble voice.

Miss Ayumi lightly shook her head. "There's nothing left for me to say when you can already play Bach's Partita that well."

I was relieved to have secured passing marks.

Kon also clapped for me with a smile.

Thank goodness! It was worth spending these past two months practicing like there's no tomorrow!

Aside from Maestro Noboru's assignment pieces, I was spending every day practicing the songs from this partita.

"There will be a large-scale student music competition around this time next year. Would you like to enter it?"

Maestro Noboru frowned at Miss Ayumi's suggestion. "…A music competition? I can't stand behind you pigeonholing Mashiro inside their closed-minded boxes at this point in her career."

"But Mashiro wants to enter them," Miss Ayumi pointed out.

Maestro Noboru shifted his gaze over to me. "The judging decisions for music competitions aren't as transparent as you think. I will stand behind you only if you are prepared to accept any result."

"I'm prepared. I want to enter."

"I see… How about you, Kon?"

"I won't enter that competition."

Miss Ayumi had a suspicious look on her face because both Kon and I had responded immediately, without taking the time to think it over.

I wanted to achieve results in this competition no matter what it took and enroll in Seio for high school. Maybe Kon wanted to avoid competing with me this time. Or maybe she believed the competition would end just like it did in *Hear My Heart* and wanted to avoid entering when her loss was guaranteed from the start. Only she knew the answer.

"Very well. Since you are going to enter, we should put forth every effort." Miss Ayumi's expression suddenly softened and she offered me a gentle smile.

Not opening up about my true motives made me feel like I was betraying Miss Ayumi and her earnest approach to music. And that hurt me.

But it didn't matter how much it hurt or tormented us; telling the truth was never going to be an option.

Interlude: Sou and Midori's War of Words (Sou's POV)

MIDORI had dropped by my place for the first time in months. I hadn't accepted it yet, but she was my fiancée on paper. Turning her away without meeting first wasn't an option.

She was as fickle as they came and didn't even think to make an appointment before visiting. Her visits were always abrupt. Not that I'd hang around at home if I knew she was coming.

"Sou! Be grateful I'm here for you!"

"I never wanted you here," I retorted within a fraction of a second, but instead of throwing her usual hissy fit, Midori started grinning from ear to ear.

Honestly, it was creepy.

"Oh, are you sure you want to say that? If you aren't nice, I won't give you your present from Japan."

That was the first I'd heard about Midori leaving England for a trip to Japan. It was a surprise and nothing more. Sure, I missed Japan, but what I really wanted wasn't sold in any store.

"Don't need it. Is that all you came for?"

I paid her the bare minimum courtesy. There shouldn't have been any reason for her to stick around any longer. As I was about to stand, my breath caught in my throat. Midori had begun lining up photos on the table across from me.

Normal photos wouldn't have elicited any reaction from me. But those photos were of the only girl I could never forget for even a moment.

There Mashiro was, smiling bashfully as Midori rubbed cheeks with her.

There Mashiro was, drinking from the same can of juice from two different straws with Midori.

The lightly dressed Mashiro had matured a great deal since I last saw her, and she shone radiantly in every picture.

"How did you—"

"I told you! I went to Japan."

The worst-possible scenarios crossed my mind when I saw the triumphant smirk on Midori's face. Before I knew it, I was on my feet, slamming my fists into the table between us.

"What the hell did you think you were doing?! Don't go near Mashiro!" I yelled in an attempt to threaten her, but Midori only snorted at me.

"Don't you for one minute misjudge me. If I'm going to do something terrible, I'm going to do it directly to *you*. Mashiro was an incredibly *goldig* girl," Midori said, tossing in German. "I completely fell for her. I adore her."

"…Hah?" I uttered, failing to comprehend what she was saying.

Midori triumphantly waved her tablet in front of me. "I can give you the data I saved on here if you promise to never do anything to tick me off again."

"Huh? What're you going on—"

"Good morning."

I heard a familiar voice from the tablet when Midori pressed the play button. Time seemed to stop. I gasped for air. *Wait. This voice is—it can't be her…could it be her?*

"It's morning now."
"Hurry and wake up."
"Have a great day today!"

My hands instinctively curled into fists. Midori's eyes went completely round at my overreaction. She seemed like she had something to say, but I had no time for her.

In a matter of seconds, my heart was filled with maddening love.
Mashiro. Mashiro, Mashiro, Mashiro!
I want to see you.
I want to see you so bad. I'm having such an overblown reaction just by hearing your voice.

I felt like I might lose my mind if I let down my guard.

"...Fine. I promise. Give me that tablet," I finally managed to squeeze out in a hoarse voice.

Midori shrugged as if she didn't know what to do with me. "I didn't think you had it this bad for her. Why'd you come out here if you love her that much?"

"That has nothing to..." I stopped myself from finishing that snide sentence. Because I saw the sly grin spreading across Midori's face as she waved the tablet in front of me.

Pushing down my desire to groan, I told myself, *you want Mashiro's voice files, don't you? You want them bad enough, right?*

"She told me to. She said it's best if I went to Germany. I've already been rejected by her."

"Hmm...I see... Looks like you can actually hold a real conversation with me." Her provoking tone rubbed me the wrong way, but I swallowed my pride. "Well, I don't mind. A promise is a promise. I'll give you the pictures of just Mashiro and her voice clips."

"Thank you," I genuinely thanked her. I couldn't care less what Midori's motives were. Mashiro's pictures and her soft, sweet voice were the ultimate reward for me right now.

Midori looked disgusted, even though she was the one who offered it to me. "Don't be so happy. You're throwing me off my game."

"Huh? What's your game here anyway?"

"...Please, please don't become a stalker and stab Mashiro when you return to Japan." Midori's face was more serious than I'd ever seen it. It appeared her remark about liking Mashiro wasn't a barefaced lie.

I'm not gonna lie and say I don't feel possessive of her, but I'd never think of destroying Mashiro's happiness. I just want to watch over her. I don't care what position I'm in, as long as I can see her happy. That's all I want.

"I'll disappear before I make Mashiro scared of me. I'll do anything to make it so she can live out her life with a smile."

"Heavy! Hold on, am I even talking to the Sou I know?! Are you some sorta elaborate clone?!" Midori shuddered. She quickly set about preparing to go home and left.

Heavy, huh? She got me there. But I'm dead serious.

The second I dropped my eyes to the pictures on the table, Midori vanished from my thoughts. My eyes locked on the picture of Mashiro sitting in front of the piano, and I decided to put that picture in my wallet.

Two and a half years left to go. Time wouldn't flow as fast as I wished it would, but I was working hard not to disappoint Mashiro the next time I saw her.

Mashiro always brightened my life, even when we were far apart. That fact alone brought me the greatest joy.

CG 25: Advice (Kou)

SECOND quarter was cram-packed with the usual school events.

It came as no surprise that Rin and Mihara, Takkun's real name, were the stars of the show during the sports festival. Calling Takkun by name instead of his childhood nickname was a hard habit to kick.

Tazaki, the bad boy with the silver piercing, was the dark horse of the day. It turned out that he was pretty popular because he was on the basketball team. His grades were questionable, but girls had a thing for athletic boys. I was impressed by the vocal power of middle school girls who cheered till their voices went hoarse during the boys' relay and athletic events.

Tomoi participated in the three-legged race with the young female school nurse.

So jealous! My heart raced for him all over again when I saw how he carefully matched his pace to hers and prevented her from tripping.

And then came the ultimate event from the gaming gods!

I had won first place in the obstacle race and was walking along the edge of the grounds to return to my classmates when Tomoi happened to be walking toward me from the opposite direction. His expression softened into a smile when he noticed me just as I was gushing internally over how cool he looked in his jersey.

"You did good out there." He patted me on the shoulder in passing.

I felt like praising myself for not swooning on the spot.

The culture festival always came after the sports festival. I was put in charge of playing the piano accompaniment during the choral competition. My class was the most disorganized out of the first-year students. Most of the boys were too nervous or shy to sing aloud, and Rei and the girls ragged on them for it.

Just like the sports festival was a place for students to show off their athleticism, the culture festival was a place for students to show off their artistry.

Our middle school band was a so-called "leisure club" that didn't partake in any competitions. They mostly performed pop and anime songs. I couldn't help but move my fingers to the beat of the trumpet music I heard through the open windows after school.

Not affiliated with any school clubs, I just watched as an observer the whole time—until the principal suddenly called me to his office after school two days before the culture festival.

"You want me to perform on stage?" I asked.

"The PTA was very vocal about allowing students exempt from school clubs a place to present the results of their hard work too. You are the only student in our school exempt from club activities right now, Miss Shimao. We have a piano in the gym. Would you mind performing a song for the school?"

Hold your horses, Mr. Principal! I understand your logic, but you should ask for something like that sooner! Do you think middle schoolers will sit through classical music? If you told me sooner, I would've arranged popular jazz numbers and anime songs into a medley that students would want to listen to!

I stamped down my desire to complain and nodded. It didn't take a genius to know he wasn't asking, but telling me to do it.

"Very good. Thank you. You will have ten minutes to perform. I look forward to hearing your performance." Evidently relieved that I'd accepted, his stiff expression gave way to a broad smile.

I bowed to him and trudged my way out of school, my feet dragging with the pressure suddenly put on my shoulders.

What should I play? How should I play it? There's no time to even run it by Miss Ayumi. I racked my brain over what to play while I walked with my bike. *Chopin's always safe. But ten minutes! "Fantaisie-Impromptu" is too short. "Heroic Polonaise" runs less than ten minutes too… But I love that song to pieces. Maybe that's what I'll go with.*

I was so wrapped up in my thoughts that I hadn't noticed the black Benz driving beside me.

Shocked by the honking horn, I nearly knocked my bicycle over.

What in the world?! My eyes darted around until they made direct contact with Kou's through the lowered backseat window.

"I thought that was you. What's with your face?"

That's my line, buddy! And leave my face alone!

"You scared me! Are you on your way home from school, Kou?"

"Yeah. Did your bike tire go flat?"

"Nope. I just wanted time to think."

"Is that all?"

"Yeah… If you have nothing else to say, can I go?"

"No. Um, well…"

I became unreasonably irritated with Kou when I saw his rare display of being lost for words. Most of my irritation had nothing to do with him, but he was a good person to take it out on. His timing sucked; we were destined to always get off on the wrong foot.

"If you have something to say, just say it already. Parking in the middle of the road is a safety hazard," I rushed him in a crabby tone.

Kou breathed a short sigh then spoke as if he'd regained his cool. "Why don't you come to my house if you have no other plans? I'll listen to your problems."

Apparently I'd been trudging down the street with such a grave expression it was noticeable from a car. I felt bad for being such a narrow-minded person that I had become annoyed with Kou for going out of his way to stop and talk to me.

"…Sorry for making you worry. Thanks for the offer." I decided to take him up on his generosity.

Being a Seio student, Kou might have a good suggestion for what I should play. The gorgeous Bösendorfer instantly came to mind.

"You're in a weaker state than I thought," Kou remarked, his eyes going round. His expression said it all—he didn't think I'd actually take him up on his offer.

Did he just offer to be polite? The thought crossed my mind, but he was the one who called out to me. I was going to take full advantage of that and consult him about my problems.

"You could say that. Let me stop by my house and drop off my bike and books first."

"Okay. I'll meet you there."

I straddled my bike and pedaled after the Benz driving ahead of me, all the while wondering why the depression hanging over me had vanished into thin air.

♪♪♪

IT had seriously been a long time since I last visited the Narita estate. The last time I went was Christmas during the fifth grade. Mr. Tanomiya's cheeks dimpled with a joyful smile when he saw me, expunging my fears that he wouldn't remember me.

"My, if it isn't Lady Shimao. What a pleasure it is to see you again after all this time."

"The pleasure is all mine, Mr. Tanomiya. I hope you don't mind me intruding again."

"You are always welcome here, Lady Shimao. The lady and master of the estate have said the same." The crinkled corners around Mr. Tanomiya's eyes deepened as he softly smiled and added, "But it is I who is very glad to see you on this occasion."

"Oh, stop! I can't do much for you even if you flatter me like that!"

Who wouldn't feel bashful when a dandy butler compliments them? Kou shot me an icy look when he saw my flushed cheeks.

Hmph! What's wrong with a girl getting excited over a compliment now and then?

The moment I entered the music room I made a mad dash for the grand piano. Its polished beauty never changed. The crystalline treble and rich bass echoed in my mind's ear.

"Um, if you don't mind, I'd like to play for a little while. Can I?"

"I thought you'd ask." Kou shrugged, but there was a smile in his eyes. "I'll let you play to your heart's content later, so can we talk first? What has you so worried?"

Ah, right, right. I was so captivated by the Bösendorfer in the room that I'd forgotten what I'd come here for. Thinking I had nothing to lose, I confided in Kou about performing on stage during the school culture festival.

"…And that's the gist of it. I need to pick my song and start practicing it today. Problem is, I can't think of a good one. Do you have any suggestions?" I asked after explaining my situation.

Kou cocked his head as if to say he didn't see the problem. "I don't get it. What's wrong with playing a song you like? It's not like you have no repertoire."

I wrapped both hands around the warm cup of café latte that Mr. Tanomiya had brought for me and clarified the reason why the song choice had me so worried. The latte art of a cat curled into a ball with its tail curled around it was absolutely adorable; just looking at it was soothing. How would I react if he admitted to drawing it himself?! I might end up falling for Kou's butler!

"Don't clump my mundane school into the same category as one of the best music academies under the sun. Only a handful of normal middle schoolers tolerate classical music, much less enjoy it. They probably won't even listen if I play one of the songs I like. It'd break my heart if no one paid attention during my performance."

Kou's teasing spirit glittered in his eyes as he pushed his crimson bangs upward. "If I was there, I wouldn't let a single note go unheard. Not paying attention to your piano is one of the most wasteful things in the world, Mashiro."

"Save the flattery for somebody else!"

"Why don't you let me compliment you for once?"

"That ship has sailed."

"Hah…"

I started laughing against my better judgment. Kou's scowl was just too cute to ignore. My laughter brought back his original expression, and he studied me with gentleness brimming in his eyes as if to say he couldn't win against me. When he looked at me like that it almost felt like I had butterflies in my stomach.

"How about you play a jazz arrangement of Mozart's Twelve Variations on "Ah vous dirai-je, Maman"? I heard one of the piano department girls playing it a while back and thought it was a fun take on the song. It shouldn't be too simple for you, and I think it's a safe bet to say the audience will like it."

"Mozart's Twelve Variations on "Ah vous dirai-je, Maman", huh? I think it's a good choice, but I don't have any sheet music for a jazz arrangement or a tone generator. It's probably impossible for me to arrange it by the day after tomorrow."

Everyone should be familiar with "Twinkle, Twinkle, Little Star",

"Baa, Baa, Black Sheep", and the "Alphabet Song", which used Mozart's twelve variations on this French melody. Playing a complex arrangement of a song composed by Mozart would increase the difficulty level too.

If only I had two more days.

Kou saw me sigh, frowned, and began reluctantly shifting through his smartphone. "Hello? Yeah. Yup, it's me. I'm so happy you could tell." Kou's sudden switch to a sweet timbre voice as he spoke to someone over the phone took me by complete surprise.

What's he doing all of a sudden? I can tell he's talking to a girl by his tone, but is there a reason he has to call her while I'm around?

"Do you have the sheet music for Mozart's Twelve Variations on "Ah vous dirai-je, Maman" that I heard you play the other day? I'll send someone to pick it up, so would you mind letting me borrow it for a bit? Of course I'll make it up to you… Thanks. See you at school."

…I misunderstood him. I finally realized that Kou made that call now to get ahold of the sheet music, but why did he go so far for me?

With one sidelong glance at me gawking at him, Kou swiftly hung up the phone. He confirmed the details on his smartphone screen with ice in his eyes and placed it on the table. His stony expression was all I needed to see to know that was a phone call he would've rather not made.

"Wait here for a bit. I'll send Mizusawa out to get the sheet music for you. You can play the piano in the meantime," he said in a businessman's tone and stood to leave. On the spur of the moment, I seized his shirt cuff. "…Hm? What's wrong?"

Even I didn't know what it was I wanted to do. *Why are you doing so much for me? Why do you care? Because we're friends? Are you this kind to all your friends?*

A long list of annoying questions crossed my mind. I pressed my open lips shut and sucked my bottom lip in between my teeth. *Asking won't do us any good*, I thought, stifling the spark of curiosity. After all, I wouldn't believe a thing Kou said, no matter what he tells me?

I gently pulled my hand back and lightly shook my head. "Sorry, it's nothing… Thanks, Kou."

"No problem. I'm happy to do stuff like this for you anytime." Tenderness colored Kou's eyes and a blissful smile overtook his face.

If only I could believe that smile wasn't fake.

Sharp pangs shot through my heart.

Heroine's Results
Target Character: Kou Narita
Event: What I Can Do For You
CLEAR

IT was past eight by the time I left the Narita estate. I took the opportunity to practice on the Bösendorfer until Mr. Mizusawa came back with the sheet music, and then, around six, I was captured by Miss Sakurako who'd just come home, and ended up intruding on their family dinner. I'd already contacted my parents about where I was, but I told the Naritas I shouldn't stay any later after dinner. Miss Sakurako went out of her way to accompany me to the front door.

"Please, by all means, come to visit again, okay? Everyone here is so much happier whenever you're around, Mashiro. Kou's always in a better mood too, and I enjoy my time with you. Isn't that right, Kou?" Miss Sakurako effused, glancing at Kou.

"Is that what you think, Mom? Seems about the same as usual to me," he smoothly evaded the question with a straight face. Every time I saw him interact like this I was impressed by how much he'd matured.

"Thank you so much for treating me to dinner. Words can't begin to express my gratitude."

"Don't mention it, dear. I'm the one who forced you to stay. Speaking of which, my husband will surely regret not being here. I'm going to brag about having the chance to eat dinner with you tonight, Mashiro."

"You are? Ehehe…" Not used to being doted on so much, I struggled with my response and hid my uncertainty behind a shy smile.

Miss Sakurako wrapped her arms around me and pulled me into a tight hug. "You're just too cute! Aww, you should just marry into our family now!"

"Mom!" Scowling with great displeasure, Kou pried me away from his mother. "C'mon, let's get going. Your parents will worry if you get home too late."

"O-Okay… Thank you for letting me come over!"

Kou tugged on my arm, hurrying my goodbyes, and pulled me into the car. Here I thought for sure he'd go on his merry way, not pile into the car next to me.

"You don't have to go out of your way to see me home. Mr. Mizusawa can handle it."

"That's not why I—" On the verge of saying something, Kou suddenly bit his tongue, shook his head, and finished with, "Forget it."

He looked depressed even as the car started driving.

Hahaha! I know what caused this look! He's all depressed because Miss Sakurako told me to marry into their family. Kou's the guy who hates women who go gaga over him. He's probably debating how to turn me down. In the past, I'm positive he would've come out and bluntly said, "Don't get the wrong idea. Know your place." The fact that he hasn't just shows how much he's grown!

Immersed in my emotional joy for his growth, I spoke up to put his fears at ease. "You don't have to be cautious around me."

"Huh? …What are you talking about now?"

"I know full-well that Miss Sakurako only said those things to tease you, Kou. I won't get the wrong idea and start throwing myself at you. You can rest easy."

Kou's eyes bulged as he scrutinized me, then he exhaled the loudest sigh known to man. "You don't know a thing."

"Yes, I do. It's a nuisance for you when people take your jokes at face value, right? You can relax because I'm the *one* person who will *never* take you seriously," I emphasized for good measure.

"…Hah. Do me a favor and stop talking."

Tch! So not cute!

Giving up on trying to brighten his mood, I directed my gaze out the car window. Watching the streetlights and house lights flicker by made me grow sleepy. Kou shot me another dirty look when he noticed I was starting to doze off. His gaze was like a knife in my side, but I decided to get through it by pretending not to notice because he was too much of a pain to deal with.

HOW LONG ARE YOU GOING TO LOOK AT ME?! We finally arrived in front of my house by the time my irritation with him grew so great it blew my sleepiness away.

"Mr. Mizusawa, thank you very much for driving me home. Thank you for everything you did for me today too, Kou."

Natsu

"Mashiro!" Kou called out to me as I rushed to leave the car.

"What?"

"Good luck at the culture festival. I'll pray for your success."

I was so shocked I thought, *is this a sign that the world is going to end tomorrow?! This is really Kou, right? Not some elaborate clone with a bad copy of Kou's personality?!* I did a double take.

"E-Err, yeah, I-I'll give it my all," I stammered. My surprise made it impossible to talk straight.

Kou hasn't been acting like himself for a while now. Did he take that huge of a hit when Sou left? But, meh, it's a waste to put too much thought into Kou. I'm scared to death of this all being some elaborate ploy to get me under his thumb!

Regaining my wits about me, I reached the conclusion that I shouldn't think too much about the sudden changes in Kou.

♪♪♪

IT was the day of the culture festival.

My piano performance was sandwiched between the choral competition and the announcement of the winners. I couldn't help feeling like I was only there to fill in an empty timeslot for the school. Less than satisfied with my slot, I ascended the steps onto the stage. The teachers had moved the Shiroyama piano from the corner of the stage to the center after the choral competition. Confused chatter could be heard from the students in the audience.

"What's going on? Is something gonna start?"

"Hey, isn't she that girl? Y'know, the one who got to ditch club activities for the piano?"

"Oh yeah, she's the girl who was the new student representative and the top of her class."

The vice principal briefly announced over the microphone why I was performing here today. Once he finished his introduction, I bowed to the audience and sat in front of the piano.

This was the same piano I'd played on during the choral competition, so I already had a good idea of what it sounded like. The tuning could use some work, but I could make do with it.

Slowly placing my hands on the keyboard, I added the primary melody with a trill to the simple fifth chord progression and strung together a sequence of arpeggios that clearly outlined the chord changes. What made this piece of music interesting were the introduction of basic themes and the offerings of variations in rhythm, harmony, and texture, which I was giving a jazz spin. Then I made lots of syncopations, interspersed with open and closed voices based on the third and seventh chords to make the arranged melody stand out.

Giving it a jazz rhythm changed the most famous phrases to sound like mature, sweet whispers, while the popular tune remained recognizable throughout.

"Oh, I know this song!"

"Isn't it 'Twinkle, Twinkle Little Star'?"

"Sounds much cooler than I remember it!"

Delighted cries rose from the students in the audience. Happy to hear that, I increased the tempo, letting it take off as the decorated melody was featured in my right hand with my left hand playing the fast running notes. My right hand made full use of the sixteenth notes and the chromatic scale. I sprinkled my ad-libbed take throughout. Skillfully making use of the opening rest notes made it sound even more like a jazzy performance.

I increased the number of notes and played the exciting finale that switches from duple time to triple time with more pizazz. Applause and cheers exploded from our spacious gym at the end of my performance.

That was so much fun!

Extremely satisfied, I tried to withdraw from the stage when, believe it or not, calls for an encore erupted from the audience. The group of delinquent third-year students who stood out from the crowd were whistling through their fingers. The teachers and school staff were going around trying to keep the students in check, but their efforts did nothing to quiet the roaring applause.

Uh, how do I handle this? Searching for help, I looked to where the teachers sat and my eyes made contact with Tomoi's.

A small smile turned up his lips and he mouthed, "Play more for them," while giving me the thumbs-up.

Oh my gosh! What is with that adorable gesture?! Here I was about to leave the stage, but now I want to play more for Tomoi!

The applause finally ceased when I sat in front of the piano again. Anticipation filled the gym.

Natsu

After a moment of indecision, I settled on playing "When You Wish Upon a Star". I had close to zero confidence in my ability to play this piece. It was a song I played by ear, arranging it to match my preferences as a breather between practice pieces. But the melody was a famous one, making it a good fit as an encore piece.

First, I played the basic melody with an unaffected chord progression.

Cries of "I know that song!" rose mostly from the female students.

The loud clamor and chatter instantly settled down as students listened, making my piano the only sound resounding throughout the gymnasium. After playing true to the melody all the way through once, I rearranged the melody and changed it to sound completely different. It didn't sound too off as long as I stuck to the original song melody and chord progression. I inserted A7 and G7 after the C and D minor part, added grace notes to the melody, and interposed rhythmical rests.

One of the most fun things about jazz music was that it allowed me to add notes and play around however I liked. Key changes could be made to sound very fluid by using a common chord through diatonic common chord modulation.

It was a soft and graceful song that everyone quietly listened to, giving me the opportunity to end my performance on a peaceful note.

In the end, I went way over my allotted performance time.

Is the principal mad? I worried as I exited the stage.

My fears were put at ease when he praised me, saying, "I wish I could knock back a few drinks during your performance, Miss Shimao."

That was meant to be a compliment, right?

When I returned to class, a hyper Rei jumped on me and bubbled, "Amazing! You're so amazing!"

My other classmates all called out to me, saying, "It was really good!"

Hearing they enjoyed it filled me with genuine happiness.

It was worth worrying over my song choice. I have to send Kou a thank-you text. The image of him appeasing the rich girl from Seio who lent us the sheet music flashed through my mind, and I slapped my hands together in a grateful prayer for his much-appreciated sacrifice.

Regrettably, our school only won second place during the choral competition, but it still turned out to be a culture festival to remember.

♪♪♪

DECEMBER came next. I scored almost all hundreds on my second-quarter finals, holding my place as the top student at school and winning the bet I had with Tomo, Rin, and Majima. Now they had to treat me to a cake set.

We decided to get together when school got out early on Wednesday. Our school forbade students from taking detours on the way home, so we each went home first and met up again at the café in front of the train station. I traded in my school uniform for jeans, a black knitted turtle neck, duffle coat, and scarf. Tomo and Eri went the complete opposite direction from my comfortable look with their adorable dresses. The motivation to dress up sure changed when boyfriends were involved.

"Is it really okay for me to tag along when I wasn't a part of the bet?" Eri shrunk down uncomfortably in her seat after we sat in the back of the café. She looked searchingly from me to Majima.

"Why wouldn't it be okay? I'm perfectly okay with you being here. I mean, coming to a place like this with Majima but not you would be outta the question."

"I couldn't agree more." Majima, having matured even more since becoming a middle schooler, gazed affectionately at Eri through his glasses.

"Ehehe. Glad to hear it." Eri broke into a relieved smile.

S-She's too cute!

Watching Tomo and Eri made me honestly think I wanted to try out falling in love too. The second the thought crossed my mind, Kou and Sou's all-too-handsome faces flashed before my eyes.

Uh, no thanks. I don't need a boyfriend with such high specs. It's too much for me to handle a love that goes hand in hand with tragic bad ends if I make the wrong move. I'd be happier with a normal love. Falling naturally in love and being fallen naturally in love with, where both sides cherish each other equally is the best... Why does that have to be so out of my reach?

"Okay, let's get this party started. I can order whatever I want, right, guys?" I flashed a wicked grin, which earned two displeased nods from the boys.

Only Tomo smiled. "I was so confident I would win this time, too."

"M'kay then, I'll have the apple pie, chocolate fondant, caramel pudding, and—"

"Y-You can eat that much, Mashiro?" Rin interrupted my order, looking completely put off.

I gave a heavy nod. "Of course I can. I calculated my calorie intake and went on a diet over the last three days just for this day. I passed on breakfast and lunch so I can eat until my stomach explodes!"

"Who the heck prepares so much for cake?!" Rin banged his head on the table and left it there for Tomo to pat him comfortingly.

See, this is why I prepared! The only thing a single girl like me can do when faced with friends in lovey-dovey relationships is pig out on lots and lots of cake! Bring on the cake!

♩♩♩

ON the Saturday afternoon of that same week, I drank tea with Kon on the couch after practice in the Genda annex. This brief respite before going home had become a vital destresser for me.

"Oh, right, I nearly forgot. Take this." Kon placed her cup on the table and handed me a white pamphlet.

"Seio is putting on a Christmas concert?" I asked, glancing over the pamphlet.

"Yup. It's on the twenty-third. Does that work for you? If you don't have any other plans, I would love it if you came."

While the word concert was in the title, they appeared to be hosting the event to allow Seio Academy's high achieving students a place to put their skills on display. The middle school department was performing on the twenty-third, the high school department on the twenty-fourth, and select students from the university were going to put on a concert with the local orchestra on the twenty-fifth.

I carefully turned the pages and checked who was performing on what days.

"Wow, this is an amazing line up! That's Seio for you, all right. The concerts and events they host are on a whole other scale."

An up-and-coming conductor who'd won a famous music competition was conducting the local orchestra. The mass media had been covering him a lot lately, so I wanted to hear what a concerto conducted by him sounded like.

Kon's expression sunk apologetically when she noticed me drooling over the program line up for the twenty-fifth. "I'm sorry. I don't have any tickets for the twenty-fifth. I can try and get my hands on one if you want to go."

"What? Nah, I'm all good! Really! I was just marveling over how impressive the whole concert is going to be."

"It's the first event Tobi is putting on. He seems to be going all out for it," Kon explained with ice in her voice.

According to Kon, Prince Tobi was currently working for the Yamabuki Group's trading firm, and starting this year, he was being added into the management ranks at Seio too. Considering how he was supposed to become the principal and director of the board at Seio in three years, that pretty much painted the picture of how much of a shrewd go-getter he was.

"He plans to run Seio by marketing the school alumni in a big way and enhancing the academy's prestige through them. Seio has tradition and history on its side, but new and improved music academies have been on the rise lately. It's creating a sense of rivalry in the board of directors, I'm sure."

"I see. Prince Tobi's an ambitious one, isn't he?"

I was about to say, "I don't think it's a bad thing to be passionate about your work," but snapped my mouth shut. Kon's expression had hardened. Wanting to change the electric mood in the room, I glanced back over the program for the twenty-third. Kon and Kou's name were both listed there.

"Neat! You're playing the third movement from Beethoven's piano sonata "Appassionata"! I can't wait to hear it!"

Kon and a girl named Yukiko Sawakura had entered the concert from the piano department.

Kon smacked the printed name "Yukiko Sawakura" with her index finger. "This girl is one of Kou's fangirls. She's the one who lent you that piano jazz arrangement."

"Oh, so it belonged to her, huh? She must be pretty good at the piano if she can participate in Seio's concert."

I wonder what her performance will be like. Never having the chance to hear anyone the same age as me play the piano, I could only compare myself to Kon's prodigious skill. When I thought about it that way, the concert sounded like a good opportunity to learn what level Seio's middle school department played at. I was getting excited now.

"Pretty good isn't quite how I'd put it…" Kon said ambiguously, studying my face. "I think it was Yukiko who saw the operetta with Kou."

"So that was her! Then that blue-haired beauty is Yukiko. Kou only has eyes for the pretty ones, huh?"

"…That's all you have to say?"

"What else should I say?"

For some inexplicable reason, Kon peered at my face as if disappointed in my reaction. Her brown hair spilled onto her cheeks when she leaned forward, stealing my breath and causing my eyes to be glued to her dizzying beauty. *Eek. T-Too bright for me!*

"…Hah," she sighed. "I know he did it to himself, but I'm starting to pity my brother."

I pried my eyes from the grumbling Kon and dropped them to read the rest of the pamphlet. Staring at Kon too much had the adverse effect of putting me in shock when I saw my own face in the mirror at home. Was I the only person who got deluded into thinking they're pretty when they're with beautiful people for a long time?

Aside from the piano department, representatives of the strings department, woodwind department, and brass department would be partaking as well. Suddenly, my eyes stopped on a familiar name.

"Clarinetist: Riko Miyaji"

Hmm, I feel like I've heard that name somewhere. Who is it? I scoured my memories until I remembered. *I've met her before too! She's that black-haired beauty with raven black eyes! That girl who acted like the captain of Kou's elite guard of groupies!*

"Is this Riko girl a member of Kou's fangirl group too?" I asked Kon, pointing to her name in the pamphlet.

"Oh? How'd you know?"

"I was right then." I recalled the time I met her at the shopping mall during elementary school and how she warned me off Kou, and briefly summarized it for Kon.

Once I finished talking, Kon grimaced. "She's definitely the type to say something like that. Speaking of groupies, look here. The violist Misa Utsunomiya and the flutist Karin Teranishi are both members of Riko's group."

Now that she mentions it, I sorta remember two flunkies flanking Captain

Miyaji back then.

"What do you know, all of Kou's fans are pretty and skilled musicians. Women should run and hide in fear of his seducing skills!" I jested, impressed by his track record.

Meanwhile, Kon was shaking her head, her expression bitter. "There are much better students at the Academy. Tobi chose those girls as members to repay their parents for their large contributions to the school."

Yikes! Now that's playing dirty. But Prince Tobi seems like the type to do something like that. He looked like the type who stood by the sayings, "Successful crime is called virtue" and "Nothing succeeds like success."

"You've got to be kidding me! Hey, Kon, why don't you give up trying to capture that no-good player?" I pursed my lips.

A slight smile made its way to Kon's lips. "I don't have a choice. My—the original heroine's romantic partner is set as Tobi."

Something about her remark stood out as awkward to me. In the past, Kon had told me, *"You are free to live as you want, Mashiro. You don't need to be manipulated by Hear My Heart."*

She said that *I* was free to live how *I* wanted. But why did that seem to imply otherwise for Kon? Why did Kon want to go down Prince Tobi's route according to *Hear My Heart?*

*No, that's not right. What if she doesn't want to, but **has** to? Then her actions up until now would flip the board completely and take on a whole new meaning.* I was starting to connect the dots around the big secret Kon was keeping and continued to mull over the meaning of what she'd said to me long after that day.

♪♪♪

THE sun set awfully early during winter. The area was already submerged in pure darkness by five. On the way to the Benz where Mr. Nonaga waited to take me home, Kon handed me a DVD.

"I've been hesitating over whether I should give you this or not. Kou told me not to." White breath escaped through Kon's pretty pink lips. Illuminated by the lit stone lantern, Kon clutched the sides of her long coat collar together as she searched my face. "There was an arts festival held in Graz, Austria while Kou and I were in Europe over fall break.

We ran into Shiroyama there."

"Into Sou?" Mention of the name I least expected startled me. Kou didn't utter a single word about it when he was giving me advice for the culture festival. "Is he doing well? Is he still playing the cello?" I quickly asked.

Kon's expression softened and she pointed to the DVD in my hand. "You can see for yourself if you watch that… Please don't blame Kou for this. My brother was only being considerate by thinking it might still be too hard on you, Mashiro."

"…Yeah, I don't doubt it," I sincerely agreed after remembering the sorry state I'd been in the day of my school entrance ceremony.

Kou often didn't seem like the type, but he was actually a considerate person. In fact, he had saved me on countless occasions since I'd gotten to know him. He'd be a great guy if his haughty attitude didn't cancel out all the good about him. I tried imagining a sincere and honest Kou, and decided it was too weird.

He was a sore loser who was a real pain to deal with because even though he was a nice guy, he hated being thought of as such. In a nonromantic sense, I'd surely fall to my knees and mourn a great loss in my life should he ever disappear from this world. One of the worst drawbacks about Kou was that I couldn't hate him even after listing all of his drawbacks…

"Anyways, weren't you wary of Sou, Kon? Are you sure you want me to see this?"

Wasn't Kon the one who'd told me not to get too close to Sou a long time ago? My curiosity getting the better of me, I put the question directly to her.

"When it comes to you, Mashiro, I get the feeling this world is no longer following the same *Hear My Heart* plot that I know of. That's why I'm neither Kou nor Shiroyama's supporter, but yours, Mashiro," Kon declared without a moment's thought. "Haven't you been curious and worried about why he hasn't written anything on any of the postcards he sends?"

"…You could tell? You can see through everything when it comes to me, huh, Kon?"

Postcards from Sou came once every week without fail. But he never wrote a reply to the letters I'd sent him. The reason for it was beyond me. Sou's feelings, which I knew like the back of my hand while we were together, were like a riddle to me now. That reality saddened me.

Regardless of how I was feeling, I never stopped sending him letters because I didn't want the connection between us to end for good. As I groaned to myself, I composed neutral, inoffensive letters to him.

"How are you doing? Are you eating well? Is Germany fun?"

Writing up letters full of nothing but bland questions was starting to become painful for me, so I began folding origami and including it in the envelope. I followed up my questions with a perfunctory summary of what was currently going on in my life and an explanation on how I made the origami.

Since my series on origami ruins seemed unpopular with him, I sent him a series of origami instruments including a cello, violin, trumpet, and trombone. I wanted to cover all the instruments used in an orchestra to accompany the grand piano I had given him when we'd first met.

"Thanks, Kon." I clutched the DVD firmly to my chest and slid into the car.

♪♪♪

I camped out in front of the living room TV the moment I got home. Hanaka's eyes lit up when she saw me. "It's unusual for you to watch TV, Mashiro. What are you watching?" She plopped down on the couch beside me.

"Supposedly a DVD of Sou."

"Of Sou?! Wow, I haven't heard his name in forever! Can I watch with you?"

"Of course you can. Let's watch together!"

Hanaka jumped off the couch and went to make hot chocolate for us. The sweet hot chocolate with roasted marshmallows on top always tasted better when Hanaka made it. It was a mystery how she pulled it off, considering how much trouble she had with cooking.

Every time I was awed by her hot chocolate she'd wink and smile at me, teasing, "The secret is love."

We sat side by side on the couch and waited for the DVD to start up. I was holding my mug in both hands, blowing on it to cool it down, when a familiar voice spoke from the LCD screen.

"Are you filming? Quit it."

"What's wrong with me filming? Don't be annoying."

The first voice was Sou's, and the second was…Midori, who seemed to be the one behind the video camera. The scenery spun around on the screen and landed on one boy.

Decked out in an attractive black jacket, Sou looked at me through the TV screen with a deep scowl. Intense sentimentality surged within me. *Sou. It's Sou!* His silky, light-blue hair hadn't changed much. *Oh, wait, maybe it's a little shorter? Maybe it's because he's taller now, but he no longer looks like the cute little Sou I remember.*

A mature young man who looked like the spitting image of Sou Shiroyama as he was pictured in my fanbook was standing there.

Midori moved the camera again, capturing another boy standing beside Sou.

"You aren't performing on stage yet. No rule says you can't be filmed beforehand. You should listen when a lady asks a favor of you, Sou," Kou, wearing a dark-brown jacket with a scarf loosely wrapped around his neck, teased.

Midori must've stepped back, because now both boys appeared on screen at the same time.

"Don't confuse me with an exhibitionist like you. I don't care for pictures or videos."

"Huh? That's a horrible way to put it. Letting people take your picture doesn't make you an exhibitionist."

Sou and Kou were lightly pushing each other around while they bantered.

Before I knew it, tears had rushed to my eyes. I frantically placed my mug on the table and wiped my eyes with the back of my hand. Hanaka quietly placed her hand on my knee.

I miss them. It's so nostalgic I can't take it. They used to always fool around like this. They nag and complain at each other, but they're both smiling.

"Hey, can I send this video to Mashiro?" Midori's voice asked over the quibbling boys.

Sou's whole face softened into a tender expression as he looked straight at the camera. "I don't mind if Mashiro says she wants to see it. Don't force it on her. I don't want to burden her in any way."

Sou's voice was a sweet alto that was slightly higher than Kou's. The love and adoration in his eyes informed me that he still had feelings for me. My heart ached. A strong desire to see him washed over me.

But if someone asked me if this feeling resulted from love, I could only deny it. He was dear to me, someone I wanted to protect, and the person I wished would find happiness more than I wished for any other. To me, Sou wasn't someone who could be constricted to the confines of the word "love."

The video went on for a while after that, showing Kou and Sou talking about inconsequential things, and then Kon showed up on screen. As tears streamed down my cheeks, I anchored my full attention on my three dearest friends.

"Looks like it's almost time for your performance. It's a real shame we can't film you playing the cello."

"Why's that?"

"I wanted to check it carefully later and search for any mistakes you made so I could point them out to you."

"Now you've gone and said it."

Sou high-fived Kou and walked off toward the stage set up in the middle of plaza. His broad back, broader than when we were kids, grew smaller in the distance before the screen went to black. The video ended there.

I agreed wholeheartedly with Kou—I wanted to hear Sou's cello. I wanted to submerge myself in that gentle, heartrendingly beautiful sound.

"Whew... Sou and Kou have both grown up to be so cool," Hanaka commented, sounding emotional. I nodded as I wiped my tears away.

They really are cool. Not just their appearance, but everything about them is dazzling.

I don't have to be romantically involved. I just want to stand shoulder to shoulder with them on stage, playing music.

CG 26: Seio Christmas Concert (Tobi & Kou)

DECEMBER twenty-third arrived in the blink of an eye.

"You're still here? I thought you said you were going to the Christmas concert at Kon's school today?" Mom asked, tilting her head at me when I came downstairs to eat lunch after playing Aine all morning.

"I'm still going. I was going to take the train and leave earlier, but I took Kon up on her offer to have Mr. Nonaga drive me there."

The concert hall was open to the public at two, but I didn't have to rush getting ready now that I was going by car. It's not like I was going to see the opera or a full orchestra, so I figured I could just wear any old dress or whatever I could fish out of the closet.

Hanaka perked up at the dining table. "You're going to a Christmas concert? Is it for a date?"

"D-Do you have a d-d-date, Mashiro?!" Dad whipped his gaze from the rugby match he was watching on the living room TV.

Straining a smile, I shook my head. "I hate to break it to you, but it's not a date. I'm going alone this time."

Kon had confirmed with me multiple times if one ticket was enough, but I couldn't find anyone to invite. Rei had club activities, Eri and Tomo had dates, and the single Sawa and Mako had plans with their families. Hanaka tended to be busy around this time of year, so I decided not to bring it up with her. Plus, it was starting to get embarrassing going everywhere with my parents like I couldn't do anything on my own.

A part of me thought it'd be great if I could go with Tomoi, but I instantly gave up on the idea. It was one thing if Hanaka and Shinji were going too, but it was obvious he'd turn me down if he knew it was going to be just me. He was the type to make a firm distinction between these things.

"Aw, really? Kou isn't going to escort you there?" Hanaka sounded disappointed.

"He can't. Kou's one of the performers today. And even if he wasn't, he doesn't have the time for me now."

"Why not?" Hanaka pressed.

I gave her a simple explanation about Kou's fanclub. Yukiko and Riko were both gorgeous. They weren't on the same level as Kon and Midori, but they weren't girls I could compete with. Or rather—I didn't want to deal with them. *I'll ignore them the next time they try to start something,* I swore to myself. I couldn't stand the thought of Kou spotting me taking on his army of spoiled, rich girls and him holding it over my head afterwards.

Before she even finished hearing me out, Hanaka sprung to her feet. "How can you say that?! It's obvious you're the cutest, Mashiro!"

How can you say that, Hanaka?! My big sister's blind doting is still going strong!

"It's not an issue of appearances. I don't want to get into a spat with Kou's fans, hence why I planned on going without making a scene—"

"Finish your food! I'm going to use my magic skills to turn you into a princess!" Hanaka avowed, not listening to a word I said.

Listen to me first!

Mom seemed to misunderstand my sigh, because even she chimed in with, "Hanaka's right. Mashiro's the cutest of them all. Use your magic on your sister, Hanaka!"

What is this, a scene from Cinderella?! Whatever. They can do what they want.

Still though, my mom and sister are scary blind when it comes to me. The Family Love Filter is absurdly powerful! I concluded profoundly.

Now that I think about it, I feel like this is similar to why Sou thinks I'm cute and amazing. He views me as a replacement for his mother Risa. Maybe his affection is just another form of the Family Love Filter… How did I end up with a thirteen-year-old son at my age?! This sucks.

Hurried along by Hanaka, I ate the rest of my omelet rice. She dragged me upstairs as soon as I finished. Her room was remarkably cleaner now than the pigsty it was during high school.

"Whoa! It's super clean in here!" I blurted.

"Hehe, I guess it is. I don't want Shin to think of me as a messy person. Besides, I'll be joining the workforce after next year. The least I can do is keep my own room tidy," Hanaka admitted bashfully as she opened her closet.

"What should we go with?" she hummed while throwing outfit after outfit onto her bed. Once she finished unloading what seemed to be her entire wardrobe, she held each piece up to me and groaned stuff like "The color isn't right" and "Hm, something cuter would be better."

No one could stop her once she entered dress up mode. It took twenty minutes before I was finally dressed in a black mini fit and flare skirt with an off-shoulder knit top that bared half my shoulders. A baby pearl necklace adorned my exposed neckline. I was trying to pull on tights when Hanaka yelled at me to stop.

"Oh no you don't! Stop right there, missy! You have beautiful legs, Mashiro. Don't hide them under tights! You can stay warm with a pair of knee-high boots instead."

"Ick. I don't wanna. This skirt is too short! You can see my underwear!"

"Don't worry. It just *looks* like you can see your underwear, but you can't!"

How much of a tease is Hanaka trying to make me?!

I wanted to reject her suggestion with every fiber of my being, but Hanaka didn't give me any time to protest before tugging me in front of the bathroom sink. She meticulously blew out my hair that'd been tied back in a ponytail and cleanly braided it. She curled the short straggler hairs with a curling iron and spread them around my face. Then she clipped a black velour ribbon barrette to the side of my head and looked me over with great delight.

"This should do it!"

Hanaka brushed some loose powder on my face, painted my lips with lip gloss, and marched me in front of the full-length mirror.

Huh... Oh my gosh!

Before the mirror stood a mature version of myself. I looked nothing like a middle schooler. When I first saw the clothes, I thought they were too gaudy for me, but once I had them on, they looked so much cuter. Appearances could be completely changed just by taking the time to do my hair and makeup.

"What do you think? It's cute, right?"

"Yeah! It's the makeover of a lifetime! Thanks sis!" I glomped Hanaka before glancing at the clock. It was almost time to go.

I hurried upstairs, pulled on my favorite white short coat, and zipped up my knee-high boots. The doorbell rang just as I grabbed my felt bag with the fur trim.

"Oh, that's probably Mr. Nonaga. I'm heading out now!" I called out to my family.

Being dressed up really had a way of making me feel excited to go out. I likely wouldn't have been enjoying myself so much if I'd just tossed on any old dress.

I rushed out of the house, feeling like I was walking on clouds.

♪♪♪

THE Christmas concert looked like it was going to be a big success. The large hall capable of seating 3,000 was nearly packed.

I confirmed my seat number on my ticket and sat down. My seat was located in the center of the fifth row from the stage. Kon had secured me a pretty good spot. Not too many people had taken their seats around my row yet, leading me to believe they were still in the lobby chatting with the performers. As I flipped through the concert program, the hall suddenly erupted with noisy squeals.

Curious about the change in mood, I looked up and instantly understood what all the commotion was about.

A tuxedo-wearing Kou was escorting Kon, dressed in her beautiful, deep-blue concert dress. I was dazzled by the beauty of Kon's white arms, exposed by the sleeveless dress. Kou had slicked back his long red hair, preventing it from getting in the way of his performance. Today, he went without the unbuttoned shirt collar. What was with this crazy world that made him look this attractive even after properly buttoning up his shirt and wearing a tie?!

The two of them were beyond beautiful.

Maybe they came out here to greet me? Nah, fat chance.

"Hey, isn't that Kou?"

"It is! Oh my gosh! He's so cool!"

"It's our Kou!"

"He gets more attractive every time I look at him!"

Girls around my age gushed over Kou, while the boys fell over themselves for Kon. Kou and Kon, however, didn't seem to care about what they said. They'd probably grown immune to hearing it. Feeling like just another fan, I watched them leisurely stroll from the stage area.

"Mashiro!" The second I made eye contact with Kon, she beamed and waved at me. Every pair of eyes in the vicinity turned on me.

Kou saw Kon waving and followed her gaze. His demure expression suddenly shifted into a soft smile. The glares burning into me upped their intensity.

"Thank you so much for coming! I'm so happy you're here!" Kon exclaimed adorably when she came over to my seat, making everyone else in the room disappear. It was pretty obvious that I was the odd one out between the two of them, but it bothered me more to act like it just because of what other people thought

"I'm the one who's grateful for the ticket. Thanks again. I'm looking forward to your performance."

"Thanks! I'll put on the best performance I can! Thank you for the flowers too. I went straight to the lobby and picked them up."

The small bouquet I'd brought for Kon was made up of miniature roses, baby's breath, and delphiniums. She blissfully held the flower bouquet up in her right hand.

As for Kou, his penetrating gaze was assessing my attire. I tightened my stomach and waited for whatever snide remark he had in store for me this time. Contrary to my expectations, his cheeks flushed light-red and he complimented, "Nice outfit. You look great."

...*Am I hearing things right?*

I waited with bated breath for the searing follow-up remark, but it never came. Baffled, I pushed off my seat. "This is my sister's outfit. I'm glad it doesn't look weird on me at least."

"...Isn't your skirt way too short?" Kou appraised my outfit all over again and frowned. He looked really irked. And he was the one who had just praised how good I looked in it too! I knew this was coming.

"I think it's fine," I said dismissively.

"And who are you trying to please with that look?" Kou asked, sounding even more irritated.

"Don't worry, Kou, I'm definitely not trying to please you with it."

"Pft!" Kon snorted, her shoulders shaking with suppressed laughter.

Was our argument really that funny? Kou shot Kon a sharp look, his mouth twisted.

"Kon?"

"What's wrong with a short skirt? It's cute and mature—a perfect look for Mashiro."

Aw, Kon! You always have my back! Teach your brother a lesson!

Kou sighed once then gave his head a small shake. "I'll accept it for now. I'm just glad I made arrangements in advance." Before I could ask him what he meant, he continued over me, "You'll be here until the end, right? Will you join us for dinner after?"

"Yes, please do!" Kon chimed in after her brother. "If you don't have any other plans, I would love to have dinner with you."

I'd originally planned on going straight home after the concert, but it seemed like such a waste after Hanaka's makeover. This was the perfect excuse to show off her work.

"Okay, I'll call home and ask. I'll join you if my parents give the okay."

"Got it. See you later then," Kou said to me then turned to Kon. "We should go. It's almost time."

Kon waved goodbye and left with Kou.

I only spoke with them for a few minutes, but that's all it took to make me the target of inquisitive and jealous stares until just before the curtain raised.

"What's that girl's story? She's not from Seio, is she?"

"What's her relationship with Kou and his sister?"

"I don't like her."

"She gives me bad vibes."

You're the ones giving me bad vibes! I tamped down my desire to let out a long sigh as I pushed down the spring seat and sat down again. The only thing that saved the night from becoming uncomfortable was the two empty seats on either side of me.

I was worried about what would happen if Kou's fans sat next to me, so it was a real relief. There was nothing worse than trying to enjoy music surrounded by negative people.

It didn't take long before the curtain rose.

The first part of the program was performed by the strings department.

The first song was a double bass solo rendition of Rachmaninoff's "Vocalise". A rich sound filled the hall, accompanied by the modest voice of the piano. According to the program, the bassist was in his last year of middle school. He sounded pretty good. He drew the audience's full attention within the first few phrases. Sergei Rachmaninoff is said to have originally written this romantic, melancholy song for double bass. Rachmaninoff composed and published "Vocalise" as the last of his *14 Songs* or *14 Romances* vocal song collection.

Because Rachmaninoff's "Vocalise" was free from lyrics, it required the listener to think of the *melody* as the conveyor of emotion, and I enjoyed performances where the instrument seemed to sing that melody. I wanted the bassist to play with more emotional intensity, but it was still an elegant and gentle rendition of "Vocalise".

The second song was a cello solo of Saint-Saëns' "The Swan".

The third song was Maurice Ravel's "String Quartet in F major".

Every song was played at such a high level it was hard to believe the performers were in middle school. This was the true ability of children gifted with a special music education from a young age. Rivalry bubbled within me. The more I admired their excellent performances, the more my desire not to lose to them grew. Since when did I become this greedy?

Kou was the final performer for the strings department.

The hall stirred to life when he stepped on stage. I thought back to the reactions I had seen before the concert started. I always knew he was popular, but his popularity still exceeded my expectations. I tried remembering what it was like for him in *Hear My Heart*, but it didn't make for a good reference because I'd only come across his character a few times. That was the worst part about RNG games.

Kou suddenly felt out of reach, forcing me to face a hopeless sense of loneliness over the distance between us. I had no right to feel lonely when it came to him, but feelings and logic rarely went hand in hand.

Kou was performing Prokofiev's "Sonata for Solo Violin in D minor".

Purposely choosing to play a song without a piano accompaniment was clearly him showing his colors as an *oresama* character. Or maybe it was just easier for him to go without one with all the piano department girls fighting for the role.

When it came to technique, there were swaths of more difficult songs he could have picked from. But Kou had his violin singing this sonata with unimaginable beauty. The high notes rung out with crystalline clarity; the double-stops richly added volume. It was a perfect performance, leaving zero room for complaint.

Kou could be the model for a painting with the way he stood with his back straight, lovingly playing his violin. Add in the fact his music sounded godly and it made sense why he had a fanclub. I hated to admit it, but his performance grabbed hold of my heart too. I didn't hold back any applause for his outstanding sonata.

Kou looked straight at me before leaving the stage—or that's how it looked to me. A smile seemed to have graced his face too. Shrill screams exploded from the audience around me—he was probably just giving them fanservice. He had the mindset of a superstar. My heart involuntarily skipped a beat.

The concert went into a ten-minute intermission.

Okay, time to use the bathroom while I can! Must not get caught by Kou's rabid fans! My desperate prayers must've reached the gaming gods—either that or I was being so sneaky it freaked people out—because I was able to make the roundtrip from the bathroom back to my seat without anyone saying or doing anything to me.

Quit being so self-conscious! I wanted to tell myself, but this world was too opportunistic when it came to cueing events. I'd tasted its power more times than I'd like to remember. Letting the tension out of my shoulders, I slowly sunk into my seat. I'd completely let down my guard at that point.

"*Bonjour*, Mashiro! *Comment allez-vous*? Can I take the seat beside you if no one else has?"

It can't be! Why's that guy here?! I awkwardly jerked my body toward the owner of that familiar voice.

My hunch was right—Tobi was here. A blond-haired, blue-eyed prince decked out in a white jacket was looking down at me with a phony smile.

I had no way of knowing if this was an event or just an irregular random encounter. Whichever it was, the choice was taken from me now. He was the big boss I had to beat in the future if I wanted to become a special scholarship student at Seio Academy.

"*Très bien, merci*. It doesn't look like anyone has those seats, so be my guest," I said politely, answering back in French.

Become like Kon, Mashiro! Put on a mask! Suppressing my panic, I lifted the corners of my lips into a polished smile.

Heroine's Results
Target Character: Kou Narita
Event: Playing For You

Original Heroine's Results
Target Character: Tobi Yamabuki
Event: Groundwork for the Future
CLEAR

I struggled to pay attention to the brass and woodwind performances during the second half of the program because I was too bothered by Tobi sitting next to me.

"I don't have a choice. The original heroine's romantic partner is set as Tobi."

The truth Kon admitted to me the other day clung to my thoughts and wouldn't let go. It swirled through my mind, trying to connect the dots with the occasional health attacks we both experienced and the fact that Kon avoided touching on what had happened in our past lives at all costs.

I'd completely assumed she didn't remember the past like me. But what if that wasn't the case? Having played or not having played the remake version of *Hear My Heart* would cease to be the sole differentiator between us.

It'd become a matter of who did and who didn't retain memories of their past life.

The real question at hand was why we were even reincarnated into a game world in the first place. I'd occasionally heard strange tales of girls who said they remembered their past lives, but none of those accounts ever mentioned anything about being reincarnated into or from a fictional story world.

And why is Kon so hung up on Prince Tobi? What will happen if she fails to finish his route?

Clarinetist Riko appeared on the stage while I was speculating. The skintight, deep-crimson cocktail dress accentuated her curves and natural beauty. Riko gracefully bowed to the crowd, her shimmering black hair spilling over her shoulders.

Poulenc – Clarinet Sonata, 1st Movement

The beautiful melody in Francis Poulenc's "Clarinet Sonata" was one of its key characteristics, but Riko Miyaji's rendition had spurts of rough notes. Her slurs failed to smoothly connect the different pitches. The overblown vibratos seemed to be her poor attempt to hide the faulty slurs.

Are my personal feelings toward Riko skewing my view of her performance? Scared that was true, I concentrated on every note she played. Kon had given me the concert program beforehand so I had the time to learn and listen to all the songs in advance. Obviously, I couldn't compare a middle school performance to the masterful performance of Paul Meyer, but there was still something off about Riko's rendition.

Prince Tobi glanced over at me as I clapped without much enthusiasm. His mouth curled into a nauseatingly pleased smile, and he brought his perfectly shaped, thin lips to my ear. "It's just not beautiful. Don't you agree?"

Tobi knew. He knew Riko Miyaji's skill level. He knew and chose her as the clarinet representative for his school anyway.

Intense disgust and repulsion crawled up my spine.

How can you tear down the performer you chose? I had always believed that even if Tobi had assumed the role of principal and director at Seio Academy as a part of his work, he had a love for music.

I refused to comment and pretended to be absorbed with the concert.

The flutist Karin Teranishi came on stage next and gave a similarly disappointing performance. Maybe they just didn't practice enough. Karin was a charming girl with a flattering pixie cut, but her performance just wasn't worth a listen.

The violist Misa Utsumiya had performed much better than the others during the first part of the concert. She had performed as a member of the string quartet and used actual technique to support the tonic key.

The concert moved into the piano department's program without intermission. According to the concert program, two performers from each school year were going to perform for a total of six performances. The program layout seemed strange to begin with, but this really solidified the feeling for me.

Normally, the best player in their senior year would perform last. Kou's performance was exquisite, but I couldn't help thinking it was weird to switch him into the final performance slot over the third-year student who'd performed a song with a much higher difficulty. All the more so when the second half of the concert ended with the best flutist who was in her senior year.

Kon was assigned as the final performer for the piano department. I had no complaints there because Kon was obviously their best pianist. But could the same be said of Yukiko Sawakura who was set to perform right before Kon?

She was playing Chopin's "Nocturne in E Flat Major".

Perhaps I was at fault for listening to Alexis Weissenberg's masterful recording beforehand, but even if I hadn't, there was no saving her performance. Yukiko played at too fast of a tempo, and her sound was flat. The excellent performance of the third-year student who had performed before her made the performance all the more disappointing.

Tobi leaned over and whispered in my ear again when he saw my shoulders droop. "You're the type to show everything you're thinking on your face, Mashiro. Miss Sawakura comes from a very wealthy family. And better yet, both of her parents love to dote on her. They are some of the Academy's finest patrons."

Tobi sounded elated. Profound sadness washed over me.

I'd always dreamed of attending the academy I looked up to as a pillar of musical learning. Someday I was going to enter Seio and enjoy every moment immersed in music. In order to make that dream come true, I had single-mindedly devoted myself to mastering the academic and music curriculum. Like a fool, I had believed that the other students attending Seio worked just as hard to be where they were. I was disgusted with my naiveté.

But my melancholy was blown far away with Kon's performance.

Kon had changed since being instructed by Maestro Noboru.

A calm aura now accompanied her passion. That new calm gave the listener room to carefully taste the world spun together by the original composer. Shining brighter than any person or stage light, Kon vividly conveyed the joy of playing music.

Wow! Wow! She shines right off the stage!

Kon's "Appassionata" moved me more than any other rendition I'd ever heard. I clapped so hard my hands hurt. Kon smiled contentedly in response to the thunderous applause. I stopped clapping once she left the stage and dragged my gaze to Tobi's face.

Kon's different. Everything about her is different from those you favor, Tobi. Her feelings toward music, her dedication, and her resolve—all of it is different. You won't win!

Tobi stared dumbfounded at the stage.

"How…how could she…how could she have changed this much?" Prince Tobi's vexed voice brought me great satisfaction. He quickly took fault with the wide grin I forgot to suppress. "You aren't very nice, are you, Mashiro? Are you that entertained by my surprise?"

"Extremely entertained. It's very refreshing."

Tobi was going to be in charge of Seio Academy in the future. I knew it wasn't smart to make an enemy of him, but I couldn't stop running my mouth. I was more pissed off with him than I thought.

I would've never put on such a disappointing and subpar performance if I was in Riko or Yukiko's shoes. I would've only taken on today's concert after putting in hours and hours of dedicated practice, set on doing whatever necessary to perfect it. If I was Tobi, I would've never picked the concert performers based on the amount of money their parents donated. I would've picked students who were seriously learning music and given them the commendation befitting their efforts.

I couldn't contain my frustration and disappointment.

"To be honest with you, aside from Kon and a select few, this concert failed to meet my expectations. I have always looked up to what Seio Academy stands for, so this concert was a real disappointment for me."

"Strong opinions for a little girl." Prince Tobi's blue eyes sharply gleamed. "You must have a lot of confidence in your piano to make those claims. Haha! You amuse me. Why don't you prove you're more than talk then?"

"…In what way?" I gasped under the scrutiny of his penetratingly cold gaze that seemed to be assessing me like a predator with a possible new prey.

Tobi seized my arm and yanked me toward him. "In exactly the way my words imply. A large-scale music competition will be held next year. Win the competition and prove your skills are more than a child's baseless boasting."

That's what this is about? Meeting Tobi here wasn't a coincidence. Interacting with him now was very likely a required event for reality to follow the game's scenario. The large-scale music competition he brought up had to be the Sadia Francesca Junior Music Competition.

It was the first piano competition held in Japan with a judging committee headed up by a famous female pianist from Vienna. This was the important storyline competition for the heroine from *Hear My Heart*'s remake.

I looked Tobi square in the eyes and answered, "All right. I accept your challenge."

I don't know how far I can go. But I do know I don't want to lose to him. I don't want to back down. I held Prince Tobi's ice-cold gaze.

Less than a minute's time passed around us. The light's clicked on in the hall while we glared at each other. The audience stood from their seats and noisily clamored for the exits.

I have to go outside and phone home. With that in mind, I silently bowed to Tobi and left our row for the aisle. I'd thought that was the end of it, but Tobi followed me out.

"Do you have any plans after this, Mashiro?" he asked me, a smile in his voice. "If you don't, how about you join me for dinner?"

Surprise hit me like a tidal wave. *What kinda person invites out the cheeky brat they were just having a staring contest with? This guy has some seriously thick skin. Everything he does is out of the norm.*

"U-Uh, um…" I faltered.

What's the right way to act here? Should I be honest and tell him about my plans with the twins and invite him along? Or should I just flat-out reject him? If this were a game, I would quick save and try out both choices, but this world is my reality, not a game. Then again, considering how every person I meet looks like an otome game character and how my life seems scripted at times, it makes me wonder sometimes if this really isn't a game…

The choice timed out on me while I was mulling over how to proceed.

"Mashiro!" a tense, deep voice called out to me from behind.

Surprised, I turned around to find Kou dressed in casual clothes skipping steps to get down the stairs faster.

Wow, Kou can run, I mused.

I wasn't sure if his arrival was going to save me or make things worse. But it took until I saw Kou's back in front of me to realize I was so nervous my legs were shaking.

"…Director Yamabuki, why were you seated in this row? You didn't have the ticket for it, did you?"

"I didn't. I was curious why the five seats you bought for row five were the only empty ones in the hall. And then who did I chance upon when I came to check it out? Mashiro, sitting in the middle of the empty seats. I couldn't resist speaking to her."

Is he telling the truth? Did Kou go out of his way to make sure no one would sit next to me? My mouth fell open from the series of surprises.

Kou kept his eyes fixed on Tobi and quietly clicked his tongue. "I bought the tickets for my own entertainment, no other reason."

There's no other reason? Ah, he scared me for a second! I nearly misunderstood his actions again!

"Heh. I was completely under the impression you did it to guard her from your rabid fans. Or maybe you did it because you wanted to locate exactly where she was from the stage?"

"I told you it was for my own entertainment," Kou dodged Tobi's goading. Then his eyes shifted to me. The moment our eyes met, Kou's tensed expression softened, his eyebrows knitting with worry. "Are you okay, Mashiro? You look pale."

"Yeah. I feel really dizzy. Maybe I should go outside for some fresh air."

I don't want to be dragged any further into this, I implored with my eyes when I looked up at Kou.

"Okay. Let's go." Kou put his arm around my shoulder and gently guided me toward the exit. "Sorry, Director. We shall be excusing ourselves here."

"I see. What a shame! I was hoping to dine with Mashiro. Well, there's always next time. See you again soon, Mashiro." Tobi winked at me. "Ñ›oubliez pas de me rencontrer dans le concours du piano."

His final words of parting were in French. Between this remark and the one earlier, it was almost as if he knew I was studying French.

How am I supposed to take this? Has he realized I've been studying different things in preparation for the music competition? My head became crowded with confusing thoughts.

Kou looked baffled too as he watched Tobi gallantly saunter away from us. "What did he say at the end there?" he muttered more to himself than to me.

"He said, 'don't forget to meet me at the piano competition,'" I translated for him.

"…He was speaking French, right? You could understand that?"

I nodded. Kou regarded me with astonishment. He suddenly leaned over until he was peering into my eyes. "What in the world is going on?"

A girl with a tense face was reflected in his purple eyes. His face was colored with suspicion and sadness.

Kou, that's the question I want to ask more than anyone else.

♪♪♪

NOT sure where I should start from, I stayed quiet the whole way to the parking lot where Mr. Mizusawa and Kon were waiting for us. Kou didn't ask anything else after that; he merely walked quietly at my side.

The tension finally left my shoulders when we met up with Kon who looked like an actress with her traditional dress and knee-length fur coat.

"What's wrong, you guys? Did something happen?" Kon asked right away. The two of us must have looked horrible.

"Director Yamabuki had Mashiro cornered when I went to get her."

Kou's explanation was simple, but Kon immediately grasped the situation. She pressed her lips in a tight line and looked to me. "Will you please tell me exactly what happened?"

Mr. Mizusawa had already handled phoning my parents. I confided in the twins in hushed whispers about my little exchange with Prince Tobi on the car ride to Miss Sakurako's favorite traditional Japanese restaurant. When I brought up the piano competition Kon only nodded and said, "I see," but the news completely took Kou by surprise.

"That's the first I've heard about a large music competition being held next fall. Has that information even been made public yet?" he asked, looking from me to Kon.

"We only recently heard about it from Miss Ayumi too," Kon quickly added.

"You did? ...So? What happens to you if you don't win?"

Kou didn't know our full story, so it's not like I could tell him the truth and say I'd reach the bad end that'd block me from attending Seio Academy. I didn't go into the specifics about Tobi either.

"I don't know. He only told me to prove to him that I can win. I don't think I'm going to lose anything either way."

"I wouldn't be too sure about that. I'd say there's little chance that Director Yamabuki would say something like that if there wasn't anything in it for him." There seemed to be a sharp bite to every word Kou uttered. I didn't know what I'd done to irritate him, but he was clearly peeved.

"I'm sorry..."

"For what?"

"For getting you involved in my problems on the day of your concert."

"That's not what I'm trying to say here!" Kou shouted.

This was the first time he'd ever raised his voice with me in all the years I'd known him. Kon pulled me into her arms as if to protect me when I flinched away from him.

"Kou, stop it. Don't take out your frustration on Mashiro."

"Sorry. I just wish you'd listen to me and be more aware of your surroundings. Our world is filled with indecent people who wish others harm for their own selfish reasons. The world isn't friendly. It's too late if you realize that fact after you get hurt," he warned in a tormented voice. My heart ached for him.

I knew very well how much he was still tormented by the agonizing memory of nearly losing his precious sister. I impulsively reached out for Kou after he made his ardent appeal. He took my hand in his and tangled his fingers through mine.

"I'm sorry for worrying you. I just lost my cool. I promise I'll be more careful next time."

How deeply was he scarred with the regret that his existence put his beloved little sister in mortal danger? A bystander like myself couldn't even begin to measure the emotional damage it had caused him. Wounds inflicted during childhood were some of the hardest to heal. It didn't matter how much people tried to comfort him by saying it wasn't his fault. He still didn't forgive himself. He was haunted by the thought, "If only I never existed."

The inability to forgive and accept oneself and move on was one trait that Kou and Sou shared.

Wanting to set his mind at ease, I squeezed his hand and received a heartrending smile in return. "…Okay. Please keep on smiling like the world is full of sunflowers and rainbows."

Is that how he thinks I see the world?! Is it just my warped view of him, or does he always ruin these moments with an unnecessary word or two?!

♪♪♪

KOU'S weak side was on full display during the car ride, but he'd regained his normal composure by the time we'd arrived at the restaurant.

We didn't have to wait long for plates of food to be carried to our table because the twins had ordered the full course in advance. All my energy had been sucked away by my quarrel with Tobi, leaving my empty stomach growling, so I was glad the food came fast.

I wanted to forget about the music competition for the time being, so I steered the conversation toward what I'd enjoyed about the concert. Kou and Kon both caught on to what my intentions were and went along with my new topic with a smile.

"Hey, Kou, why did you choose to play Prokofiev's Sonata? I was surprised by your choice. I thought you'd pick a more standard, sweet song that'd fit the Christmas season," I mentioned.

Kou's eyebrow twitched. "No reason—"

"The piano department girls nearly went to war over who should play his piano accompaniment," Kon explained over Kou's answer. He protested by scowling at his sister.

"Aha! I thought that was why."

Words couldn't even begin to describe Kou's expression when he saw me accept that answer. He had his poker-face on, but the pain of betrayal flickered in his eyes.

"End of story," Kou said sullenly. He changed the mood by switching topics with a cheerful voice. "Anyways, I nearly forgot to give you this. Here." He pushed a gift bag sitting on the corner of the table towards me.

"Oh? What's this?"

There wasn't a logo on the shiny gift bag. I peeked inside to find a foot-tall rectangular box.

"It's a little early, but this is a Christmas present from me and Sou."

"Seriously?!"

Why is he giving me a present?! And why is it a present that includes Sou?! There were so many points to nitpick at, I struggled to speak at first.

"I-I didn't bring anything for you," I finally managed to say, pathetically.

Kou burst out laughing. "We're not looking for a gift exchange. We just wanted to give you a present, Mashiro."

Am I speaking to the real Kou? Not his friendlier clone?! I slammed my mouth shut before I accidentally asked. That was about as rude of a response as I could give in return for someone's kindness. Kou was growing up. That's all there was to it.

"Thanks. Can I open it here?"

I can't accept it if it's something ridiculously expensive.

"Go ahead," Kou consented, holding his palm out toward the gift bag.

I removed the wrapped box from the gift bag and gingerly untied the ribbon, revealing a mini tabletop Christmas tree within. A cute white and baby pink tree stood on a purple, rectangular base. Delicate looking ornaments hung from the string lights wound evenly around the tree. The Christmas lights were connected to a clear battery pack on the bottom of the base. When I flipped the switch to try it, the LED lights clicked on all at once, giving off the vivid colors of the casings. Kon and I raised our voices in awe over the whimsical and colorful Christmas tree.

"It's lovely. Way to go, Kou." Kon poked Kou's shoulder.

"I wasn't the only one who picked it out," Kou corrected, being unusually modest for once.

"I love it! It's super adorable, and I can put it anywhere because of the battery pack!" I thanked him from the bottom of my heart.

"Yeah. I thought the battery would help with that," he said proudly, his cheeks flushing. He looked his age when he made that face.

"I wonder where I should put it in my room. I'll take good care of it. Thank you so much!"

I was ecstatic about the surprise present. I would've been nowhere near as happy if they'd given me some high-end brand item that cost an arm and a leg. It was the best present they could have picked out for me.

"Sou found the tree in Germany and sent it to me. I picked out the Christmas lights."

"What? D-Didn't Sou send that to you as a present then? Is it really okay to pass it on to me?"

Kou stared at me then heaved a massive sigh. "Haah... Do I have to explain everything to you? Do you know how to read the mood?"

"Of course I do! Don't be rude!" I rebutted.

"Liar. No way you know how."

"I do too! I don't mind if you gave it to me after getting Sou's permission."

"There are some things you should just pick up on without them having to be said. Do you honestly believe Sou would send me a white and pink Christmas tree as a present? With a purple gift box for a base? Fat chance."

"...I guess he wouldn't. But then why did he send it to you, Kou? I could've sent him a present back if he'd sent it directly to me."

"That's what he didn't want to happen."

"He didn't want a present from me?"

"He didn't want to put you out. That guy doesn't want to burden you in any way...haah," Kou sighed midsentence and suddenly stopped talking. "Why do I have to be the one to tell you this?" he groaned, shoving his bangs up with annoyance. My slowness to catch on seemed to frustrate him.

"Sorry. I won't bring it up again. Anyways, I'll just take it as a gift from you both. Thank you very much. I happily accept," I said, bowing my head.

Kon, who'd silently watched over our conversation, gently rubbed Kou's back during the car ride home.

♪♪♪

SPENDING winter break studying and playing the piano like I usually did over long breaks made it go by fast. Having become much more social than I was in elementary school, I acted like a proper middle schooler and watched movies with Rei and ice-skated with Eri and the gang.

"Three cheers for my little sister graduating from being a shut-in!" Hanaka had teased me.

Going out more often didn't mean my goal to win next year's big music competition had changed. Panic always haunted the edge of my thoughts, telling me that I didn't have time to play around. But I'd matured enough not to let those thoughts rule over me like before.

Shinji stopped by our house after visiting the shrine with Hanaka for New Years. He and Dad were drinking beer and chatting about work while an ekiden race played on the TV in the background. Apparently, Dad had thrown out all the doubts and reservations he had towards Shinji.

Us women of the house were putting away the rest of the traditional New Year's food at the dining table while we watched the men bonding in the living room.

"It happened so fast," Mom blurted out as she reached for the red-skinned and white *kamaboko* with her chopsticks.

"What did?" Hanaka asked with a puzzled look.

Mom giggled. "Giving birth to you and raising you as my precious only child. Then just around the time I thought you didn't need to hold my hand anymore, I gave birth to Mashiro and things became hectic again. We aren't a wealthy household, so I started working too, making my two favorite girls feel lonely. I was just thinking all of that happened so fast," Mom said emotionally.

The tone of her voice squeezed my heart in a tight vise.

"It happened so fast. I can't believe R-- is going to be a university student now too!"

"Only if I pass the exams, you know? Don't put more pressure on me."

"You'll do just fine, R--. Won't she, Mom?"

Tears began rolling down my cheeks without me realizing it until Mom and Hanaka gaped at me.

"Wh-What's wrong, Mashiro?!"

"Silly girl. This isn't something for you to cry over. Here. Take this tissue."

I yanked several tissues from the tissue box Mom held out to me and blew my nose after wiping my tears. The tears took even me by surprise.

But I'm certain I felt an intense wave of sadness crash over me for a second. What in the world was that?

"Sorry about that. But Mom, aren't you the one feeling lonely since you brought it up?" I teased.

Mom's expression softened into a tender smile. "No, not in the way you think. Even if you girls get married and move out, it doesn't change the fact that you are my dearest daughters. Your dad and I have been discussing going on an international trip once we're empty nesters. I'm looking forward to that just as much."

"Okay, okay, thanks for rubbing it in. But marriage is still far off in the future for us. Don't try to get rid of us too soon!" Hanaka cried out in a pathetic whimper that got both Mom and me laughing.

♪♪♪

WITH the end of winter break came the start of the third quarter.

I spotted Tomoi during the opening ceremony for the first time since going on break. He was standing in the corner of the gym with his usual cool expression. He had gotten out of the car wearing a fluffy scarf around his neck and over his down coat in the ultimate combo to combat the cold. Once he entered the school building he abandoned his warm wardrobe for a suit, falling in line with the other male teachers.

A coat wasn't necessary in the classrooms because they had heaters, but the unheated gymnasium felt like a freezer. He probably really wanted to wear that coat right now. He was facing the principal on the stage with a neutral expression, but upon closer inspection, I spotted him discretely rubbing his hands together for warmth. I couldn't stop the stupid grin from reaching my face.

When I got back to class I shared my discovery with Rei, hoping she'd agree with me. "See? Isn't he super cute? He was trying to endure the cold like that!"

It only earned me a pitying look. "…You watch Mr. Matsuda park and get out of his car every morning…?"

"Yup. I can see him from the classroom window. It's the best spot to observe him! How lucky am I to have secured it twice in a row?!"

"If you say so. I have nothing left to say. I've finally come to understand why they say, 'to each his own.'"

"Aw, don't be a spoilsport! You're missing out!" I protested, depressed with her criticisms of my crush.

Rei comforted me by patting me on the shoulder. "Sorry, sorry. I can't get all worked up over him with you, but I can share some secret information about him to make up for it."

"Oh? What is it?"

Eyes sparkling, Rei lowered her voice to a secretive whisper. "This is something I heard from one of the badminton club girls, but word has it that Mr. Matsuda can often be found at the shopping mall in front of the station during the afternoon on Sundays when he doesn't have to coach the club."

"He can?" I dropped my voice to a hushed whisper too.

"The badminton girls said they spot him mostly around the bookstore and electronics store. Isn't it super sad for an adult man to be spending his precious day off all alone? That's what everyone thinks when they see him wandering around the mall alone." Rei shrugged.

I don't think he has a girlfriend, but I know he has friends and isn't a loner. I fought back my desire to defend Tomoi. I couldn't share that information with Rei. It'd make her wonder why I knew that much about him.

Shinji once told me that Tomoi still hung out with friends from university and that he occasionally joins him for a drink out at night. He sounded disappointed when he told me, "A middle school teacher is really busy work. We can't hang out as much as we did in our uni days."

It was too difficult for me to share the information that Tomoi was my sister's boyfriend's best friend with friends from school. Not that I didn't trust Rei and Eri and the girls, but I'd feel bad if weird rumors about him favoring me spread in the off-chance that the information leaked.

I know! Kon is the perfect person to tell! I wonder what kinda face she'll make if I tell her that I actually have a crush on someone. Will she be surprised then smile like she always does while teasing, "I want to see who won your heart!" My mood brightened as I imagined Kon's reaction.

I felt like I could tell her anything after she had declared that she was my ally, not Kou or Sou's.

"Thanks a million, Rei! I'll look around for him the next time I go to the mall."

"Don't mention it. I hope you can bump into him."

At the time, I didn't understand anything at all. Not even for a moment did I consider that Tomoi might be connected to Kon somehow. There's no point in what-ifs after something has happened, but if I'd known about it in advance, I would've never, ever gone out that day.

CG 27: ???

THE day I could go to the shopping mall came sooner than expected. Kon had called my cell phone and invited me to go shopping for Valentine's Day chocolate with her.

"When should we go? Want to head over to the mall after solfège on Saturday?"

I hesitated with my answer before throwing caution to the wind. "Could we go on Sunday instead? Do you already have plans then?"

"No, I don't. Is there something special about Sunday?"

"There is and there isn't... Ehehe. I'll tell you all about it when we meet up."

"Okay. Sunday it is then. I'll pick you up."

After hanging up, I clutched my cell phone to my chest and reveled in the excitement. *I'm really looking forward to picking out chocolates with Kon! I was going to make chocolate for Dad again this year, but it's too soon for me to give Tomoi homemade chocolate.* Feeling grateful for Kon and her perfectly timed phone call, I contemplated what chocolate and ingredients to buy.

Tomoi said he likes alcohol, so maybe a whiskey bonbon would be a good fit for him. Oh and I should buy chocolates for Mr. Mizusawa, Mr. Nonaga, and Kou's and Kon's dads as thanks for all they do for me every year. Kou will definitely receive more chocolate than he can eat, and it's not like he'd want cheap obligatory chocolate bought from the store anyway. And I can't send any to Sou at this point.

Is it just me or is there a real problem with the average age of the men I'm giving chocolate to being decades older than me? Oh, well. Not like I can help it. Yeah, let's just go with that.

Happily humming away, I sat in front of my desk.

What should I do if Rei's information is solid and I bump into Tomoi on Sunday? It wouldn't bother him if I said hi, right? I sure hope I get to see him.

Bubbling with energy, I sped through my homework at twice the usual speed. Crushes gave girls amazing powers. *Now that I think about it, I get the feeling it was the same way for me in my past life too.* The memory tickled the edge of my mind, but I shook my head hard. *2D crushes don't count!*

♪♪♪

UNFORTUNATELY, it was snowing on Sunday.

Hanaka had already left the house, leaving me to try and dress up without her help while I waited for Kon. Afraid I looked weird, I kept going back to double-check my appearance in the mirror. Even I was amused by how stupid I was acting. Here I was, getting all excited and hopeful when there was no guarantee I'd see Tomoi at the mall.

Today I went for a long-sleeved, tight-fitting dress tied at my waist with a belt and long boots over my thigh-high socks. Aiming for a more mature look, I abandoned my usual up-do and let my hair fall around my shoulders after loosely curling it with the curler. Hearing the doorbell ring, I carefully navigated my way downstairs and to the front door— boots with heels were dangerous!

Because our destination was a public shopping mall in front of the train station Mr. Nonaga came to pick me up in a casual Lexus. I didn't think there was anything wrong with me checking that Kou wasn't inside first.

"Sorry for making you go out of your way for today, Kon."

"I don't mind at all. I was concerned about the bad weather, but it shouldn't be a problem if we stay inside the mall." Kon gently wiped the snow off my head and shoulders with a large handkerchief when I rushed inside the car next to her. "There you go. It'd be such a shame if your cute hairstyle was ruined by the wet snow."

Kon had on a knit shirt and cardigan combo, paired with a Burberry plaid print pleated skirt. Her lace-up boots were totally adorable.

"It's been so long since we last went shopping together."

"You know what, I think you're right. I feel like Kou has gotten in the way every other time."

"Right? Is he at home today?"

"Nope. I think he's busy catering to his fans again. If I remember right, he said something about going to an art museum with Riko and the girls."

"Catering, huh? He puts in the hard hours even on the weekend!"

"He's the one wrapping the noose around his own neck like that, so I've decided to let him be," Kon laughed. "That reminds me, even at school he…" Kon started, going into stories about Kou and how he was digging his own grave when it came to his groupies.

I can just tell her about Tomoi while we have tea later, I thought as I listened to Kon's stories with a big smile. She was much more talkative than usual today. The shopping mall was practically dead because of the bad weather keeping people home. Not everyone had the benefit of being driven here.

"It's so nice being able to browse without anyone else around," Kon exclaimed. She didn't do well in crowds. It made me happy to learn about this side of her when I had always thought that she was a social butterfly.

"Honestly, I don't like being in crowds either," I admitted.

"Hehe. Isn't that because you're afraid an alien might be mixed in the crowd and you'd never be able to tell the difference?"

Kon's teasing grin put a stop to all the gears in my mind.

That was undeniably the reason why I hated being around crowds. But the one time I'd confessed it to Eri, she made fun of me, saying, "No normal person thinks that way!" I had kept it to myself ever since.

"That's why I told you to stop watching movies like that! Whenever you do, you come to my room in the middle of the night saying you're too scared to go to the bathroom alone!"

"I can't help it! The trailers always make me want to see it! Can I…sleep with you tonight?"

"My bed is too small! So no!"

Ever since I saw the horror movie about an alien that blended into human crowds and preyed upon them one by one, I'd developed an innate fear of being swept away by crowds. My older sister Hanaka watched that movie with me even though she'd complained about it.

But wait a minute. Hanaka was in middle school when I was in elementary school. Why is the hand holding mine in this memory so small and unreliable?

"—shiro! Mashiro!"

"Ack! You scared me!" Kon's beautiful face was right in front of mine.

"What's wrong? You were completely out of it just now." Kon frowned when she saw me blinking back at her, confused.

"Hey, Kon? Did I tell you the reason why I hate crowds before? I can't remember," I asked her directly, bothered to no end by it. Kon's expression crumbled as if she'd messed up big time. She quickly schooled her features and tilted her head at me.

"Yeah. I'd heard about it."

"...You did?"

Her expression just now was the real answer. Kon had heard about it, just not from *me*.

Why are you lying to me?

That was the first key that resulted in unraveling the tight cord wrapped around my memories. The ends of that cord had been chopped off. All that was left was for me to figure out how to make it come undone.

This wasn't a conversation worth prying into and ruining the day over, so I headed to the chocolate store to wrap up our shopping. Kon fell in line beside me as if nothing had happened.

We roamed around the brightly decorated Valentine's Day chocolate section assessing and rejecting all sorts of chocolates together. Kon turned an envious gaze on me when I told her how I made chocolates at home every year.

"Lucky. I couldn't cook even if my life depended on it. Mother and the chefs forbade me from ever entering the kitchen to cook."

When I saw the disappointment clouding Kon's features it instantly brought my family's kitchen-destroyer to mind. *She sounds just like Hanaka. Actually, this isn't the first time I thought they were similar, is it?*

When was it? Ah, right, when I was in the car heading to the Genda estate to hang out for the first time. I learned how Kon likes the idol group SAZE. I thought her tastes for fads were similar to Hanaka.

...I thought they were similar.

Cold sweat dripped down my back. Intense uneasiness washed over me. I felt like I was overlooking something very important. But I didn't know what it was. Not knowing the source or meaning of what felt like a titanium door sealing away something deep in my heart tormented me.

…Stop it.

If I keep thinking, it's going to activate another "attack." I'd learned the signs from prior experience with the attacks. I held my hand to my head and forcefully changed my line of thought.

"Who are you buying chocolate for, Kon?" I asked, looking for a way out of my head.

"My fathers and Kou. I also plan to buy friendship chocolate for my friends at Seio. How about you, Mashiro?"

"Same as you. Oh, but I also plan to give some chocolate to a teacher at my school."

"What?! To your teacher?!" Taken by complete surprise, Kon's eyes popped. I went ahead and told her all about Tomoi.

"He's my math teacher, but don't let that fool you, because he's a great guy! The rules at my school are pretty lenient on this stuff, so plenty of students give chocolates to their teachers."

"Really? You're so lucky! None of the teachers at my school are worth giving chocolate to. I'm so jealous!"

I smiled at Kon as she repeated saying how lucky I was while we shopped. I splurged on Tomoi and bought him champagne truffles. Only four truffles were in the box, but they cost a good chunk of money, which hopefully meant they tasted amazing. A smaller box seemed like it would be easier to give and for him to accept. Kon chose all brand-name chocolates for her gifts.

Kon called Mr. Nonaga on her smartphone when we finished up our shopping and entrusted him with our shopping bags so we could go for tea.

"Oh yeah, is it okay if we drop by the bookstore first?" Kon asked.

"For sure! There are a couple of magazines I wanted to check out too," I happily agreed. She had just reminded me that I wanted to check the bookstore for Tomoi. The whole reason why I had picked Sunday to go out was because I wanted to look for Tomoi and observe him on his day off! *I can't believe I almost forgot.*

We took the escalator upstairs while chatting away about fashion magazines. Things got weird once we got to the front of the big bookstore. Kon suddenly stopped dead in her tracks next to me.

"…It can't be…" she rasped in a deathly whisper.

Her cheeks tensed, and her jaw was set in such a hard line it forced me to look in the same direction to see what was bothering her so much. My gaze landed on Tomoi and Hanaka together. Even my eyes bulged at the unusual pairing.

I totally thought she was on a date with Shinji today. I was wrong?

The pair was looking at the same book together. Hanaka puffed out her cheeks and poked Tomoi in the side. Tomoi had a big frown on his face, but his joy showed through the farce as he looked admiringly down at my sister.

Why doesn't Hanaka notice? How can she not read his body language and see his feelings for her?

I knew my sister's personality better than anyone else. She wasn't the type to flirt with her boyfriend's friends. She was a natural airhead with a few loose screws, but she possessed a stronger moral compass than most. It wasn't feasible for her to betray Shinji by having a secret rendezvous with his best friend.

I quickly pulled myself together and stepped forward to call out to them when Kon's dainty hand pulled me back.

"I can't…I'm sorry, I just can't do it…" Her voice was on the verge of falling apart, and it ripped the air out of my lungs. The light and life died in her gorgeous eyes. It was as if all of her feelings had been whisked away to some faraway place.

My shock was accompanied by what felt like a physical blow to the head. My brain felt rattled.

I KnOw. I KnOw SoMeOnE wHo MaDe ThIs SaMe FaCe.

"Why didn't you tell me?" I'd demanded in the ugliest burst of anger.

Your face froze over and crumbled.

I'm sorry. I'd become stubborn halfway through our argument.

I had thought that you, the person I cared about the most, had left me behind.

Halfway through our argument, I was just being a brat.

He was just someone I'd admired. I already knew what his answer was.

It was never my intention to hurt you until you made that face.

I'm sorry. I'm so sorry, Hana.

Everything before my eyes was buried in a blindingly bright, white light.

I had regained the sealed memories of my past life.

I should've turned right around and led Kon far away from there. But all I could do at the time was stand dead still like an idiot. Remembering the other Tomoi and how ugly I was in my moment of cruelty towards my sister left me unable to do anything other than squeeze Kon's trembling hand.

The one who noticed us rooted to the spot first was my "current" sister Hanaka. Her hair was bright pink, her eyes an olive brown. The lack of black hair and eyes completely changed her image from the sister I knew in my past life. Of course it'd be different—it was almost like she was wearing a disguise.

"Hey, Mashiro!" Hanaka smiled like a sunflower and happily walked over to us.

Kon slammed her eyes shut before assuming her usual mask. She greeted my sister with a sweet smile. "Hello. It's nice to see you again."

"Hi there! I think I last saw you at the piano recital? You've gotten even prettier since then!"

Tomoi followed Hanaka over to us. He waved to me, then shifted his gaze to Kon. "Hello. You're the girl who attends the same piano lessons as Shimao, right? It's nice to meet you. My name is Tomoi Matsuda."

Kon's hand was noticeably shaking. Her heartbreaking state made me gnaw on my bottom lip.

"I-I'm Kon Genda… Nice to meet you."

I hadn't remembered everything yet. My hypothesis could've been wrong too. I mean, when you think about it carefully, it's a strange theory. How could there be two versions of my sister from my past life in this world? One had the exact same appearance. And the other was—

How could this have happened?

But I was certain. I knew with certainty exactly what Kon was feeling in the moment and the pain she kept hidden away in her chest.

Now I understood why Kon was so thrilled that day we met for the first time at Miss Ayumi's house. The reason why she always worried about me. The reason why she was in so much shock after meeting Hanaka for the first time. The reason why she always shut her mouth in despair every time she was about to say something more. The answer that solved all the mysteries was presented in front of me, telling me the truth.

Kon, you were my "Hana" all along, weren't you?

…How could this happen? How was it possible? If my conjecture was right, then the god, or whatever it was that reincarnated us into this whacked world, was a cruel bastard.

"HOW can this be? There are still three years left until the routes split."

Flabbergasted by the error in *his* calculations, he took out his irritation by chewing on his nails. They had no taste or feeling. The general concept of nails slid over the illusion of his lips.

He held out his hands again and again to recast the memory erasure spell, but Mashiro Shimao repelled every attempt.

He gave up, yanked his finger from his conceptualized teeth, and summoned the parameter screen into the air in front of him. The friendship events with the original heroine should've been shut down a long time ago.

His eyes widened in horror when he saw the numbers that appeared in the air.

Current Heroine's Trust Level For the Original Heroine⇒MAX

Original Heroine's Trust Level For the Current Heroine⇒MAX

"…They got me good!"

Mashiro had gone and cleared the conditions required for one of the game's endings—the Friend End. He couldn't count on feeding off her energy anymore. He'd no longer be allowed to do anything to Mashiro until the day she turned eighteen.

He glowered at the sky for a while until a dark smile eventually curved his lips.

"Meh, it doesn't matter."

He absorbed the endless supply of despair, hopelessness, sorrow, and burning love from Kon Genda until it filled him. The swell of power within him brought relief.

"You truly are magnificent… How very sweet."

The brave girl frantically gathered together her shattering heart to stand her ground and turn an equally kind smile toward her former love. Even though that very same love of hers was infatuated with another person who looked just like her.

"Guess what, Kon? This is the critical juncture. After all, even Mashiro will become mine if I win my bet with you."

He hugged his contractor from behind and planted a kiss on a lock of her silky brown hair.

HANAKA explained that she'd come with Tomoi to pick out a birthday present for Shinji. My original theory was proven correct when she informed me that they planned on meeting up with Shinji in the evening once he finished running some errands.

"Would you girls like to join us?" Hanaka invited us then looked innocently up at Tomoi. "You don't mind, right?"

"Yeah, I don't mind," he responded.

Everything felt like it happened just yesterday now that I got my memories back. Hana, Tomoi, and I often went out to eat together. In that world, I was much closer in age to them than I was now. Both Hana and Tomoi treated me kindly whenever I took advantage of my position as the little sister and followed them around.

Was the crush I had on Mr. Matsuda during these middle school years a result of lingering feelings from my past life? How could I fall for the exact same person even after being reborn? Sure, it sounded romantic in the storybooks, but it was nothing more than a bad comedy if that love never came to fruition.

My fleeting crush on Tomoi the teacher had cleanly disappeared once my memories came flooding back. Nostalgia was the only feeling I had for him now.

I loved everything about you, Tomoi, from your dead serious personality to your no-nonsense stubbornness—all of it.

"Sorry, Hanaka. Kon has to go home soon. Tell Shinji hi for me," I turned down her invitation.

"That's too bad. Hopefully we can do something together next time then!"

I waved goodbye to my disappointed sister and the teacher who stood by her side with a warm expression then turned on my heel and left.

I led the silent Kon, with a smile still plastered on her face, away from there at a brisk pace. I brought her to the elevator and pressed the rooftop button. Her hand was still trembling.

No one was on the rooftop as I suspected.

The lightly falling snow dusted the benches and potted plants in white. The air was biting cold, but it felt just right on my skin warmed from the heaters inside the mall.

It was in the middle of the rooftop that I finally released Kon's hand and stood directly in front of her. "You're Hana, aren't you?"

"……"

"I finally remembered. I'm sorry for making you suffer alone all this time."

Kon's eyes opened wide, and then the tears came. She shook her head over and over again as she silently wept. Afraid to make this magic moment end, she refused to speak.

"You know, I've always wanted to apologize to you properly for what happened with Tomoi," I admitted, speaking when she couldn't. "... You see, I knew—I knew that you two were dating. But then you lied to me that you weren't. And that drudged up the nasty desire in me to be mean to you. I've got the worst personality, don't I? I only confessed to Tomoi to harass you both. I wanted to put him on the spot for having eyes only for you, Hana."

"Don't lie!" Kon shouted in a hoarse voice as she took hold of my hands. "You had real feelings for Tomo, Rika. Don't try to pull one over me. I know that much about you."

"My feelings weren't as strong as yours, Hana," I responded. It was the truth. "I regretted that you stopped seeing Tomoi altogether so much that I wanted to die. I kept going back to him, begging him not to give up on you. What do you think he said each time?"

It didn't take long before my cheeks were wet too. The burning hot lump lodged in my throat caused my voice to quiver.

Two girls were sobbing on top of a freezing cold rooftop under the dancing snowflakes, talking about the fate of their first loves in their past lives. Putting the situation into perspective like that made the whole thing so ridiculous.

"'I could never give up on her,' he told me."

Kon broke down. "Tomo...Tomo," she whispered over and over again. I tried my hardest to help her stand up as she sank onto her knees in the snow crying out the name of her love who no longer existed.

"Shh, it's okay. My current sister is in love with her boyfriend Shinji. I'm sure if this Tomoi realizes that you're his Hana, he'll fall in love with you, *Kon*. Come on, why don't you give up on Tobi? That man gives me the creeps. He's no good for you," I desperately strung my words together in a bid to bandage her broken heart.

Kon finally let me help her to her feet and wiped the tears off her face in one quick motion. "Mr. Matsuda won't fall in love with Kon Genda," she said decisively, a small smile on her lips.

"You don't know that for sure!" I protested.

How can she say that like it's a fact? This world might be scripted for Tomoi to fall in love with this Hanaka, but Kon is also my big sister Hanaka!

"I do know for sure. Because he——" Kon stopped midsentence and glowered at the empty space behind me with a hard face.

Is there someone behind me? I instinctively turned to look, when Kon tightly grabbed hold of my shoulder and forced me forward.

"Listen to me, Rika. Please find happiness. That's the only thing I want in the whole world. I'll definitely make it in time this time. So please, believe in me."

What in the world is she talking about...?

"Today is the last time we will ever speak about our past lives," she continued when I stared dumbfounded at her. "Don't bring it up ever again. I am Kon Genda now. Not Hanaka Takeshita. ...Promise me, Rika. This is important."

Nodding was the only option left for me faced with Kon's intensity. She probably wouldn't explain anything to me even if I pressed her. Her stunningly beautiful eyes were frighteningly serious.

"Cherish the family you have now. Your parents and Hanaka are the ones who have loved and cared for you ever since you were born."

I put my hands on my hips. "Of course I will. My past has nothing to do with my love for my current family."

The tears threatened to burst forth again if I didn't joke around at this point. Reuniting with Hana should've been a happy occasion, but I couldn't shake the sense that things beyond my power were circling around her, ever closing in.

Kon placed her hand to her chest as if relieved by the joking. "Glad to hear it. I'm really, truly happy to know that you're happy."

I feel the same way. I'm always praying for your happiness, Hana—Kon.

But Kon was hiding something that wouldn't let me be openly happy for her.

"It's getting cold out. Shall we head back in?"

I softly took hold of the hand she held out to me. Circumstances had shifted since we first came to the rooftop—it was my hand that was trembling this time. There were so many things I didn't understand, it made it impossible to see what was ahead.

Darkness fell on our surroundings without me noticing. We decided to save our teatime for another day, and I had her take me home.

"Thank you for today. See you next time, Kon."

"See you later, Mashiro."

I stepped under the umbrella Mr. Nonaga held out for me. Obeying the surging impulse, I turned back to Kon in the car. "We'll continue to be together from now on, right?"

An unsettling uneasiness took root within me over the way Kon was acting overly cheerful as if she'd gotten over everything. Her gaze lingered on my face, and she flashed a killer smile.

"Of course we will. We'll be together forever."

Even now, I wonder how she felt as she said that to me. The answer continues to elude me no matter how many times I reflect on it.

The only thing I could say for sure was that our paths were forked from the beginning. It was a terrible, horrible fact, but the outcome was set in stone since the day I'd fallen into that open manhole.

But not once have I ever wished I hadn't met Kon.

I wouldn't give up those joyous, dazzling days together for any treasure in the whole universe.

♪♪♪

REI was baffled when I stopped bringing up Tomoi's name as if he'd been exorcised from my life like an evil spirit.

"Have you finally seen the light?" Rei asked, peering at my face after I ended up not giving Mr. Matsuda any chocolate on Valentine's Day.

"Never. I still think there aren't many men out there as amazing as Mr. Matsuda."

"You think that highly of him?! Then why in the world did you quit stalking him in the morning?"

Don't call me a stalker. Those were the adorable actions common to a middle school girl with a one-sided crush. Or so I'd like to think.

"Because Mr. Matsuda has had feelings for someone else for forever... Oh, but don't ever share that with anyone else, 'kay? I'll be ticked if weird rumors get around about him."

"I'd never do something as scary as make an enemy of you, Mashiro," Rei retorted with a grimace, but she was still unnaturally nice to me for a while after that. She seemed to be trying to comfort me in her own way for what she believed was a broken heart.

She'd lent me her copy of a historical novel tilted, *Onihei Hankachō*. I was slowly reading through it during my breaks between piano practice, but the sheer number of proverbs in it made my brain go numb. But our shared knowledge of the series made for fun times mimicking the characters and storyline.

"What? You haven't done any of your homework yet? You'll be the one who's troubled in the future if you don't study properly while you're a student, Rei."

"Listen to me closely, Lady Mashiro. Those known as women have no past, and even less of a future—all we have is our present selves," Rei recited with great pomp.

"Who are you, Hasegawa Heizō?"

We played around like that a lot. I'd forgotten that middle schoolers spent their days laughing away at absolutely ridiculous stuff like this.

This feeling was incredibly nostalgic to me.

I ended up saving the extra chocolate to eat myself. The extra ended up being the almond chocolates I'd bought for Mr. Mizusawa. I planned to give him the champagne truffles I'd purchased for Mr. Matsuda instead.

On my way home from school on Valentine's Day, Kou called out to me as he was on his way home too. Normally, I would've been on guard, but I was honestly grateful to him this time around. I had been debating how I should get in touch with Mr. Mizusawa to give him the chocolate.

Kou stepped out of the car once it parked on the side of the road with its flashers on. Through the backseat window I spotted a mountain of wrapped presents stacked up to the car ceiling.

"Hi, Mashiro. I'm glad I ran into you."

"Hello. You stopped with really good timing!" I put on a wide smile and leaned down toward the passenger's seat window, careful not to scuff up the cleanly polished car. "Mr. Mizusawa, can I have a moment of your time?" I called his name in a loud voice so he could hear me in the driver's seat. Surprised as he was, Mr. Mizusawa immediately stepped out of the car and walked around to the sidewalk.

I pulled a tiny gift bag from my schoolbag and held it out to him with both hands. "This is for you. You always take such good care of me; this is just a small token of my appreciation."

"For me?" Mr. Mizusawa confirmed, pointing to himself and stealing a glance at Kou. Perhaps it was just my imagination, but for a second, a wicked smirk seemed t0 flash across his face. "Thank you very much, Lady Mashiro. I will thoroughly enjoy them."

Kou glared down Mr. Mizusawa as if he had just become the greatest enemy in his life. Despite his car overflowing with enough chocolate to fill a swimming pool, he appeared to want more.

"Just for Mizusawa? Don't have any for me?"

"None for you. I can't even come close to buying the expensive chocolates the kids at Seio exchange with my allowance. And you're the one who once told me, 'Spare me the handmade crap,' so I didn't waste my time on it."

Kou sighed and gave me a look words couldn't even begin to describe. *Save the suggestive wiles for your fanclub members, will ya?!*

"YOU seem like you've been having a blast every day, Mashiro," Dad commented, happily watching me during dinner.

"Do I seem that way? I guess you could say that. Studying and playing the piano are just so much fun. All of my friends are great, and I have a sweet family, too. Recently I've started thinking about how incredibly blessed I am."

"You've finally grown up, huh, Mashiro?" Mom chimed in with a grin. "You hear all these horror stories about when kids are going through puberty in middle school, but I think our Mashiro might be an early bloomer."

"I think you're on to something there. She was always more on edge and uneasy than she is now," Dad wholeheartedly agreed with Mom.

"Ugh…it hurts because you're right. Sorry?"

I definitely couldn't tell them that it wasn't an early onset of puberty, but the result of a jumble of things related to my past life. Wanting to dodge where this conversation was heading, I directed the focus onto Hanaka.

"How was Hanaka? During puberty?" I asked casually. Our parents burst out laughing in unison. Hanaka turned tomato-red and fanned her face with both hands.

"You don't have to talk about me! Stop right there! End of topic! Period!"

"Okay, okay. We won't talk about it. Mashiro doesn't seem to remember anyway."

"Good for you, Hanaka. Aren't you glad your little sister didn't catch you wearing black leather gloves and a cape while you pretended to have superpowers?"

"GAH! I can't hear you! I can't hear you!"

Who knew that Hanaka had Chūnibyō, the disease that makes middle schoolers think they have superpowers!

"PFT! Black leather gloves…and superpowers!" I laughed.

"Sheesh! I kept hoping you guys had forgotten about it by now!" Hanaka stomped her feet in frustration.

Surrounded by everyone's cheerful laughter in the living room, I swore to never do anything that'd make my family in this life grieve.

♪♪♪

THE fun times flew by, and I was in the second year of middle school.

October's music competition overview was announced publicly, and I was getting nervous about how close it was now.

The rainy season was afoot now that it was June. This month was notable because I spent most of it making recordings at Miss Ayumi's house for my music competition application.

The Sadia Francesca Junior Music Competition worked like this: first, the applicants would be reduced down to just thirty for each of the school divisions during the preliminary round. The quarterfinal round would eliminate another fifteen, then another ten would be let go during the semifinals. The remaining five participants would contend for the win during the finals.

In most student competitions, the degree of difficulty for the song selections was divided by the school divisions. The Sadia Francesca Junior Music Competition worked differently though. The song selection was the same across all divisions from middle school to university. That was the first point that tended to get most middle school contestants eliminated.

Although the song selection for the preliminary round hadn't been announced yet, I knew what it was, having read Kon's *Hear My Heart* notebook. Among the several songs available to choose from, I planned to pick Chopin's "Etude Op. 25 No. 11".

Sorry for cheating, I internally apologized to the rivals I'd yet to meet.

Miss Ayumi picked out the piece for my application. She had given me the new sheet music about a month ago.

"While there are no specific guidelines for sound, Sadia Francesca will be presiding over the judging committee as its chairman. So I believe you should choose something from Tchaikovsky's '18 Pieces'."

"If we're talking about Tchaikovsky's '18 Pieces', would 'Scherzo-Fantaisie' work?"

"That one wouldn't be a bad choice, but I recommend this one." Miss Ayumi gave me the sheet music to Tchaikovsky's "Meditation, Op. 72 No. 5".

I thought that "Scherzo-Fantaisie" would be ear candy for the audience, but Miss Ayumi's recommended "Mediation" was the more famous of the two.

With my entry piece decided, I spent the entire month practicing Tchaikovsky's "Mediation". Sadia Francesca became famous after winning first prize in the International Tchaikovsky Competition. She was always quoted saying that Tchaikovsky was her favorite composer. Choosing "Mediation" as my selection piece might have been a strategic choice on Miss Ayumi's part to leave a stronger impression on her.

Speaking of the International Tchaikovsky Competition made it impossible not to think of Risa Morikawa. The "Piano Concerto No. 1 in B-flat minor" she had performed with the Moscow Symphony Orchestra remained the best piano concerto performance I had ever heard. I'd replayed the CD so many times I worried I was going to wear out the disc.

Risa Morikawa's breathtaking piano music hadn't lost its hold on me even after I'd learned she was the horrible mother who'd abandoned Sou. I liked to keep a person's nature as a human being separate from their skills as an artist.

Tchaikovsky – 18 Pieces Op. 72 No. 5, Meditation

"Meditation" begins tenderly but becomes quite impassioned by the end. The intro opens with a relaxed tempo. The sweet theme that appears constantly throughout the piece is romantically supported by arpeggios breaking up the left hand chord. And then you reach the verse where powerful rising sound appears, and the melody is played dynamically through Tchaikovsky's characteristic octaves. The tempo drops again during the refrain.

I tried playing this part with lots of emotion. I added a decrescendo to the final trill, careful not to muddy up the sound, and gently removed my fingers from the keyboard.

Holding my breath, I glanced at Miss Ayumi. She gave me a thumbs-up and quietly stopped the recording device. "That was very good. It's just like you to pull it off on your first try, Mashiro."

"Thank you very much."

By all appearances, my performance had passed. My cheeks dimpled with a relieved smile.

"I highly doubt you will be eliminated from the preliminary round.

I'll turn your application in for you. We already explained it to your parents and received their blessing, so all that's left is to keep your condition up while we wait for the main competition."

"Thank you so much for everything." I collected my sheet music and bowed to Miss Ayumi. I felt so bad for depending on her for everything.

"Don't make that face. All you have to do is concentrate on giving a beautiful performance, Mashiro. Oh, and I heard that they will be holding a seminar on the song selections over summer break. Some of the judges will be randomly assigned to give public lessons."

"They're holding a seminar? Will Sadia Francesca be there too?"

"No one knows. It hasn't been announced yet, so there is a possibility. There is a participation fee, but I will speak with your mother if you would like to attend."

Participation fee… I just know it's going to be outrageously priced.

As it was, I was stretching my parents' wallets thin with piano tuning fees, sheet music costs, and lessons. I had little doubt they would smile and say okay if I asked them to pay for it. I would have loved to take part in the seminar, but I had much stronger feelings about not wanting to burden my parents anymore.

Miss Ayumi quietly watched me as I internally struggled with how to respond, the corners of her eyes suddenly softening. "It's okay. There's still time until the application deadline. You don't have to give me an answer right now. I will try to come up with some ideas of how to reduce the cost in the meantime."

"I'm sorry for the trouble. Thank you for helping," I said, leaving the soundproof lesson room with my bag.

Ugh. I want money. If I had money, I could've applied for the seminar without a second thought. Depressed, I plodded for the front door.

"Mashiro," a deep, resonating voice called out to me from behind.

"You're here today! It's been ages since we last met here." I stopped descending the spiral staircase and looked up at Kou on the top step. The muscled curve of his arms exposed by his short-sleeved white school uniform shirt was too good on the eyes. He was looking older every time I saw him.

"I came because I heard you were recording your song for the competition here today. How'd it go?"

"You went out of your way to check on me? Are you worried about me or something?" I asked wide-eyed.

Kou strained a smile at me. "You can put it like that. But I also came to see Ayumi about something. You're just an extra."

"It figures. Phew. You scared me for a second. Ahaha." Relieved by his answer, I laughed even though it wasn't the mood for it. Kou's gaze lingered on me for a while, his expression mixed, before he lightly shook his head.

"You're way too easy to understand... So? How'd it go?"

"I think I played pretty well for the recording. Miss Ayumi even said she thinks I'll make it through the preliminaries."

"She did? Good for you."

I couldn't help but be captivated by his soft smile. It wasn't that calculated, swindler smile. This one had a youthful innocence to it.

"Why are you staring? You're awfully docile today."

"N-No reason, really."

There wasn't anything for me to feel ashamed of, and yet I felt the heat rush to my cheeks. Kou was being terribly kind to me lately. He stopped tearing me down with his sarcastic remarks and didn't tease me anymore. He had completely thrown me off my game.

Was it just my imagination that a sweet mood seemed to be flowing between us? No, it had to be my imagination! Absolutely that! A quick retreat was the best course of action in these situations.

"Okay, I'm heading home now."

"You aren't waiting for your ride?" Kou asked, skeptical.

I waved him off. "Mom only came to pick me up while I was in elementary school. I've been commuting by bicycle since starting middle school."

"Huh? I never heard anything about that."

"Well duh, I never told you. I'm not obligated to tell you things, Kou," I huffed.

"I'll have Mizusawa drive you home. He can take your bike back for you later," Kou stated, dismissing my comments.

"You don't have to do that for me! I've gotten home just fine on my own after every other lesson," I protested.

"...You do remember my warning that it's too late once something already happens, right?"

His voice was naturally deep, but he sounded like a demon when he purposely deepened it further. Going against him here wouldn't be smart. All the years I'd known him had taught me that much at least.

"I-I remember."

"…Wait a minute then." Kou heaved a pretentious sigh and pulled his smartphone out of his back pants pocket. He called Mr. Mizusawa over in less than thirty seconds.

"May I accompany you home, fair princess?" Kou placed his hand on the car roof and peered down at me after he helped me inside the Benz's back seat. The faint orange light lingering in the evening darkness illuminated his silky hair.

"I humbly decline, my dearest lord," I answered with deliberate pomp and grace, so as not to lose out to Kou's little charade.

When he heard that, the playful glimmer in his eyes wavered visibly. "…You can be very cruel sometimes, Mashiro."

"What does that—"

—Mean, I tried to ask, but he roughly slammed the door in my face. My nose nearly got smacked!

Dang it, Kou! Figure out if you want to be nice or mean already!

CG 28: Homesick (Sou)

Letters (Sou's POV)

DEAR Shiroyama,

I was very happy to see that you are doing well. I watched the DVD Midori shot. I'm really happy that you are continuing to play the cello to this day.

I'm doing well. Is it weird to write that when you never asked how I'm doing? But I feel like I should at least fill you in on how I'm doing too. Seems kind of unfair for me to keep my life a secret after I got to see how well you're doing. Umm, what was I trying to write again?

School is fun. I've made a lot of friends. I wonder if you heard from Kou about me playing the piano during my school's culture festival. I played a jazz arrangement of Mozart's Twelve Variations on *"Ah vous dirai-je, Maman"* and "When You Wish Upon a Star" for the encore piece.

What songs have you been practicing recently, Shiroyama? Ah, don't feel like you have to respond to me, my curiosity just got the better of me. I probably shouldn't ask questions.

Thank you for sending me tons of picture postcards. Europe has lots of pretty cards, huh? I love both the real pictures of scenery and the illustrated ones. Midori sends me cards too. She's an interesting girl to say the least.

I'm sorry this letter is just a lot of random rambling.

This time I folded an origami Christmas tree to match the season. I folded it in a way you can stand it up later. Please refer to the separate paper I included when you assemble it. What probably looks like small scraps of paper are the ornaments. I folded it so you can use tweezers to decorate the tree with them. Please try your hand at decorating it when you have time on your hands and feel bored (which I doubt ever happens to you).

Please be careful not to catch a cold. Take good care of yourself.

Sincerely,
Mashiro Shimao
December

♪♪♪

I had received a letter from Mashiro.

I rushed back to my room, dropped my bag on top of my desk, and took a deep breath.

I carefully sliced the envelope open with a letter opener and peeked inside. Most of her letters contained only origami lately, so my breath caught in my throat when I saw letters written on the other side of the semitransparent stationery. Mashiro's handwriting had a cute roundness to it. I remember the one time I complimented her on it, she got angry and huffed at me, saying, "It bothers me like crazy so don't remind me."

The included origami looked like…a Christmas tree. *I wonder what the tiny scraps of paper with it are for.* For now, I removed only the letter, careful not to spill any of the little pieces in the process.

The name she addressed the letter to saddened me. But I was the one who'd gone and thrown away my right to be called "Sou" by her. I was such a stupid, spoiled brat; I'm amazed Mashiro still wants to be my friend. Chances were, she would never call me Sou again in order to keep a clear line between us. I loved how she was serious to a fault like that.

Frankly, I was envious of Kou who could stay by her side, having her say his name. He had finally worked up the nerve to confide in me about his feelings when he visited Germany over fall break.

"I'm only telling you this because I doubt I can hide it from you—I love Mashiro."

I thought it'd come to that eventually.

He could say whatever he wanted, but until he met her, Kou never believed a woman who he could be the real him with existed.

Mashiro was the only girl out there who didn't treat Kou special and acknowledged every piece of him as he was, faults and all. In all likelihood, she was the only one who wouldn't chain down the willful Kou and would forgive him for his hopeless selfishness that had him presuming upon other people's kindness.

He said he was having a real hard time when she avoided him like the plague for a while after I left. "Serves you right," I sneered at him. He just shrugged.

Who knew he was capable of that expression too? It was the first time I'd ever seen my best friend show insecurity. It had the unfortunate effect of letting me know just how hard he'd fallen for Mashiro for real.

I kicked down the impulse to ask him if he was going to confess to her and just went with, "I still love her."

"I thought so," Kou replied with a resigned smile.

♪♪♪

DEAR Mashiro,

Thanks for the Christmas tree. The ornaments were a fun surprise. You used red lame paper for the candle fires, right? The tree found its new home on my windowsill. Our maid was speechless when she entered my room to clean. I overheard her talking to the other help exclaiming how amazing the Japanese are.

I did hear about your culture festival from Kou. Sounds like you took Mr. Yamabuki down a peg or two during Seio's Christmas concert. Kou told me about that too. It made me think you haven't changed one bit. In a good way, of course.

I know a lot of things go into competitions, but I want you to put on the performance that best represents you. I'm rooting for you from Germany.

Nothing much has changed on my end. If I have to list one thing, maybe it's that I've gotten better at speaking German. Well, of course I would, living here and all. I'm still playing the cello. I've been playing Brahm's "Cello Sonata" a lot lately. Number 1 and 2 are my favorites.

Schubert's "Arpeggione Sonata" is fun too.

Cold days are going to continue through the winter, but I hope you don't catch a cold either, Mashiro.

Sincerely,
Sou Shiroyama
January

I erased all the lines where I wrote things like "I hope we can make music together again someday," "I want to see you," and "I miss you."

By reading and rereading the letter, I made sure nothing went outside the bounds of a letter sent to a friend. *This shouldn't be too bad.* Finally satisfied with my finished product, I slipped the stationery into the envelope.

I stepped outside to put the letter in the mailbox. Powdered snow covered the ground. I went back inside to retrieve my scarf from the coat hanger and wrapped it around my neck. It was the scarf Mashiro had knitted for me. I buried my nose in the soft knitted wool and squeezed my eyes shut.

In my heart, I was constantly composing the letter I really wanted to send her.

I want to see you. I want to see you smile, Mashiro. I miss the sound of your piano.

People often say feelings fade with time. Would I be able to forget about her someday too? Would I be able to choose another person like Father did? I still didn't understand Father's feelings that drove him to remarry another woman just one year after the woman he loved with all his heart, the woman he'd married after spending years upon years wooing her, left him.

If my stepmom was the log he latched onto in his final moments before drowning then—

Halfway through that thought, I shook my head. It was painful knowing that it resulted in neither of them being happy.

♪♪♪

DEAR Shiroyama,

Thank you for writing me back! I never thought you would write me a letter! It took me by complete surprise. Not much has changed, has it? I'm very happy to hear that you are doing well.

Thank you for telling me what cello songs you are playing. I went straight to the CD shop and searched for them both. They're lovely songs. It's been a lot of fun for me to listen to them while imagining how you would interpret them, Shiroyama. Please let me know if there's a specific cellist you recommend. Ah, but don't force yourself to reply if you don't want to.

I'm also getting along just the same. This time I included an origami trombone and horn. The horn was a challenge! I had to redo it several times. It's official—the horn's shape wins the difficulty medal in the wind instrument collection.

Speaking of horns, Mozart's "Horn Concerto" is famous, but I have a thing for Rössler-Rosetti's "Horn Concerto". Oh, but I guess that's too much unnecessary information, huh?

Sorry that I can't ever seem to write anything that's not completely random and boring.

I wish I could write about something more interesting. On another note, I'm a bit late to the game, but I've recently become addicted to Shotaro IKENAMI's novels. Historical novels are so sophisticated. Something about them slips into your mind and leaves a lasting impact. I've been reading the copies I borrowed from my friend Rei, so I'd like to collect the novels myself someday.

Kou has seemed like a sad, lonely little puppy ever since you left, Shiroyama. I feel like his word choice and actions are getting stranger by the day. If you happen to meet him during one of your breaks, please give him the time of day even if it's a pain. It will probably make him happy.

Sorry for writing such a long letter. Look after yourself.

Herzliche Grüße←Am I using this greeting right?

Mashiro Shimao

March

♪♪♪

DEAR Mashiro,

Thanks for the origami. The rotary valves on the horn definitely seem difficult to recreate. But I was shocked by how insanely high quality it is. The maid I told you about in my last letter was practically jumping with joy over the new additions to the collection. She even asked if she could take a picture of them to show her husband later, but I told her not until I got permission from the creator. If you're okay with it, I hope you can give her permission.

I'm no good at coming up with interesting things to write about either.

Midori came over during spring break and dragged me all over the place like a madwoman. When I told her about your competition, she became enthusiastic about going to see you play in person. Please let her know the details once the dates are set.

It's spring here now, so the park I often go to is colored with lots of flowers.

April 24th is Easter, and it seems like a special day in Germany. Father was thrilled that he gets the day off from work. He said he's inviting my stepmother over from Japan just to throw a house party. Frankly, I'm not up for it, but he asked me to put on a cello performance. Midori told me she "refused with gumption." She's my stepmother's niece, but they have a horrible relationship and are always at each other's throats, so I'm grateful she's not coming.

Sorry this is about the only thing I can talk about.

I'll try looking around for the books you recommended and see if I can get a hold of them over here. It seems like fun to have friends you can chat about the same books with.

Your closing line was the correct German phrase. I'll use it too.

Herzliche Grüße

Sou Shiroyama

April

♪♪♪

MY once a month letter exchange with Mashiro ended up continuing for three whole years. Though I knew there was no way the conscientious and kindhearted Mashiro would ever stop replying to me, I just couldn't be the one to cut off contact with her. Her kind letters became my emotional support.

I'd learned from a text message from Kou that Mashiro had passed the competition's preliminary round. It was beyond frustrating that I was so far away, I couldn't even congratulate her when it mattered.

Midori called me all excited after she'd received a similar text from Kou's sister. There wasn't much of a time difference between England and Germany, so Midori always called me the moment she had something she wanted to talk about. She blabbed on and on without letting me get a word in, and then suddenly hung up once she had her fill. That used to tick me off in the past, but it didn't bother me anymore now that the majority of her conversations revolved around Mashiro.

"I plan on going to Japan during summer break! Come with me, Sou. I hope you don't plan on staying cooped up at home all break like you did last year. It's ridiculous for you not to enjoy our rare vacation time!"

"Leave me be. I won't return to Japan. I plan on participating in a summer program, so I won't be at home either."

"Hmph. Uncle is ever the workaholic, I hear. He should at least spend his summer vacation with his only son. Well, whatever. I'll just go with my brother. I'm so looking forward to seeing Mashiro again! Bye!"

I wanted to tell her not to bother Mashiro, but she suddenly hung up the phone like usual. I'm of the belief that the word "overbearing" exists solely for Midori's use.

A year and a half to go.

I had no intention of returning to Japan until the day I returned to Seio for good.

Heroine's Results
Target Character: Sou Shiroyama
Event: Love Letters
CLEAR

♪♪♪

SADIA Francesca ended up not participating in the summer seminar. Her schedule couldn't fit everything in.

Miss Ayumi caught wind of that news faster than anyone else and asked me again, "What do you want to do?"

"I'll pass," I said, shaking my head.

Receiving direct guidance from members of the judging committee on what points to watch out for when performing the selection pieces was an amazing opportunity that would be hard to come by, but the venue was a good hour away, and the participation fee was so outrageous it made me wonder if this was really for a junior music competition.

I loved classical music and the piano. But I was often left thinking that pursuing this path was reaching beyond my station, having been raised in a normal middle-class family.

Miss Ayumi seemed to have seen through me deciding to pass on the seminar as a result of it not weighing up to the costs. She carefully studied my face and put her hand to her cheek. "You have been like this since the day we met, Mashiro."

"Like what, Miss Ayumi?" I asked with a blank look.

Miss Ayumi took my hand and led me to the couch. "There is absolutely nothing wrong with having a strong sense of purpose. However, in a sense, I think it's very scary to make your choices based solely on whether it's necessary or not, or if you should do it or not."

I couldn't wrap my head around what she was saying at first. But the fact she was deeply worried about me came across.

"Anyone who has their heart set on pursuing any of the performing arts professionally can't take it on with halfhearted dedication. In that regard, your wholehearted devotion is a virtue. But why don't you try broadening your horizons some more? Those things you disregard as worthless at a glance have a way of broadening our horizons as people and by extension, our performances."

"Um…are you telling me that I will gain necessary experience if I take the seminar?" I timidly ventured, scared that I had made the wrong choice by passing on it.

She answered me with a somber smile. "No, I'm not. Passing on the seminar doesn't pose much of a problem for you." Miss Ayumi reached out with her slender arm and gently stroked the top of my head. "I wonder if you will be able to break out of your shell someday if you experience a love that makes everything else in the world feel meaningless."

"WHAT?! No, thanks."

I've had my fill of love for the time being, thank you.

I slapped my hands over my mouth to stop from accidentally letting my real thoughts slip out. I was the girl who once ruined her dear sister's true love. The bitter memory of crushing her relationship with Tomoi crawled its way up the back of my throat in the form of a hard lump. I couldn't answer right away if someone asked me if my feelings for him were really love. How I wish that I'd torn their relationship apart because of burning love and passion for him instead of out of shallow stubbornness and ugly jealousy.

But that's not what happened. I had been a shallow child. And I knew that side of me hadn't changed yet.

Miss Ayumi saw me suddenly fall silent and changed topics in a cheery voice. "In that case, you won't mind if I continue to look over the songs you will be playing until the quarterfinals in September, yes?"

"Of course! Please do!"

Nothing would make me happier than to undertake Miss Ayumi's Spartan training lessons.

The lessons would prevent me from having to think too much. It would push back those haunting thoughts surrounding the mystery of why this world resembled *Hear My Heart* and why only Kon and I had any memory of a past life. All the thoughts about what Kon was hiding from me and why she seemed to be suffering now—I didn't have to think about any of it while I was playing the piano.

Perhaps that's the reason why I became so engrossed and devoted to playing. Not that I would continue playing if I didn't actually love it too. The music world wasn't generous enough to allow people with half-baked feelings to aim for the top.

Get a hold of yourself! I took several deep breaths and gave myself a small pep talk.

Everything from my feelings to my thoughts affirmed that I was really here. Humans had nothing more than that to prove they actually existed in any world. And the me that was here chose the music path, so I had to continue down this road giving it my all.

That was the *only* path, right?

♪♪♪

COINCIDENTALLY, Miss Ayumi's old piano mentor was going to be serving on the competition's judging panel.

Thanks to the information he shared with Miss Ayumi, I was able to throw myself into piano practice without having to worry about the small details. Miss Ayumi even asked her mentor about the judging criteria when I told her of my desire to play Chopin's "12 Etudes Op.10" for the quarterfinals.

Her mentor came back and asked if I was capable of accurately adhering to and expressing the composer's tempo and dynamic markings. Precisely because this song is suitable for measuring the musical technique of performers, the judges were looking for a performance that emphasized accurate touch and the beauty of the tone over free musical expression. Practicing a piece became significantly easier when I knew exactly what the judging panel was looking for beforehand.

And then came summer break.

Midori contacted me when she arrived in Japan just as she'd promised, so Kon and I went to hang out at Maestro Noboru's house for the first time in a long while.

The quarterfinals were just around the corner after summer break. A piece of me honestly worried whether now was really the time for me to be hanging out with my friends. I hated the part of myself that always had a habit of thinking, "Ugh! If only I hadn't made plans, I could be practicing right now!"

I kept repeating the advice I'd received from Miss Ayumi about broadening my horizons and was mumbling to myself in the back of Kon's car. "This counts as broadening my horizons. Everything in life is experience!"

Kon looked freaked out by my muttering. "Mashiro... What weird thoughts are possessing you this time?"

"I plan to broaden my horizons through trial and error."

"Broaden your horizons how?"

"I've heard that even the things I think aren't worth doing could actually help my music if I try doing them."

"Hey!" Kon scolded me, frowning. Whoops, my real thoughts on this outing slipped out. "Haven't you been completely absorbed in nothing but the piano lately, Mashiro? Both Midori and I are worried about you. You have a bad habit of becoming like this."

Kon put her hands on both sides of my face, to which I forced a smile and admitted, "You think so too? Sorry. I'm not really sure why, but I feel panicked when I'm not practicing the piano."

"You're way too stoic! Well, that's just like you, Ri—" Kon gasped and bit her lower lip. Pretending not to notice, I directed my gaze out the window. "That habit is just like you, Mashiro."

Rika. Kon, who was about to call me by that name, manifested a remarkable force of will to work past that hiccup and continue speaking as if it'd never happened.

"Yeah, I'll try to be more conscious of it."

Never again could we bring up our past. I made sure to keep my end of the promise we'd made on that snowy day.

Midori flew out the door the second we rang Maestro Noboru's doorbell. "Long time no see! I've been dying to see you both!"

I stood bolt upright as she welcomed me with a bear hug and a kiss on the cheek before letting us inside. She'd become completely steeped in overseas customs from her long stay abroad. I couldn't fathom the possibility of her turning into a normal Japanese high school girl like in the game.

Should I tell her that it's not okay to casually touch people in Japan?

"Where's Maestro Noboru?" I asked, curious as to why Midori was the only one at home.

Her lips curled into a Cheshire cat grin. "He said he has a date with Ayumi today."

"You're kidding?!" Kon and I both blurted at the same time.

"Right? It's a complete shocker, isn't it?!" She nodded along with us. "I've already pinned down exactly where they're having lunch. Say, why don't we go spy on them?"

Oh no, here it comes! Midori's brother complex in full gear!

Midori loved and adored her older brother to the point that she even admitted to wanting to marry someone like him in the future. She wanted to marry a genius pianist not attached to the things of this world (while being from a rich family). Finding another person out there like that was going to be quite the feat.

"You shouldn't ruin their date," Kon chided with an exasperated expression as she stuck her straw in the iced tea Midori served us.

"But I'm so curious! Wouldn't you be curious if Kou said he was going on a date with a girl, Kon?"

"Not one bit. Kou goes on dates with different girls more than he changes his shirt," Kon remarked calmly.

"Sugar!" Midori cussed.

I bet she wanted to say shit there, I mused as I watched over their conversation, keeping out of it.

That's when Midori's eyes flashed, and she turned the conversation on me. "What about you Mashiro?"

"What about me?"

"Are you okay with Kou flittering between girls?"

"…Hmm. I feel bad for him and the girls to be honest. I understand how he feels since he's trying to do whatever he can to secure Kon's safety. It's not really a matter an outsider like me has any right to comment on," I answered truthfully.

"If you say so. That's the extent of your feelings for him, eh? Then Sou still has a chance. You know, you should just forget about an unfaithful player like Kou and go with Sou instead. He's like scary loyal to you. Like scary, scary, loyal. Any woman aside from you, Mashiro, is less than trash in his eyes."

Midori's constant use of the word *scary* made it questionable whether she was honestly recommending him to me. Besides, it's not like I wanted to be with someone who treated people like trash either. I was starting to pity her because her hatred for her engagement to Sou was so great she'd endorse me getting together with him every time she saw me.

"Midori, you know what happened between us already, don't you? I treated Sou so horribly it's amazing he was ever willing to speak to me again, you know? Nothing can happen between us now."

"…Mashiro, are you actually this cruel?" Midori asked me, her tone serious, eyes narrowed in on me.

Huh. I feel like Kou said the same thing to me before.

"Cruel…huh?"

"I love how cut and dry you are, Mashiro, but you're so matter-of-fact and detached from things. Don't most people worry and lose their way while they're young?"

"If worrying and being lost would help me find the answers, I'd do that, but it can only get you so far. Isn't it a shame to waste time worrying?"

Midori exchanged looks with Kon and sighed. "Both Kou and Sou have lost epically to the piano."

"That's the biggest problem right there. The piano dominates Mashiro's top ten priority list. There's no room for love to wiggle its way into her life."

"You're absolutely right. I don't have the time or energy for such things," I huffed, puffing out my cheeks at my friends who seemed to be on the same wavelength.

♪♪♪

TWO days before Midori returned to England, Kon invited her and Maestro Noboru to the Genda estate where she was throwing them a going away party. Kon frantically fought to prevent her mother from interfering with the party. According to her, it'd become a party of unimaginable proportion if she hadn't stopped her involvement.

She'd even begun saying things like, "If Noboru Misaka is coming over, we should hire a full orchestra and have them put on a concerto together!"

But since the occasion presented itself, Kon and I planned to put on a two-piano performance as a farewell gift.

With his hemp blazer on and properly shaved beard, Maestro Noboru was a 100 times more attractive than usual. Seeing as Kon and I had accidentally blurted some rude things last time that'd hurt him, I restricted my comment to, "You look great today," and swallowed my real comment of, "you'd look even better if you did something about that mop of wild hair on your head."

Rachmaninoff – Suite No. 2 for two pianos, Op. 17, II. Waltz

After four years of inactivity caused by the emotional damage he had received from negative reception towards his first symphony, Rachmaninoff rediscovered his confidence and composed this piece, confirming the comeback of his creativity. An elegant waltz took up the piano's tenor voice amid a flurry of activity. The unique rhythm of the mingling triple and duple meter created a kind of Russian pathos. The dynamic chords and arpeggios played colorfully, painting the romantic primary melody. Even when an expansive melodic line unfolded in one of the pianos, the other maintained a driving pulse.

Kon and I had practiced the piece after discussing how the song created this image of young couples dancing through a ballroom under the dazzling light of a crystal chandelier.

Spending all my time practicing the songs for the competition created this incessant need to play any other song. Performing at the party gave me the break I desperately needed and the enjoyment I didn't realize I was missing.

It'd been three years since I'd last sat across from Kon on a different piano.

I matched my breathing with hers and conversed through the music. The conversation was filled with the sweet memories of the distant past where we once giggled and told each other all our secrets, nearly bringing me to tears. I even saw an illusion of Kon leading me by the hand, running into the bright sky during the middle of the song where the crescendo took off as a fortissimo.

Maestro Noboru and Midori stood in applause after the performance.

"Magnifique!" Midori exclaimed in French, her cheeks flushing as she ran over to her flute case. "I can't sit still and do nothing after hearing a performance like that! Noboru, accompany me!"

"Sure. What song?" Maestro Noboru stood with a resigned smile and headed for the piano. Midori was about the only person in the whole world who could designate Noboru Misaka as her accompanist for a sudden ensemble. Aside from Miss Ayumi, of course.

"It's gotta be Bizet's 'L'Arlésienne'. Let's go with the Minuet," Midori said in a singsong voice while she assembled her solid gold flute.

Holy smokes! The golden light is dazzling! It looks like it costs about 5 million yen. Hmm, 5 million. The mortgage left on our house could be mostly paid off if we had 5 million yen to spare.

"Mashiro, your mouth is hanging open." Kon elbowed me. I hastily snapped my mouth shut.

Midori laughed at me then slowly raised her flute. She played the relaxed, beautiful melody with very little breathiness. Her performance took center stage. Maestro Noboru played a mellow and diffident accompaniment, so as not to outshine her.

She's good. Her performance is outstanding.

Midori played a million times better than any of the flutists I heard during Seio's Christmas concert. Her flute tone not only had a centeredness to the sound, but also rang like a bell and possessed the purity and flexibility of a beautiful, pure soprano voice. It was like she was playing the melody of the heavens.

Kon and I applauded until our hands hurt.

After we wrapped up our musical performances, we snacked, picked different CDs out, and kept putting in requests for Maestro Noboru to play different songs. It made for an extremely fun and fulfilling time.

"I'm sorry I can't see you off at the airport."

"That's okay. It's not a big deal."

When I left the Genda estate, I said my farewells two days early to Midori and Maestro Noboru.

"I'll be back in October to see you in the finals, Mashiro!" Midori winked at me.

I still had to get through the quarterfinals and semifinals first. Midori's words of encouragement got me laughing.

"You can look forward to my rendition of Ravel's music." I winked back, earning a smile out of Maestro Noboru too.

♪♪♪

THE new school quarter began.

My sunburnt friends and I filled each other in about what we did over summer break. Our middle school placed a huge emphasis on club activities, so most of the conversation surrounded club related stuff. From the sound of things, they all had it pretty rough going to school for their practice and on away trips when it was supposed to be their vacation time. Rei told me she had competed in the singles match for the junior high soft tennis tournament. Her match landed on one of my piano lesson days with Miss Ayumi, which prevented me from going to cheer her on.

"It's all good! Just come and see my match during my last tournament next year, and we'll be even!" Rei laughed and forgave me.

I didn't realize how much I was holding out on my friends until the first morning of the new quarter.

On the way to school I was telling Eri about how I went to see the fireworks with Mako and Sawa, drawing an earful of complaints from her.

"I would've went with you guys!"

"Really? I didn't invite you because I thought you would go with Majima instead. I didn't invite Tomo for the same reason," I explained.

"I get that you were just trying to be considerate, but still." As we were waiting for the intersection light to change, Eri murmured, "It makes me feel lonely," and dropped her gaze to the street.

"You and I won't be together in high school, you know? My grades aren't that great, and I know you've had your heart set on Seio since forever," she said sadly, lifting her gaze to my eyes. "That's why I believe right now is the only time we'll have together like this. Invite me along the next time you go somewhere. I want to make more memories with you, Mashiro."

"Eri… I'm sorry."

Since we lived in the same neighborhood, Eri had been a great friend of mine since long before I'd regained my memories of the past. Eri stayed by my side with a smile even when my personality drastically shifted in the second grade and when I struggled to fit in during the fifth grade. All the days I'd spent with her flooded into my mind. I bit my lower lip as I recalled Miss Ayumi's advice.

I have to practice the piano! I have to work harder at my studies! Stuck in the vortex of my own little world, I didn't stop once to think seriously about how my best friend was feeling.

"I'm so embarrassed. A part of me just always assumed that you and I would be together forever. Your house is nearby and I know your parents well. But that's not how it works in reality, is it? I'm really sorry," I apologized.

"What? C-Come on, now. You don't have to take it that seriously! I'm just sulking that I didn't get to go with you!" Eri was flustered by my tone.

I was made aware of how often Eri, with her offbeat friendliness and kindness, had saved me. I loved laughing at stupid things with her. And I never even realized it.

"The fireworks were really pretty. The three of us watched them wondering if you were enjoying them somewhere together with Majima," I quickly reverted the conversation back to the fireworks because I felt like I was about to cry.

Eri cracked a relieved smile. "I didn't make any plans with Majima that day because he had summer lessons. I ended up catching the last half from the bank near my house."

"Are you serious?! Oh my gosh! I am really sorry!" I felt so bad I wanted to hop off my bike and prostrate myself before her.

"Seriously," Eri laughed. "I thought about texting you, but I stopped myself because I know your piano comp is coming up soon. You're so cruel!" She puffed out her cheeks.

T-Too cute! She's so cute it hurts! And I hate how shallow I was being. Stupid, stupid! I could've confirmed her plans in a few seconds if I really wanted to!

I definitely didn't want her finding out about how Mako, Sawa, and I ranted about how envious we were of her. The conversation went something like this:

"I'm so envious of couples! I bet Eri and Tomo are all dressed up in their yukatas being told how good they look in them by their boyfriends!"

"Stupid Majima!"

"Stupid Kinose!"

As soon as I get to school I have to swear them to secrecy!

During break, I nervously checked with Tomo. To my relief, she and her boyfriend had successfully seen the fireworks as a couple. *Thank goodness!* If Tomo told me that she'd ended up watching it alone too, it would've been a blow to my conscience that I couldn't recover from for a while.

It didn't take long after the start of the new quarter for the sports festival and school trip to become the hot topic at school. But the competition's quarterfinal round just so happened to land on the same Saturday as the sports festival, which resulted in my first authorized absence from a major school event.

When Tazaki, the cute delinquent with piercings, heard about it, he pursed his lips and grumbled, "Tch! I was planning on showing you how cool I am too!"

"You're always cool," I teased back. He shoved the hair off his face and gave a satisfied smile.

"She's right. We'll be cheering you on with all our heart," Sawa added for good measure.

"Yippee!"

His innocent display of joy got us smiling along with him.

I knew it was horrible of me to compare, but Kou didn't even have an inkling of Tazaki's cuteness. They both fit into the playboy mold, but Tazaki's flirting didn't annoy me. How do I put it? The way he showed his love for girls was kind of endearing. Kou, on the other hand, generally didn't trust anyone other than Kon. He was especially distrustful of the opposite sex.

But isn't it about time he starts treating me like a real friend after how long he's known me? Why has he been unnaturally kind to me lately? He used to interact with me as his real self, without holding anything back. He's the one who used to taunt me and call me names. That ticked me off in and of itself, but I preferred him being straight with me to lies and deceit. Had I done something to upset him without realizing it?

Just as I was getting depressed over how possible that was, my cell phone vibrated.

"Your quarterfinals are right around the corner. I'll go to cheer you on. Good luck."

One glance at Kou's text message pulled a sigh from me.

"Prioritize your dates," I texted back, purposely implying he didn't have to come.

An extremely happy sounding text came back in response. "It's rare for you to be jealous. Don't you worry, there's nothing I'd ever prioritize over your competition, Mashiro."

What is with this text? Kou, I just don't get you lately.

♪♪♪

REI ran over to me as I was cleaning up my desk before heading home. It was the day before the quarterfinals. "Thank goodness! You're still here!" she panted, still dressed in her soft tennis jersey. She must've come from her club. "I spent all that time making this, and then I forgot it at home! I just ran back to my house to get it."

Rei pressed a small good luck charm into my hands as she gasped for air. "Good luck tomorrow! I know just how hard you've been working at the piano, Mashiro. You'll do amazing!"

"Rei…"

Oh no, I feel like crying. I actually felt nervous to the point of being sick when I thought of the quarterfinals coming up tomorrow.

Miss Ayumi had given me her stamp of approval when she said, "You can take it easy until the finals with your skill level," but this was my first time participating in a music competition. Truth be told, I was a bundle of nerves.

What should I do if I make a mistake? How do I get by if my mind blanks on me and I forget how to play the next note? Those thoughts gnawed at me.

All of my schoolteachers rained encouragement on me when I turned my absence permission slip in to the teacher's lounge. Even the principal had encouraging things to say. Mr. Matsuda was about the only person who smiled and said, "Don't make yourself too nervous."

The panic inside me grew and grew the more I wanted to live up to the expectations placed on me.

"Whoa! D-Don't cry, Mashiro!"

"I'll try… Sorry, I just wanted to say thanks too."

I opened up my right hand and examined the good luck charm with a warped shape. I could tell Rei had put everything she had into embroidering the material. The embroidered words "Prayers for Certain Victory" brought tears to my eyes. Rei's fingers were covered in Band-Aids. And I couldn't even make myself take time off to go and see her singles match.

"Don't look at it too close! Ugh, I should've taken home ec more seriously."

"Hehe… This is why I'm always telling you that keeping up with your schooling will—" I paused in the middle of repeating my usual saying as I wiped the tears from my eyes with a handkerchief.

"Will only make life easier for me, right? It really hit home for me this time," Rei conceded, beating me to the punch line. We both laughed.

Chatting with Rei had taken the load of tension off my shoulders, allowing me to return home with a little hop in my step. I was pedaling my bike with a dorky grin as I squeezed the good luck charm in my pocket, when one of the older men in my neighborhood saw me on his way home from work and joked, "Oh! Somebody's happy! Did you get a boyfriend?"

"I got something even better than that!" I giggled back.

Eri dropped by my house that night to give me a fancy square cardboard letter that all of our friends had written in. I squeezed the colored cardboard to my chest that had messages from my group of friends saying things like, "Believe in yourself" and "You're definitely number 1, Mashiro!" and cried again.

Why did they do so much for me when I was such a hopeless friend? I could kind of understand why Rin and Majima would leave a message because of how long we knew each other, but there were even messages from Tazaki and Hirato.

"GOOD LUCK!"

"YOU'D BETTER WIN!"

♪♪♪

AT long last, it was the day of the quarterfinals.

I followed Miss Ayumi through the Arts Center's backdoor to the waiting room. Today was the middle school division, tomorrow the high school division, and the university division was to be held on the third day. A large group of reporters had gathered at the Arts Center since today was the first day of the competition. Sadia Francesca had earned herself a lot of fans in Japan when it became widely known what a Japanophile she was. There was probably a lot of demand for articles covering her time here.

"Are you all right? Though you look calm enough I don't have to ask. You look confident." Miss Ayumi peered down at my face and smiled with relief at what she saw there.

The only reason why I wasn't as nervous as I thought I'd be was because of Miss Ayumi and everyone else there for me. Dad, Mom, and Hanaka had come to cheer me on from the audience as well. I wanted to convey my gratitude to them as best I could through my performance.

Each waiting room was assigned to a group of five participants. Some had come with their guardians, while others came with their mentors like me. Competition staff members were giving instructions at the stage wing. They informed us that we were free to do what we wanted while we waited for our names to be called.

I'd already confirmed what the piano I would be playing on sounded like during the public practice session held beforehand. As one of the sponsors for the competition, the Shiroyama group had provided one of their newest model concert grand pianos for us. I had spotted several participants I hadn't seen before during that practice session. There were kids wearing Seio's uniform, as to be expected. I wanted to chat with them, but everyone was stuck in their own world, shutting out everyone else they viewed as rivals. This was the time to read the mood and behave myself.

Several other participants aside from me had chosen to play Chopin from among the song selection. No one in the middle school division had chosen to play what was considered to be one of the most difficult etudes, Chopin's "Étude Op. 10, No. 1 in C major", which is why Miss Ayumi strongly suggested I pick it. I still didn't have the confidence to pull off that challenging piece of music with the perfection required of a competition.

I always ended up struggling to add the accent onto the intro's arpeggio. It was hard to play passionately until the end when my fingers were exhausted halfway through the piece.

In fact, Chopin had surprisingly small hands and had to come up with some imaginative fingerings for his music in order to play it. I'd read somewhere that they were so small he could only reach ten keys, but he made up for it with extremely limber palms.

Some of the participants were wearing concert dresses, but I came in my middle school uniform. I didn't think it would pose a problem since even Miss Ayumi told me it was fine. I listened to a recording of my performance on my cell phone while I went through the sheet music in my head.

All of the repeat signs are omitted to make the performance more compact for the competition, right? Okay, I'm good. After all, I've been practicing long and hard for this day, I reminded myself. The good luck charm was secure in my chest pocket and the cardboard letter from my friends was tucked away in my lesson bag with my sheet music.

"Miss Shimao, please get ready."

"Ah, okay."

I entrusted my things to Miss Ayumi and followed the competition staff lady. I'd arrived at the stage wing by the time the person before me had finished their performance. The spotlights were blinding. Taking several deep breaths, I held my hand over the good luck charm.

I'll do the best I can.

My name and song were being announced. I took one big step onto the stage.

Chopin – Etude in A flat major, Op.10, No.10

This etude was a technical study composed by Chopin that placed huge demand on the performer in varying a single pattern by changes of accent and touch. As a practice piece, this etude was designed to develop and stretch the right hand, specifically between fingers. The ludic melody took flight on the lively rhythm in an endless continuum of sixths sonorities. With carefree feeling, I danced my fingers over the keys.

This is fun! The piano truly is loads of fun!

Putting my whole body into it, I gracefully and lightly let each note ring out. I clearly defined each stress, careful not to shake up the tempo. Happiness exploded inside me when the sound I was aiming for reached my ears. Only the melody stood out from the notes strung together like a pearl necklace when the accents were pulled off correctly.

Just like this.

I was able to play the song with more concentration than ever before, playing through to the end without a single mistake. I gently placed my fingers on the keys for the last chord.

I rose from the bench, picked up the handkerchief I'd left on the side of the piano music rack, and turned to face the audience where I bowed once and hobbled quickly from the stage.

I was already off the stage by the time applause erupted from the audience that had been stupefied into silence moments earlier.

CG 29: Dinner Party (Kou & Tobi)

I was informed that I had passed the quarterfinals a while after all the performances had ended. Tears threatened to burst forth when I heard that the judges evaluated my performance as having great expression and a mastery of the technical work.

Sadia Francesca gave me an A- according to the interpreter. "Your performance would have been perfect if you played with more love."

Love, huh? Maestro Noboru often told me the same thing. *I thought I played with love. I wonder what's missing.*

I mulled over that question the entire time I was getting ready to leave and even after I exited the waiting room. Lost in my thoughts, I skidded to a halt when I spotted Kou and Kon. They were both standing in the main hall outside of the waiting rooms.

"Ah," I uttered stupidly.

"Don't 'ah' me. You were trying to walk by us just now, weren't you?" Kou was scowling, arms folded. That expression, that pose, they were all I ever wanted to see. They tickled me pink.

"Sorry… I was lost in my thoughts. Thanks for coming today!"

"My pleasure! Your performance was breathtakingly good, Mashiro. You've improved again." Kon squinted at me as if I was glowing. Kou seemed to have pulled himself back together as his expression reverted to normal.

"Ayumi wanted to see if we could all have dinner together. Your family came too, right? She already invited them."

"Oh? Is it okay for us to join you?"

"Yeah. I was waiting for you here because I wanted to tell you that. Everyone has already gone ahead to the parking garage. We should head over there too."

"If I'd known about this I would've worn a dress instead of my school uniform," I mumbled.

Kou flashed me a smile. "You look just as cute in your uniform, Mashiro."

Oh, darn. He's reverted back to host Kou.

Kon burst out laughing when she saw the disappointment on my face.

♪♪♪

MISS Ayumi had made reservations for us at a quiet, unconventional French restaurant thirty minutes from the Arts Center by car. My jaw dropped at the sudden appearance of lush greenery in the middle of a residential area. Surrounded by hedges, the section ahead was totally blocked from view. It was a forest, a freaking forest! Was there really a restaurant in there?

Mom, Dad, and Hanaka were also staring with eyes rounder than saucers. A chic wrought-iron gate was situated in a gap between the hedges. Birds, vines, and roses decorated the lovely design.

"Ayumi, I'm amazed you secured a reservation."

"I was lucky. Come along. Let's head in." Happily nodding along to Kou's comment, Miss Ayumi confidently pushed open the gate and stepped inside.

Kon and Kou calmly followed Miss Ayumi like they'd been here before. Worried we'd be left behind, we quickly chased after them.

Can we just walk inside?

Past the hedges and wrought-iron gate was a garden straight from Burnett's *The Secret Garden*. A brick promenade overflowing with rustic beauty wound its way from the gate through the garden. Meticulous care was paid to pruning the vines and rose thorns closest to the promenade to prevent possible injury. Evenly spaced garden lights led the way like footlights at the theater. The sky overhead was dyed in gradations of purple. Before me was a green garden covered in roses from all four seasons.

Yup, I've walked into another world.

"Mashiro, Hanaka, take a look over there!" Dad directed in a hushed voice, looking over his shoulder at us. I squinted in the direction he pointed and saw a reddish-brown bird perched in a grove of trees.

"Wow! Cute!"

"Is that a sparrow?"

Extremely fond of all things cute, Hanaka and Mom both gushed over the bird. Surprised by their voices, the small bird took flight in a flurry of flapping wings. Dad looked disappointed.

"It was a long-tailed rose finch. I would have brought my camera from the car if I had known we were coming to a place like this."

"You can't take pictures without permission," I promptly chided. Dad restlessly swept his eyes around the area as if he couldn't give up on the prospect.

We eventually arrived at a small, white, cube-shaped building while we were sight-seeing. Taking views of the garden into consideration, the building had gigantic windows on three sides. Inside, comfortable armchairs were positioned around a large, white table. From outside I also spotted napkins for several people decorating the top of the table. The strange thing was…nobody was seated inside.

I ran up to Kon and Kou and whispered, "Are they not open today?"

They laughed at me with the exact same tone that implied, "Aren't you cute?" Annoying twins!

"This restaurant accepts one party a day by reservation only."

"That's why I told Ayumi I was amazed she'd secured the reservation."

"I see. I thought that might be the case," I nodded along in all seriousness, and Kou patted me on the head. Argh! When will he stop with that stuff!

A very petite woman was waiting for us when we entered the restaurant. "Welcome. Please come right this way."

The woman wore a white shirt and black pants. She had her brown hair pulled back into a tight bun and her bangs pinned back. You couldn't guess her age by looking at her. She looked like she was in her mid-teens and her mid-twenties. Eugen Cicero's jazz music played casually in the background.

I was staring at the small flower decorating a cup on the table when Kou informed me, "That's a star swertia."

"It's cute. I love this kind of flower," I answered.

Kou's expression sunk for some reason. "Sou said he loves that flower too."

"He did? Cool."

He's sad because I reminded him of Sou. My mistake.

The restaurant felt more like a secret hideaway than a five-star luxury restaurant, which helped my family feel more at home.

"The last member of our party will arrive later," Miss Ayumi explained to the woman, who I assumed was the waitress.

"Okay. Would you like to order first? Or would you rather wait?"

Miss Ayumi began placing orders with the waitress. There weren't any menus around, so with nothing better to do, we looked around the restaurant and at the garden through the windows.

"Are you certain it was all right for me to order the courses at my discretion?" Miss Ayumi worriedly confirmed with Mom and Dad after the waitress disappeared into the back.

"Well, we've never come to a place like this before, so you are actually doing us a big favor by ordering."

"No one in our family is a picky eater. We're looking forward to eating new foods. Aren't we?"

Miss Ayumi looked relieved by Dad and Mom's answers and enthusiastic smiles. Dad and Miss Ayumi both drove here, so they weren't going to order any wine.

"How does Perrier sound?" Miss Ayumi checked with Dad.

"Noncarbonated for me," Dad responded, and the waitress brought him normal mineral water.

She had arrived with such perfect timing it made me wonder if there were hidden cameras in the restaurant. The waitress was extremely professional.

Hanaka leaned over and whispered in my ear, "Hey, do you think there will be dessert too?"

Kou overheard from his seat on the opposite side of me and answered in my place. "This is a full course meal, so there should be. The desserts are delicious here. You can safely look forward to the *dessert sucré.*"

I flinched from the rich timbre of Kou's baritone voice—his post-puberty voice.

I used to love the sound of this voice in the game. I love it even now. His looks too. Maybe I'll join Kou's fanclub if I get accepted into Seio.

Imagining Kou's disgusted frown made me laugh out loud.

"What's *dessert sucré?*"

"It means a sweet dessert in French," I whispered to Hanaka.

"I had no idea! Oh gosh, that's embarrassing!" Her cheeks turned red.

"*Dessert sucré* isn't usually used after all. We normally just call it dessert." I thought that Kou would laugh at my sister's reaction, but he didn't even crack a smile. "Your family is made up of great people, huh?" he quietly commented out of the blue.

"You think so too? Ehehe, thanks."

Hearing my family complimented brought me instant joy. All the more so because Kou's tone didn't have a hint of sarcasm in it.

"They don't have any ulterior motives. They're honest and have this warmth about them. I can relax around them. ...I'm not lying."

The fact he felt the need to add that last part on was like a knife to the chest for me. *I don't think he's a liar—nah, that'd make me the liar. I think he's a big fat liar only when it comes to women.*

"...Are you okay?" I asked him.

"Why wouldn't I be?"

"Aren't you worn out? Don't push yourself too far. You should take it easy now and then."

"Right back at you—is what I want to say, but...you're right. I'd do just that if it would actually change things."

"And things will change if you leave them be?"

The smart and intuitive Kou immediately caught on to what I was talking about. Being surrounded by his fanclub all the time had to be like living on pins and needles for him.

"They're satisfied with just a little superficial attention. Those girls aren't serious about me either. It's just that it'd be too late if their pent-up feelings exploded and they went after Kon."

"Yeah...pretty scary."

I quietly chatted with Kou as we ate the food the waitress brought to our table. Curiously enough, my heart was at peace. This might have been the first time I was ever able to relax this much with Kou.

The hors d'oeuvre, pumpkin potage, and main fish dishes were all delicious. The gentle seasonings brought out the flavor of the base ingredients. They had cut the ingredients into beautiful shapes, making it just as much a feast for the eyes. Everyone enjoyed the meal over friendly conversation. We didn't have to worry about what others thought of how we looked or what we were saying because there were no other customers. No wonder the restaurant was popular.

As for Kon, she was in the midst of listening to Hanaka gush about Shinji. She'd made the grave mistake of casually mentioning, "I heard you have a boyfriend. You're so lucky."

Hanaka was definitely going to prattle on for a long time because she'd been too busy to see Shinji lately.

Oh dear, now she's pulled out her smartphone. Seriously, Hanaka, please don't put on a slideshow of all your date pictures with Shinji.

"Wow! He's cool!"

"Oh no! If I tell Shin that you called him cool, I won't be able to bring him back down to Earth! Too dangerous!"

Kou's shoulders shook with laughter when he saw me sighing.

I was honestly dreading having Hanaka and Kon together in the same place. In the back of my mind I worried that as long as Kon was my *Hana*, being together with Hanaka would torment her. But from the look of things between them, it was needless worry on my end. They were now talking up a storm about SAZE. In summary, apparently their youthful vibrancy during their debut years was hard to pass up, but now that they'd grown up, they were "seriously bad news."

"Mashiro has zero interest in boy bands, so I'm ecstatic you're a fan, Kon. Let's go to their next concert together!"

"I want to go!"

An instant reply?! You want to go that bad?!

"Mashiro barely watches any TV either. Public broadcasting is about the only thing she watches. She watches it so seriously while taking down notes. Hey, Kon, what do you think of that?"

Failing to hold in his laughter, Kou pressed his napkin to his lips, his shoulders shaking even harder. *He's been laughing way too hard since this conversation started!*

"Mashiro's a very serious person."

"I agree. That's one of her super adorable points, but still," Hanaka said in an emotional tone.

Kon partially closed her eyes and nodded with a faint smile.

By the time everyone had polished off the main course, Tobi showed up with calculated timing.

Shocked, Kou arched his perfectly groomed eyebrows. "Director Yamabuki? You're the last party member?"

It was a surefire thing in my mind that he was going to show up after how much he challenged and goaded me during the Christmas concert. Kou glanced at me out of the corner of his eye, his wariness towards Tobi on full display. I blinked once to let him know I was okay.

Not even batting an eye at Kou's attitude, Tobi flashed his princely smile. "That's right. Ayumi didn't tell you? Don't look so scary. At least let me greet my beautiful contestant." He held out the bouquet of pink roses he had in his right hand. "My apologies for arriving late. There was a meeting I couldn't get out of. In any case, hearty congratulations to you for passing through the quarterfinals. You were the only contestant to receive an A from Sadia Francesca today, Mashiro."

"Pardon?" Forgetting to even say thanks, I held the bouquet he handed me and stared back into his glimmering eyes. Surprise surpassed my joy, rendering my brain incapable of wrapping around the situation. The third-year student from Seio I saw in my waiting room had put on a terrific performance. I was positive he had received an A as well.

"You seem to have great affinity for Chopin, Mashiro. But I wonder if the same can be said of Bach in the next round. I can't wait to see."

"Th-Thank you."

Tobi flashed me a subtle smile then went around greeting the members of my family. Mom and Dad responded to the blond-haired, blue-eyed prince with awe when they learned that he was the director of Seio Academy. I mentally prepared myself for Hanaka to fawn all over him, but she acted surprisingly composed.

Wh-What happened? Why is she so calm? The strength drained from me later that day when she told me the reason why. Apparently she was irked when Tobi challenged me about Bach. "Mashiro is obviously amazing at Bach too!" she ranted as soon as we got home. She was way too much of a doting older sister.

Hanaka couldn't tell the difference between Bach and Vivaldi. For example, the chord progression in Pachelbel's "Canon" was beautifully arranged in such a way that a number of modern pop songs adapted the same chord progression. I could understand how someone might get that confused, but was it really possible to confuse Bach and Vivaldi? Whenever I let Hanaka listen to Vivaldi's "Spring" she would boast, "I know this song! It's by Bach," while wiggling her eyebrows. As cute as she was, she was still wrong.

Once he finished his pleasantries with my family, Tobi ordered wine and cheese, and comfortably sat down beside Kon.

"I'm happy to see you again, Kon. You become more beautiful every time I see you."

"Thank you, Director."

The waitress placed a wineglass in front of Tobi. He skipped ordering the bottle since he had driven there too. Tobi carried a strip of cheese to his mouth and brought the wineglass to his lips with an artful slowness.

He's someone who eats like he really enjoys food, I thought, gaining new insight into his personality.

"You make me feel like an outsider when you call me Director. It's very lonesome. It would make my day if you would just call me by my name, Kon."

Oh gosh. Gross. Is this an event for the original heroine?

Goosebumps prickled across my arms. I turned toward Kou and implored him to do something with misty eyes. *Do something about that pervert! PLEASE!* To which Kou responded by swiftly averting his eyes. His ears were red. *What are you BLUSHING over?! Please save the cheap gimmicks for when we aren't in dire straits! Forget you! I just have to take matters into my own hands and snap the flags leading to Tobi's route. I won't stand behind giving Kon over to a creeper like Tobi!*

"I think you should stick with calling him Director, Kon. He's a *MUCH* older man in charge of your school. It's out of the ordinary for you to call him by his name. Don't you agree?"

"M-Mashiro."

Kon and Tobi both looked at me wide-eyed and stupefied when I cut into their conversation.

"Haha! I don't know about that. Don't girls of her age look up to older men?"

"Even if some do, it tends to cap off at guys who are in high school or university. A man FIFTEEN years older going after an underage girl is a CRIME, no?" I emphasized, glaring provocatively at Tobi.

I don't know what you're planning mister, but I won't let you get away with perving on Kon!

"...Tobi. What in the world did you do to Mashiro?"

Tobi and I had been locked in a death stare, neither willing to relent, until Miss Ayumi's exasperated voice broke us up. Sparks had been flying. If this was a game CG, I knew the artist would have drawn them in.

Heroine's Results
Target Character: Kou Narita
Event: I Understand

Original Heroine's Results
Target Character: Tobi Yamabuki
Event: An Unexpected Interruption
CLEAR

◆◆◆◆◆

♪♪♪

THE moment I entered the classroom on Tuesday, Sawa and the gang surrounded me. I didn't come in on Monday because the school gave it off to me for being at the competition all weekend.

"Congrats for making it through the quarterfinals!"

"It's all thanks to the card you guys gave me! Thank you so much!"

I had texted the good news and my thanks to my group of friends yesterday. Kids outside of that group had seen my name and the results announced in the news too. I was bombarded with questions during break.

"How was it?"

"Were you nervous?"

"What was it like?"

Tazaki came over to my desk and pestered, "What were the other participants like? Just tell me about the ladies, I don't care about the dudes."

"Every girl was cute. I guess you could say there were a lot of girls with that rich young lady feel."

"The prim and proper type, huh? Dang! I should've gone instead of gettin' all sweaty runnin' around the school grounds!"

"Stop right there! Don't go to her performance for gross reasons!" one of the girls in class quickly cut in.

"You seriously have a one-track mind," Majima marveled.

I wholeheartedly agreed with him.

♪♪♪

SATURDAY came ridiculously fast. This was the day of the semifinals where the fifteen semifinalists were going to be narrowed down even further. The song selection was Bach's "Sinfonia No. 9 in F minor". To the listener, this song might sound simple and uncomplicated depending on the performer, but Bach's counterpoint was the most pronounced in this piece. The sigh motif began with a rest, giving it a breathless urgency. The dissonance born of the descending chromatic figure that came from combining the other two motifs played to the listeners' angst and grieving. The last three chords were a symbol of hope. This Sinfonia, masterfully composed as a complex, tightly knit two-minute piece, was a song pianists must learn to play if they were to tackle Bach in any way.

The competition rules stated that participants must pick a different composer from the quarterfinals for their free song selection. Many of the participants were likely to select Chopin for their free piece with the high technical demands his music placed on a performer while still allowing them to put a unique spin on the music. Chopin was no longer an option for me.

"As far as I can tell from looking at the free song list, your song choice doesn't clash with any other participant." Miss Ayumi looked with satisfaction at the song list handed out before the semifinal.

"What a relief. Is it mostly Chopin?"

"For the most part. Rachmaninoff and Liszt make up the rest."

That's exactly how I thought it'd turn out.

My selected song, "Pavane for a Dead Princess", wasn't a technically difficult piece. Some people might think that the nostalgic lyricism would come back to bite me, with its unsuitability for competitions.

But I chose this piece exactly because I would be performing before the same judging committee. Performing a song that gave a totally different impression from the quarterfinals was a strategic way to stand out from the crowd.

For the semifinals, I abandoned my school uniform for a pale-blue short-sleeved dress.

Miss Sakurako and Miss Chisako actually went out of their way to bring this dress to my house. They were both disgruntled that Kon had prevented them from going crazy with it, which was why it ended up being a simple knee-length dress.

"We'll have an even more gorgeous concert dress prepared for the finals!" they effused with flowery smiles and disappeared from our house, leaving Mom and I feeling grateful and sorry at the same time.

They were actually coming to see my performance today too. I sincerely wanted to put on the best performance I could to show them my gratitude for doting on me as if I was another daughter.

Eyes closed, I ran my hands down the silky satin sleeves. My concentration was at an all-time high. *I want to get on stage soon.* I was registered to play last in the morning.

A tall boy was performing Liszt's "Mephisto Waltz" when the competition staff led me over to the stage wing. The percussive violence of the bass arpeggios and the tempo speed left nothing for want as might be expected from a boy with lots of physical strength. He brilliantly pulled off hammering out the tetrachord in fortissimo arpeggiated figures.

His performance came to an end while I was marveling over how the people left in the semifinals were truly skilled. He departed the stage with a satisfied expression over the roaring applause. Only five participants would be left in the finals. Thinking about that fact made the fear well up inside me, so I slammed my eyes shut and drove the wicked thoughts from my mind.

"Number 8, Mashiro Shimao. Performing Ravel's 'Pavane for a Dead Princess' as her free song."

The audience clamored over the announcement. My song choice was probably a real shock after the long, difficult pieces from composers like Brahms, Chopin, and Liszt. Worry surged within me for a moment, but there was nothing I could do after coming this far already. Eyes locked on the piano, I walked on stage. I took a bow and raised the bench's height. Placing my hands on the keyboard, I took a deep breath.

Bach – Sinfonia No.9

The tempo played slowly, while keeping the momentum standing against the steady plodding of the lament motif. I let this song, where a crescendo and decrescendo coexisted in one measure, ring out with hope. It painted the picture of mass at a cathedral; like a sliver of light shining in through the stained-glass windows. Imagining those people who struggled in the pursuit of happiness, my hands raced across the keys. Music spread through the concert hall sounding exactly how I imagined it.

Without stepping on the pedal, I accentuated a series of notes in the legato. Legato phrases required all of the notes to be smoothly connected with the same tonal quality, with no intervening silence. Otherwise, the two notes wouldn't flow together. Connecting two notes without a moment of silence was far easier said than done. Going the extra mile to practice that part paid off—I played it pretty well.

I took a breath and centered myself.

The concert hall had fallen silent.

The free song was to be played next.

Ravel – Pavane for a Dead Princess

Ravel wanted to create his own music free from the classical harmonic progression, but it's said that he didn't achieve the sound he was aiming for with this song. How ironic it must have been for the composer that he had instead succeeded in capturing a nostalgic primary melody capable of strongly moving the listener. The secondary melody played as if placed on the other side of a mirror. The excellent balance and refined composition of this song was part of what made it appealing.

I kept the volume to a bare minimum according to the Tres lointain (very distant) notation. Rather than just play the pianissimo as is, I stroked the keys with the intention of changing the notes into the dazzling light hidden far beyond the cracks in the clouds. And then, towards the middle, I emphasized each note at a volume close to forte.

This same melody existed in two different worlds at the same time. The people I could never reach again were reflected beyond the mirror. Lending my ear to the faint whispers I heard, I screamed with the piano on this side of the glass. Only this music could freely transverse between the two worlds that could never converge.

Please, reach them. I pleaded with the piano. *Please reach the dear people I can never touch again. I'm right here, beyond the mirror.*

To the father, mother, and friends and family I will never see again: the time I spent with those of you I left behind makes up who I am today. But I still can't stop thinking of you. I long to see you again.

Focusing every fiber of my being into my fingers, I wrote my feelings into this song.

Letting the final note ring out, I lifted my arms and returned my hands to my lap.

Sporadic applause broke the tranquility. All at once, the light clapping spread through the concert hall like a thunderstorm. Some people even stood as they applauded. Surrounded by unceasing applause, I bowed and left the stage.

I wanted to play more. I wanted to make even more beautiful music with that piano. It was the first time I had ever felt this way.

I returned to the waiting room and dashed over to Miss Ayumi. "How did I do?" I panted out.

Miss Ayumi wiped the tears at the corner of her eyes with a slender finger. "It was a superb…performance."

I took a reflexive step back. My knees buckled under the ultimate praise from my mentor, who rarely gave compliments.

"Um, I guess I didn't make any mistakes then!"

"It's not even within the realm of not making mistakes. You were just eight years old, you know? When you first came to my lessons and faltered your way through Bayer with tiny fingers. You've come this far in just six years, Mashiro." Miss Ayumi put both hands on my shoulders and searched deep into my eyes. "Let's take this road together. You have the talent to pull it off. Expand your horizons as far as they can go then broaden them some more, and change that into your music. Then let the world hear your music."

"Yes, Miss Ayumi." I was baffled by her word choice that made it sound like she was positive I would make it into the finals.

The afternoon half of the performances still remained. Only five of the fifteen who performed today would make it into the finals.

I waved goodbye to Miss Ayumi who said she had some business to attend to and then went with my family to a nearby diner for lunch. It felt weird having my overly excited parents piling praise after praise on me.

"That's our Mashiro," they said together.

"That's Daddy's girl," Mom giggled.

"No, no, that's Mommy's girl," Dad insisted.

Why did their compliments always devolve into them complimenting each other like a dorky, lovey-dovey couple?

"Okay, we have to head home first. Give our regards to Miss Ayumi."

"Sure. Thanks for coming today."

"You did a great job out there, Mashiro. Let's splurge and go out for sushi tonight."

"Woohoo!"

I watched Dad's sparklingly clean car drive off before returning to the concert hall.

I showed my participant pass to the doorman and entered the concert hall. Almost all of the seats were taken, but some seats were specifically set aside for participants, and the usher escorted me there.

Now I was free to relax and enjoy the performances as just another member of the audience.

If I'm not wrong, the third year from Seio is performing last in the afternoon half. Oh, he picked Liszt's "Études d'exécution transcendante d'après Paganini No. 6" huh? Nice! Very nice!

Paganini's original violin song was known as a difficult piece to play, but Liszt's etude also proved to be quite the challenge. The technically demanding work abounded with rapid octaves, scales, and arpeggios, which made it easy to mess up, but it was practically guaranteed the performer would receive high marks if they were able to pull it off with zero mistakes and with ample volume during the fortissimo.

His performance during the quarterfinals was fantastic too. It was him who should have taken the stage during Seio's Christmas concert, not Yukiko Sawakura. I ran my finger down the list of performers until I landed on his name.

His name is Kakeru Tominaga, huh? Throwing a likely winner with real ability into the music competitions is just like Prince Tobi.

Every contestant was fantastic. For every contestant who played faithfully and accurately to the sheet music, there was one contestant who put their own surprising, unique twist on the song that made you think, "aren't they straying too far from the original?" Of course, some were swallowed whole by the atmosphere of the competition and made a series of mistakes that had me come close to covering my ears.

Aw, I understand how you feel! You get nervous the more people tell you not to.

Before I knew it, it was time for the last performance of the day. I was seriously sick of hearing Bach by this point. I might've lost my mind if not for the free songs.

"Number 15, Kakeru Tominaga. Playing Liszt's 'Études d'exécution transcendante d'après Paganini No. 6' as his free song."

Hooray! It's his turn! I thoroughly observed Kakeru play a textbook rendition of Bach like he was the star of the day's performances. He had also abandoned his school uniform for a black suit and a pale blue, pinstripe shirt. He wasn't especially tall, but his balanced proportions made him look slender. His short, fluffy orange hair accentuated his sharply drawn eyebrows and pretty black eyes.

Liszt – Études d'exécution transcendante d'après Paganini No. 6

The introduction opened with a striking arpeggio. Every keystroke had significant weight behind it. The fortissimo packed an impressive punch. This was the performance of a pianist with fairly large hands. He pulled off the chord consisting of ten continuous notes with his left hand with ease. I was overwhelmed by the sound of the piano I felt reverberating through the pit of my stomach.

I struggled to stay seated while listening to it. *Oh, wow. This is amazing! I want to play like this too!*

The mournful ring of the high notes toward the middle ignited within my chest. If I had to describe his performance in a word, it'd be passionate. He made three mistakes, but his power of expression was more than enough to compensate for it. It was frustrating to admit to myself, but I wasn't capable of producing a sound like his. My hands weren't strong enough yet to make the fortissimo shake through the hall like thunder. There was a limit to how far putting my body weight into it could make up for the lack of strength in my small hands.

I balled my hands into tight little fists. *I want to grow up faster. I want more strength to play like this.* I kept my eyes locked on the boy on stage as a fierce fighting spirit blazed within me.

All of the middle school performances were over, so the judging committee commenced their decision making. I left the concert hall and scanned the area for Miss Sakurako and Miss Chisako to thank them for coming.

Odd, I don't see them anywhere. I wonder if they went home after my performance.

I had plans to get together with Kon and Kou after the results were announced. I fished through my bag for my cell phone to confirm the time with them. *Where is it?* My hands came back empty.

Gone…it's gone?!

I scoured through my bag again and again, but my cell phone didn't turn up. I didn't use it when I went out to eat with my parents. *When did I use it last…um…the waiting room!* I had thought I turned off the power and slipped it into my bag before my performance. That would make the waiting room the only place I could have dropped it. Panicking, I spun around and headed back the way I came.

I nearly rammed into a boy when I rushed around the hallway corner. Forcing my feet to come to a quick stop had been a bad idea.

"Ack!" The boy I was trying not to run into caught me just as I was about to fall on my face. "I-I'm so sorry!"

I-I'm saved! Scratching up my face didn't bother me, but it'd be terrible if I banged up my hands or arms.

"Thank you very much! I am really sorry!" I deeply bowed my head and took off in search of my phone. The boy called out to me from behind after I'd gone no more than a few steps.

"Hey, you."

"Yes?"

"Are you possibly looking for your cell phone?" The boy held up my pink cell phone in his right hand.

"AH! That's mine!"

The cute panda charm hanging from the phone was something I'd made. There was no mistaking that the phone was mine.

I'm so glad I found it! Overcome with relief, I felt like squatting on the ground when I finally took a good look at the boy's face. *K-Kakeru T-Tominaga?!*

"Here you go. Also, sorry if this is meddlesome, but you should really lock your phone. Then again, it's only thanks to you not locking it that I knew it was yours right away," Kakeru said, handing me my cell phone.

The heat rushed to my cheeks. He had seen my wallpaper screen! I'd recently switched my wallpaper to the selfie I took with Sawa and Mako when we went to see the fireworks display during summer break. It was a crazy shot we had drawn heart marks and weird faces on. It was so embarrassing to have that seen!

"Sorry again. And thank you very much for picking it up for me." I took a full ninety-degree angle bow and tried to make my way back to the lobby.

"Wait up," Kakeru called out to me, stopping me for the second time. "We still have time until the results are announced. If you don't mind, want to chat for a bit?"

Hostility was absent from his tone. I could sense he just wanted to talk to another participant in the same competition. More than happy to oblige, I agreed on the spot. I was dying to know what kind of lesson plan he followed to be capable of producing that passionate, powerful sound.

"There's a vending machine in the lobby. Let's go there," Kakeru suggested.

The eyes of the other participants and the audience members followed us as we walked side by side. They were scrutinizing us hard. I instinctively looked myself over. My stockings weren't ripped and my skirt wasn't flipped up.

Why are they staring so much?

Contrary to my anxiety, Kakeru was the picture of calm. "Don't worry. You look fine."

"Uh?" I uttered stupidly from the sheer shock of him reading my thoughts. If I was Kakeru, I would've been a little put off by how weird the girl I was with was acting.

Kakeru, however, simply shrugged and explained, "They're probably curious why the two sure picks for finalist are walking together." He searched my dumbfounded face with great interest.

"Sure pick for finalist?" I repeated.

"You really have no self-awareness after putting on such a groundbreaking performance, huh? Top off your performance with the fact that your mentor is *the* Ayumi Matsushima, and it's no wonder you were marked as a sure pick for finalist from the beginning."

"Hah. If you say so," was all I managed to say in response.

Miss Ayumi is even more famous than I thought, I mused while trying to come up with a more intelligent answer.

Kakeru stood in front of the vending machine and asked, "What will you have?"

"Oh, warm tea for me."

Kakeru held out his left hand, stopping me from pulling my wallet out of my bag, and purchased both of our drinks. "Don't worry about it. You're a second year, right? Let your elders treat you." There was nothing pushy about his eloquent smile. This was one of those occasions where firmly refusing was ruder than accepting.

"Thank you. You've done so much for me since the moment we met."

He returned my cell phone and even treated me to tea. *He's a good guy. Now that I think about it, he even matched his pace to mine when we were walking. I don't think there are many boys our age who are conscientious enough to walk in step with a girl. Does he have an older sister? Or maybe a girlfriend?*

Then again…maybe every student at Seio is like this. I wouldn't be surprised if someone told me that they have a class on "how to escort a lady" as a part of their main curriculum.

At the gentlemanly Kakeru's suggestion, I sat across from him on the couch next to the vending machine.

"I was shocked when I saw your profile. You attend a normal public school, right?"

"Yeah. I'm from a normal household that can't afford to pay for a private school," I answered honestly. Pretending otherwise wouldn't do anything for me.

Kakeru smiled broadly. His difficult to approach, stalwart image crumbled before my eyes, giving way to a cute boy. "You're funny, Mashiro."

I don't get rich people humor, I thought, sighing aloud in response to his comment.

He quickly rushed to amend his statement. "I wasn't making fun of you. I'm sorry if it sounded that way."

"Nah, it's okay," I laughed this time.

He actually seems like the type who cares. We looked at each other and smiled, creating a sudden openness between us.

"Um, is it all right if I ask you some questions?" I asked, fully aware of how rude my frankness was.

"I'd be happy to answer if it's something I know," Kakeru gladly assented.

"How much do you practice on average?"

"Hmm. I practice the basics for about thirty minutes, then go on for a total of two hours or so playing songs I like and studying sheet music for new songs, I'd say."

"That's it?!"

He only plays two hours a day?! He can play that well with that little practice?! Isn't he a little too amazing?!

"Yup. I struggle with concentrating for long periods of time. It's a bad habit, I know. You heard the few mistakes I made today, right? My teacher always nags on me about that part, but I still failed to pull it off when it counts." He gave a roguish smile.

"Wow," I breathed in awe.

I wanted the mindset that allowed him to laugh off screwing up the same part when it counts out of lack of practice instead of just nerves getting the better of him.

Just try messing up a section Miss Ayumi points out to you. She doesn't give second chances... I shivered.

"How about you, Shimao?"

"About four hours during the week and all day long on the weekends."

"Holy crap! Are you freakin' serious?!" It was Kakeru's turn to be shocked half out of his chair. He slipped into a more casual tone, sounding more like a boy his age. "Are you the type to hash out the same song for hours?"

"Mm-hm. I'll keep practicing until I can play it well."

"Makes sense to me. Your Bach was dead on and you played Pavane with attention to every subtle nuance. I thought it was the result of the emotion you put into it, but turns out you're actually someone who works hard," Kakeru laughed.

Hey! What does he mean it turns out I'm actually someone who works hard?! I don't see my results as anything other than from hard work. I must look like a real space case to him.

"I'm an ordinary person. Hard work is all I have going for me."

"Where'd you come up with a funny idea like that?" Kakeru asked.

I confided in him about the way a certain person used to tease me and give me weird nicknames.

"S-Space case? Poor girl?"

"Yeah! Isn't it horrible?"

"Pft!" Kakeru cracked up. Through his chuckles he asked, "Was it a boy who called you those names?"

How did he know? I nodded.

"He called you names in elementary school?" he continued. "Isn't that a case of teasing a girl because you like them then?"

"ABSOLUTELY NOT! Never in a million years."

Kakeru could come to such a horrifying conclusion because he didn't know better. That triumphant look on Kou's face when he called me those names was ingrained in my mind. He always had this look that implied, "A mere normo like you dares to think you can ever defeat me? Hah!"

Huh? I actually can't remember the last time he called me names.

"Thank you very much for waiting. The judging committee has finished making their selection. Participants please return to the concert hall."

The announcement over the loudspeaker gave us the push to gather up our things and stand.

"Aaaaaah. I'm so nervous," I moaned.

"You are? I'm fairly positive you and I will be finalists, Shimao."

His apathetic manner of speaking only fueled my nervousness. *I wonder if he's used to competitions. Lucky him. It'd be so much easier on me if I could take it easy like him.*

I walked back to the concert hall together with Kakeru. Out of the corner of my eye I spotted Tobi lying in wait for us next to the doors.

Geh! I've bumped into the worst possible person at the worst time.

I grimaced, while opposite of me Kakeru cheerfully greeted Tobi, "Director Yamabuki! You came to see me?"

"Of course I did. A representative of our school is participating in this competition. I could never miss it."

I barely managed to tamp down the impulse to strut by him with a casual, "Yo." Doing that in front of Kakeru would've ruined his image of me. Tobi could hate me for all I cared, but I didn't want to upset Kakeru after the lovely conversation we just had.

"Your performance today was most elegant, Mashiro."

"Thank you. I believe Miss Ayumi is waiting for me inside, so if you will excuse me," I said in perfunctory greeting, forcing a smile as I tried to pass by him, but Tobi gracefully held out his left arm.

"Then allow me to escort you to your seat, *my little princess*." He had a soft demeanor, but the smile didn't reach his eyes.

Determining that pushing him away here would only lead to him doing something horrible to me later, I helplessly placed my right hand on his arm.

"You know Shimao?" Kakeru asked, wide-eyed.

"Yes. She's someone I have known since she was just a little girl." Tobi winked at Kakeru and opened the door to the concert hall.

It wasn't a lie, but something about that explanation didn't sit well with me.

We entered the main concert hall, and he escorted me all the way to the reserved seating. He helped me take my seat beside Miss Ayumi then sat on the other side of me. He had Kakeru sit on the other side of him.

"You were with Tobi?" Miss Ayumi asked me in a hushed voice.

I shook my head. "I was chatting with Kakeru."

"With Seio's Kakeru?" Miss Ayumi blinked in surprise.

Just as Kakeru predicted, we both made it into the finals. Roaring applause congratulated us before the judges' comments were announced.

Sadia Francesca gave me an A this time as well. Some of the judges expressed concern that my song choice wasn't difficult enough, but when I later learned that Sadia appointed me as a finalist before anyone else, I felt a mix of joy, gratitude, and humbleness.

"See you at the finals."

"I'm looking forward to your performance."

"Thanks. Let's put on the best show we can."

Kakeru held out his right hand, and I firmly shook it. His hand was one size bigger than mine. He had a soft palm and slender, angular fingers.

This is a pianist's hand. I don't want to lose!

Preferences for composers and interpretations of the piece varied per the judge. But I hoped to perform in such a way that surpassed all those things and moved their hearts.

Naturally, Kakeru received a praiseworthy evaluation too. During the car ride home, Kon told me that after the results were announced, everyone in the lobby was whispering about how it was going to be a showdown between the two of us.

"You have to play a sonata for the finals. I think it's safe to say that Tominaga will play Rachmaninoff. That's his favorite composer. I often see him performing pieces composed by him at Seio." Kon closely studied my face in the car. "Are you still planning to go with Schumann, Mashiro?"

"Yeah. I kinda hate to follow *Hear My Heart*'s plot at this point, but I love that song, and I've been practicing it all this time. I'm going to play Schumann's 'Piano Sonata no.2 in G minor'."

"Okay. Good luck. Your performance today was exceptional too. I'm looking forward to hearing you play in the finals."

Kon's encouragement was more reassuring than anything else. I was honestly happy just to have a calm talk alone with her like this. The pesky interrupter was absent this time. Kon told me that Kou was captured by the upperclassman groupies from Seio who came to cheer Kakeru on.

"Kou never lets his displeasure over the girls show on his face like he did today. He must have really wanted to come home with us," Kon giggled.

I gave one big nod. "Well, duh. It's obvious he'd pick you if it's a choice between pandering to the groupies or spending time with his beloved sister."

"Uh…" For some reason, Kon was speechless.

Was she disappointed by Kou's sister complex again? *But I'm pretty sure she should just accept her fate. Kou has a hardcore sister complex. Not like I'm one to speak.*

CG 30: Direct Confrontation (Heroine)

THE third Saturday since quarterfinals had arrived.

The green leaves decorating the roadside trees in the last vestiges of summer were already beginning to change color in front of the concert hall. The breeze caressing my cheeks had developed a shuddering chill, accompanied by the tormenting reminder of how fast time passed.

Midori, who was on fall break, came to Japan just as she'd promised.

"You came all this way just to cheer me on during the competition?" I asked her on the phone, feeling guilty.

She laughed it off. "Silly, Mashiro. You make it sound like such a big deal when it's not."

Midori made traveling the vast distance between England and Japan sound no different than a trip from Tokyo to Osaka. *I'm pretty sure there's close to 6,000 miles between them. The rich and famous are scary!*

Supposedly her family owned a lavish mansion in Denenchofu, but Midori had come to love Maestro Noboru's quaint house in the woods. She told me over the phone on Friday that she would be staying there for her duration in Japan.

"Can you cook, Midori?" I asked.

"Of course I can't," she responded in a pointlessly confident voice over the receiver. "Whenever I need something, I'll just call one of the maids over from the main house."

She's going to have the maid come over every time she wants to eat, wash her clothes, and clean? Poor maid… I put my hands together for a moment of silence for the maid I didn't know. *I hope her family adds extra pay for all that commuting!*

"Hey, you're free on Sunday, right? Let's invite Kon and go hang out somewhere! It can double as a party to celebrate your victory!"

"Please stop tripling the pressure on me by saying stuff like that! What are we going to do if it turns into a pity party instead?"

I could just imagine myself sitting there with the gravity of depression weighing me down, while two beautiful girls sat on either side trying to comfort me. The image alone was just too pathetic.

"There you go again! I know being humble is a Japanese virtue, but it's going out of style these days, girl. I saw the video of the semifinals uploaded on the competition website. You were the best one there, Mashiro. As long as you don't epically screw up, the championship is as good as yours."

What would be an epic screw up? Her praise went right through one ear and out the other, leaving only the discomforting thoughts behind to haunt me. I could just see myself forgetting the sheet music and drawing a complete blank in front of an audience in the thousands.

"Yeah…I'll try."

"Take it easy, Mashiro!" Midori hung up after leaving those last words of encouragement.

I glanced over at the pale-green concert dress hanging on my wall. Miss Chisako and Miss Sakurako had dropped it off just before Midori called. The sleeveless, simple A-line dress dazzled with shimmering pearls inlaid along the golden embroidery, accentuating the chest and hem. This dress alluded to the mothers' true efforts after they were forced to prepare a simple dress for the quarterfinals under Kon's watchful eye.

They really looked disappointed the first time. I wonder how much this cost. The thought alone made my stomach churn.

Sleep eluded me. I rolled over in bed, tossing and turning until my sheets wrapped around me. I reached for the good luck charm from Rei and the colored card from my friends that I kept next to my pillow. Hugging Becchin at my side, I read and reread their messages.

Everything was going to be decided tomorrow.

I probably won't get to attend Seio if I don't win. There are some professional pianists out there who never attended music school, so it's not like that path will be closed off forever.

But still…it'd kill me not to accomplish the dream I've been striving toward for years. I don't want to fail the expectations of everyone who has supported me until now. What should I do? Will I really be able to play properly?

The sound of Kakeru's powerful music during the semifinals beat in my ears, keeping me awake until the wee hours of the morning.

♪♪♪

SEPARATE waiting rooms were prepared for the five finalists.

I changed into my concert dress and had Hanaka put up my hair. My pale complexion reflected in the mirror was a far cry from looking healthy.

"You still have time before you're up. What would you like to do in the meantime?" Miss Ayumi asked.

I breathed a sigh. "Is it all right if I go outside for some fresh air?"

My performance was the last of the day. *Is the first finalist already on stage?* I didn't have it in me to listen to the other finalists. I was scared it'd influence my own performance.

"Sure. Come back in fifteen minutes."

"Okay."

"Good luck, Mashiro! I'll be cheering you on from the audience!"

"Okay. Thanks, Hanaka."

Pinching the corners of my dress to keep from stepping on the hem, I left the waiting room. *I think there's a rest area in the garden behind the hall. I'll get some fresh air and refresh my mood there.*

Destination in mind, I walked around the hallway corner and bumped into the person I wanted to see the least. Tobi. Kakeru Tominaga was written on the nameplate hanging on the door he had stepped out of.

"Hello, Mashiro. You look quite stunning in today's dress," Tobi complimented with a smarmy smile while he assessed me with his eyes.

"Hello. Thank you," I said briefly, trying to make my way by him. My faint hope that I'd be able to escape him this time was dashed by the hovering presence I felt directly behind me.

Dang it! Why the heck is this guy following me?!

At all costs, I had to avoid accidentally falling right before the biggest performance of my life. *If only I was wearing sneakers, I would run away from him at maximum speed!* I walked on in silence, internally layering curse after curse on him.

I slipped out the automatic doors connecting to the back garden, where an invigorating breeze tousled my hair. There wasn't a single cloud in the clear blue sky. *The weather is great today.*

Taking several deep breaths, I tried my best to shut Tobi out of my thoughts, which soon proved impossible.

"Excuse me…should you really be here right now?" I blurted, my ability to handle his presence past its limits.

He stepped beside me and stared down at my face with phony affection. "We are only minutes away from the critical performance of a lifetime. I can't leave you all alone at a time like this, Mashiro."

"Is that so? I would much rather be left alone though." I walked over to the bench, mulling over how I could get rid of him.

"Wait. Your dress will be sullied if you just sit down." Tobi pulled a large white handkerchief from his suit pocket and spread it over the wooden bench. He looked like such a perfect gentleman with those smooth gestures of his.

Dang it! He got me. Now I have to sit next to him.

"Thank you," I reluctantly said, perching on the edge of the bench. Tobi sat down beside me.

"How are you faring today?"

"…Not very good," I admitted, since it wasn't like I could hide it.

Tobi's eyes bulged as if he couldn't believe his ears. "Mashiro, are you an idiot?"

"Excuse me?"

He's the one who started this fight, but I'll happily go to war with him.

"See, you always let what you're thinking show on your face. I'm on the side of your rival today. Do you even understand that?"

Is he trying to compel me to view him as the enemy? Ha! I don't need you to tell me that now. I've viewed you as the enemy for years, pervert!

"I understand. But I won't lie. I'm not in a good state right now. So I wish you would leave me alone."

Go away, would ya?! I insisted with my eyes.

Tobi, who was by no means dumb or dense, ignored me. "I was planning on asking you a favor today, but it appears I won't have to." A derisive sneer curled the corner of his lips.

"What favor?"

"I want you to let Tominaga win. That's what I was thinking about asking of you."

I was too shocked for words. Was he insane?!

I flayed Tobi with my eyes, but he merely shrugged.

"It was merely a thought. Don't get the wrong idea. Hear me out."

I sprung to my feet and swiped the handkerchief from the bench. "I will wash and return this to you later. Goodbye." Glaring at him with every ounce of contempt in my body, I tried to get away by walking past him.

"What if I said I'll make you a scholarship student at Seio if you help me save face today?" Tobi bluntly offered while crossing his legs in front of me.

The shock was like a punch to the head. Dizzy, I staggered and was held up by his hand of all things. Tobi's sweet cologne made the bile rise in the back of my throat, and I quickly pressed the handkerchief to my mouth.

"I took the opportunity to investigate your aspirations. Don't you want to attend Seio? I could easily make your dreams come true. It's not a bad offer, is it?" Tobi's voice was sickeningly gentle.

This...this nauseating joke is the competition event I'd been waiting for? Is this the only way for me to achieve my dreams?

"Is it really all that startling? But I guess in your current state, tackling the final is beyond you now. Dropping out before you set foot on stage is another option." Tobi's singsong voice sent my thoughts into disarray.

This is so frustrating! Get a hold of yourself, Mashiro! I ordered my trembling legs to move, but they wouldn't listen to me.

"Let's take this road together. You have the talent to pull it off."

"Good luck! I know just how hard you've been working at the piano, Mashiro. You'll do amazing!"

My fingers wouldn't stop trembling. *Everyone has gone above and beyond to encourage me. I don't have the time to clear out my thoughts. I have to stand on stage in less than half an hour. Can I do it in this state?*

What should I do? What can I do?

"So this is where you were, Mashiro. You have to get ready to go on stage soon. Let's head back in together."

It was Kon who saved me from the brink of breaking down. From beginning to end, she was always my guardian angel.

Seeing Kon show up behind the concert hall brought me so much relief my knees nearly buckled. She walked swiftly over and rescued me from Tobi's hands.

"It's okay. Hold on to me." Kon wrapped her arms around me when all I could do was nod, and guided me towards the automatic doors.

Not once did she acknowledge Tobi.

I should've treated Tobi like that too, I absently thought.

Kon handed me a chilled bottle of mineral water back at the waiting room. I took a sip and washed away the bitter taste permeating my mouth. I was informed that Miss Ayumi had already moved to her seat in the audience.

Kou and Midori were waiting for my return in the waiting room, and they gasped when they saw my face.

"What the—"

"Mashiro?!"

A knock on the door stopped them from saying more as the competition coordinator popped her head into the waiting room. "Miss Shimao, please head over to the stage wing now."

"...Okay." It took me until that moment to realize that I had been clutching Tobi's handkerchief.

Disgusting! I threw it reflexively on the floor. Kou's whole countenance changed when he caught sight of Tobi's initials embroidered in the handkerchief's right corner.

He grimly picked up the handkerchief, confirmed the initials, and swore, "Damn it."

"Use this, Mashiro." Midori handed me her handkerchief. I accepted it from her with a shaking hand. She pressed her soft hands around my right hand. "I know Sou is cheering you on right now. He was super ecstatic about watching it live online."

"You're amazing, Mashiro!" The image of a younger Sou squinting at me like I was the most dazzling light in his world crossed my mind.

Ahh, he's the one person I don't want to see me like this.

"I've got to go." I paused at the door and looked over my shoulder at my three friends.

I'm so ashamed. Tears are blurring my vision.

Kon was practically staring a hole through me as she clenched her teeth. Kou was scowling with an expression that captured a mix of emotions: worry, regret, and intense anger.

It's my first time seeing him make that face. My first time seeing Kou without any composure. I couldn't help myself from letting out a small giggle.

The second I laughed, the memory of that day I longed for, to play music side by side with Kou, Sou, and Kon, came rushing back to me in full color.

That's right. That was my true dream. Not winning this competition or enrolling in Seio.

I'll muster everything I have and climb to new heights with my own ability.

My hands had stopped shaking.

Heroine's Results
Target Character: None
Event: Determination
CLEAR

The finalist performing right before my turn was already on stage. Kakeru's rendition of Rachmaninoff's "Piano Sonata No. 2" drifted down the hallway as I made my way to the stage wing.

"Please hurry," the coordinator rushed me.

I walked as fast as possible without tripping. The pearls on the hem of my dress glittered in the dim backstage lights.

As I thought, the resonance of Kakeru's lower register notes is exceptional. He's extremely talented with the way he uses the pedal, vividly laying on the next phrase while letting the prior note trail behind it.

Rachmaninoff's "Piano Sonata No. 2" has three versions in circulation: Rachmaninoff's original version, his revised version, and finally the Horowitz's revision which combines elements from Rachmaninoff's original and revised versions. I was very curious which version Kakeru would play. It turned out to be the revised version.

The second movement had a relaxed tempo that could come across as boring depending on the player. Kakeru maintained the high tension of the first movement, transforming its softness into a captivating whisper. He had a dramatic way of adding the stresses, making the fortissimo especially prominent.

Natsu

I listened carefully, allowing myself to become lost in Kakeru's Rachmaninoff. The heavy chords that are said to have the sound of church bells as the motif, reverberated at the bottom of my stomach. Choosing a song that required him to play for twenty minutes without pause allowed him to display his physical strength for the judges.

He's really good.

Kakeru's passionate play style was a perfect fit for Rachmaninoff's piano music, which idealized masculine sound. The most frustrating thing about his performance was the inevitable mistakes I heard throughout it. His slip-ups on the irregular arpeggios and arpeggiated descent were particularly painful to sit through. I had no idea how it would affect his final evaluation, but I was relieved.

I'm horrible. How could I rejoice over my rival's failure? But those ugly feelings were undeniably a piece of me too. *What right do I have to rag on Tobi when I'm just as bad? Maybe anyone can become a monster if they let jealously, vanity, and self-importance rule them. If I don't want to become like that, I'll have to resist with my whole being and work toward the person I do want to become.*

A whirlwind of applause burst from the audience after the final note faded from the stage. Relief spread over Kakeru's face as he took a bow and left the stage.

"Number 5, Mashiro Shimao."

The announcer's voice echoed through the concert hall as I pinched the sides of my dress and headed straight for the piano on stage. Only five people were allowed the honor of playing this piano today.

When I put it into perspective, it's pretty amazing I was even picked as a finalist in a major music competition like this.

The audience looked dark from the bright stage, but I could tell it was a full house. Somewhere in the silence sat my family, Miss Ayumi, Miss Chisako, Miss Sakurako, Kon, Kou, and Midori. No doubt Sou was sitting in front of his computer waiting for my performance too.

Thank you, everyone.

I bowed to the audience then adjusted the bench height.

My heart was at peace, almost as if the chaos from before was a figment of my imagination. Taking a deep breath, I laid my fingers on the keys.

Schumann – Piano Sonata No.2 in G minor

There were two particularly difficult, or rather, compelling aspects to this sonata.

The first was the tempo speed. Straightaway the pianist was asked to play "so rasch wie möglich" (as fast as possible), only to find in the coda the marking "schneller" (faster), and, in the concluding bars, "noch schneller" (even faster)! It made the pianist want to ask, "just how fast do you want me to play?!" But speed was essential to this song as it demanded the pianist play "appassionata" (passionate).

The second difficulty was the percolating arpeggiated texture in the left hand. It's said that this sonata puts a great emphasis on the size of the pianist's hands. Schumann was known to have large hands, so it's assumed he composed the song using his hands as the standard.

He had supposedly composed this song after giving up on following the road of a pianist and resolving to live as a composer. He'd composed the song around the same time he was distressed by Clara Wieck's, the future Mrs. Schumann, father opposing his marriage to his daughter. But Schumann never gave up no matter the setbacks and failures he went through.

How painful that must've been for him. But he never once stopped reaching for music and his distressing love.

The first movement was played with a sorrowful cry from the heart and a sweep of passion. *I can play this fast?* I marveled, surprised by how my repeated strikes of the keys gathered the notes into a twinkling gem that rolled through the air.

And then the second movement came. The C major's romantic motif was played as if singing about one's love with the piano. Letting the chords sing, my hands raced over the keys as if I were weaving together a love letter to those dearest to me.

I wonder if this letter will reach Sou in Germany. I sure hope it does. I hope my prayers for your happiness reach you.

The third movement returned to G minor with the Scherzo. It featured a rapid tempo, a brief trio section, and an urgent melody that reversed the gentle impression from the second movement. I struck the keyboard with all my strength for this part.

The third movement gave way to the final movement. *Just how beautiful can I make the octave tremolo sound?* Mustering the last of my strength, I added accents to the theme, bringing it to the forefront, and sprinted through it with the image of swaying waves in mind.

I won't lose. Knock me down as many times as you want, I'll always get back on my feet and work my way back here. With those feelings, I earnestly fought to reproduce the beautiful series of notes Schumann had composed. I let the last chord ring out and lifted my arms.

As if finishing a marathon at full speed, I panted for air.

Fighting back the desire to flop over, I picked up the handkerchief I left on the music rack at the same time an ear-piercing rumble shook the ground. It was applause. I stood from the bench and faced the audience, where I witnessed member after member standing from their seats clapping. Some people even shouted, "Bravo!" The audience was delighted by my performance in a way I never thought possible for a student competition.

Overjoyed beyond measure, I dropped into a deep bow and slowly walked off the stage. Excitement vibrated through my entire body. My feet were so unsteady on the ground it was hard to believe I didn't step on my dress and fall flat on my face.

♪♪♪

Sadia Francesca Junior Music Competition: Junior High Division Finals: A Critique

EACH of the five finalists enchanted the audience with their talent, showing a glimpse of what they have in store for us in the future. The world still has this outdated notion that Japanese pianists put on mechanical and uninteresting performances, but I have no doubt that these young contestants will obliterate that false image once they grow up.

Kakeru Tominaga and Mashiro Shimao's performances in particular stood out as impressive. Kakeru Tominaga's dynamic rendition of Rachmaninoff's contemplative "Piano Sonata No. 2" possessed the power to suck the listener right in. The rough parts stood out, but the stately and beguiling nature of his music was truly worthy of Rachmaninoff.

On the other hand, Mashiro Shimao, paying careful attention to detail, showcased a deep understanding of Schumann's music. I know I wasn't the only one whose socks were knocked off by the sheer speed she played with during the first movement. If I were to make any critiques, there were certainly a few parts I would comment on. However, not only does she have a technically advanced foundation, she also possesses a unique world unimaginable for a fourteen-year-old. By no means did she bring about a new interpretation, and yet, that can be the only explanation for why her music has a newness to it that makes the listener think they are hearing it for the first time.

(Some pieces of this critique have been omitted for space. The rest of the music critic's comments will be published in the next magazine issue.)

♪♪♪

THE finalists gathered in the stage wing after a thirty-minute break. The final results were going to be announced soon. Kakeru smiled when he saw me. The calmness behind his smile took the weight right off my shoulders and made me think, *Phew, the competition is over at last.*

"Your performance was great."

"Your performance was phenomenal too. I wish I could've performed before you," I confessed with pursed lips.

Kakeru deliberately twisted his lips and pretended to glare at me. "Good one. You didn't even feel a tad nervous, did you?"

"I wish. I was shaking in my boots."

Thanks to that evil Director of yours, I continued in my thoughts. *Trying to tear me down right before my performance, that jerk.*

If I had ended up putting on a shameful performance because of him, I would've flown into a rage and tried to tear Tobi a new one. I shuddered imagining the headline in the next day's news saying: "Junior Music Competition Finalist Assaults Rival's Mentor?!"

All the other contestants exuded an unapproachable aura with their faces set in hard scowls. Unfriendly glances were sent our way by people who weren't too happy with us standing there holding a friendly conversation, but I stopped caring what others thought. Sure, we were rivals during the competition, but we were also two people who loved the piano. There weren't any rules stating we had to be cold to each other.

As we burned time chatting, Sadia Francesca stepped on stage, followed by the rest of the judging committee. Silence suddenly fell over the boisterous audience. Sadia walked to the middle of the stage and began speaking into the microphone set up on top of the podium. The interpreter standing beside her translated her quickly spoken Italian into Japanese.

"I am honored to have the opportunity to hold a large-scale music competition in Japan like this. I especially felt rejuvenated after having the chance to listen to all of your performances, filled with your youthful spirit. I want to say a special thanks to the finalists who put on lovely piano performances."

Sadia was supposed to be in her fifties. I expected her to have a low, authoritative voice, but she spoke with a sweet, feathery voice that reminded me of a young girl. She dropped her gaze to the list in her hand once she finished the opening pleasantries. At last, it was time to announce the winner.

Holding my breath, I waited for her to announce the name of the winner next. Even the nonchalant Kakeru had his fists clenched and his eyes focused on the stage.

Though I had been obsessed with wanting to win up until my performance, now that it was over, I had this enlightened mindset that I didn't care who won. There was no point in complaining now that it was done and over with. Maybe I felt that way because I'd done everything I could.

I can go home with my head held high, knowing that I gave it my all.

"Choosing a winner today was exceptionally difficult. Opinions were divided until the end, and no second and third place winners were chosen. Instead, two participants tied for first place," the interpreter explained, sending waves through the audience.

Nobody expected two first place winners to be selected during the first year of a new music competition. Surprise ran through the finalists standing in the stage wing. Reactions varied from sighs to squeezing handkerchiefs until they wrinkled.

I probably should've felt something more about it, but my thoughts were preoccupied with how badly I wanted to go home and get some sleep after barely sleeping last night. My fancy heels were crushing the tip of my toes and rubbing the back of my heel raw.

I want to get home, strip off my heels and this heavy dress, and jump in the tub. Then I'll take the rest of the day off from the piano and studying and dive into my bed. Yup, sounds like a great plan to me.

"*Mashiro Shimao* and *Kakeru Tominaga*," Sadia fumbled out two names in broken Japanese.

I absently watched Kakeru fist-pump the air. I didn't realize my name was called until he smacked me lightly on the shoulder.

"C'mon, let's go!"

"Erm?" I squeaked.

Ever the gentleman, he urged me to walk in front of him. Loud applause surged from the audience, welcoming us onto the brightly lit stage.

"Congratulazioni!" Sadia shook my hand then pulled me into a friendly hug. Praised by the piano virtuoso I'd always looked up to, I lost all bearing on where I was in the moment. Only the sound of thundering applause rang in my ears.

♪♪♪

I returned to my waiting room carrying the certificate of commendation, the gold trophy, and the cash award. The commemorative photoshoot was over, but I was expected to participate in interviews with the newspaper and music magazine reporters in the lobby afterwards.

It was a real relief when the coordinator told me I could change first. I wanted to hurry up and throw on a more comfortable dress and flats.

Though my body was exhausted, my mind was whirling from the excitement of winning. Strolling down the hallway feeling happy enough to skip, I opened the door to my waiting room. Already waiting inside was my family, Miss Ayumi, Kon, Kou, and Midori who had run there from the main hall. Even Miss Sakurako and Miss Chisako were inside. The fairly small and narrow room was tightly packed with people and an insane amount of flowers.

"Congratulations!" Hanaka was the first person to throw her arms around me. I could tell she had been crying the whole time because her foundation was smeared. She narrowly escaped looking like a panda thanks to her waterproof mascara.

"Thanks, Hanaka." I tried to give her a big hug back and laughed—all the stuff I was carrying got in the way of our hug.

"Congratulations. Here, why don't I take that off your hands? Is it okay on the table for now?" Kou swiftly came over and held out his hands.

"Yeah, thanks!"

Kou's timing was perfect, as always. I handed him my stuff, thinking with conviction that he was popular simply because everything about him was made to be popular.

"You were seriously…great! Like earth-shatteringly awesome! You were crazy good!" Hanaka became emotional as she told me her thoughts on my performance.

"Thanks. I was really happy you were here to hear me." I waited for Hanaka to calm down before turning to Kou and Kon. "I'm sorry you guys had to see me break down earlier. Thank you for putting me back together," I thanked them from the bottom of my heart.

Kou softly smiled and rested his hand on my head. He patted me twice before pulling his big hand away. Pathetic as it may be, his touch brought me ultimate relief. My expression melted into a dorky smile as Kou's hand overwrote the disgusting feel of Tobi's. He stared at my face.

"…Don't do this to me," he wrenched out in a husky whisper I just barely caught. This was where I'd normally get angry at him, but I ended up grinning instead because I noticed his red ears.

Kou's embarrassed! Now that's rare!

Kon looked from Kou to me and giggled behind her hand.

"Mashiro, you went out there and gave it your all!" Miss Ayumi's hands were clammy. I only ever knew her hands as being soft and dry. I immediately realized she'd been worrying about me to the point of having sweaty palms. There was no doubt in my mind that I would've never made it this far without her guidance.

"All of my success is thanks to you, Miss Ayumi. Thank you so much. I will strive to get even better!" I held Miss Ayumi's right hand in both of mine and deeply bowed to her. Seemingly lost for words, she nodded several times as she returned my handshake.

I responded to everyone's congratulations in turn and then finally got a chance to bring up the standing vases overflowing with flowers in the room.

"Um, what's with the flowers...?"

"What's wrong with them? You won the competition. A congratulatory flower wreath is a requirement."

"Chisako is right. We actually ordered them in advance. We were positive you would win, after all."

The two rich mothers answered in unison. Kon put her hand to her head and groaned.

A generous number of white, purple, and light-pink moth orchids decorated the extravagant two-tier flower stand. I felt like face-palming. Worst yet, there were five flower stands with different types of flowers decorating the tiny waiting room.

What is this? The ceremony to celebrate the opening of an influential politician's new office?! I won't ask the price. Yeah, no need to know.

Midori was talking to someone on her smartphone. When our eyes met, she flashed a toothy grin and said, "Here," as she passed me the phone.

Could it be...? I gingerly took the phone and held it to my ear.

"Hello?"

"...Congratulations."

A lump caught in my throat at the voice ringing in my ear.

It's Sou! I knew it'd be Sou!

"It's pretty early there. It's not a problem for you to be up right now?" My voice trembled despite my best efforts to talk normally. Tears welled up in my eyes, and I blinked them back several times.

"No problem at all... You've gotten better, Mashiro. Your performance was breathtaking." I heard his gentle, deep voice through the phone.

Thank goodness I saw him talking on that DVD before this. His matured voice would've made him sound like a completely different person otherwise.

The way he spoke was much calmer now too. He stopped being the adorable little Sou in my memories.

I bit my lower lip and thought of the space and time separating us. The closeness between us as children seemed like a dream now. Loneliness washed over me.

Staying quiet the whole time just because I was absorbed in sentimentalism wasn't a good idea. I pulled myself together and spoke cheerfully.

"Midori told me before my performance that you were cheering me on from Germany, So—Shiroyama," I barely stopped myself from saying his first name. "Knowing that really bolstered my confidence. I felt like I couldn't perform poorly with you listening, Shiroyama."

"...I see. I'm glad to hear that," Sou said softly after a short pause. "Congratulations again. You deserve it. Also, thanks for the letters. That's all I wanted to tell you. You don't have to give the phone back to Midori. I'll just hang up," he continued. My heart felt like it was being strung up and hung upside down.

I want to talk longer. I don't care if it's just small talk, I want to hear Sou talking in person, not just through a video.

...Uh, wait. This is an international phone call! ACK! And even worse, I'm using Midori's phone!

An insanely expensive phone bill haunting my thoughts, I quickly said goodbye. "No, I'm the one who wants to thank you. I'll write you another letter soon!"

"I'll be waiting. Till next time."

"Yup. Until next time."

We didn't have to say goodbye anymore. That alone made me unbearably happy. It gave me this delusional sense that he and I were connected forever, even if we never saw each other again.

"That's it? And what the heck is this Shiroyama business...?" Midori frowned and raked her gaze over my face.

I felt like I couldn't properly explain to Midori why I called Sou by his last name. A proper explanation would require speaking of that sad, snowy day. That was the one thing I never wanted to do.

"Thanks for letting me use your phone. I'm glad I got to speak to him after all this time," is all I said as I held out her smartphone.

"Is this your doing?" Midori pursed her lips with disdain and turned on Kou for some reason.

Kou accepted her glare head-on and lightly held up his hands. "Hardly. She's just awkward when it comes to these things. I haven't said anything... Not yet, that is."

"Hmph. So you say."

The mood between them took on a sharp, sparking edge. *Does Midori dislike Kou? I've always thought that almost every girl fell for Kou's looks and suave moves. This is like a breath of fresh air. Kou and Midori, huh? They look like a picture-perfect couple when they stand next to each other with their mouths shut.*

They both shot me questioning looks when I started grinning like an idiot.

"What's with you, Mashiro? You're creeping me out with that look in your eyes."

"I bet you're getting the wrong idea in that flower-filled head of yours again."

Two surly gazes slammed into me like bullets.

Boo. Why is everybody able to see right through what I'm thinking?

♪♪♪

I had everyone leave the room so I could change and head for the lobby. I greeted Kakeru who was already seated and took the interviews alongside him. They asked us a basic set of questions including stuff like: "How do you feel right now?" and "Were you nervous on stage?" The questions were practically identical to what I'd asked Kakeru last week. I glanced up at Kakeru just as he was looking down at me. We exchanged funny looks and laughed despite ourselves.

"Oh, what's this? You two look quite friendly with each other even though you attend different schools and piano lessons," one of the reporters noted.

As I was trying to think up an answer, that chance was taken from me—

"They might be attending the same high school." Tobi stood right beside Kakeru.

"Director Yamabuki!" Kakeru happily stood from his chair and shook hands with Tobi as if this were the first time he saw him since winning.

I, on the other hand, felt like removing my metaphorical glove and slapping him across the face with it.

"I apologize for interrupting the interview. I am Seio Academy's director, Tobi Yamabuki," Tobi greeted the reporters with a swindler's smile.

"Oh, so you're Director Yamabuki! I hear your name quite often."

Kakeru looked equally perplexed by the business card exchange party that took place between Tobi and the press. Once he finished greeting everyone, he patted both of us on the shoulder in a friendly gesture you'd expect out of a guardian or mentor.

The body's reaction tends to be more honest than the mind's—all my hair stood on end the moment he stood behind me. I struggled to endure the impulse to get up and flee the room.

"To be up-front with you all, I am in the middle of negotiations with Miss Shimao to see if she will enroll in Seio Academy as a special scholarship student. I have known her personally since she was a little girl. I was deeply torn over who I should cheer on during the finals."

LIAR! YOU BIG FAT LIAR!

The cameramen snapped lots of pictures of Tobi as he told that brazen lie. He was something else all right, trying to connect even my win into promoting his school. A mix of feelings whirled within me.

"You're going to Seio for high school, Shimao? Cool! I'm looking forward to seeing you there!" Kakeru's face lit up brighter than the sun.

Gah...your innocence is blinding. You shouldn't get any closer to your black-hearted school director. A black heart is extremely contagious!

"I sure hope she does. What do you think, Miss Shimao? Will you accept my offer?" Tobi was trying to get me to commit in front of all the reporters.

I was furious. *How dare he make all of this stuff up? He never brought this up with me before! I won't let him get away with it scot-free! Two can play at this game!*

"Good question. I would love to if my parents agree. You did promise me that not only would the tuition be free, but also my uniform, textbooks, and all my school-related costs as well, right? Oh, and the dorm fees too, yes? It was a very appealing offer."

Tobi's polished smile twitched at the corners. I had publicly extorted him in front of all the reporters. *Serves you right! ...Huh, I guess I'm the one who has contracted a black heart.*

"Does that mean Seio Academy is revising their policies on scholarship students?! This is great news!"

The crowd of reporters began taking notes and snapping pictures. Tobi quickly amended the situation by saying, "The decision isn't finalized yet, so please keep the information off-the-record for now."

I crossed my legs and flashed an innocent smile at him.

ONLY the middle school division had ended so far. The competition coordinator explained to me that they would send information about the special concert put on by the winners at a later date. Performing with the orchestra was a special privilege granted only to the winner of the university division.

Yet another thing that ended up differing from Kon's notes. As it was, the remake version's heroine was supposed to be the only winner.

It dawned on me all over again that this world was gradually deviating from *Hear My Heart*'s storyline. Kon had mentioned something about that ages ago too. *What did she call it? The butterfly effect?*

Not knowing anything about what made up this world or why I was reincarnated meant the only thing I could do was live out each day as it came.

♪♪♪

THE interviews and information session had ended, so I said my goodbyes to Kakeru and left the lobby.

Oh yeah, Miss Chisako and Miss Sakurako were all excited about going out to celebrate. Going out to eat with everyone sounds like fun. I was happily walking toward the door, when Tobi chased after me for the umpteenth time.

I figured he'd come. I stopped and turned towards him.

The dubious smile from earlier was wiped clean off his face as he stared right at me. "Congratulations on your win."

"Thank you. Congratulations on Tominaga winning as well. Are you satisfied now, Director?"

"…Satisfied? Far from it." Tobi bent down from his high view of the world and brought his perfectly drawn lips to my ear.

Revulsion rippled through me, screaming at me to pull away from him, but I didn't want him to see what bothered me. I knew he'd use it to his advantage later. I planted my feet firmly on the ground and stifled my emotions.

"Tominaga's win was decided from the start. I made the necessary arrangements long in advance."

"…What?"

His unexpected confession rooted me to the ground. *Then, what? The winner was decided from the start? Why did he have to say all of those horrible things to me then?*

"But Sadia Francesca only gave you As. Female pianists are so difficult to control," Tobi spat bitterly and straightened up. His usual calm composure returned to his clear blue eyes. "And that's why I am congratulating you on your win... Say, why don't we call a truce, Mashiro? Why don't you come to me as a scholarship student?"

I answered his honeyed, catlike voice with a derisive smile. *I will never be broken by you again.*

"You honor me with your high evaluation of my skills. I will take your offer under consideration." I gave a light nod and walked by him. A quiet smile played across his face.

Interlude: A Certain Woman's Confession 2

MY little sister remained quieter than the dead during my nineteenth winter. Spring arrived, I turned twenty, and then another year circled around, I turned twenty-one. So much stuff should've happened during that time, but not a single clear memory of it stayed with me.

Did I take part in the coming of age ceremony? I sort of remembered Mom's puffy red eyes when she made me a long-sleeved kimono for the occasion.

Dad and Mom slowly began giving up on Rika ever recovering. Their daily visits to the hospital became every other day and then every three days. It almost seemed like a ceremony to bid their beloved daughter farewell over the years.

"You did nothing wrong, Hanaka."

"Hanaka, please don't blame yourself anymore."

I was aware that it wasn't Rika causing my parents to suffer but me. But I just couldn't give up on my little sister for the life of me.

She had barely just turned eighteen.

She had been studying like her life depended on it.

She was driven to the depths of death before she had the chance to enjoy the best part of her youth, before she ever tasted the joys of being loved back by the man she loved.

◇◇◇◇◇

"RIKA!" I shouted as loud as I could from the other side of the road.

"Hana?" She stopped with the brightest smile on her face. She wasn't swallowed up by the black hole at her feet.

Ah, thank God! I made it this time!

I always awoke from the dream just as I rejoiced.

Staring at the faint outline of the ceiling in the dark, I sluggishly pushed myself out of bed and turned the doorknob to the room next door.

An empty bed. An organized desk.

Where did that silly girl go? It's already two in the morning.

I stood there in a drowsy daze for a while before that horrible memory settled in. The difficult to face reality that Rika would never again return to this room permeated my thoughts.

How many times did I have that exact same dream?

After the tenth time, the tears stopped coming. After the hundredth time, I stopped counting.

I was living in a waking nightmare that never ended.

THE chances of Rika recovering from being in a vegetative state were close to zero. Her body would slowly atrophy, and her immune system would weaken. A lot of long-term coma cases like hers had patients dying within a few years from catching the slightest contagion.

Whatever the scientific diagnosis, Rika simply looked like she was sleeping when I saw her.

"Rika…I'm here." I entered the hospital room after going through the sterilization process and held her pale hand.

See, her hand is still warm. How can they give up so easily on her?

"Call me Hana, Rika. Say it. Say H-a-n-a."

Rika pretended not to hear my request.

You can't react. Right. Sorry.

I switched my approach and told her about everything that came to mind, from the color of today's sky to the type of flowers I brought to what our parents were doing. By the time I ran out of things to say, it was time for me to go home.

Leaving the hospital room was the hardest thing of all.

"…Just so you know…I'm waiting for you, Rika. I'll always be waiting for you." I reluctantly let go of her hand and left the room, constantly looking over my shoulder at her. I hated this moment the most.

I traveled all over the place confirming information I had found online or rumors I'd heard from others between my visits to the hospital. There were all sorts of weird things out there like a phone that allows you to speak with the dead or a mailbox where you could receive letters from the deceased.

Rika was still alive. Perhaps that was the reason I failed to find a way to bring her back no matter how hard I searched.

The turning point came during my twenty-fourth summer.

I had finally managed to find "him."

That day, I went to this bridge in the neighboring prefecture where it was rumored I could see the person I wanted to see most in the world. Placing an offering of pomegranates at the bottom of the bridge on a specific day during the Obon Festival, the several-days-long festival dedicated to honoring ancestors, was said to grant you the ability to see someone you could never again meet in this lifetime.

I headed there at the exact time given in the rumors, placed an offering of pomegranates, and fervently chanted Rika's name.

Please, Rika. Come back to me.

The bridge was famous for being a place where people came to pray, so people quietly walked away when they saw the pomegranate in my hand.

It was the devil's hour of eventide when the cicadas cried the loudest.

Not a single soul was around.

A man appeared out of thin air upon the bridge where there was no one before. He materialized with the casual ease of the summer sediment drifting through the air.

"That wish of yours surpasses the realm of what is allowed for humans, *Hanaka*." Golden hair tousled by the wind, the corners of the man's perfectly shaped lips curled up. Every hair on my body stood on end, warning me of his inhumanness. "Do you still wish it regardless? Wish for the return of Rika."

"I wish it."

Those clear blue eyes that were like looking into the deepest ocean turned blood-red in the evening sunlight.

"We have a deal then. Play a game with me with your little sister and your very own life as the prize." The man grinned from ear to ear with blissful rapture and began detailing the rules of this game.

My heart and mind had long since broken, for I swallowed that man's existence and the words he said hook, line, and sinker. I listened attentively to the sweet promises he whispered in my ear.

January of the next year—on the same day of Rika's accident—I was going to break away from this world. I was going to move over to a new world of his making and participate in a game of his choosing. My excitement dissipated the second he mentioned another world.

"You want to send me to another world? I don't believe you're capable of something like that. Give me a more realistic deal," I demanded.

He shrugged it off. "You've greatly insulted me, but I'll play nice for now. You haven't become my contractor yet, after all. Only God is capable of making a world from scratch. But it isn't too difficult to make a new world based off of a template that already exists."

"…It's not? Are you a demon or something?"

I didn't understand even a fraction of the man's logic, but he didn't appear to be lying through his teeth either. *If he is a demon, I might be able to exchange my soul in return for Rika.* I stared at the man with that desperate hope.

"Call me whatever you wish. Judging what is good and evil is a task too great for humans. You can think of me in whatever way suits you."

Perhaps he was just a megalomaniac who was getting kicks messing with my mind. But there was nothing else for me to cling to. Out of sheer desperation, I decided to take on this deal of his.

"…Explain how it works to me in more detail."

"Now you're talking. Hm, let me think," he paused and rubbed his chin between his thumb and index finger. "Why don't we set the stage as a music love simulation game? The one and same game Rika was obsessed with. Doesn't that make things more entertaining?"

The man had a creepy level of knowledge about Rika. The more we spoke, the more my faith in him grew. I asked him an array of questions and confirmed the roles assigned to Rika and me.

"You win if you clear the music school director's route," he explained. "Upon winning, you will reveal the truth about everything to Rika, and she will be granted the opportunity to choose. Does she want to stay in that world or return to her old world?"

The man seemed to be having the time of his life. "My blood is boiling with excitement over my first legitimate bet in eons," he admitted. I wasn't even listening to him at that point.

It's a chance for Rika to relive her life. There's no way I'd pass this up. I agreed on the spot.

"Fine. I'll do it."

"Good, good. Such a good girl. You're such a sweet, gentle girl it makes me want to barf. Just for that, I'll mix fragments of myself into the character you have to win over. I can enjoy myself more that way. You can rest easy knowing that he is a very beautiful and cruel creature. Don't you forget, *Hanaka.* You must become a cute little girl who falls madly in love with that creature."

"...I'll try my best."

Tomoi's face came to mind. Five years had passed since I dumped him, and yet, I still loved him dearly. *Can I be more shameful?* I tightly balled my fists, using the pain of my nails digging into my palms to stop from thinking further.

He licked his lips at the sudden pain flashing across my face. "Haha. Marvelous. Your despair and selfish desire to sacrifice yourself shall taste most delicious."

He dug his long nails into my neck as a sign of our contract. The sound of his nails piercing through my flesh was followed by the sensation of dripping blood. The pain was so agonizing I thought I would die; tears sprung to my eyes in a visceral reaction to it. But I viewed even that pain and suffering as proof that I was paying the price in Rika's place.

The man slowly thrust his blood-soaked nails into his heart. "With this, the contract is formed. I will protect both *you* and *Rika* from death in that world until you turn eighteen. But don't ever forget—I will be with you at all times."

To this day, I can vividly recall his honeyed voice that sounded like he was whispering sweet nothings to a beloved new pet.

"...n. Kon!"

"Mnh?"

Someone was shaking my shoulders. Dazed, I shifted my gaze to my older brother beside me, peering at my face with worry. The clapping that sounded like roaring waves showed no signs of stopping. The entire audience continued to clap as though they longed for an encore from her.

"Are you okay?"

"Yes, I'm fine."

Without another word, Kou pressed his large handkerchief into my hand. Wondering why in the world he did that, I tilted my head, and felt the tears stream down my cheeks. My brother averted his eyes, pretending he didn't see my tears.

The sound of her piano had the uncanny ability to directly capture the soul.

That girl always laid herself bare and tried to convey what she was felt to us. The deep ocean of my memories seemed to have sucked me in while I was listening with rapt attention to the Schumann she played with her heart and soul. The various things I had tried my hardest not to remember came crashing back into my mind at once.

Indeed, that world was not my "former life." It was my "past" connected to and continuing into my current present.

Every time I saw that girl smiling away as she had fun, frowning, pouting, vivaciously playing the piano, and just living and breathing and moving, I couldn't not see my other little sister in her.

I don't care if we never meet again now. I don't mind if you forget all about me. Please, please live happily ever after.

If someone has to pay a cost for that to happen, I will pay every last drop.

CG 31: School Trip (Heroine)

SCHOOL became insanely hectic after the competition. After school, I was called straight to the teacher's lounge where they showered me with words of praise. They informed me of their plans to publicly acknowledge my achievement during the next school-wide assembly.

"I knew you would take home the win, Miss Shimao!" Cheeks flushed with excitement, the principal gave my hand a strong squeeze.

"Thank you very much. I only made it to where I am today because of my teachers." My gratitude seemed to move him as he shook my hand up and down in wide arcs.

Oww, my elbow and shoulder hurt. Please be gentler with a pianist's hands.

From a few steps back, Mr. Matsuda watched the other teachers flock around me. A gentle smile touched his face when our eyes met. I later heard that he came to see the finals with Shinji.

"Congratulations," he mouthed from the back of the room. The difficult-to-approach aura surrounding him melted away whenever he smiled. That was one of the things I used to love about him.

Able to confirm that my feelings for him were already a thing of the past brought tremendous relief. *It's all good now. My feelings for him exist within the realm of nostalgia.*

Yes, even the most intense emotions fade over time. Patiently waiting for the intensity to die down is the only option sometimes.

If only I had realized that fact sooner.

♪♪♪

"MASHIRO, you're so totally awesome! Congrats!"

"I watched you online, and it still moved me to tears! You're seriously way too freaking good!"

During break, my usual group of friends crushed me in bear hugs, and I squeezed them back just as tight.

"It's all thanks to you guys cheering me on! I can't even begin to tell you how encouraging the lucky charms and cards were! Thank you so much!"

Majima and Rin watched us girls squeezing each other and giggling with wry smiles, while Tazaki shrewdly slipped into our circle.

"Okay, Shimao, it's time for my hug."

"It is *so* not!" I decisively shot him down and took a big step back.

"Why not?! A little hug never hurt anybody! Stingy!"

"Make that cute pouty face all you want! It won't change a no into a yes!"

"That's discrimination!"

Sawa rolled up her printout and whacked Tazaki on the head with a loud ka-thwack.

♪♪♪

"CONGRATULATIONS! Sadia Francesca Junior Music Competition Junior High Division Winner: Miss Mashiro Shimao (Tada Middle School Second Year)" was printed in big letters on a banner hanging from the school building. Heck, the same banner was hanging from town hall too!

Are they trying to embarrass me out of town?!

News channels ran a special segment on the competition, turning me into an overnight local star. I was grateful for their words of encouragement and congratulations, and equally embarrassed by them.

"Congrats, Mashiro! Let this old geezer hear you play someday!"

"Ahaha. Thank you!" I waved to my older neighbor, who'd recently switched professions from liquor store owner to convenience store owner, and finally arrived at home.

I changed into more comfortable clothes and was about to work on my homework when there was a knock on my door.

Now in her fourth year of university, Hanaka's class days had decreased, and she spent most of her time at home studying for employment exams and teaching credentials. She practiced Bayer on Aine whenever I was out.

"Welcome home, Mashiro. The paperwork from the competition office arrived for you. Looks like the commemorative concert will be held in December."

"Hey. Thanks. I'll check it out later. Oh, and before I forget, thank you for doing my laundry."

"No problem! You have a lesson with Miss Ayumi tomorrow, right? Don't forget to bring the concert paperwork with you."

"Thanks for the reminder… I have to consult her about what song to play."

Students from Seio Academy had won both the high school and university divisions. Combine that with the middle school division, and they took home all three gold trophies. The media was running elaborate features on Seio's outstanding achievement.

Tobi's shrewdness was frightening. Here was a man who put rich kids on stage during his school's Christmas concert for the sole purpose of emptying their parents' pockets, while choosing only his best players to enter into official music competitions.

According to what Kon told me, Tobi had more influence over the school board than the current board chairman did. He undoubtedly took care of the legwork necessary to lure the other board members to his side. It didn't take a genius to know that he alluded to the powerful family backing him whenever he needed to add pressure.

Hahaha! That's the black-hearted prince for you!

A special concert where I'll be the odd woman out, huh? I have to be on full-alert against Tobi. I just know he will appear on the scene with a smug smirk. Kakeru is my only oasis among the other winners.

Sighing, I opened Aine's keyboard lid. No matter how depressed I was, once I started playing the piano, all worldly thoughts were driven from my head. The only things left in the world were my fingers, the music born from them, and the sheet music guiding me.

Time whisked by in a flurry whenever my fingers flew over the keys, chasing the music.

♫♫♫

AND then it was November. Yes, this was the month with the biggest event of them all—the school trip!

Believe it or not, I actually looked forward to it this time around even though I was so set against going during elementary school. How could I not when middle school would be the last time I could enjoy events like this with Eri and the gang?

Supposedly Tobi had contacted my parents right after the competition. One night, Dad called me to the quiet living room where the TV was switched off.

"According to Mr. Yamabuki, he's willing to take care of all your school-related expenses until university if you are interested in becoming a special scholarship student at Seio Academy, Mashiro. We asked him lots of questions about it, and both your mom and I think it's an extraordinary offer."

"It is."

"But you must know," Dad suddenly reached across the table and pulled my hands into his, "when they say they want you for your ability to play the piano, it also means they don't want a Mashiro who doesn't play the piano. You will be the one who inevitably gets hurt if you enroll with halfhearted feelings. Your mom and I are worried that it's not right for you to have to decide your entire future at your age. But we respect your opinion. So please tell us. What do you want to do, Mashiro?"

A hot lump formed at the back of my throat when I saw Dad's serious and sincere expression.

I have to properly explain my feelings to Dad and Mom who are always doing everything they can to protect me. My goals haven't changed since that day when I regained memories of my past life at age seven.

"I want to become a pianist. I know it's an unforgiving path. I know it isn't easy to make it big. But I don't want to give up on my dreams without trying. I want to attend Seio Academy!"

"…I see. Okay." Dad stared at my face as if blinded by what he saw there and took a short breath. "You are loved by the Naritas and Gendas like you are another one of their children. Even Mr. Yamabuki wants to hold out his hand to you. You are a blessed child, Mashiro… You are our pride and joy."

Despite wanting to hold back the tears, they gushed forth on their own volition. *He could've left Tobi out of the mix of people helping me out.*

Dad. Daddy. My dear father who hasn't changed one bit from my past life. I love you so much.

I had once asked my dad if he didn't find life boring spending all of his money on his two daughters instead of going out to play golf and to drink like my friends' dads. It hurt seeing him as a busy worker bee, spending every day in the vicious cycle of just going from home to work and back again. Out of our guilt, Hana and I once apologized to him. He was furious with us for it.

"Never say something like that again," he scolded us. He bent down, patted us both on the head, and added, "I'm very happy you were born my daughters, Hanaka, Rika. I'm the happiest a man can be."

And yet, I had to go and leave the world before him.

"I'm sorry. I'm really so sorry."

My current dad began to panic over my tearful apology.

I wasn't just crying about the stuff dealing with Seio, but I couldn't explain the real reason why without sounding crazy, so I rubbed my cheeks with the back of my hand in a bid to stop the tears. But the memories with my family flooded my mind, surrounding me and not letting go.

Mom came out of the bath and took one look at me sobbing and Dad's flustered attempts at comforting me and casually remarked, "Wow! Things descended into mayhem fast without me!"

Dad and I burst out laughing.

I want to live a full life this time around. At the very least, I don't want to leave my sweet family behind to mourn me.

To do that, I have to take good care of my health and pay attention when I'm walking! I took it to heart to watch out for manholes.

♫♫♫

AND so, it was decided that I would attend Seio for high school. I planned to let Eri and the gang know once things were set in stone. Kon was the one person I called up right away.

"I see. Then we can attend high school together." Kon's voice sounded happy yet somewhat lonely over the phone.

"What's wrong? Is something bothering you? Is it Tobi?" I asked without thinking.

"No," Kon promptly answered. "...I was just thinking that we'll be fifteen soon."

"Yeah. I can't believe we're this old already. At this rate, we'll be graduating from high school in no time." I only saw a bright future ahead.

Kon quietly giggled. "Speaking of school, isn't your school trip coming up? Where are you going?"

"Kyushu. We're going to board the ferry for Nagasaki. Then we're going to travel around Hakata and Kumamoto before coming home. What do you want me to bring back for you?"

"Hehe...let me think. I would love it if you brought me back something made of glass from Nagasaki."

"Okay! I'll pick out something cute!"

I thought she would turn me down for sure, so I was ecstatic when Kon made an actual request for something.

I guess I'll look for a pretty picture postcard for Sou. Kou will definitely sulk if I only buy souvenirs for Sou and Kon... That said, I'll only get sarcasm in return if I give him something he doesn't want when he's so picky.

After thinking it over, I decided to text him.

Subject: Souvenir

"I'm going to Kyushu for my school trip. I'm currently taking requests for what you want me to bring back. Please don't respond if you don't want anything."

That should do it. When you don't know, it's best to ask the person directly.

I placed my cell phone on the end table next to my bed and scuffled over to my desk.

Lately, I had fallen into a pattern of practicing the piano as soon as I got home, taking a bath once it got dark, and then studying after that. Once I wrapped up my homework and self-assigned workload, I made a point of watching the French language lessons I had recorded on the living room TV. I had completely forgotten about the text I'd sent while I was immersed in my studies.

I started getting sleepy around eleven.

I thoroughly rubbed leave-in conditioner into my hair and crawled into bed. Hanaka had given me different hair care products, but I was particularly fond of the not-too-sweet apple scented conditioner. I planted a goodnight kiss on Becchin's nose and pulled the comforter up to my shoulders. Then I noticed my cell phone flashing.

Oh? Who texted? In the dark I reached out, grabbed my cell phone, and checked the screen.

…There were five texts and two missed calls. All from Kou.

"What the heck?"

I instantly snapped awake. I rolled onto my stomach and blearily blinked as I scrolled down the bright screen.

Subject: None

"Where are you sightseeing in Kyushu? I hope it's a fun trip for you! Thanks for asking what I want. I think I'll take you up on the offer."

Kou's texts were always like this. I was suspicious that his butler Mr. Tanomiya was writing them on his behalf.

In short, he was basically saying, "I'm happy with anything you pick out for me, Mashiro."

Come on now, boy. Be honest with me! I thought as I read through his next text message. This time it seemed like Mr. Tanomiya (or perhaps it was Kou himself) wanted to ask if he was too late to make a request because I never responded to his prior text.

By his fifth text, he threw off all pleasantries. "Just buy me something." That cleared my suspicions that it wasn't actually Mr. Tanomiya all along. I knew beyond a shadow of a doubt that this arrogant text belonged to Kou.

He probably called me twice because he wasn't getting anywhere with texting.

Do you want a souvenir from Kyushu that bad?! I had an insatiable urge to karate chop his head. *You want more stuff when you already have so much?!*

This reminds of that one time in elementary school with the scarf. I cracked up laughing at the memory of Kou stubbornly not letting Sou have the scarf I had made for our Christmas present exchange. *He's all grown up now, but this side of him hasn't changed.*

Subject: Scary

"I know I'm partially to blame for not noticing your texts while I was studying, but that's an annoying number of texts and phone calls from you in a short period of time. Please don't ever do it again. I'll try to find a souvenir that I think you'll like, so don't complain to me later about it. I'm going to sleep. Don't respond. Goodnight."

I quickly typed up my text and turned off my phone. *Now that should take care of that!*

I'm really looking forward to my school trip!

♪♪♪

IT was finally here: the school trip! This was going to be my first time riding a ferry—former life included. I was brimming with excitement long before boarding. I sighed a word halfway between "wow" and "awesome" that kinda sounded like "wawesome," before the large white ship. It was so big, the entire ship didn't fit into view when I looked up!

"Shimao, your mouth is hanging open," Majima pointedly warned me.

Tch! Curse you for being observant!

"Anyone else curious about what the baths onboard are like? I heard dinner will be a buffet."

"I can't even picture what a bath on a ship would be like. You know, I'm actually looking forward to having to sleep together in tight quarters."

"Me too! That's like something you can only do on a trip like this."

Boarding time came quickly as I chatted with girls in my same group, took motion sickness medicine, and went to the bathroom.

Walking up the gangway onto the ferry brought me right to the escalators. That was the first thing that took me by surprise. Oohing and aahing on the inside, I dragged my suitcase behind me as I confirmed my room location in the guidebook and headed for it. Our school had rented out several traditional Japanese-style rooms that fit twenty.

One teacher was assigned per a room.

"Okay, girls! Once you put down your bags, head to the bath in order starting from group A. Be sure to secure your valuables in your luggage. The rest of the teachers and I will watch your stuff for you."

Female teachers were assigned to the girls' rooms. Mr. Matsuda was serving as chaperon too, but the boys' rooms were on a different floor, so I hadn't spotted him yet.

"Mashiro, let's go! It's our turn for the bath!" Sawa hurried me.

I quickly snagged my change of clothes and a towel, and headed for the bath. The onboard bath was large enough to be one of those super deluxe bathhouses, tricking me into thinking I had stepped off the boat! Hot water gushed from the showers by the buckets. How in the world did this thing work?

"Look! We're leaving port!" one of the girls shouted from where she sat in the bath with her forehead pressed up against the large window. The rest of the girls clustered around the window.

"Eek! Won't people see us naked from outside?!"

"They wouldn't make it work that way!"

Everyone was full of excitement. Girls burst out laughing every time someone said something, turning it into the liveliest bath I'd ever taken.

It was financially unfeasible for the school to charter a boat this size. Other passengers should've been somewhere onboard, but it was anyone's guess where they were. Being the middle of the day on a workday probably had something to do with why I only saw middle school jerseys everywhere I went. Maybe the other passengers were holed up in their rooms, trying to avoid the noisy students on their school trip. I'd feel bad if that was true.

"There are other passengers on this ship! Please don't shout, run on the deck, or do anything to cause problems for the people around you! With that said and out of the way, let's eat!" The teacher in charge of all of the classes for the year gave us that brief reminder before dinner.

"He's the one who's shouting," one of the boys at the table next to ours joked. Sawa overheard and nearly spit out the juice she had just taken a sip of.

After dinner, we went out on the deck and enjoyed the white capped waves and twinkling stars until curfew.

On my way back to my room, I spotted Mr. Matsuda standing at the edge of the deck. He looked terribly lonely as he absently gazed out at the ocean. Was he thinking about Hanaka? Or was he troubled by some other worries? Whatever the case, there was nothing I could do for him.

Even after I graduate, I don't think we'll ever get beyond the student-teacher relationship. Nor do I want to. My connection to him in this world was infinitesimally shallow. *Good luck, Mr. Matsuda.* I mentally cheered him on, completely graduated from my second first crush.

We returned to our cabin, flopped back on the tatami mats, and pulled our covers up, but nobody tried to sleep yet. What began in the dimly lit cabin was the school trip standard affair: exchanging love stories and talking about boys!

In our class, the popularity vote was split between Majima and Tazaki. Majima and Eri's close relationship was common knowledge at school, so you'd think that it was a winner-take-all situation for Tazaki, but there weren't any undaunted girls willing to confess to a boy who flirted with every girl. Confessions of love were only further put on hold by rumors he had a girlfriend from another school.

"He said he's dating a girl from the girls' basketball team at the school next to ours," one of the girls shared, drawing disappointed sighs from across the cabin.

"Haaah. I want a boyfriend," Sawa grumbled, triggering a round of girl talk about what kind of boy would make a good boyfriend.

"A tall boy. He's gotta be handsome too!"

"One with a swoon-worthy voice and who's loyal to his girl."

"He's gotta be smart and athletic."

The long list of impossibly high specs eventually ended in laughter.

"No boy like that exists in reality."

"Let's turn to games then!"

"Oh, but maybe not all hope is lost! The guys who appeared on the TV special with Mashiro all had high specs!" one of the girls from my group suddenly mentioned.

I actually hadn't watched the special yet. My parents had recorded it with zeal, but it was too embarrassing for me to watch myself on video.

I ended up holding a one-person viewing party of the other contestants' videos that I had downloaded from the Internet. Though I could've gone without the video and been happy with just the audio. I had to hold back my desire to ask the contest staff for audio files instead.

"Totally! Wasn't that hottie with the red hair too hot for TV?! I felt the heat coming off my screen!"

"I'm all for the blond who looks like he's only half-Japanese! He was like a real, living, breathing prince!"

"Those two were both eye candy, but I have a thing for the orange-haired boy. You know, the smart-looking one who tied for first with

Mashiro?!"

They were going gaga over Kou, Tobi, and Kakeru.

"I'm so envious of you, Mashiro. No wonder you don't fuss over the boys at our school."

"I should've taken up piano lessons."

"I bet you would've dropped it in three days!"

Just as the conversation was picking up, there was a knock on the door and our teacher came in.

"Hey, girls! You're being loud! You're going to suffer tomorrow if you don't sleep soon!"

"Crud!"

Everyone pulled their covers over their heads and pretended to sleep. I squeezed my eyes shut and curled into a ball.

I agree that those three look good. The girls would've really made some noise if Sou had been in the camera shot next to Kou. Simply imagining Kou and Sou together made me emotional. *I miss the times when being together was the obvious thing. Never again will the three of us argue about stupid things.* That sad truth cut deep into my chest.

♪♪♪

THE next day we disembarked in Nagasaki and hit sightseeing spots such as Heiwa Park, Glover Mansion, and Oura Church while fighting back our seasickness. An exotic atmosphere permeated the area that had served as a trade port for centuries. When we came to Meganebashi, the bridge said to look like a pair of glasses, I was astonished that it really did look like its namesake.

I had a friend take a picture of me in front of the bronze statues of opera singer Tamaki Miura and Puccini in Glover Garden. *I have to show this to Kon when I get home!*

I also wanted to hunt for souvenirs along the way, but our group's sightseeing schedule was packed tight. Our shopping excursion had to wait until our free time at Huis Ten Bosch tomorrow.

We stayed the second night in a famous hotel. The girls and I were disappointed we wouldn't get to have a pillow fight in a *ryokan*, but the hotel's glamour made up for it. After finishing dinner with my group and splitting into pairs of two for our rooms, I opened my window curtain and stared out at the night scenery.

"Wow!"

Spread out as far as the eye could see were the beautiful lights centered around the port below. The fantastic view of what looked like a floating, shining city out of a fairy tale book excited me more than anything else on the trip.

I looked over my shoulder and called for Sawa. "Sawa! The view is awesome! Hurry over here!"

"Okay, okay! Coming! Oh my gosh! This is amazing!"

Sawa and I pressed together in the window and gazed in silence at the picturesque scenery.

It really is beautiful to look at! If I was to compare it to music, it's like an octave tremolo, a trill, an arpeggio. I listened to the piano music playing to the scenery in my ears.

All of a sudden, our room bell rang.

"It's open!" Sawa shouted right next to my ear, bringing me back to reality.

I want to play the piano. I miss Aine with a vengeance.

"It's confirmed: your true love is the piano, Mashiro," Sawa laughed when she saw my fingers subconsciously playing on an imaginary keyboard.

"You guys were checking out the great view too?"

Eri, Tomo, and Mako strolled into the room wreathed in smiles. Eri tilted her head to the side when she saw me staring wide-eyed at the surprise visitors. "We didn't get to hang out with you or Sawa at all during the ferry ride or today's sightseeing. So we took matters into our own hands and barged in!"

Eri's cute gesture nearly knocked me off my feet. Irrational anger at Majima for monopolizing her time surged within me again. *I'll never forgive him if he doesn't treat her well!*

"This is supposedly one of the three major night views of the world. When I heard about that, I was like, it can't be compared to the rest of the world! But yeah, this is totally world-level scenery."

Mako's comment got the rest of us laughing.

"It's a world-class view!"

"Dude, we're on top of the world!"

We joked around as we snapped pictures with our cell phones.

"Hey, we should totally visit the other two major night views together when we're older."

"The other two are in Hong Kong and Monaco, right? What country is Monaco in?"

"What country? It's the Principality of Monaco, duh! Did you seriously not know, Mako?"

"How could I?! I suck at geography!"

Mako made a silly remark after Tomo's suggestion, and Sawa swiftly corrected her.

It was tons of fun having a good time with the group of friends I'd been with since elementary school. Merely seeing them laughing and smiling together brought on a wave of tearful sentimentalism.

"…Mashiro, what's wrong? Tired?"

I vigorously shook my head at Eri's kind smile. *I'm sad because it's so, so, so much fun, but I know it can't stay this way forever.* I swallowed back my mood breaking thoughts and linked arms with Eri.

"Nah, I'm fine. I'll never, ever forget you guys. No matter how far apart we are, I won't forget."

"…Don't make me cry, stupid." Teardrops misted Eri's eyes.

I hadn't told them about attending Seio for high school yet. But everyone seemed to have some idea I was headed that direction. They flocked around me any chance they got as if holding on tight during the last few moments before having to let something important go.

A little more than a year left to go. I hope I can make lots and lots of memories with them.

♪♪♪

THE third day had perfect weather without a single cloud in the sky.

My friends and I went crazy checking out Huis Ten Bosch theme park. I was so hyper that the cool November wind felt nice. Afraid of risking an injury on the thrill rides, I sat them out and watched my friends' stuff. I had fun just watching them celebrate clearing the Maze and sliding through the sky on the Rail Coaster in the Sky.

"Boy, was that satisfying!"

"It was hecka fun! This is too good to be a school trip!"

"You can say that again. Hey, why don't we go look for souvenirs now?"

We didn't stop talking even as we walked around for hours. We went from store to store looking predominately at cute things and sweets.

"...I wonder what boys like," I blurted in the middle of our shopping trip.

My group of friends jumped on that comment like a bloodhound on the trail.

"Hold up! What's this I hear? Are you giving a boy a present?!"

"No way! Mashiro gifting a boy?!"

"Who is he?! What lucky boy finally stole your heart from the piano?!"

I averted my eyes from the excited faces looking at me and cleared my throat. "It's for a friend I'm just sorta stuck with. Anyways, he has hecka annoying tastes. Should I just play it safe and go the sweets route?"

"Sweets? That's a horrible gift choice for a guy friend."

Mako's instant rejection got me to put back the box of shortbread I was holding. She had a point.

I can't imagine Kou eating sweets that are popular with the masses.

"If you want to play it safe, why not go with a cell phone strap? Check out this glass bead strap. It's pretty and chic," Eri suggested after watching me roam through the shop, struggling to find something. She pointed out a strap with three gorgeous glass beads dangling from it.

Oh, wow! This is so neat! I decided to fish through the variety of designs for ones with colors that matched my friends' names.

For Kon, I picked out one with white flower petals drifting across the dark-blue glass. For Kou, I went with the one that had chic stripes through light-crimson glass. And then I chose one with a cute polka dot pattern on light-blue glass for Sou.

I hope they like them.

That series of straps was just too cute to pass up; I ended up buying one for myself too. I went with the pink glass bead flecked with gold dust.

I'm thrilled that the four of us will have matching straps, but I wonder if Kou will be upset... I'll just give his to Mr. Mizusawa if that's the case. Yup, that's the plan.

"You really care for the people you're buying for, huh?" Mako smiled softly at me when I returned from the register. "You looked like you were on cloud nine while you were picking out the straps," she clarified.

Heat rushed to my cheeks. *Huh. That's what I looked like?*

"Yeah. You're right. They are very dear friends to me like you and the gang, Mako," I declared aloud, and it really hit home with me.

Kon was obvious, but Kou and Sou were also very near and dear to my heart. I had finally realized that truth anew. They weren't love interests in some game for me to capture—they were friends and fellow musicians I had spent the better half of my childhood with. They were the people I wanted to reach their happiness.

Whatever fate awaits me in the future, I pray with all my heart that these bonds never fray or sever.

Heroine's Results
Target Character: Every Target Character
Event: Making Memories
CLEAR

Interlude: A Souvenir from Mashiro (Kou's POV)

THE Saturday after she came back from her school trip, Mashiro arrived at the Genda estate with a paper bag hanging from her wrist, looking shocked to see me in the annex with Kon.

"Oh, you're here too, Kou?"

"Yeah. I needed to see Kon about something."

I didn't need to see Kon about anything. But Mashiro would never ask me what that something was, so I didn't have to worry about her seeing through my crummy lie.

Relief and frustration hit me at the same time. I was tormented by the schism between us and how it seemed to never repair with time.

But I knew she wouldn't give me the time of day if I told her how I really felt. My frivolous behavior in the past was what kept Mashiro forever out of reach. What situation fit the saying "you reap what you sow" better than this?

"I see! I'm glad you're here though! I was going to give Kon yours for later, but I'll give it to you since you're here." Mashiro rummaged enthusiastically through the paper bag and pulled out two tiny wrapped packages. "Let's see...this is Kon's, and this one is Kou's."

She looked seriously from one identical package to the next before handing them to us. "Here you go!"

Kon smiled brighter than the sun. "Yay! I'm so happy! Can I open it right now?"

"Go right ahead!" Mashiro's eyes glittered with anticipation as if she couldn't wait to see how we'd react to her present choice. She was so adorable, my expression unknowingly softened into a smile.

I opened the package to find a glass bead strap inside. The combination of braided cord strung through three glass beads was clean and beautiful. It couldn't have been too expensive, but I fell in love with its chic design at first glance.

"You went with glass beads from Nagasaki? Nice choice! It's absolutely beautiful!"

A big smile blossomed on Mashiro's face when she saw Kon's over-exaggerated delight. "That's right! I'm so glad you like it!"

That unguarded, defenseless expression raked at the center of my heart.

Why is it you? Why did it have to be you?

I long for more with you every time we meet. I can't stop thinking about you when we're apart. This is textbook lovesickness.

It didn't matter that I had given up on ever falling in love for the rest of my life—I was head over heels in love with Mashiro to the point I wanted to laugh at myself.

"I actually bought one for myself too. I also got Sou a strap from the same series for his souvenir, so the four us will have matching straps... Do you think that's too childish?" She turned and asked me.

Was she uneasy because I hadn't said anything yet? Her eyes were just a tad watery.

Kon and Sou don't need to match with us.

How great it'd be if I could tell her these feelings directly and shake her up so I was all she could think about? How amazing it'd be if she believed what I told her.

"I don't see anything wrong with that. I like it. Thanks. I'll use it now." I defaulted to the most innocuous remark. Mashiro took a good, hard look at my face as if startled by what I said. "What? Is it that unusual for me to say thanks and mean it?"

I seriously wish I could do something about feeling hurt by her reaction every single time. That's what my head thought, but my lips twisted in self-mockery.

I was fully aware of all the teasing and bullying I'd put her through. I had attacked her to her face at first, then halfway through, I wanted to know what made her different from other women, so I kept testing her. On more occasions than I could count, I put my arm around her shoulder and whispered in her ear like I did with other girls. Each time Mashiro firmly spurned me though her face was bright red.

I wish I had never done that. From the very beginning, Mashiro only ever said what she meant, yet I didn't believe her.

It was only natural that she wouldn't even consider me now. I couldn't stop wondering about what I had to do to make it up to her and earn her trust again. What would it take for her to believe that the things I say now are how I really feel about her?

Mashiro's silent contemplation over how to react was broken by a sudden smile. The smile meant only for me stole my breath away.

"Nope. I was just happy that you liked it, Kou. I debated a ton before picking it out for you."

My heart trembled as a bashful Mashiro didn't avert her eyes from me. I was positive she wouldn't believe me this time either, but she went and accepted what I said at face value.

I swallowed back my sigh and mustered every last piece of restraint to give the short answer of, "I see."

It was so easy for me to reenact the behavior my self-proclaimed fans wanted from me, and yet, when it came to this one girl, the one girl who mattered, I was like a fish out of water.

"...Hey, Kou, you're acting kind of weird today. If you have something to say, just say it. Okay?" The way she emphasized her words with a tilt of her head was irresistibly adorable.

I want to confess every feeling I have for her. I desperately suppressed my emotions. It would be fine if those feelings just annoyed her. I already figured she would reject me.

But what if she became afraid to be around me? What if she avoided me? Scorned and hated me? I knew with certainty I wouldn't survive it.

"Are you sure it's okay if I say it?" I asked back.

She tilted her head and stared back at me puzzled.

Interlude: A Souvenir from Mashiro (Sou's POV)

IT was snowing that day. I heard my chauffeur's flustered voice when I grabbed my bag and hopped out of the car.

"Master Sou, your umbrella!"

"The house is right there. Thanks though."

Snow would fall on him during the time it'd take to hand me the umbrella. The me of the past would've thought of that as just another part of a servant's job. But ever since I had realized Mashiro hated that kind of arrogance, I made every effort not to create extra work for them. I also started consciously saying thanks.

"It's not natural for someone to do something for you."

I think it happened right after the summer school camp in elementary school. Mashiro felt bad about making Mr. Mizusawa drive us everywhere. To which Kou pointedly declared, "I'm compensating him for it."

Mashiro's expression turned cold and she retorted, "That compensation isn't paid by you. It's your parents' money."

I had never thought about it that way before. But she was right. Both Kou and I were children, and our household staff didn't obey us simply because they valued us as people worth serving.

I ran to the front door and shook my head several times to shake the snow off my hair under the awning. I removed my coat in the heated entryway and greeted the butler awaiting my return.

"Welcome home. The snow fell quite suddenly."

"Yeah. Just a sign it's already December."

He waited a few steps away from me as I removed my scarf and gloves. Our eyes suddenly met. Something was off about the look in his eyes—it seemed like he had something more to say.

"…Is something wrong?"

"No, it's just that…" It must have been something hard for him to say, because his face crumpled apologetically. "A package for you arrived from Japan just past noon, but the snow had soaked the paper, and the exterior ripped slightly when I accepted it."

That's it? I cocked my head, relieved it wasn't something more. "I don't mind if the contents are safe."

"I am greatly relieved to hear you say that, Master Sou. I left it in your room."

"Thanks. I'll check it out."

I was freezing to the bone, so I requested a cup of hot coffee and marched upstairs.

On the table in my room was a cute brown letter package wrapped in white lace. A piece of me got my hopes up when my butler said it came from Japan. I carefully picked it up and felt my hopes transform into joy when I saw the sender.

It's from Mashiro.

What appeared to be white lace was actually a complex cutout of glossy white paper. While I admired Mashiro's signature elaborate wrapping job, it was ripped here and there because of the snow.

Everyone who worked in this house knew how much I looked forward to her letters. So that must've been why my butler acted like he was walking on thin ice. True, I was disappointed to find my package from Mashiro ripped, but it's not like I was going to throw a hissy fit over it.

Smiling sadly, I carefully unwrapped the frayed package.

Is this a strap wrapped in Bubble Wrap? I saved opening the smaller packet secured firmly by tape for later and unfolded the letter first.

♪♪♪

DEAR Shiroyama,

Hello.

I was happy we got to talk on the phone after my competition. I successfully made it through the commemorative winners' concert. You might have already watched the video uploaded online, but I played Rachmaninoff, and Kakeru played Schumann as a part of this special program called "Finalist Song Shuffle!"

Kakeru and I complained that it was a lousy program. Mr. Yamabuki came up with the whole thing. Do you remember him? He's Miss Ayumi's friend—the one she invited to the Christmas party that one year. He is currently serving as Seio's director.

It was popular with the audience members who were all of the opinion that, "it's entertaining to hear the performers' individuality." My Piano Sonata failed to sound anything like Rachmaninoff. I want the strength to play more dynamically and expressive! Kakeru's Schumann was really great. Especially when it came to the second movement. His rendition was so heartrending it gave me the baseless suspicion that he has a coldhearted girlfriend.

After the concert, I introduced Kakeru to Miss Ayumi at his request, but he got an earful from her, with the added bonus of a scary smile. "Your performances are almost guaranteed to be full of mistakes. It bothers me to no end," she chided him. It was pretty entertaining seeing how easily it depressed him.

♪♪♪

I read up to there and stopped—I was bothered by the constant mention of Kakeru Tominaga in Mashiro's letter. He was the boy who won alongside her at the competition.

I kind of remember someone like him in the year ahead of me... I think he was famous on campus for being crazy good at the piano.

Frankly, his unrefined, emotional play style wasn't my type, but I understood why Mashiro admired a skill she didn't have. That guy's masculine sound had a completely different flavor from Mashiro's delicate and graceful music.

For as smart as Mashiro was, she tended to have her head in the clouds when it came to other people—she wasn't on guard around them. She easily trusted others, became attached, and cared for them. I should've more than known that she would become friends with all sorts of people because of her personality, but my chest still hurt.

How does it feel for you, Kou? Do you feel nothing having to watch her with other people when you're right there with her?

I always thought that if she was going to pick someone, it'd be Kou. This letter forced me to realize that was a selfish wish on my half.

I had this stupid idea that if she picked Kou, I could watch over her for the rest of our lives as the best friend. No one had to tell me I was expecting too much—I knew it.

Who Mashiro chooses to become friends with or date is up to her and her alone. All I could do was smile and wish her the best. I didn't want to put Mashiro in a bad spot again because of my selfishness.

I repeated that to myself to calm down and took several sips of the hot coffee the maid brought me. I finally returned to reading the rest of the letter.

♪♪♪

INCLUDED in this package is a slightly belated souvenir from my school trip. It's a strap that I bought as part of a matching set for me, Kon, Kou, and you. I hope you don't mind that we match.

I fell in love with the lovely design and just had to send you one too. To tell you the truth, I wanted to have a matching set with you. Sorry that it's such a self-centered present.

I would be ecstatic if you like it, but if not, please give it to someone else. It's from Japan, so maybe someone in Germany will enjoy it!

All right, that about wraps it up. I'll write you again.

It's getting colder by the day. Please be careful not to catch a cold.

Sincerely,

Mashiro Shimao

December

P.S. I searched high and low for a glass bead strap that's the same color as your hair!

♪♪♪

Natsu

I reread the last half of the letter over and over and over again.

I'd never mind having something that matches with you, Mashiro! I can't believe she said she wants to have a matching set with me! Ah, gosh darn it, she's cute!

I felt like I was going to go out of my mind with happiness.

Spurred on by my high spirits, I pried the packing materials off the packet. She must've been super worried about it breaking, because the tiny strap was wrapped in layers of Bubble Wrap. Colorful orange and ultramarine polka dots decorated the transparent light-blue glass beads.

I wonder where she bought it. I instantly imagined her carefully choosing it in some gift shop.

I dangled the beautifully crafted strap in front of my face and stared at it for some time. The miserable feelings brewing deep inside had vanished without a trace.

"Mashiro," I unconsciously said her name aloud. Once I said it, I couldn't stop. "Mashiro...*Mashiro*. I want to see you. I want to be near you."

I love you. I love you this much even now.

It's okay if you don't return these feelings. I feel so much happiness just from the attention you're giving me.

During my third year since leaving Japan, the yearning love I felt for Mashiro refined into its purest form and tried to change into a quiet, calm attachment.

CG 32: Choice (Kou & Sou)

"**HEY,** Mashiro, how do I look?" Hanaka stood in front of me and uneasily sought my opinion.

The kindergarten near our house was holding its entrance ceremony today. This day also doubled as Hanaka's teaching debut. She was wearing the cream-yellow suit Dad bought to celebrate her new job. Minimal makeup touched up her face and her hair was tied back in a loose ponytail.

"You're rocking the look! You give off that gentle beauty teacher vibe," I told her.

Her cheeks turned a bashful red. "Ehehe. Thanks! Okay, I can do this!"

"Yeah! You can! Have a good day!"

Once she got her new job, Hanaka attended driving school until she earned her driver's license. Amazingly enough, she had already purchased a k-car with the money she had saved up working part-time while still in university. Her credit wasn't good enough to get a loan, so the contract was signed in Dad's name, but Hanaka swore she'd pay the monthly payments from her salary.

Our parents were past the point of impressed and were more astonished by how reliable Hanaka had become—it seemed like her days of leaving everything up to chance in middle and high school were behind her. Dad often sat in the passenger's seat next to Hanaka and had her practice driving through the neighborhood with the "Student Driver" sticker stuck firmly on the back of her car. I was pretty sure she would be safe driving on her own by now…

I walked to the front door to see her off. Mom clenched the hem of her apron beside me.

"Don't rush, Hanaka. Drive safe, okay?"

"Okay. I'll be careful. I'm leaving now!" She slipped her feet into her brand-new white pumps, spun her keys around her finger, and cheerfully waved at us.

The house felt very quiet when the door shut behind her.

I can't believe my sister is a working adult now.

The Hanaka who used to roll around on her unmade bed in her untidy room, procrastinating on the things she didn't want to do was gone. I felt a hole form in my chest.

I'm definitely going to cry on her wedding day.

"…They grow up so fast," Mom sighed. I put my arm around her shoulder, and we returned to the living room together.

I couldn't rag on Hanaka for growing up—I stood a head taller than our mom now.

♪♪♪

MY school held its opening ceremony for the new quarter yesterday.

Students in their last year of middle school had farewell matches for their clubs waiting for them before they had to focus on studying for exams to get into high school. Most of spring break was eaten up by club activities, which only gave us the chance to see one movie together.

Of all the third-year students, I probably had it the easiest.

I already had an established pattern of practicing the piano and studying on a daily basis, so I wasn't burdened by that load, and I didn't have to worry about taking entrance exams because I already knew where I would be attending. For Seio Academy, I just had to submit my application at the beginning of the year, go to an interview in the middle of January, and the admission procedure would be completed at the end of the month. My heart was heavy with sadness over having to part from Eri and my friends, but I was also hopelessly excited to enroll in the music school of my dreams.

I was going to attend the same school as Kon, Kou, and Kakeru! Just imagining totally immersing myself in music, competing with lots of rivals, and growing as a person through diligent work filled me with excitement.

In the past, I used to dream about falling in love in high school, but I had completely stopped thinking that way. Did remembering the sad fate of my love in my last life have an effect on me? Not even I knew the answer to that.

Falling in love with someone from the bottom of my heart and being thought of in the same light by the object of my affection—I couldn't help but feel detached from the normal ideals of love and romance. They just seemed unreal to me.

The story might be different if there was a tolerant weirdo who said he would happily accept the piano-obsessed, small-minded, and quick-to-pick-a-fight me. Yeah, that's a tall order.

I checked my sailor uniform tie in the mirror and shouted, "I'm heading to school," to Mom in the kitchen before heading out.

♪♪♪

FIRST quarter of my third year in middle school could be summed up as "testing hell." Days cycled from studying your butt off, midterms, studying even harder, and then finals. We only had a two-week interval between tests. Kids attending cram school and taking mock exams were swamped in even more tests.

You could feel how serious the school took testing with its schedule that screamed, "Stop slacking! Hop to it! You're third years trying to get into high school! We're going to up your standard test scores until you cry high scores!"

I, for one, was pretty happy to apply my results from one test to the next at a fast speed. I had enough common sense not to share my unpopular opinion with my groggy and cranky classmates.

On the piano lesson side of things, I was rehearsing Beethoven's sonatas, Chopin's etudes, and Bach's partitas in order. Ravel and Scarlatti, among others, were tossed into that mix. Sometimes I replayed songs I'd played before or practiced just the piano part from a concerto.

"I'm sure you are ready to start practicing with an orchestra, Mashiro. You won't need brass or wind instruments if you go with Chopin's chamber music or you can join an orchestra of just 20 members with

Poulenc's music."

I hopped onboard Miss Ayumi's suggestion without missing a beat. "I would absolutely love the challenge of playing with an orchestra!"

"Then making that happen comes down to if we can arrange things with an orchestra. Even if we can't work anything out this year, I will make something happen by next."

"Thank you so much!"

Being a solo instrument, I never grew bored of drumming away at piano practice by myself, but an extra level of enjoyment is added to music when you play with others. Having only experienced playing with other pianos and string instruments, performing with wind and brass instruments sounded like an awesome opportunity to gain new experiences.

"By the way, isn't Noboru's little sister coming this summer?"

"You mean Midori? Yes, I heard she is."

"I've heard she is extraordinarily talented with the flute. Why don't you ask her to play with you over the summer?"

Good idea! I can't believe I never thought of that myself. The "Minuet" she played with Maestro Noboru last year was sensational!

Wanting to strike while the iron was hot, I wrote a letter to Midori as soon as I got home. She called me less than a week later and happily accepted my request.

"Hehehe. Sou will be *so* jealous! I have to get Kon to video us!" Midori sounded awfully hyped up on the phone.

"Video, huh? I like that idea! Then we can check through the performance for mistakes together! As for the song, how does Borne's 'Carmen Fantasy' sound?"

"I don't want the video for *that* purpose, but whatever. I'm great at Carmen Fantasy. You can look forward to it!"

"I will! I'll practice hard to catch up to you!"

"Okay, talk to you more this summer, Mashiro! See you soon! *Tschüs*!"

♪♪♪

THE hectic and productive first quarter ended, plunging me right into summer break.

More than half of August was gone. The seething heat didn't relent after sunset. It couldn't have been completely windless outside because I saw the smoke trailing from the mosquito coils I left burning next to all the open windows in my room. If only the wind blasted through the windows with the power of an electric fan!

To cool myself down, I wiped my forehead, arms, and legs with the wet towel I left to chill in the freezer. This was how I got through the hot summers. Air-conditioning jacked up the electric bill and tended to make me lazy. Once I felt nice and cooled off, I normally pulled my hair back and plopped down in front of my desk or popped open my piano keyboard lid.

Truthfully, ever since I cleared my goal of winning the competition, my motivation had dropped. Being aware that "I can't keep going on like this!" made me even more panicked and less motivated. Luckily, practice became fun again after I decided to play with Midori.

I glanced at my calendar. My plans with Midori were tomorrow. Her voice was filled with its usual power and energy when she called me to say she had safely arrived in Japan.

I can't complain about the summer heat! I have to pull my own weight!

♪♪♪

THE next day I slid into Mr. Nonaga's Benz for the Genda estate. Maestro Noboru was busy following Miss Ayumi on her Europe tour and hadn't returned to Japan this year. Miss Ayumi's mentor Mr. Saito looked after my piano lessons while she was away.

Mr. Saito was the one who gave me tips during the junior music competition. The disadvantage I had from not attending the seminar was counterbalanced by his detailed advice as a member of the judging committee.

He was a well-groomed older gentleman in his early sixties who courteously instructed me. His method of teaching stayed true to the music score, the complete opposite of Maestro Noboru's eccentric style.

During our first lesson, Kon had whispered in my ear, "I feel both relaxed and like something is missing with his style. What do you think, Mashiro?"

I agreed with her on the whole but resisted fully accepting it because it felt like we had been trained by Maestro Noboru to think this way. I'd feel horrible towards the serious Mr. Saito if I agreed wholeheartedly with Noboru's crazy, nonsensical lessons.

Midori was staying at her family's main estate since she couldn't use her brother's house while he was out of the country. "I seriously don't want to go home because that old man is pigheaded and the house is stuffier than living in a capsule," she complained on the phone before coming to Japan.

The rich and powerful have all sorts of problems unique to them... How many times have I thought this exact same thing? At least it doesn't seem like celebrities have a life full of rainbows and kittens either.

I was walking towards the Genda annex wiping the sweat from my brow with a handkerchief, when I received Midori's passionate welcome.

"MASHIRO!"

"Whoa! Welcome back, Midori."

"There's nothing that makes me happier than to hear you say that to me, Mashiro! I'm home!" Arms coiled around my neck, she rubbed her soft cheek against mine.

"Okay, okay! I get it. But I'm sweating and smell, so let go."

"Aww, you always smell good Mashiro."

"That's not the problem here!"

Finally satisfied, Midori released me from the bear hug. Her frank display of affection made me happy, but I was pretty sure I'd never get used to these Western-style greetings as long as I lived.

"Hi, Mashiro. Don't worry, I received the exact same treatment." Kon smiled sympathetically as she put slippers on the floor for me. She wasn't kidding—her silky brown hair was tousled. I pulled a comb out of my purse and we fixed up each other's hair after surviving the hugging wars.

"...Oh, Kou's here too!"

I saw a tuft of red hair over the couch when I walked into the main annex room. *Is the siscon Kou camping out at Kon's house because he loves his sister too much? I've been bumping into him a lot here lately, so I guess it's not too weird that he's here today too...*

"Welcome, Mashiro." Kou stood up and sat back down once I sat on the couch.

What a gentleman! This guy is seriously always too cool for real life!

"Hi, Kou. Is it just me or have you been cutting back on the dating business lately? Everything okay?"

"Can you please quit treating me like a host every time you see my face?" His bright smile fell and a clearly disgruntled frown took its place.

I can't stop myself from teasing him every chance I get because I love this look on him much more than that shady smile. I should really get help.

"Sorry. I was just curious because I've seen you here a lot since the beginning of the year. Are you hanging out with the fanclub girls on Sundays instead of Saturdays?"

"…Does it bother you that much?" Kou combed back the hair that fell on his cheeks and stared intently at me. All of his gestures were just too sexy, it made me dizzy.

I barely managed to stop myself from crying out, "How are you so perfect?!" and went with, "Yeah" instead.

"…Wha-?" The great and mighty Kou's mouth fell wide open. A good-looking guy had the ability to make even that facial expression wildly attractive.

"It bothers me," I declared in a strong voice. "Tell me if there's a reason for it."

This was something I would've never admitted when I first entered middle school. Back then, I was constantly on guard around Kou. But close to three years have gone by. As time went on, my opinion of him changed dramatically. I honestly believed he no longer viewed me as an outsider. I became capable of believing that he cared for me like I cared for him.

Kou held my gaze and let out a small sigh. "…No real reason for it. I just grew sick of going through a lover a day."

Though he wasn't telling the whole truth, I still laughed out loud at the way his real thoughts slipped in.

"I get that. My condolences." I gave a little bow and Kou chuckled. Midori and Kon were watching us with strange expressions.

"…I don't really get the whole picture, but isn't this where you should find fault with him?" Midori thrust her thumb at Kou and angrily added, "He's the scum of the Earth, toying with the feelings of the girls who like him. I think Sou's still the better choice over Kou. At least he isn't a manwhore!"

I could see why people who knew nothing about his situation like Midori would interpret his actions that way. But Kou would never pursue a girl who was serious about him. He was the type to firmly reject someone who seriously confessed their feelings to him.

Did the members of his fanclub truly like Kou as a person? I doubted anyone who had real feelings for him would agree to share him with other girls. The fanclub members planned their date schedule whenever they got together for fun, presenting it to him only after they ironed out the details. A convenient boyfriend who's good-looking and only whispers sweet nothings in their ear—that's what they viewed Kou as.

Prouder than most, Kou set aside that pride and became their plaything, all to protect his precious little sister. And that ticked me off to no end.

I shook my head and corrected Midori. "You have him wrong, Midori. Kou's usually an arrogant narcissist, but he's not the type of guy who enjoys cruelly hurting others. He's doing what he's doing to protect Kon and the fangirls know that. Outsiders have no right to find fault with him for it."

The thought probably never crossed Kou's mind that I'd stand up for him. He gaped at me, dumbfounded. Embarrassed over what I had said, I suddenly became uncomfortable. *What am I getting all worked up for?*

"Sorry, I went too far. I'm just as much of an outsider here."

"…No, don't apologize. Everyone has reasons for what they do. Kou, I'm sorry for running my mouth when I don't know anything about you." Midori took what I said to heart and apologized to Kou.

"It doesn't bother me. You have a right to be uncomfortable with it, Misaka." Kou waved it off and smiled.

Kon watched over our conversation on the edge of her seat. A relieved smile overtook her face upon seeing us resolve the matter without issue.

"Okay, enough of this topic. I want to make music now!" I piped up in a cheerful voice, trying to change the mood.

"Sure. I'm looking forward to playing with you, Mashiro!" Midori agreed in a bubbly voice.

Borne – Carmen Fantasy

French flutist François Borne composed "Carmen Fantasy", also known as "Carmen Fantasie Brillante", based on themes from the opera "Carmen" by Georges Bizet.

In about twelve rapidly paced minutes, Borne covers seven of the great themes from the opera. The fantasy begins with the music from Carmen's first entrance in the opera, goes to the "Fate Motive" theme, the cigarette girls' song from Act I, the "Habañera", and then builds up in excitement for the "Chanson de Bohème" (Gypsy Song). Just as the piece seems ready to close, Borne ends with a flashy finale, the "Toreador Song".

Most people are familiar with the "Habañera" and maybe the "Toreador Song". A lot of musicians choose to play just those parts.

As this was our first time playing together, Midori faced me with her flute, not our audience consisting of Kon and Kou. The mood completely shifted from playful to tense enough you could hear a pin drop.

I dropped my fingers onto the keyboard and rang out the first series of notes. Beating the same chord with both hands, I waited for the flute to join in.

Face set in a serious expression, Midori listened closely to my piano, until her part came around and she inhaled and entered the music with an original lyrical melody followed by winding arpeggios and large leaps.

I was amazed at how long she could hold her breath during the long trill taking us from the ominous "Fate Motive" in triple meter, to the dazzling quadruple meter. The clarity of her high notes was heavenly, and the bewitching nature of her low notes was sensational. We looked into each other's eyes while adjusting the tempo for the accelerando (gradually increase speed) part.

Ah, you want me to play faster? Sorry about that, Midori.

Next came the "Habañera" theme from the aria "L'amour est un oiseau rebelle". Embarking on the unique rhythm, the flute and piano shared the same motif. Expressive and rhythmic freedom was given by a slight speeding up and then slowing down of the tempo in the rubato tempo portion. I accompanied the waves of music Midori created as she slightly rocked with her flute, her cheeks flushed with life. This was the perfect spot to give people goosebumps once we got the song down pat.

After covering the whole theme once, the same melody was repeated with a terrific sprinkling of grace notes. This was the flute's moment to shine. I was overwhelmed by Midori's transcendent technique.

The last section, the lively "Chanson de Bohème" (Gypsy Song), contains grace notes and oscillating sixteenth notes. It's highly embellished with arpeggios, a jaunty melody, and playful rhythm.

I played a crescendo, supporting the ascending flute. Letting the final chord resound noticeably, I lifted my hands from the piano.

Kon and Kou applauded without holding anything back.

"Midori, you're incredible!" I was the one who leapt into a flying hug for Midori this time—after she put down her flute, of course. It wasn't an exaggeration to say I couldn't sit still. That's how amazing her "Carmen Fantasy" was.

"What did you do to become capable of playing like a goddess?! How long can you hold your breath for? That's some record-breaking lung capacity you've got!"

"S-Slow down, Mashiro. Sich beruhigen (calm down)!" Midori lightly rapped on my back, pulling me back down to Earth.

"Sorry," I apologized, taking a step back. I was like a dog that was too excited to wait.

"It's super easy to play alongside your piano, Mashiro. I haven't had such a good time playing since Noboru. I can't believe that happened on our first time, too!"

I giggled with a bashful smile.

For some reason, Kou's mood suddenly soured. "I thought your obsession was limited to the piano, but it looks like any instrument will do for you. You'll have to watch out who you play with if you have a habit of hugging the other player every time a performance ends, Mashiro," he snorted, sounding exasperated.

I stuck my tongue out at him. "I don't hug just anybody! Only those who are terrifically talented!" I returned his scowl with one in kind.

Midori slipped in between us. "Okay, children. You've proven just how much you like each other."

What part of that argument implied we like each other? I contemplated it. *Meh, we won't get anywhere if we carry on like this.*

I pulled myself together and asked Midori, "Hey, why don't we practice each part separately next? I think we can play better doing it that way first."

"Good idea. But can we take a break first? I'm thirsty."

Kon stood up and asked for drinks through the intercom. Once she finished talking to the maid, she walked over to Midori and whispered in her ear. "Good luck, Midori. Mashiro won't relent now that she's got you. She's a perfectionist to a frightening degree."

Kon, I can hear you.

"Are you serious? I only accepted as a means to torment Sou, but… right…she's a pianist. There's no way she's not a weirdo."

I hear you too, Midori! What's with that biased view on pianists?! I opened my mouth to object, when Maestro Noboru crossed my mind. *…Mm, then again, she might not be wrong.*

♪♪♪

I spent my last middle school summer vacation indulging in leisurely activities. Midori ended up staying in Japan until the end of August and dragged me all over the place with her. Theme parks, art galleries, museums, and fireworks displays punctuated my vacation.

Meanwhile, Midori experienced her first taste of fast food with me. My insistence that we hang out within the means of my allowance resulted in Midori and Kon carrying trays with hamburgers and soda to the plastic table and chairs, where they hesitantly sat.

The girls stood out like super stars, walking into a fast-food joint wearing what anyone could tell was brand-name clothing at a glance. The people around us stared hard.

On a side note, the flavor was too much for the girls and their acquired tastes.

"Is it really okay for us to play around so much? I'm starting to feel guilty because I'm supposed to be drowning in exams like my friends," I muttered.

"Why not?" Midori puffed out her cheeks. "This might be the last year the three of us get to play to our heart's content, you know?"

"Why would it be the last?"

"Because if you start going steady with a boy in high school, you'll prioritize him over us. I fear the consequences from said boyfriend when we get in the way of your dates."

"You don't have to hold back on the account of a hypothetical boyfriend," I laughed.

Midori sent a meaningful look Kon's way.

"I agree with Midori. Whoever you pick will end up monopolizing your time, Mashiro."

"Ha! Monopolize is too cute of a word! She'll be under complete lockdown!"

…*Uh, they're so not making me want a boyfriend.* Their whispers sent chills crawling down my spine.

♪♪♪

FALL came peacefully.

The days were packed with the final school events of middle school: the sports festival and culture festival. Everyone took the events super seriously as if it was their only outlet from the daily test stress.

"Go, go, class 3!" My classmates huddled together during the sports festival and shouted cheers from the sidelines with overwhelming intensity. Well, it's obviously more fun to put your heart and soul into the things you have to do, whatever they may be—especially when taking brain-numbing tests is the alternative.

The girls changed into cheerleading outfits and cheered on the boys playing capture the flag. Many students came to school at six in the morning to practice for the choral competition. Every day felt like what you'd expect from adolescence.

Following the events of last year, I was asked to play the piano at the culture festival again, but the teachers had specific requests of me this year, turning it into a showcase of Chopin's "Grande Polonaise Brillante" and Liszt's "Un Sospiro".

My worries over whether it was okay to just perform classical pieces ended up being for naught. Only the sound of the Shiroyama piano I played rose up in the quiet gymnasium. My mini recital concluded with loud applause.

♪♪♪

WINTER arrived even faster than fall.

Days immersed in testing came back in full fury, thrusting the entire school into a one-note testing mood. I also decided to participate in more solfèges in preparation for my interview with Seio in January.

Tobi told me it was going to be a simple interview, but it couldn't hurt to be perfectly prepared for it. I mean, it was Tobi who told me that. I absolutely couldn't do such a dangerously stupid thing as take him at his word. I doubled down on practicing sight-reading as well. It was practically a given that a music school test would include sight-reading.

Sight-reading started by checking the tonality, rhythm, steady beat, and tempo, before quickly glancing over the note arrangement. Growing accustomed to sight-reading helps musicians think on the spot. A song none of the test takers knew was required to assess their skill, which was why they normally consisted of handwritten music scores by the teachers.

The student would be placed in front of a row of interviewers, given a short score of music and several minutes to read it, and then they would be asked to play. Not only was the skill to quickly pick up on a score being tested, but also how the student performed under pressure.

Fortunately, I didn't have trouble with sight-reading or memorizing music.

♪♪♪

I had plans to spend Christmas on a lunch cruise with Kon. Didn't the name Christmas cruise have an incredible ring to it? Even better, a string quartet was going to perform live onboard! No one could blame me for getting excited, right?

By the hands of my pumped-up sister, I was transformed into the replica of a noble family's proper young daughter. I met up with Kon in her shiny cream dress and we boarded the ship holding hands.

The lunch was prepared in a spacious dining hall, and guests, dressed up in fancy gowns and suits, shared in pleasant conversation under the bright chandeliers.

A porter, decked out in a white uniform, pulled out my chair for me. The string quartet waiting on standby at the front of the dining hall began playing their elegant melody when the porter placed the aperitifs on top of the starched tablecloth.

We were underage, so the glasses we lifted to toast were filled with sparkling soda.

"Getting to listen to Schubert while eating delicious food is the greatest thing ever!"

"Hehe. It sure is." Kon looked more beautiful by the day. She smoothly brushed her cascading brown hair behind her ear and gracefully cut her steak. "By the way, Mashiro, are you going to perform in a concerto?"

"Miss Ayumi said she would have one arranged for me by next year. How about you, Kon?"

"I've already played several times with Seio University's orchestra."

"Oh my gosh! Lucky! I wish I could've been there!"

A small smile graced Kon's lips as she watched me blissfully imagine her performance. She intently locked her eyes on me as if trying to sear my expression into her memory.

"...Um, it's kinda embarrassing for me when you stare," I surrendered, unable to withstand it any longer.

It hurts being picked apart by a beautiful woman's gaze. I don't have a zit, do I? When did I last pluck my eyebrows?

Kon pressed her napkin to her mouth and laughed. "Silly, Mashiro. You're usually so aloof, but shy when it comes to the oddest things." After she finished her laughing fit, Kon talked to me about Seio with a sunny smile.

According to her, Kou had stopped entertaining the fanclub. She said he turned down their date invitations using his status as a busy third year as an excuse. Lately, he had increased the frequency with which he asked them to leave him alone at school as well.

"Has it finally gotten around campus that you two are twins even though you have different last names?" I checked with her.

"Yeah, our relationship finally clicked in everyone's heads after three years of pounding it through the gossip circles. There's no one who doesn't know about us now," she cheerfully relieved my fears.

Thank goodness!

While we were filling each other in on our lives, we polished off the last dessert.

The time to disembark came all too soon.

"...I don't want to go home," Kon muttered, suddenly stopping.

"What's wrong?" I walked over to the wall to avoid being swept up in the wave of people leaving and looked back at Kon who had stopped behind me.

Kon clutched her coat in front of her chest with her right hand and shrunk in on herself like she was freezing. She was framed in the ephemeral aura of someone who could disappear at any moment. Opening and closing her mouth several times, she finally managed to squeeze out, "Because I'm having so much fun... I wish time would just stop here and now."

"I don't hear you say stuff like that often, Kon. Are you feeling lonely? I had a blast too. And I feel the same way about not wanting it to be over. But, you know, it's practically guaranteed lots of fun things are ahead of us. We get to attend the same school in April, and we can always go out like this again. Right?"

"...Yeah. You're...right."

Not knowing any better, I offered her clichéd words of comfort, and gently rubbed her back. Thinking back on it now, that was the first and last time Kon ever voiced her tormented feelings.

♪♪♪

THE calendars switched to a new year, bringing about January.

The entrance exam for Seio Academy's sponsored scholarship students ended without a hitch. When one of the interviewers asked me what ambition would drive me once I enrolled in the academy, I answered, "Wanting to become a better pianist." Laughter broke out across the room. What did I say wrong?

Seated in the center of the interview panel with his elbows on the table and hands folded like he knew he was the most important man in the room, was Tobi. "I look forward to seeing how you grow." With his words of approval, the interview ended. The other interviewees were going to be tested on sight-seeing, aural skills, and actual performance next. I was sent home right after as a special exception though.

A simple map of the Academy's layout in hand, I finally arrived at the front of the school. My first impression of Seio Academy was that it was ridiculously large and spacious. It boasted a campus size that ran contrary to the knowledge that it was built in a prime location downtown.

Since Seio Academy had an old history, its buildings were built with a very classic and elegant architectural style. Stepping inside the buildings was like stepping from the past into the present, as the interior was modernized with seismic retrofitting. Commercial-sized elevators were available for use in different locations too.

Are they used for carrying bigger instruments? I wondered. *I wish I could explore since I'm already here!*

Torn by the desire to look around some more, I ran to Mom's car parked in the parking lot.

"Sorry for the wait!"

"You finished up fast! Is it okay for you to go home now?"

"Yup, that's what they said. They'll be sending me the enrollment paperwork next week." I couldn't resist laughing at Mom who looked like she couldn't believe it was that easy.

Dad was anxious for me this morning too. Only Hanaka was brimming with confidence for me. "There is no way Mashiro won't get in!" Where in the world did her confidence come from?

♪♪♪

THEN came February.

Snow had been falling since morning. I was keeping my feet warm with the electric heater while playing the piano, when my phone rang. I lifted my hands from the keyboard and picked up my flashing cell phone. Cocking my head at the name on the display, I answered the call.

It was from Kou. Surprising since he rarely called.

"Hello? Kou? What's wrong?"

"Hi. Sorry for the sudden call. Do you have any plans today? If not, can you come over?"

"Come over to your house? Why?"

"Because I want to see you." His straight answer caused me to lock up.

Turning him down would be easy. Sorry, I'm playing the piano right now. Just saying those words probably would have gotten him to say, "You are? That's too bad," and hang up the phone.

"…Tell me the truth. What's wrong?"

I couldn't push him away. His voice sounded very different from usual. *Is he sending out some kinda SOS with this call?*

"Do you need to talk?"

"…Yeah. I do." Kou's voice was frighteningly calm and quiet. It was different from sounding cold. The clerical tone bothered me to no end. "This is the one area you always pick up on," he added teasingly.

Under normal circumstances, I would've countered him with, "What the heck?! I won't go if that's how you're going to be!" But the weirdness I sensed wouldn't allow for that.

"Okay. I'll head right over," I replied.

"I'll send Mizusawa to get you. Wait until he gets there," Kou said briefly before hanging up.

Anxiety stirring in my chest, I arrived at the Narita estate in the car driven by Mr. Mizusawa. Kou was waiting for me in the foyer. Mr. Tanomiya was nowhere to be seen.

"Hi. Where's Mr. Tanomiya today?"

"Hey. Thanks for coming. I gave him the day off… Follow me," Kou urged, spinning on his heel and briskly walking in front of me.

Kou, a professional when it comes to ladies first, is walking in front of me? Things were getting weirder by the minute.

Contrary to my expectations that we were headed for the parlor on the second floor, he brought me to a Michelin 3-Star Restaurant! Or rather, a kitchen that was a close second to one. Lined up on the sparkling clean counters was a row of cookware, flour, butter, milk, and so on.

"D-Don't tell me you want me to…?" I glanced up at a wicked smirk on Kou's handsome face.

And so, I got roped into making a chocolate cake in the Narita kitchen. Yes, of course it was per the selfish demands of the high and mighty oresama Kou.

"I can't believe you invited a guest all the way over to your house just to have them make you cake! You're unbelievable!"

"Who might this guest be?"

"Me, obviously!"

Once our customary bickering was done and out of the way, I snapped my mouth shut and set about cooking. I used the whisk to beat the eggs until they formed stiff peaks and gently combined it with the flour and cocoa powder I had mixed beforehand. Then I added melted butter and milk and poured the mixture into a round cake mold.

Kou pulled a chair over from the other side of the kitchen, spun it around backwards, and sat down facing me with his arms resting on top of the backrest. The unusually gruff gesture made my heart pound against my wishes.

Kou's clearly not acting like himself today. What in the world happened?

I pounded the mold against the counter to get the air bubbles out of it, shoved it into the preheated oven, and set the timer for forty minutes.

The job finished, I finally made my complaints known. "And you even had the nerve to watch me do all the work! Did it not even cross your mind to lend me a hand?"

"You did everything so perfectly, I thought I'd just get in your way." Kou partially inclined his head, his red hair smoothly falling on his face with the movement.

Cunning! Pushy! Cool! And so not fair! I stamped my feet on the ground and groaned.

Kou laughed before finally getting to the point of why he called me over. "Sou's coming back from Germany."

"…Come again?"

What a relief he waited to tell me until I finished cooking. If he told me a few minutes sooner, I would have dropped the glass bowl and the batter would've splattered on the kitchen floor.

I just heard him say Sou is coming back.

"I thought you'd have a heart attack if you suddenly ran into Sou at Seio. I called you over here to prepare you mentally."

"I see. Thanks…for that."

My knees buckled. Kou jumped to his feet and supported me by the elbow to a different seat. I wanted to thank him, but only a hoarse wisp of air left my throat.

Sou will never come back to Japan. I had convinced myself of that. It was because of that understanding that I had forced him away from me with the cruelest method at my disposal.

Had I known he would be back in just three years, I would have persuaded him in a better way. I could've smiled and comforted him by saying, "I'll be waiting for you to come back! So do your best over there!" Our parting wouldn't have become one of the hardest moments in my life.

"Don't you even think about saying, 'Welcome back, Shiroyama.' I get that was your way of drawing a line between you, but it'll only hurt Sou."

I couldn't see Kou's face. All that was before my eyes was his torso clad in a white shirt.

"…What choice do I have? Don't you know what I said to him? I told him that I *hate* him. That I hate his guts! I even told him not to place the burden of his future on me. I can't say his name like I did in the past. I don't have that right!" I became emotional as I spoke. I curled my hands into tight fists and punched them into my thighs. "What was the point of getting all emotional if he was coming back in just three years anyway?!"

Kou clapped his hands around my cheeks as I fell into a state of panic over the sudden news. He dropped down to a crouch and looked up at me from a lower position on the floor.

"You are the only person who can't say that. Sou adored you. Just three years? That time was like an eternity for him."

Kou was angry. His low voice censuring my selfish complaints sliced into my ears. I was so wrapped up in my own feelings, I didn't stop to think about how Sou felt.

"…Sorry… I'm so sorry," I faltered, biting my tongue to stop from crying.

Kou's expression fell and he frowned apologetically. "No… It's my fault. I wasn't trying to be that hard with you. Did it hurt when I brought my hands to your cheeks?" He shot to his feet and walked over to the sink. He soaked his handkerchief with cold water and returned to a crouch in front of me where he gently pressed it to my cheeks.

"Your cheeks aren't red at least. Sorry."

What an overreaction. It's not like he hit me. Both Kou and Sou are too kind for their own good. I'm the cruel one. Guilt toward Sou tore my heart to pieces.

"No, I'm sorry too. For losing it. Also, thanks for telling me. Do you know what day he flies in?"

"Yeah, I already asked… I figured you'd want to know." Kou pulled a folded piece of paper out of his jacket pocket and pressed it into my hand. "What else needs to be done to this cake after it bakes?"

His sudden question took me by surprise. "Um," I mumbled, shoving the paper into my pocket as I thought through the recipe. "Once it cools, whip up some ganache, ice it, and it's done."

"I see." Kou pulled me to my feet with a radiant smile. "I'll have the help take care of pulling it out and setting it to cool. Is about two hours long enough?"

"Yup, that's good."

"Then why don't we play together on the second floor?"

My mouth fell open at his suggestion. Too many surprising things had happened for my brain to keep up. *By play together...he means in an ensemble, right?*

If that's what he meant then...is he asking to accompany me on the violin?

"Sure—if you become skilled enough to win a music competition somewhere."

The promise we made as little kids hit me full force. Nostalgia and joy over him remembering slammed together inside me.

I swiped at my eyes with my sleeve, holding back the tears threatening to burst forth. "That reminds me of the time you agreed to accompany me once I won a music competition."

"Yeah. You remembered."

Kou smiled so blissfully it made the stupid tears I had under control blur my vision.

♪♪♪

I went right for the music sheet shelves inside the music room on the second floor, but Kou grabbed my arm and shook his head.

"Love's Sorrow. How about it?"

"Oh wow! Now that's nostalgic! Ah, but the sheet music you gave me is at my house."

"It's okay. I downloaded it online... Need practice time?" he asked teasingly.

I arched an eyebrow and protested, "Oh, please. I mastered that song ages ago. I'm able to play the difficult notes I couldn't back then."

"Good to hear. Then why don't you prove it?" Kou chuckled, pulling his violin out of its case. He swiftly finished tuning with practiced ease.

While he was getting ready, I placed the printed sheet music on the Bösendorfer's music rack and glanced over at him to cue I was ready whenever he was. The music score that had given me so much trouble back then was a piece of cake now.

Kou slowly tucked his violin under his chin and brought up the bow. I was temporarily captivated by his dignified pose. The sweet tones of the elegant violin filled the room as he drew his bow. Seemingly having memorized the music, Kou looked at me and me alone as he played. Not once did he glance at the sheet music or at his hands.

Emotion blazed in his earnest gaze. The more I attempted to concentrate on the music the harder it became to pry my eyes from him. Realization suddenly dawned on me just as the song reached its climax.

Kou loves me.

The way his violin entreated with a plaintive melody and the reluctance to part glimmering in his eyes spoke eloquently of those feelings.

I probably would have never believed him if he told me with words. But the tone of his violin laid his heart bare for me to see.

Today was February fifteenth. Did he forcefully invite me over and insist I had to make a chocolate cake for him because he wanted Valentine's Day chocolate from me? What was the point a day late?

Did he tell me about Sou returning and give me the note with the day he'd arrive to make me choose? Choose him or Sou.

What an awkward and hard to understand man you are, Kou.

"I love you. You are everything to me, Mashiro."

Sou's direct love confession rung in my ears. I kept every letter and postcard from him as precious treasures.

I must come to an answer.

Using the pretense that I couldn't choose either one because both Kou and Sou were dear to me wasn't a conceivable option. I think I knew that a long time ago. I simply used the justification that I wanted nothing to do with *Hear My Heart* as a way to turn a blind eye on my feelings.

The one I love is—

Heroine's Results
Target Character: Sou Shiroyama & Kou Narita
Event: Crossroad
CLEAR

THE common route is now over. The next two volumes are contained stories where Mashiro ends up with the boy she picks! Both stories contain a unique standalone route just like an otome game. Kou and Sou both hope you will pick their route first!

◇**Choose Kou's Volume** ⇒ **Kou Route**
◇**Choose Sou's Volume** ⇒ **Sou Route**

Afterword

HELLO, Natsu here.

I'm thrilled you read Obsessions of an Otome Gamer Volume 2! Thank you very much for picking up a copy and adding it to your collection!

This volume deals with the Middle School Years, so I wrote about the slightly older Mashiro and gang's struggles, friendship, and the current direction of their love. I hope you were able to enjoy the awkwardness of Kou and Sou at the height of puberty with the mentally older Mashiro.

The secrets about the world Mashiro finds herself in are finally revealed in this volume. At a glance, Mashiro seems like the main character of the story, but in all actuality…there is a greater plot at hand you can look forward to.

I am extremely curious about what you think about the story. If it's not too much trouble, please leave reviews and comments so I can hear your opinions! I used an English to Japanese dictionary to read through every review left on the previous volume.

Your warm words conveying how much you enjoyed the story are the greatest source of encouragement for me!

The next volume to come out will be determined by a reader poll on whose route you would rather read first: Kou or Sou. They will both be eventually released either way, so you can look forward to that!

Both routes are complete, contained stories, but I have written them in such a way that the reader will gain a deeper understanding of Mashiro and Kon's world by reading them both.

Natsu

They aren't just sweet, lovey-dovey endings. The original title for this story is *The Maiden Can't Save through Music Alone* and that plays a critical part in the end. I do, however, promise you that all of Mashiro and Kon's hard work will certainly pay off in the end.

Last but not least, I want to offer up my deepest gratitude to the talented illustrator of this series, Shoyu-sensei, and to everyone at Cross Infinite World involved in publishing it. Thanks to you, I was able to deliver this series to readers overseas in the best possible way.

Until we meet again in the next volume. I hope to see you until the end of the series!

Natsu
April, 2019

LITTLE PRINCESS IN FAIRY FOREST
STORY BY: TSUBAKI TOKINO
ILLUSTRATION BY: TAKASHI KONNO
STANDALONE | OUT NOW

Join Princess Lala and Sir Gideon as they flee for their lives from the traitor who killed the royal family and wants to wed Lala! Gideon is willing to do anything to protect his princess, even if it means engaging the mighty dragons in combat! Tsubaki Tokino's fairy tale inspired Little Princess in Fairy Forest!

BEAST † BLOOD
STORY BY: SATO FUMINO
ILLUSTRATION BY: AKIRA EGAWA
VOL. 1 OUT NOW

Biotech Scientist Euphemia's world suddenly gets flipped upside down when her sister hires a sexy alien mercenary to be her bodyguard!

THE ECCENTRIC MASTER AND THE FAKE LOVER!
STORY BY: ROKA SAYUKI
ILLUSTRATION BY: ITARU
VOL. 1 OUT NOW

Yanked into another world full of dangerous magic and parasitic plants, Nichika does the one thing she can to survive: become the apprentice to an eccentric witch!

THE CHAMPIONS OF JUSTICE
AND THE SUPREME
RULER OF EVIL
STORY BY: KAEDE KIKYOU
ILLUSTRATION BY: TOBARI
STANDALONE | OUT NOW

Mia's a supervillain bent on world domination who lacks tact in enacting her evil schemes! Will the lazy superheroes be able to stop her?

THE WEREWOLF COUNT
AND THE TRICKSTER TAILOR
STORY BY: YURUKA MORISAKI
ILLUSTRATION BY: TSUKITO
VOL. 1 | OUT NOW

"I don't care if you are a man, let me court you."
Rock's whole life is shaken when a werewolf shows up at her shop in the middle of the night...asking for more than just clothes!

OF DRAGONS AND FAE: IS A FAIRY TALE ENDING POSSIBLE FOR THE PRINCESS'S HAIRSTYLIST?
STORY BY: TSUKASA MIKUNI
ILLUSTRATION BY: YUKIKANA
STANDALONE | OUT NOW

After being dumped by a dragon knight, Mayna sets out to prove that fairytale endings aren't only for princesses! See how this royal hairstylist wins over the dragon kingdom one head of hair at a time!